DEBBIE MACOMBER

Back on Blossom Street

MIRA

MIRA®

ISBN-13: 978-0-7783-1796-8

Recycling programs
for this product may
not exist in your area.

Back on Blossom Street

Copyright © 2007 by Debbie Macomber

For questions and comments about the quality of this book, please contact us at
CustomerService@Harlequin.com.

www.MIRABooks.com

Printed in U.S.A.

To Bob and Joan McKeon
Treasured Friends

Also by Debbie Macomber

Blossom Street Books

The Shop on Blossom Street
A Good Yarn
Susannah's Garden
Back on Blossom Street
Twenty Wishes
Summer on Blossom Street
Hannah's List
The Knitting Diaries
  "The Twenty-First Wish"
A Turn in the Road

Cedar Cove Books

16 Lighthouse Road
204 Rosewood Lane
311 Pelican Court
44 Cranberry Point
50 Harbor Street
6 Rainier Drive
74 Seaside Avenue
8 Sandpiper Way
92 Pacific Boulevard
1022 Evergreen Place
Christmas in Cedar Cove
  (*5-B Poppy Lane* and
  A Cedar Cove Christmas)
1105 Yakima Street
1225 Christmas Tree Lane

Dakota Series

Dakota Born
Dakota Home
Always Dakota
Buffalo Valley

The Manning Family

The Manning Sisters
The Manning Brides
The Manning Grooms

Christmas Books

A Gift to Last
On a Snowy Night
Home for the Holidays
Glad Tidings
Christmas Wishes
Small Town Christmas
When Christmas Comes
  (now retitled *Trading
  Christmas*)
*There's Something About
  Christmas*
Christmas Letters
Where Angels Go
The Perfect Christmas
Choir of Angels
  (*Shirley, Goodness and Mercy,
  Those Christmas Angels* and
  Where Angels Go)
Call Me Mrs. Miracle

Heart of Texas Series

VOLUME 1
  (*Lonesome Cowboy* and
  Texas Two-Step)
VOLUME 2
  (*Caroline's Child* and
  Dr. Texas)
VOLUME 3
  (*Nell's Cowboy* and
  Lone Star Baby)
Promise, Texas
Return to Promise

Midnight Sons

VOLUME 1
(*Brides for Brothers* and
    The Marriage Risk)
VOLUME 2
(*Daddy's Little Helper* and
    Because of the Baby)
VOLUME 3
(*Falling for Him,*
    Ending in Marriage and
    Midnight Sons and Daughters)

This Matter of Marriage
Montana
Thursdays at Eight
Between Friends
Changing Habits
Married in Seattle
    (*First Comes Marriage* and
    Wanted: Perfect Partner)
Right Next Door
    (*Father's Day* and
    The Courtship of Carol Sommars)
Wyoming Brides
    (*Denim and Diamonds* and
    The Wyoming Kid)
Fairy Tale Weddings
    (*Cindy and the Prince* and
    Some Kind of Wonderful)
The Man You'll Marry
    (*The First Man You Meet* and
    The Man You'll Marry)
Orchard Valley Grooms
    (*Valerie* and *Stephanie*)
Orchard Valley Brides
    (*Norah* and *Lone Star Lovin'*)
The Sooner the Better
An Engagement in Seattle
    (*Groom Wanted* and
    Bride Wanted)
Out of the Rain
    (*Marriage Wanted* and
    Laughter in the Rain)
Learning to Love
    (*Sugar and Spice* and
    Love by Degree)

You...Again
    (*Baby Blessed* and
    Yesterday Once More)
Three Brides, No Groom
The Unexpected Husband
    (*Jury of His Peers* and
    Any Sunday)
Love in Plain Sight
    (*Love 'n' Marriage* and
    Almost an Angel)
I Left My Heart
    (*A Friend or Two* and
    No Competition)
Marriage Between Friends
    (*White Lace and Promises* and
    Friends—And Then Some)
A Man's Heart
    (*The Way to a Man's Heart*
    and *Hasty Wedding*)
North to Alaska
    (*That Wintry Feeling* and
    Borrowed Dreams)
On a Clear Day
    (*Starlight* and
    Promise Me Forever)
To Love and Protect
    (*Shadow Chasing* and
    For All My Tomorrows)
Home in Seattle
    (*The Playboy and the Widow*
    and *Fallen Angel*)
Together Again
    (*The Trouble with Caasi* and
    Reflections of Yesterday)
The Reluctant Groom
    (*All Things Considered* and
    Almost Paradise)
A Real Prince
    (*The Bachelor Prince* and
    Yesterday's Hero)

Debbie Macomber's
    Cedar Cove Cookbook
Debbie Macomber's
    Christmas Cookbook

KNIT TRIANGULAR PRAYER SHAWL

Finished Size: 65" wide x 33" deep (165 cm x 84 cm)

MATERIALS
Bulky Weight Yarn   Icon 5
[6 ounces, 185 yards (170 grams, 169 meters) per skein]:
3 skeins

29" (73.5 cm) circular needle, size 13 (9 mm) or size needed for gauge

GAUGE: In Garter Stitch, 10 sts and 16 rows = 4" (10 cm)

Gauge Swatch: 4" (10 cm) square.
Cast on 10 sts.
Knit 16 rows.
Bind off all sts in knit.

SHAWL

Cast on one st.

Row 1: Knit into the front and the back of st (increase made): 2 sts.

Row 2: Increase, K1: 3 sts.

Rows 3–6: Increase, knit across: 7 sts.

Row 7: K3, YO, knit across: 8 sts.

Repeat Row 7 until piece measures approximately 32" (81.5 cm) from cast-on edge, ending with an even number of stitches.

Next Row: K3, YO,*K2 tog, YO; repeat from * across to last 3 sts, K3.

Next 4 Rows: Increase, knit across.

Bind Off Row: K2 tog, *K1, pass second st on right needle over first st; repeat from * across to last 2 sts, K2 tog, pass second st on right needle over first st and finish off.

Design by John Feddersen for Leisure Arts

ALIX'S LACE PRAYER SHAWL[1]
Copyright © 2006, Myrna A. I. Stahman,
dba Rocking Chair Press[2]

Introduction to Lace Knitting

Many knitters are under the impression that knitting lace
is difficult. It's not—knitting lace is simply using knitting
needles and yarn to connect a series of holes in a pleasing
fashion. The holes are so easy to make. Just put the yarn
over your right needle—voilà, you have made a hole. Often
the hole made with the yarnover is paired with a decrease.
The most common decrease is that of simply knitting two
stitches together. When knitting two stitches together, the
stitch you first place your needle into lies on top of the
second stitch. For most knitters, when two stitches are knit
together the stitches end up leaning to the right.

Alix's prayer shawl includes right-leaning decreases, the
mirror image left-leaning decreases and reducing three
stitches to one stitch. For a left-leaning decrease (1) insert
your right needle into the next stitch on the left needle as
if you are going to knit that stitch, but instead just slip that
stitch onto the right needle, (2) knit the next stitch and then
(3) lift up the slipped stitch and pass it over the newly made
stitch. The 3-to-1 decrease combines these steps: (1) insert
your right needle into the next stitch on the left needle as if
to knit that stitch, but instead just slip that stitch onto your
right needle, (2) knit the next two stitches together and then
(3) lift up the slipped stitch and pass it over the newly made
stitch.

A great way to practice knitting the lace stitch pattern is by
knitting a triangular dishcloth. Use worsted weight 100%
cotton yarn and size 8 knitting needles so you can see exactly
what happens with each stitch as your lace pattern develops.
Knitting a dishcloth is a great way to practice casting on, the
lace stitch pattern, the bottom border and the bind-off. Even
if you make a few mistakes in your practice, the cloth will be
fine for washing dishes.

Shawl Instructions—The Preliminaries

Before beginning your shawl, take these instructions, including the chart, to a copy machine and enlarge them so they are easy to read. Be sure to make the chart nice and big.

Any yarn you enjoy working with may be used. I knit both a stockinette stitch shawl and a garter stitch shawl using Blue Moon Fiber Arts[3] lightweight "Socks that Rock" yarn, and a garter stitch shawl using Haneke fingering weight merino/alpaca yarn. Either a hand-painted/variegated yarn in a colorway with low contrast and color changes every four to six inches or a solid color yarn works well when knitting lace.

Many lace knitters prefer knitting from a chart, rather than knitting from the written word. The chart is a picture of your knitting as one looks at the public side of the shawl. The chart is read from right to left, and from the bottom to the top, just as your knitting progresses. The chart shows only the odd-numbered rows on which the pattern stitches are worked; the even-numbered rows are worked plain. By knitting from the chart you will soon learn to "read your knitting." After a bit of practice you will be able to see if something has gone wrong with your stitch pattern.

Alix's prayer shawl is constructed using a four-stitch beginning border, two triangles joined by a column consisting of just one stitch, and a four-stitch ending border. Each triangle begins at the point and increases in size as the shawl increases in size. Because the two lace triangles are identical, the same chart is used for each triangle.

[1]To see pictures of a number of shawls knit with these instructions, and for more detailed line-by-line instructions, go to www.DebbieMacomber.com.
[2]Myrna is the author, publisher and distributor of *Stahman's Shawls and Scarves—Lace Faroese-Shaped Shawls from the Neck Down and Seamen's Scarves* (Rocking Chair Press, Boise, ID, 2000). She is currently working on a second book, *The Versatility of Lace Knitting—Variations on a Theme*. She may be contacted at stahman@aol.com.
[3]Go to www.bluemoonfiberarts.com for information on yarns available from Blue Moon Fiber Arts.

The chart shows one half of the shawl; it does not show the center stitch that is between and connects the two halves, nor does it show the four border stitches at the beginning of each row and at the end of each row. Work the beginning four border stitches; work the chart one time; knit the one center stitch; work the chart for a second time; work the ending four border stitches.

The first four stitches and the last four stitches of every row form the top border of the shawl. Although it works to just knit the first stitch, I recommend the chain selvedge: (1) With the yarn in front of your working needle (2) slip the first stitch as if to purl, (3) move the yarn to the back of your work by passing it between the tips of your needles and (4) work the next three stitches; always knit the last two stitches of every row. In the written instructions the four border stitches are referred to as B4 at the beginning and the end of every row.

I recommend using stitch markers in three places on your needle: (1) immediately after the first four border stitches; (2) immediately before the center column of stitches; and (3) immediately before the last four border stitches. Attach about a 12-inch thread to each marker; the thread keeps the marker from flying across the room if the marker accidentally jumps off the needle. The symbol ^ is used in the written instructions to show where a stitch marker is placed.

Alix's Stockinette Stitch Lace Prayer Shawl

<u>Casting On</u>—Leaving a tail of yarn approximately 10 inches long, cast on 11 stitches.[4]

<u>Setup Row</u>: K2, p1, k1, ^, p3, ^, k1, p1, k2. [11 sts]

<u>Using the Chart</u>—Go to the chart. The chart is a picture of your knitting as you look at the public side of your work. The chart is read from right to left and from the bottom to the top. Only the odd-numbered rows, which are the public side rows, of the lace stitches of your shawl are shown on the chart. Although only three stitches are shown on row 1a of the chart, row 1a of your knitting is worked on 11 stitches, and ends with 15 stitches. The stitches not shown on the chart are: (1) the first four stitches of every row, which are the border stitches of one side of your shawl; (2) the center back stitch of your shawl; and (3) the last four stitches of every row, which are the border stitches of the other side of your shawl.

Beginning with row 1a, and for every odd-numbered row thereafter, work B4 at the beginning of the row by slipping the first stitch as if to purl, k1, p1, k1; work the chart one time; knit one stitch; work the chart a second time; work B4 at the end of the row as k1, p1, k2. For every even-numbered row work B4, purl across to the last four stitches, work B4.

To assist you in understanding the chart, the following detailed written instructions are given for rows 1a through 16a and 1b–4b. Every odd-numbered row is a pattern row. In every pattern row there is an increase of four stitches.

---

[4]Alix used a provisional cast-on. When she completed her shawl Alix took out the provisional cast-on and, using the tail of yarn, wove the live stitches together using the Kitchener stitch. You may use your favorite cast-on and then sew the cast-on stitches together using the tail of yarn after you complete your shawl. For instructions on the provisional cast-on see *Stahman's Shawls and Scarves* or another good knitting reference book.

Each increase is made by working a yarnover. One increase is made directly inside each four-stitch border and one increase is made on each side of the center back stitch. The center back stitch is written in **bold.**

Row 1a: B4, place a marker on your needle, [yo, k1, yo], place a marker on your needle, **k1,** [yo, k1, yo], place a marker on your needle, B4. [15 sts]

Row 2a and all even-numbered rows: B4, purl across to the last four stitches, B4.

Row 3a: B4, ^, [yo, k3, yo], ^, **k1,** [yo, k3, yo], ^, B4. [19 sts]

Row 5a: B4, ^, [yo, k5, yo], ^, **k1,** [yo, k5, yo], ^, B4. [23 sts]

Row 7a: B4, ^, [yo, k7, yo], ^, **k1,** [yo, k7, yo], ^, B4. [27 sts]

Row 9a: B4, ^, [yo, k9, yo], ^, **k1,** [yo, k9, yo], ^, B4. [31 sts]

Row 11a: B4, ^, [yo, k11, yo], ^, **k1,** [yo, k11, yo], ^, B4. [35 sts]

Row 13a: B4, ^, [yo, k13, yo], ^, **k1,** [yo, k13, yo], ^, B4. [39 sts]

Row 15a: B4, ^, [yo, k15, yo], ^, **k1,** [yo, k15, yo], ^, B4. [43 sts]

Row 1b: B4, ^, yo, k1, (yo, sl 1-k1-psso) three times, k3, (k2tog, yo) three times, k1, yo, ^, **k1,** yo, k1, (yo, sl 1-k1-psso) three times, k3, (k2tog, yo) three times, k1, yo, ^, B4. [47 sts]

Row 3b: B4, ^, yo, k1, (yo, sl 1-k1-psso) four times, k1, (k2tog, yo) four times, k1, yo, ^, **k1,** yo, k1, (yo, sl 1-k1-psso) four times, k1, (k2tog, yo) four times, k1, yo, ^, B4. [51 sts]

Continue by following the chart.

<u>Making the Shawl the Size Desired</u>—Repeat rows 1d–18d as many times as necessary to make the shawl the size desired. For every 18 rows worked, the shawl increases in width by 36 stitches.

<u>Bottom Border</u>, worked after completing row 18d for the final time:

Row 1, the eyelet row: Work the four border stitches, (yo, k2tog) until you reach the pattern repeat just before the center back stitch, (yo, k2tog) eight times, (yo, k1) three times, (yo, k2tog) until just four stitches remain on your left needle, yo, work the four border stitches.
Row 2: Work as you have worked all even-numbered rows.
Rows 3, 5 & 7: Work in seed stitch to the center back stitch, work a closed increase by making a half-hitch on your needle with your working yarn, k1, work a closed increase, work in seed stitch to the end.
Rows 4 & 6: Work in seed stitch.
Row 8: Bind off, using a larger needle for your right needle.

Wash and dress your shawl. A shawl is a knitted hug. Enjoy giving your completed lace prayer shawl to someone who is in need of a comforting hug. Knit a second shawl for yourself or for another friend.

Alix's Garter Stitch Lace Prayer Shawl
Follow the instructions for the Stockinette Stitch Lace Prayer Shawl, with the following modifications. When working in garter stitch, work the setup row by knitting all stitches. B4 at the beginning of every row is slip the first stitch as if to knit, k3. B4 at the end of every row is k4. All even-numbered rows are worked as Sl1, knit across.

Alix's Lace Prayer Shawl

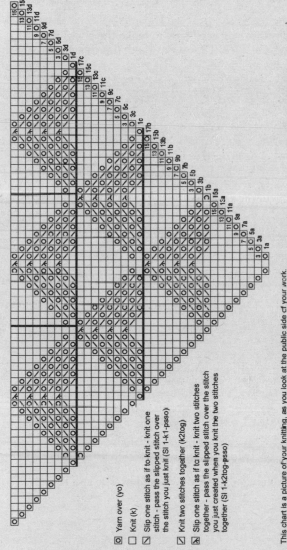

- ⊡ Yarn over (yo)
- ☐ Knit (k)
- ⟋ Slip one stitch as if to knit - knit one stitch - pass the slipped stitch over the stitch you just knit (Sl 1-k1-psso)
- ⟍ Knit two stitches together (k2tog)
- ⋏ Slip one stitch as if to knit - knit two stitches together - pass the slipped stitch over the stitch you just created when you knit the two stitches together (Sl 1-k2tog-psso)

This chart is a picture of your knitting, as you look at the public side of your work.
For detailed line-by-line instructions for this chart, and to see photographs of shawls knit using this pattern, go to www.debbiemacomber.com.

Copyright 2006 by Myrna A.I. Stahman dba Rocking Chair Press

One

"One of the best kept secrets in the knitting world is that knitting lace appears to be much more difficult than it is. If you can knit, purl, knit two together and put the yarn over your needle to form a new stitch, you CAN knit lace."

—Myrna A.I. Stahman, Rocking Chair Press, designer, author and publisher of *Stahman's Shawls and Scarves—Lace Faroese-Shaped Shawls From The Neck Down and Seamen's Scarves,* and the soon to be published *The Versatility of Lace Knitting— Variations on a Theme*

Lydia Goetz

I love A Good Yarn, and I'm grateful for every minute I spend in my shop on Blossom Street. I love looking at the skeins of yarn in all their colors and feeling the different textures. I love my knitting classes and the friends I've made here. I love studying the pattern books. I love gazing out my front window onto the energy and activity of downtown Seattle. In fact, I love *everything* about this life I've found, this world I've built.

Knitting was my salvation. That's something I've said often, I know, but it's simply the truth. Even now, after nearly ten years of living cancer-free, knitting dominates my life. Because of my yarn store, I've become part of a community of knitters and friends.

I'm also married now, to Brad Goetz. A Good Yarn was my first real chance at life and Brad was my first chance at love. Together, Brad and I are raising our nine-year-old son. I say Cody's *our* son, and he is, in all the ways that matter. I consider him as much my child as Brad's; I couldn't love Cody more if I'd given birth to him. It's true he has a mother, and I know Janice does care about him. But Brad's ex-wife is...well, I hesitate to say it, but *selfish* is the word that inevitably comes to mind. Janice appears intermittently in Cody's life, whenever the mood strikes her or she happens to find it convenient—despite the parenting plan she signed when she and Brad divorced. Sadly, she only sees her son once or twice a year. I can tell that the lack of communication bothers Cody. And Janice's cavalier attitude toward motherhood angers me, but like my son, I don't mention the hurt. Cody doesn't need me to defend or malign Janice; he's capable of forming his own opinions. For a kid, he's remarkably resilient and insightful.

On a February morning, my store with all its warmth and color was a cozy place to be. The timer on the microwave went off; I removed the boiling water and poured it into my teapot after dropping in a couple of tea bags. The rain was falling from brooding, gray skies as it often does in winter. I decided it was time to start another knitting class. I maintain several ongoing classes and charity knitting groups, and I usually begin a new session four or five times a year.

As I considered my new class, I was also thinking about my mother, who's adjusted to life in the assisted-living complex reasonably well. In some ways, I suspect that moving her was even more difficult for my sister, Margaret, and me than it was for Mom. Although Mom hated giving up her independence, she seemed relieved not to have the worry about the house and yard anymore. I wept the day the house was sold, and while she never allowed me to see her tears, I believe Margaret did, too. Selling the house meant letting go of our childhood and all the reminders of growing up there. It was the end of an era for us both, just as it was for our mother.

While I drank my tea, I flipped through the new patterns that had arrived the day before. The first one to catch my eye was a prayer shawl. Lately, I'd seen several patterns for these shawls, some more complex than others. I could easily envision knitting this one for Mom.

Prayer shawls have become popular in the last few years—and not only for prayer. They offer comfort and warmth, emotional, as well as physical. I'd received several inquiries about them and thought perhaps one of these shawls would make for an interesting class. I decided to discuss it with my sister, Margaret, who has a keen business sense and a good feel for which class I should offer next. I didn't appreciate that about her until after she'd come to join me at the shop. Margaret worked for me part-time, which has now turned into full-time. She's not as good with people as I am, but she knows yarn and, surprisingly, has become an excellent employee. She's also my friend. Not so long ago, I couldn't have said that; we might be sisters, but the tension between us was unbearable at times. Our relationship changed for the better, and I thank A Good Yarn for that.

Margaret wouldn't arrive for another thirty minutes, since the shop officially opened at ten. Any number of tasks awaited my attention, things I should be doing, like paying bills and ordering new yarn. Instead, I sat at my desk, with my teacup between my hands. I felt so incredibly blessed.

Needless to say, I didn't always feel this tranquil. When I was in my early twenties, a second bout of cancer struck with a viciousness that had me reeling. I survived, but my father didn't. You see, he fought so hard for me, and when it seemed I'd make it after all, he died, suddenly and unexpectedly, of a heart attack. It was almost as though my recovery meant he could leave me now.

Before I lost Dad, I tended to approach my life tentatively, afraid of happiness, fearing the future. It was a void that loomed hopelessly before me and filled me with dread. Dad was the one who gave me strength. With him gone, I knew I was responsible for my own life. I had a decision to make and I boldly chose…independence. I chose to become part of the world I'd retreated from years before.

The ceiling above me creaked and I knew Colette was up. Colette Blake rented the small apartment over the shop. For the first two years, that tiny apartment was my home, my very first home away from family.

After I married Brad, I wasn't quite sure what to do with the apartment. It stood empty for a while. Then I met Colette, and I'd known instantly that she'd be the perfect tenant. The apartment would console her, give her a place to regain her emotional balance. A bonus— for me—is that she looks after Whiskers on my days off. My cat is a much-loved feature in my store, which he considers his home. I've had customers stop by just to visit him. He often sleeps in the front window, curling up in the afternoon sun. Whiskers generates lots of comments—and smiles. Pets have a way of connecting people to life's uncomplicated joys.

Colette reminds me of myself three years ago, when I first opened the store. I met her shortly before Christmas, when Susannah Nelson, who owns the flower shop next door, brought her over to meet me. It wasn't cancer that shook her world, though. It was death. Colette is a thirty-one-year-old widow. Her husband, Derek, a Seattle policeman, died a little over a year ago. When I mention that, people usually assume Derek was killed in the line of duty. Not so. Following a Seattle downpour, he climbed on the roof to repair a leak. No one knows exactly how it happened but apparently Derek slipped and fell. He died two days later of massive head injuries.

In the weeks since she'd moved here, Colette had only referred to the accident once, as if even talking about her husband was difficult. I've learned that she's an easygoing person who laughs readily and yet at times her grief seemed palpable. Overwhelming. I understood how she felt. I remembered all too well that sense of anguish, that terror of what might happen tomorrow or the next day. Colette approached life fearfully, just the way I once did. I longed to reassure her, and I hoped my friendship provided some pleasure and solace. Friends like Jacqueline and Alix had done the same for me.

The apartment has an outside entrance, as well as

the one leading into the store. Susannah Nelson had hired Colette soon after Susannah purchased what used to be known as Fanny's Floral. Colette's mother once owned a flower shop, and Colette had worked there as a high-school student. Her house sold practically the day it was listed, and Colette needed to move quickly. My tiny apartment was vacant, so we struck a deal. I assumed she wouldn't be there long. Most of her belongings were in storage and she was taking the next few months to decide where she'd live and what she'd do.

The stairs creaked as she ventured down. Since Colette became my tenant, we sometimes shared a pot of tea in the mornings. She was always respectful of my time and I enjoyed our leisurely chats.

"Tea's ready." I reached for a clean cup. Without asking, I filled it and held it out.

"Thanks." Colette smiled as she took the tea.

She was thin—too thin, really. Her clothes were a bit loose, but with her aptitude for style she cleverly disguised it. I noticed, though, as someone who's done the same thing. Part of what I liked about her was the fact that she was lovely without seeming consciously aware of it. Despite her occasional silences, Colette was warm and personable, and I could see she'd be a success at whatever she chose. She hadn't said much about the job she'd left, but I gathered it was a far more demanding position than helping customers in a flower shop.

This job change obviously had something to do with her husband's death. She told me he'd died a year ago January fourteenth. She'd waited for the year to pass before making major changes in her life—selling her home, moving, quitting her job. These changes seem drastic in some ways and completely understandable in others.

Colette wore her long, dark hair parted in the middle. It fell straight to her shoulders, where it curved under. She seemed to achieve this effect naturally—unlike some women, who spend hours taming their hair with gel and spray.

In the short time she'd been here, Colette had made a positive impression on everyone she met. Everyone except my sister. Margaret, being Margaret, shied away from Colette, instinctively distrusting her. My sister's like that; she tends to be a naysayer. She insisted that renting out the apartment had been a huge mistake. In Margaret's eyes, a tenant, any tenant, wasn't to be trusted. She appeared to think Colette would sneak into the shop in the middle of the night and steal every skein of yarn I owned, then hock them on the streets and use the money for drugs. I smiled whenever I thought about that, since not only did I trust Colette, I have a fairly expensive alarm system.

Margaret is, to put it mildly, protective of me. She's older and tends to assume more responsibility than is warranted. It's taken me a long time to understand my sister and even longer to appreciate her, but that's a different story.

Colette held the teacup close to her mouth and paused. "Derek would've turned thirty-three today," she said quietly. She stared into the distance, then looked back at me.

I nodded, encouraging her to talk. She'd only told me about Derek that one other time. I believed, based on my own experience, that the more she shared her pain, the less it would hurt. "Derek wanted children…. We'd been trying, but I didn't get pregnant and now…"

"I'm sure you'll have children one day," I told her. I was confident that she wouldn't be alone for the rest of her life, that she'd marry again and probably have children.

Her smiled was filled with sadness. "Derek and I talked about a baby that morning. The next thing I knew, I was choosing his casket. Ironic, isn't it?"

I didn't know how to comfort her, so I leaned over and gave her a hug.

She seemed a little embarrassed by my show of sympathy and focused her gaze on the floor. "I shouldn't have said anything. I didn't mean to start your day on a sad note. Actually, it wasn't until I glanced at the calendar on your desk that I realized the date."

"It's okay, Colette. I'm just so sorry."

"Thank you," she said, shrugging lightly. "Life is like that sometimes, you know?"

"Yes…" And I did.

Colette set the empty cup in my sink.

The back door opened, then shut with a bang. Margaret, of course, muttering about the weather. After Colette moved in, Margaret had taken to parking in the alley, apparently to keep an eye on my tenant's comings and goings. After dumping her huge felted purse on the table, she hesitated, stiffening at the sight of Colette.

"Good morning," I said brightly, pleased to see her despite her bad mood. "It's a fine morning, isn't it?" I couldn't resist a touch of sarcasm.

"It's *raining*," she replied, eyeing Colette almost as if she were an intruder.

"Rainy weather's good for knitting," I reminded her.

For me, there was nothing more satisfying on a rainy afternoon than working on my current knitting project with a cup of tea by my side. People looked for something productive to do when it rained and—fortunately for me—that sometimes included knitting.

Margaret removed her coat and hung it on the peg by the back door. "Julia dropped me off this morning," she said in passing.

I caught the significance right away. "You let *Julia* drive the new car?" Only the day before, Margaret had said that her elder daughter, a high-school senior, had been asking to take the car out for a spin. If I recall, Margaret's exact words were *Not in this lifetime.*

Margaret's hot-from-the-showroom vehicle was a first for the family, since she and Matt had always purchased their cars secondhand. Margaret's previous car was well past repairing, and she was excited about buying a brand-new vehicle. They'd looked for weeks before deciding on one that was in high demand and said to get incredibly good mileage. Once the decision was made, they'd waited two months for the vehicle to arrive. Which it finally had in all its metallic-blue glory.

"I know, I know," Margaret grumbled. "I said I wasn't going to let her take the car, but I couldn't help myself. She has something going on after school and somehow managed to convince me that her entire scholastic future rested on driving my car." Her mouth twitched as she admitted how easily Julia had finessed her way past her mother's objections.

"I don't even have a hundred miles on that car," Margaret said. "That's how fast she broke down my defenses. Sad, isn't it?"

Colette laughed. "Kids can do that."

Margaret responded to the comment with a dismissive nod, barely acknowledging Colette.

Colette's eyes momentarily met mine. "I'll catch up with you later, Lydia," she said and headed back upstairs.

Margaret's gaze followed Colette. "You like her, don't you?"

"She's great." I wished my sister would give Colette a chance. Hoping the sympathy factor might work, I added, "Today's her dead husband's birthday. She'd started telling me about it when you arrived."

Margaret had the grace to look ashamed. "That's tough," she said, her own eyes returning to the stairs. The door had been left open and Whiskers wandered down.

"I know the rental income's a plus, but frankly I don't trust her," Margaret said.

I sighed; I'd heard this far too often and it still made no sense to me.

"Why not?" I asked defensively.

"Think about it," Margaret said. "Colette's obviously far more capable than she's letting on. Why is she working in a flower shop? She could get a job anywhere."

"She just lost her husband," I muttered.

"A year ago. Okay, that's tragic and I'm sorry, but it doesn't mean she has to go into hiding, does it?"

"She isn't hiding." I didn't know that for sure. But I argued with Margaret because I sincerely liked Colette; my sister was overreacting and it troubled me that she went through life seeing everyone as suspect.

"Then why's she working next door for minimum wage?" Margaret pressed. "There's more to her than meets the eye and until we find out what it is, I don't think it's wise to be so chummy."

"Everyone handles grief differently," I went on to explain, although I didn't have the answers Margaret wanted. It was true that Colette had made a lot of major changes in a short time. Equally true that I didn't know much about her circumstances.

"I doubt any of this has to do with her husband, anyway," Margaret said, still looking in the direction of the stairs. "Mark my words, Colette's hiding something."

My sister sometimes shocked me with the things she said. "Oh, for heaven's sake, that's ridiculous!"

Margaret raised one shoulder. "Maybe, but I doubt it. Something about her doesn't sit right with me. I know you like her and apparently Susannah does, too, but I'm reserving judgment until we learn more about her."

I shook my head stubbornly. My instincts told me Colette was a good person.

Margaret frowned at my wordless response. "Just promise me you'll be careful."

Careful? She made Colette sound like a fugitive. "You've been reading too many detective novels," I teased, knowing how much my sister enjoyed reading suspense fiction. She kept a paperback tucked inside her purse and enjoyed discussing the plots with me. I tend to listen to audio books; that way, I can "read" and knit at the same time. That's my idea of multitasking.

"Has Colette ever mentioned where she used to work before Susannah's Garden?" Margaret asked.

"No…but why should she?"

Margaret cast me one of the looks that suggested I was far too trusting.

Clearly Margaret had a more vivid imagination than

I did. "I don't think she's in the witness protection program, if that's what you're implying." I walked to the front of the shop, rolled up the shade on the door and turned the Closed sign to Open. I saw that the rain had intensified in the last while. Whiskers immediately leaped into the window and curled up, purring softly.

"I wanted to discuss another knitting class," I said, remembering my thoughts of earlier that morning. I flipped the light switch and through the steamy windows of the French Café across the street, I saw my friend Alix Townsend, who worked there as a baker. The rain came down in a torrent, falling so hard it bounced against the pavement and ran in the gutters. It'd been nearly two weeks since Alix and I had talked and I'd missed her. I knew she had less free time these days, since she was in the middle of planning her wedding.

Many changes had taken place since I'd come to Blossom Street. The French Café, of course, and Susannah's Garden. There was a new bookstore three doors down from me now, and directly across from that was the old bank building, which had been turned into ultra-expensive condos. They sold so fast, even the real estate people were shocked. A few of the residents had taken my knitting classes and I was beginning to know them.

"Maybe I'll go and see Alix this morning," I said casually. I rarely ate breakfast but I was in the mood for something sweet. If I timed it right, maybe Alix would be able to join me for a muffin and a cup of coffee.

"You're changing the subject again," Margaret said from behind me.

"I am?" I tried to recall what we'd been discussing.

"I didn't mean to. I was just thinking about everything that's happened on Blossom Street."

Margaret glanced at me. "It all started with you and A Good Yarn," my sister said. "You set the tone for this neighborhood. People like it here."

Praise from Margaret was rare indeed and I felt a surge of pleasure at her words.

Despite the rain and despite our disagreement about Colette, I knew we were going to have a good day.

Two

Alix Townsend

It was raining—again. Alix Townsend dashed across the street, already drenched by the rain that had been coming down steadily since the Thursday before. She needed a cigarette. Bad. After more than two years without one, she could hardly believe how intense the craving was. She felt blindsided by it. The damn wedding—that was the problem. A whole vocabulary of swearwords raced through her mind. In less than four months, on June second, she would become Reverend Jordan Turner's wife, and frankly, that terrified her.

Alix Townsend a pastor's wife! It was almost laughable. Although few people knew it, her mother was in prison for a variety of crimes, including forgery, passing bad checks and attempted murder. This wasn't her first stint in jail, either. Tom, Alix's only brother, was dead of a drug overdose and she hadn't had any contact with her father since she was twelve. As far as she knew, he'd made no effort to get in touch with her. When it came to family, Alix definitely felt cheated.

She didn't consider herself a fancy-church-wedding candidate, but somehow, almost without noticing it, she'd become immersed in this whole crazy mess. This...this *sideshow* of a wedding.

"Alix," Jordan shouted, running after her, his feet pounding hard as he crossed the road and splashed his way through the puddles on Blossom Street.

Alix had visited Jordan's office during lunch break. They hadn't actually argued, although they'd come close. She hated what this wedding had turned into, hated having no control, hated that no one seemed willing to listen. Not even Jordan. When she realized he wasn't hearing her, she'd rushed out of his office with a huge lump in her throat. The stinging tears surprised her as much as the craving for a cigarette.

She ignored Jordan's shout. With the rain and wind, it was easy to pretend she hadn't heard him.

"Alix!" he yelled again and a moment later caught up with her.

She slowed her pace and he fell into step beside her. "What just happened back there?" he asked. He was obviously confused by the way she'd hightailed it out of his office.

"What do you mean?" she asked, annoyed that he couldn't figure it out.

"Why'd you leave like that? We were right in the middle of a conversation and all of a sudden, you're gone."

"You weren't *listening* to me," she said, looking up at him, not caring that the rain had drenched her short hair, dripping down her face and onto her chin.

"I don't know why you're so upset," he began. "I—"

"You don't *know?*" she cried, struggling not to get emotional. "Shouldn't I have some say in my own wedding?"

"You do." He still seemed befuddled. "The last thing I remember was you telling me Jacqueline and Reese had decided to hold the reception at their country club."

"And you think that's a good idea?" she asked him.

"I think it's very generous."

"It is, but…" Jacqueline and Reese had been wonderful—about everything. Alix owed them far more than she could ever repay.

She'd met Jacqueline in a knitting class at A Good Yarn, and after a rough start the older woman had taken Alix under her wing. Alix had signed up for that class in order to work off community service hours on a trumped-up drug charge; she'd decided to knit a baby blanket and donate it to charity. Her caseworker had approved the project and that was the beginning of her friendship with the Donovans.

Through Reese Donovan's business connections and the Rotary Club, Alix had been able to attend culinary school. The Donovans had provided part-time employment, as well. She'd filled in as their housekeeper when needed, and they'd let her move into their guesthouse, where she still lived. Jacqueline and Reese were about as close to family as Alix ever hoped to have. They'd given her the love, encouragement and support her own parents never had, and Alix loved them in return. She'd asked their daughter-in-law, Tammie Lee, to serve as her matron of honor. Jordan's brother, Bret, was to be his best man.

"From what my mother told me, Jacqueline had to

call in all kinds of favors to get the country club for a Saturday in June," Jordan said.

"I know." The guilt was even stronger than her craving for a cigarette. "But, Jordan—the country club?"

Her fiancé placed his arm around her shoulders. "Let's get out of the rain." He led her under the awning outside the French Café. The rain beat against it and the water fell in a solid sheet over the edge.

"Mom was really pleased when I told her what Jacqueline had done," Jordan continued.

Alix lowered her head. Jordan's mother was a subject best avoided. Susan Turner would've preferred a more traditional bride for her son. Her future mother-in-law hadn't said or done anything overt, but Alix wasn't stupid. She *knew*. Jordan was close to his parents, though, and Alix would never mention any of this to him.

"Kiss me."

Jordan's eyes flared wide. "Here? Now?" He glanced over his shoulder through the large picture window at the café filled with customers.

Alix nodded, not caring who saw them or what anyone thought. "And not a peck on the cheek, either. I need a *real* kiss."

"All right." He clasped her shoulders with both hands and bent down to cover her mouth with his. His lips were warm and moist as they touched hers, his mouth slightly open. Relaxing, she savored his taste, his feel. She did her best to remember that while a big fancy wedding wasn't what *she* wanted, it would make a lot of people happy—people like Jordan and his family and Jacqueline and Reese. She'd do it; she didn't have to like it. With that in mind, she slid her arms around Jordan's neck and leaned into him. She wanted him to know how much she loved him. She *must* love him if she was willing to go through with this craziness.

When he broke off the kiss, she sighed and instantly felt better.

"You have to talk to me, Alix," he whispered, holding her tight, nuzzling her neck. "Tell me when you're worried about something...."

"I did. You weren't listening."

"I was trying," he said in a low voice. "Do you want to call off the wedding? Is that it?"

"No!" Her response came fast and vehemently. "I love you. I want us to be married."

He brushed the wet hair from her forehead, his eyes intense. "And I love you."

She looked away because the love shining from his eyes confused her and made it difficult to speak. "As soon as you gave me the engagement ring, I should've known everything would change."

"In what way?" he asked.

"Before...before, it was just you and me—and your teens, of course." As a youth pastor, Jordan planned church-related activities with the teenagers in his congregation. Alix often tagged along to help. It was understood that once they were married, her role would continue in a larger capacity. That was fine; she enjoyed working with that age-group. She related to a lot of the temptations they faced in the world and found it gratifying that she was able to steer some of them away from making negative choices, choices she'd made as a teenager and come to regret.

Then the minute he'd slipped the engagement ring on her finger, life as she knew it changed.

As soon as she heard the news, Jacqueline had instantly started talking about the wedding. In fact, for Christmas, Jacqueline had presented Alix with a huge hardcover book titled *Planning the Perfect Wedding*. At the time, Alix hadn't given the actual ceremony much thought. She figured she'd marry Jordan with his family and a few friends in attendance, open gifts, eat cake, and that would be it.

Boy, was she wrong. The wedding was turning into a production, like a Broadway musical or something, with a dinner that cost more per plate than she'd earned in a week back when she'd been employed at the video store.

That wasn't all. The dress—correction, *gown*—had become a major issue. Each one she'd seen came covered with expensive lace or hundreds of tiny pearls. Or both. Jacqueline had taken her to a boutique, and Alix had made the mistake of glancing at the price tag. She'd nearly fainted. People bought cars for less money than those dresses!

"Can't we elope?" she pleaded, her face buried in Jordan's chest. She knew the answer; still, she had to ask.

"Sweetheart, I can't do that."

"Why not?" She looked up, hoping he'd give her the confidence she needed to see this through. The acceptance the resignation—she'd felt earlier had faded. She was no longer sure she could be Alix Townsend, Perfect Bride. The wedding was four months away and already she could feel the panic rising inside her.

More than anything she wanted to be Jordan's wife. She'd fallen in love with him when they were in the sixth grade; he embodied everything she'd ever longed for in life. Then she'd met him again three years ago, shortly after she'd joined the knitting class. She remembered every single fact about Jordan from grade school.

She remembered what she'd learned about his family, too. His mom and dad loved each other and cared for their children. They weren't drunks and losers like her parents. They had regular meals, during which the entire family sat down at the table and talked about their day. In Alix's home, no one did anything together. If her mother was inclined to cook, dinner was left on the stove and everyone dished up their own meals. Most nights Alix ate alone in front of the television while her parents argued in the background. More often than she cared to count, the fights turned physical and she hid in the closet, where she'd invented a fantasy world—a whole family of parents and siblings like the ones on TV. Or the ones at Jordan's house…

The contrast between her life and his didn't stop there. Alix's mother had once fired a gun at her father and landed in jail. By the time she left school, Alix had gone through a whole series of foster homes. During those years she'd been in plenty of trouble, too. But when Tom died of a drug overdose, it had hit her hard. Alix knew she was headed for the same fate if she didn't change her life. From that moment, she swore off drugs. They were death with a capital *D*. She'd been tempted more than once, but had always found the courage to walk away.

"The wedding's just one day out of our lives," Jordan pointed out.

Alix sighed. Twenty-four hours—actually, less than that—she could handle. The wedding was scheduled for five o'clock in the afternoon, followed by a dinner and reception at the country club. Jordan already had reservations at a hotel in Victoria, British Columbia, for their honeymoon. If enduring a formal wedding meant she'd be Jordan's wife at the end of that day, then she'd do it without another word of complaint.

"I know this isn't your kind of thing," Jordan said, kissing the top of her wet head. "The truth is, all I care about is being married to you."

"Really?"

He smiled. "Really."

"Then why don't we just get married by ourselves and tell everyone after the fact?" Even as she said it, Alix knew that would never happen.

"We can't, sweetheart, I'm sorry. My mother would feel we'd cheated her and...there'd be talk."

"Talk," she repeated, her voice numb.

"I work in a church," he reminded her unnecessarily. "Eloping isn't a good example to pass along to the kids in the congregation. You might not realize it, but they watch everything we say and do."

This wasn't news to Alix, since she was well aware of how the teens looked up to Jordan and consequently, to her. She remembered the first time she'd seen Jordan with a group of church kids at a local skating rink. He'd made her think of the Pied Piper leading children through the town. Those kids thought the world of him; they idolized him and had sent frequent glances her way, apparently shocked that he was associated with her. They weren't the only ones.

It'd taken Alix a long time to believe that Jordan loved her. Even now, she wasn't sure what had attracted him to her. Whatever it was, she felt deeply grateful.

"It'll be a small wedding," Jordan promised.

She nodded. Her guest list was limited to a few friends, most of whom she'd met through the knitting class. Maybe twenty people.

"Mom's putting together her list this week."

At the mention of his mother, Alix tensed. She liked Jordan's mother but couldn't shake the feeling that she was a disappointment to Susan Turner. In truth, Alix didn't blame her and was determined to do whatever she could to make this relationship a successful one.

She derived some comfort from knowing that Jacqueline hadn't liked her daughter-in-law in the beginning, either. Jacqueline couldn't understand why Paul, their only son, would marry someone like Tammie Lee, whose southern background was so dissimilar to his own.

If Alix recalled correctly, Jacqueline had had another woman in mind for Paul. Tammie Lee had persevered, though, and eventually her kindness and charm had won Jacqueline over. By the time her first grandchild was born, Jacqueline had wholeheartedly accepted Tammie Lee. Now they were as close as…well, family. And Alix considered Tammie Lee one of her best friends.

Susan Turner might well have another woman in mind for her youngest son, too. If so, Jordan had never mentioned anyone. One Sunday, three years ago, Alix had slipped into the back of the church without Jordan's knowledge. As part of the service he'd sung a duet with a beautiful blonde—who'd turned out to be his cousin. But seeing him with someone else, even in church, had infuriated Alix. Jordan had been equally upset with her for jumping to conclusions. He was right. Not once in all the time they'd dated had Jordan given her reason to suspect he was interested in anyone else.

That didn't mean his mother shared his certainty about Alix, though. Still, Susan had always been polite, if a bit cool. Jordan got along exceptionally well with his parents, and the last thing Alix wanted to do was mess that up for him.

"You need something to take your mind off all this wedding business," Jordan said.

"Like what?" She was eager to do anything that would help her get through the next few months.

"What about another knitting class?"

Alix bit her lip as she considered the idea. She nodded slowly. "Lydia was in the other day and we chatted for a few minutes. She's always got classes going and she's starting a new one for a prayer shawl."

"What a great idea."

"Who would I give it to, though?" Alix asked.

"What about my grandmother Turner?"

Alix knew immediately that this was the perfect suggestion. She'd met his grandmother for the first time over the Christmas holidays, shortly after Jordan had given her the engagement ring, and had felt an instant connection with the old woman. They'd talked for hours, finding that their views were surprisingly alike and laughing at the same corny jokes. Although well into her eighties, Grandma lived on her own and still managed to keep a large flower garden. Alix had called Grandma Turner several times since and been out to see her last month with Jordan.

"I'll sign up for the class after work," Alix told him.

"Good." He sighed, as though relieved the matter was settled.

Alix leaned into Jordan and kissed him again. She wanted him to know how much she appreciated the fact that he'd come after her. She'd left before he'd begun to really listen to her. Before he'd taken her doubts and fears about this wedding seriously. But he was listening now.

She must have put a bit more emotion into the kiss than she'd realized because Jordan was breathing hard when they broke apart. He cleared his throat. "That was nice."

"Yeah," she agreed in a soft voice. "It was."

Jordan pulled her back into his arms. "June can't get here too soon as far as I'm concerned."

"I second that," Alix said with a laugh.

Three

Colette Blake

Colette suspected that Margaret from the yarn store had never meant for her to hear that comment. The truth was, she was running away; she was hiding…from Christian Dempsey, from her past and—mostly—from herself. Colette had been halfway up the stairs when Margaret's words hit her square in the back and now, a week later, those words continued to sting. She felt an overwhelming urge to explain, but she resisted. How could she tell these two women she'd been a widow for a year but was two months pregnant? Life was full of ironies, to say the least. Bitter ironies…

For three years she and Derek had tried to have a baby with no success. Then…one slip. A one-night stand, and here she was, carrying the child of a man she'd hoped never to see again. The very thought of Christian Dempsey filled her with dread. How could she have worked as his personal assistant for five years and been so naively unaware of the kind of man he was?

Losing Derek, her shocking discovery about Christian and now this unexpected pregnancy—it was enough to drive anyone to the brink of emotional collapse.

Memories of her dead husband always brought her a pang of loss. It shouldn't hurt this much after a full year and yet it did. His death made no sense to her. Her guilt over the fight they'd had just before his accident, another fight about their fertility problems, didn't help. Nevertheless, her husband was dead, and she had to deal with that reality. She hated it. She hated every minute of life without Derek.

It was so *stupid* that he'd died. So incredibly stupid. For the first few weeks, her anger at the unfairness of it had consumed her. Derek should never have gotten up on that roof in the first place. All it would've taken was a simple phone call, and a professional repairman could've come out to take care of the leak. Derek had no business even attempting it. However, he'd said that any delay would cause more damage and claimed the job was a "no-brainer." Before she could stop him, he had the ladder up against the side of the house and a tool belt slung around his waist. This was his opportunity to use the tools he'd gotten for Christmas; she wondered if that was his real motivation, or part of it, anyway. So pointless. So foolish.

If there was one thing to be grateful for, it was the fact that Colette hadn't witnessed his fall. A neighbor friend had been there, talking to Derek, when he lost his balance and slid off the roof onto the concrete driveway. The neighbor called 911 from his cell phone before Colette even knew anything was wrong. Derek had been rushed to the hospital and never regained consciousness.

Initially Colette had been in shock, and then, as soon

as the fog cleared and her numbness dissipated, she became angry. Deeply, furiously angry. The anger was followed by a feeling of sadness and overpowering loss. But none of this was a good reason for what she'd done a couple of months ago.

Her cheeks grew hot with embarrassment as she sat at the round oak table in her tiny kitchen. Covering her face with both hands, she relived the night of the company Christmas party.

Colette had been Christian Dempsey's personal assistant for five years. That had come about in a completely unexpected way.

After working at Dempsey Imports in customs clearance, she'd been transferred to another floor near the corporate offices. Recently married, she was excited about her promotion to broker and the raise that went with it. She and Derek were just setting up house and with the added expenses of the honeymoon and the wedding, which they'd paid for themselves, the increase in pay had been a blessing.

Although she'd been with the company for two years, Colette had only seen Mr. Dempsey briefly and in passing. He was a man who exuded authority and power. He was frequently away from the office on foreign buying trips, and whenever he made an appearance, he seemed remote and preoccupied. This had probably contributed to the mystique that surrounded him. It didn't hurt that he was six-three, solidly built and exceptionally good-looking. Heads turned anytime he walked into a room; he commanded that kind of respect and attention. Her first day on the second floor, Mr. Dempsey had arrived at work soon after she did and Colette, standing in the corridor between his office and her own department, had greeted him.

"Good morning, Mr. Dempsey."

Those four words would forever change the course of her career—and her life.

He walked past her, with only the slightest acknowledgement of her greeting. It was then that she noticed everyone in the room watching her.

She waited until Christian Dempsey was inside his office, then gazed around her. People simply stared. Jenny, her boss, had a coffee mug half raised to her lips, her expression one of disbelief. Mark Taylor stood in front of a filing cabinet, shaking his head.

"Why's everyone looking at me like that?" Colette asked.

Jenny set the coffee down on her desk and answered in a hushed whisper, "*No one* talks to Mr. Dempsey."

"No one," Mark reiterated.

Colette couldn't imagine why not. He was flesh and blood like everyone else. Wishing him a good day was just the polite thing to do. But when she asked about it, she didn't get a satisfactory response. Jenny sputtered, "Because he's…because." And Mark said, "Well, he's *very* busy, you know." None of which, in Colette's view, justified the staff's awed—or was it fearful?—reaction.

An hour later, she was summoned to Mr. Dempsey's office by his assistant, who came to ask if she was the person who'd greeted him that morning. Her fellow workers cast her sympathetic looks as Colette rose from her desk and followed Dempsey's assistant into the inner sanctum. Glancing over her shoulder, she noticed that Jenny was biting her lip. Mark waved as if to bid her farewell. Karen Christie and the others shrugged mournfully. Colette hadn't known what to expect…except the worst.

Christian was working on his computer when she was ushered into his office. His assistant announced her name and left her standing there. Mr. Dempsey didn't look up. Consequently, Colette felt like some minion called in, awaiting his notice. Her mouth had gone dry and she resisted blurting out that she loved her job and didn't want to lose it. In nervous agitation she clenched her fists at her sides. When he finally deigned to glance in her direction, his eyes held hers.

"Are you the one who spoke to me?" he asked.

"Yes, sir." She probably should've apologized but she couldn't make herself do it. The thought of losing her job because she'd been polite to her employer was ridiculous. And yet… She and Derek had made an offer on a house and needed her income to qualify for the loan. Everything would fall apart if she was fired.

"Why?"

"Why did I wish you a good morning?" she repeated, wanting to be sure she understood the question.

He gave her a half nod.

"Well," she murmured, "I was just being courteous."

"Are you new to the company?"

"I've worked here for two years." Her throat felt scratchy but she refused to let him see how nervous she was by clearing it. Dempsey's was currently the largest Seattle import company and one of the biggest on the West Coast.

He frowned as if he didn't believe her. "I haven't seen you before."

Colette squared her shoulders. "I received a promotion from customs clearance on the fifth floor to working as a customs broker."

He studied her in silence, and when he spoke, she found his question surprising. "Is that a wedding band on your finger?"

"I was married a few months ago."

"Congratulations."

"Thank you." She didn't know how to respond. Anything she said might be considered crossing the line between professional respect and what could be perceived as excessive familiarity.

"Peter is leaving my employment and I'm looking for a personal assistant. You'll do."

"Me?" Colette slapped her hand over her heart in astonishment. "What about HR? Shouldn't they be sending you people to interview?"

"Do you want the job or not?"

"I...sure. Only..."

"I prefer to hire my own assistants. Now, are you interested?"

At that point, she should have asked any number of questions; instead, she nodded.

"Good. Peter will train you. I don't know what you're earning per hour, but from this point forward you'll be salaried." He named a figure that was three times more than her current rate. Colette nearly fainted.

"Thank you," she managed to mumble. Before leaving, she almost curtsied, such was Christian's effect on her.

That had been the beginning. For the next five years, she made Christian Dempsey's travel arrangements, screened his calls, wrote his letters, did research of various kinds, checked contracts and hired translators.

She also booked his tee times at the local country club, made reservations for his dinner dates and set up all his appointments. When it came to the business, she was aware of every detail. Or so she'd assumed. She even purchased corporate Christmas gifts on his behalf. The one thing she knew next to nothing about was his family. His mother was dead, although how she'd learned that she couldn't remember. Probably gossip she'd heard from Jenny or Mark. But in all that time Christian had never said a word about his father or any siblings.

For the past five years, Colette had spent nearly every work day looking after the details of his business life—and his private life. She dealt with the women, too, and there was no lack in that department. This was hardly surprising, since Christian was rich, powerful and dynamic, not to mention attractive. Equally unsurprising, these relationships never lasted long.

She and Derek were grateful for the money she earned, which they spent on things for the house and traveling. They'd taken trips to Australia and New Zealand, Europe and China, purchased new cars and dined out often. Colette enjoyed the benefits of her job. Then they'd decided to start their family and that was when her marital troubles began. She couldn't get pregnant. There seemed to be no obvious reason, but Derek refused to seek medical help. In his opinion, if a pregnancy happened, it happened and if not, that was fine by him, too. It wasn't fine with Colette; she wanted children, and her inability to conceive had devastated her.

After her husband's death, Christian had been exceptionally kind. The biggest and most elaborate floral arrangement at the funeral had been from Dempsey Imports. He gave her a month off with pay, of which she'd taken two weeks. After that, it was either go back to work or go crazy. As much as possible, her work life returned to normal—until the company Christmas party.

Colette had handled all the arrangements for the party, which was held at a posh downtown hotel and took place on the third Friday of December. Dinner was followed by entertainment and dancing. It was her first Christmas without Derek, so her parents had wanted her to join them in Colorado. Colette's flight was leaving late Saturday afternoon.

To blame alcohol for what happened would've been too easy. Yes, she'd had too much to drink. She'd always been fond of champagne and there'd been plenty of it available. Christian had been drinking, too. Perhaps more than a few glasses; she hadn't kept count. They were both a long way from being clearheaded and sober, *that* was for sure.

At the end of the party, in the wee hours of the morning, she and Christian were the only people left. He'd thanked her for her part in making the evening a success. She'd already received her Christmas bonus but he surprised her by presenting her with a gift—a cameo on a delicate gold chain. Colette hadn't known what to say. She couldn't imagine Christian actually taking the time to shop for her. She was the one who always purchased gifts on his behalf. The gesture had touched her deeply. With this gift, Christian was telling her how sorry he was that she'd lost her husband. He was letting her know he appreciated everything she'd done for him and for the company.

Her eyes had clouded with tears. He tried to dismiss her gratitude but she wouldn't allow him to do that. Impetuously she stood on the tips of her toes and kissed his cheek. Christian clasped her shoulders and stared down at her, his brow furrowed. Then slowly, as though he was waiting for her to stop him, he lowered his mouth to hers. The kiss was explosive, not at all the gentle expression of thanks she might have expected. Colette was knocked off balance, physically and emotionally.

When the kiss ended, they were both breathing hard. He looked at her as if he'd never seen her before. He murmured something she couldn't quite hear; a moment later, she realized he'd told her he was getting a room. No one needed to spell out his intentions, or her own. She wanted him to make love to her. Her head was spinning and even as he led her to the elevator and then to the suite, she knew this was a mistake. Yet she couldn't make herself walk away. She'd been lonely for so long.

When Christian unlocked the door and they entered the room, she made one feeble effort to introduce a note of reason.

"Are you sure we should be doing this?" she'd asked, barely recognizing her own voice.

Christian had responded with a soft laugh. Then they were kissing again, his mouth warm as his tongue found hers. The passion in him left her trembling. They broke apart only long enough to breathe. In a brief moment of sanity, she tried to talk but all that escaped were incoherent sounds that seemed to encourage him.

He led her to the bed, stripping off her clothes as they made their way across the suite. They literally fell onto the bed. The ache in her was so powerful, so strong, that she couldn't think, couldn't speak. A sob rose in her throat but his deep, openmouthed kisses swallowed any sound. Then he was making love to her....

He was an accomplished lover, she'd grant him that.

Her body hummed with pleasure, her senses completely alive. Christian knew how to satisfy a woman. Despite knowing what she did about his history with women, she was a willing participant in their lovemaking.

He turned her face toward his so she couldn't avoid his gaze. His eyes burned into hers and he brought his mouth to Colette's, kissing her again and again. She didn't want to respond and yet she found it impossible not to.

Afterward, he drew the covers over both of them, and they fell asleep. He drifted off first. Colette was harassed by doubts and regrets but she chased them away, refusing to listen. At least, not then... They would return later, the next day and the next. Even now, months afterward, she could hear them echoing in her mind, asking how she could have dishonored Derek's memory that way. How she could have acted so irresponsibly. How she could've let such a thing happen...

At some point during that night she awoke, disoriented. She raised her head from the pillow; the room was still dark. As soon as she realized where she was and who she was with, she opened her eyes wide and her entire body tensed. She tried to slip silently away but the second she moved, Christian rolled over to face her.

"You're awake," he whispered.

She blinked uncertainly but he didn't give her a chance to respond.

Instead, he leaned closer and gently pressed his lips to hers. Colette wanted to tell him they'd made a terrible mistake. She tried, she sincerely tried, but it was useless. He distracted her with his hands, his mouth, and she forgot her protests. Their lovemaking was passionate and uninhibited. And it didn't end there. Twice more they made love.

The next afternoon, when they finally left the hotel room, Colette barely had time to race home, shower, grab her suitcase and fly into Denver to meet her parents.

It was the worst Christmas of her life. On Christmas Eve she and her parents watched their church's reenactment of the Nativity, complete with live animals and a newborn baby. The service had her sobbing uncontrollably. Her parents assumed her tears were related to Derek's death and how dreadfully she missed him, and they were. But it was more than that. She wept for reasons she had yet to fully understand.

Another worry nagged at her. In their rush and foolishness, neither one had bothered with birth control. Colette had never done much praying until then. A quick glance at the calendar told her that a pregnancy could result from her night with Christian.

When she returned to work, it was embarrassing for both of them. Christian treated her as if nothing had happened and for a while she pretended, too. Then one day while he was out of the office, she received an important call from one of the customs brokers and needed to get onto his computer to find a contract service code. His system was shut down, although he'd never turned it off before; she'd frequently needed to refer to files in the past and he always left his computer on for that reason. Knowing him as well as she did, it didn't take her long to discover his password, which he'd listed on his Rolodex under *P*. She'd explain when he got back. She retrieved the necessary information and was ready to close when a file with an odd name caught her attention. It consisted of several Chinese words, none of them familiar. Christian was fluent in Mandarin, but he named his files in English. Not only that, these words didn't seem to correspond with any of their suppliers in China. What made her open the file she'd never know. Their relationship was strained as it was and neither of them had ever spoken of that night. For whatever reason—idle curiosity or latent suspicion—she did open the file. A hundred times since—no, a thousand—she'd found herself wishing that she'd left well enough alone. In that moment, she learned more than she'd ever cared to know about the man who was her employer. She hadn't immediately understood what she was reading, but then it became all too apparent. Christian Dempsey was involved in smuggling illegal aliens from China, using his import business as a cover. At first she refused to believe it. But as she considered his actions since Christmas, certain details started to add up. She'd assumed his uncharacteristic behavior was because of their night together. Now his activities seemed more sinister. He'd begun to close the door between their offices, too, with strict orders that he wasn't to be disturbed. He was away for lengthy periods without explanation. And sometimes, always late in the day, he had guests who weren't announced by Reception. Guests he didn't introduce.

Then, three weeks into the new year, Colette knew she could no longer ignore the obvious. A pregnancy test from the drugstore confirmed it. Under normal circumstances Colette would probably have discussed the situation with him. Not now. She wanted no further contact with Christian Dempsey. The biggest struggle was what to do with the information she had. For several sleepless nights, she debated the best course of action. Her conscience wouldn't allow her to ignore the fact that he was trafficking in humans. At the same time, she wondered if she could put the father of her child behind bars. In the end, she wrote an anonymous letter to the Immigration and Naturalization Service. One thing was certain—she couldn't work for Christian anymore. As far as she could see, leaving was the only solution. Early one morning, she typed up her letter of resignation and placed it on his desk.

Colette wasn't sure how he'd react when he read it. She soon found out. He called her into his office and glared at her. Then with a look so scornful it cut straight through her heart, he suggested she take her two-week vacation now and leave immediately. She nodded, convinced that he was aware of exactly what she'd uncovered. Without a word, she turned and walked out. That was the last time she'd seen or heard from Christian Dempsey.

Her house sold right away and she'd obtained the job in the flower shop the next week. Fortunately, real estate in her part of Seattle moved quickly. When she heard about the apartment above the yarn store, it had seemed perfect. She was hiding from Christian, praying he wouldn't ever look for her. What she earned at the flower shop covered her meager expenses. The insurance money she'd collected after Derek's accident, plus the proceeds from the house, had paid off her car and given her enough to make a few sizable investments. She was financially comfortable.

Too nauseous to eat, she swallowed the rest of her tea, washed her cup and dressed for the day. Colette had a new life now, a brand-new beginning. She was doing

her best to prepare for her baby, trying to eat properly
and taking prenatal vitamins. She'd bought a copy of
What to Expect When You're Expecting from the bookstore down the street, wishing she could have shared
this whole experience with her husband. No one knew
about the pregnancy yet, not even her parents. Until the
authorities arrested Christian, she'd keep it to herself.

When she got to work, Susannah Nelson was already
there, cataloging a shipment of fresh flowers. The scent
of roses filled the shop.

"Good morning." Susannah greeted her absently,
intent on her task.

"Morning. Those smell gorgeous."

"They do, don't they?" Susannah looked up with a
smile.

With Valentine's Day the following week, they'd
received a huge shipment of roses, in addition to the
flowers that arrived every other day. Colette's favorites
were the antique roses with their intense fragrance, although they tended to be smaller and less colorful than
the hybrids.

"I expect we'll be extra busy today," Susannah said.
This was her first full year of owning Susannah's Garden and she was learning as she went. "Oh, before I
forget, there was a phone call yesterday afternoon, just
after you left."

A chill went up Colette's spine. She'd told only a few
people where she'd gone. "Who was it?"

Susannah frowned. "I don't remember the name,
but I wrote it down." Leaving the counter where she'd
been working, she walked over to the phone and sorted
through a stack of pink message slips until she found
the one she wanted.

"The call was from a Christian Dempsey. He said it was personal."

Colette's hand felt numb as she accepted the slip. She glanced at the phone number, one she knew so well, and with her heart pounding, crumpled the note and tossed it in the garbage.

Four

"When individual fibers are knitted together with a thread of emotion, they become an original, personal design. This creative process is my joyful obsession."

—Emily Myles, Fiber Artist. *www.emyles.com*

Lydia Goetz

One of the joys of owning my yarn store is the pleasure I derive from teaching people how to knit. I wish I could explain how much delight it gives me to share my love of knitting with others. I know machines can create sweaters and mittens and other things cheaper, faster and far more efficiently. That's not the point. The projects I knit are an extension of me, an expression of my love for the person I'm knitting for. And—something else I love about knitting—when I'm working with my needles and yarn, I link myself with hundreds of thousands of women through the centuries.

I was on my lunch break, sipping a mug of soup in my office as I reviewed the names on my latest class list.

I think if I'd had a normal adolescence, I might have decided on teaching as a profession. Don't get me wrong, owning A Good Yarn is a dream come true for me. It's part of the woman I am now, the woman I've become not *because* of the cancer, but in spite of it. I'm proud of that.

What I especially love about my classes is getting to know my customers, some of whom are among my dearest friends. For example, in the very first beginning knitters' class I formed three years ago, I met Jacqueline Donovan, Carol Girard and Alix Townsend. We still see each other often, and they're as close to me as my own family. Over the last three years, I've taught dozens of classes, but that first one will always hold a special place in my heart.

Certain of the other classes are also special to me. Like the sock-knitting class two years ago. That's where I met Bethanne Hamlin, Elise Beaumont and Courtney Pulanski. Bethanne is so busy with her party business these days I rarely see her, but Annie, her daughter, often stops by while she's running errands for her mother. Her friend, Amanda Jennings, another cancer survivor, comes with her whenever she can. Bethanne and I don't communicate regularly, but I consider her a good friend. Elise, too, although most of her time these days is spent nursing her husband, Maverick, whose cancer has taken a turn for the worse. Her tender patience brings tears to my eyes. I don't think I've ever seen a couple more in love. Foolishly, I assumed that kind of love was reserved for the young, but Elise and

Maverick have shown me otherwise. The way they love each other is what I pray for in my marriage with Brad.

Courtney Pulanski is at college in Chicago and teaching everyone in her dorm the benefits of knitting. She keeps in touch; I also hear how she's doing from Vera, her grandmother. After her mother's death, Courtney's dad took a job in South America, and Courtney went to live with her grandmother in Seattle for her senior year of high school. It wasn't an easy transition. I'm proud of Courtney, who's become a lovely and well-liked young woman with a strong sense of her own potential, although I have little claim to her success.

It seems to me that each woman who signed up for one of my knitting classes taught *me* a valuable lesson. I suspect that's another reason I feel so close to many of them.

This new class, the one to knit a prayer shawl, has a good feel, although I wish more than three people had enrolled. The first person to sign up was Alix Townsend, which surprised me until she mentioned that she needs something to help with the prewedding stress. Because she's an experienced knitter, I suggested she attempt a more complicated pattern, and she agreed. She chose a beautiful lace shawl.

I certainly understand why Alix is feeling anxious. My own wedding was a low-key affair with just family and a few friends in attendance, yet I was an emotional wreck by the time Brad and I were officially married. Margaret didn't make things any easier. She fluttered around me with questions and criticisms and unwanted advice until I thought I'd scream. But *she* was the one who broke into uncontrollable sobs halfway through the ceremony. My sister, for all her gruff exterior, has a soft heart and genuine compassion for others. I didn't figure that out until I was over thirty.

That's because, until recently, my entire existence revolved around me. It was all I could do to deal with my disease. I was so focused on myself, I failed to notice other people as I should. That knowledge opened my eyes in any number of ways, and I've learned to listen to others, including and perhaps especially Margaret. She still has her irritating mannerisms but I overlook them now —for the most part—and I try to ignore her suspicious reactions to people like Colette. I understand she's trying to protect me (patronizing though that is), I've become much more tolerant, too. And I find myself reaching out more, getting involved in my neighborhood and business community.

Anyway… Alix signed up for the class; Susannah Nelson did, too. With Susannah's Garden she's brought a new energy to the retail neighborhood. She has such interesting and inventive ideas. In the beginning, she gave away more flowers than she sold but the strategy paid off and her shop's doing well. Since Susannah and I hadn't had much opportunity to know each other, I welcomed her presence in the knitting class.

Colette Blake, my tenant, enrolled, too, with Susannah's encouragement. She'd stopped coming by for tea in the mornings and I knew why. She'd obviously overheard Margaret's comment. Ever since that morning, our conversations were brief and a bit stilted. She'd started using the outside entrance right afterward. I missed her.

Because Susannah and Colette were both taking the class, I'd purposely scheduled it later in the afternoon. At four-thirty, Susannah's college-age daughter, Chrissie, would be available to work at the flower shop and Alix would have finished her shift at the café.

The bell above the door jingled and I was distracted from my lunch break. Thankfully, Margaret was out front. She's increasingly more comfortable dealing with customers, although she can sometimes seem brusque and unfriendly. That's a shame because she isn't really like that.

A minute later, Margaret came into the office. "Do we have any yarn made from soy beans?" she asked, frowning. "I never heard of such a thing."

I swallowed my soup. "I have some on order."

Margaret's frown darkened. "You're joking! There's actually a yarn made from *soy?*"

I nodded. "You wouldn't believe the fibers being used for yarn these days." Margaret should've known all this, but she prefers wool, as do I. However, I can't discount the incredible ribbon yarns and some of the newer acrylics. There's even buffalo yarn—or should that be bison?—and I've heard about a yarn from New Zealand that's a blend of wool and possum fur, of all things.

My sister shook her head in wonder and left me to my lunch and my thoughts once more. I'm so grateful the shop has brought Margaret and me together after all the difficulties we faced in our relationship. A few years ago I would never have believed that possible.

Margaret hadn't supported my efforts in the beginning and in retrospect I can't blame her. I'd never taken a single business class or even worked at a full-time job. Margaret was afraid I'd set myself up for failure; as it turned out, she was wrong. Later I could see how much I'd absorbed about business from my father. He'd taught Margaret and me a strong work ethic, too. Our dad had his own business for years, and almost by osmosis I learned a lot from him without even realizing it.

After I finished my lunch, I joined my sister. We did a steady business for the rest of the afternoon. I counted up more than forty sales by four o'clock, which is excellent for a two-person shop. Another bonus—the days pass quickly and pleasurably when we're busy like this.

"Julia's late." Margaret glanced at her watch for the fifth time in the last minute.

"You let her take the car to school again?"

Margaret nodded curtly but wouldn't look at me.

I didn't remind her that she'd sworn the new car was hers and Julia wasn't going to drive it *ever*. She hadn't owned the car for more than a few weeks and already my niece was behind the wheel more often than my sister.

"She was supposed to come by for me right after school," Margaret muttered.

"I'm sure there's a good reason she's late," I told her. Julia was a high-school senior and so involved with myriad activities her schedule made my head swim.

"Not today. She's got a dental appointment at four-thirty and I'm going with her."

I glanced at my own watch and noticed it was four ten. "She'll be here any minute."

Margaret nodded.

"Since she's late, why don't you get your coat and purse and wait outside?"

Margaret hesitated, but finally agreed. She disappeared into the office only long enough to collect what she needed.

"She'll be here soon," I reassured Margaret again.

Julia was a responsible girl and I didn't think for an instant that she'd forgotten her mother.

"It's twenty minutes to the dentist's office from here," Margaret worried.

"Would you like me to phone ahead and let them know you might be late?"

Margaret considered that, then nodded. Her frown grew even fiercer, and I didn't envy Julia once she did arrive. The wrath of Margaret was something to behold. My sister didn't lose her temper often but when she did she could clear a room.

"Go ahead and step outside. I'll contact the dentist's office right now."

Margaret pushed open the door, and the bell chimed as she left the shop.

Stepping up to the counter, I reached for the Rolodex and flipped to the *D*s, where Margaret had filed the dentist's number.

The receptionist answered on the second ring. "Dr. Wentworth's office. How may I help you?"

"Hello," I said, "I'm calling on behalf of Julia Langley. It looks like she's running late and I wanted you to know."

"Can you tell me how late she's going to be?"

"Ah… I'm not sure."

"If it's going to be more than ten minutes, the appointment will need to be rescheduled."

"I don't think it'll be that long, but it depends on traffic," I said, although I had no idea when Julia would show up. I could see Margaret pacing back and forth in front of the display window. Every step she took conveyed nervous agitation.

"Please call again to reschedule if it is later than ten minutes."

"I will," I told her and replaced the receiver.

I remembered then that Julia had a cell phone, one she paid for with money she earned from a part-time job at the movie theater. I'd driven five miles out of my way to take Cody to the theater where Julia worked. Cody had loved seeing his cousin behind the counter. Julia had given him extra butter on his popcorn and my son had been thrilled.

"Margaret," I called, poking my head out the front door. "What about her cell?"

"It's at the house," Margaret snapped. "She let the battery go dead." Her frown told me she saw this as another example of Julia's lack of responsibility. My poor niece was about to get an earful.

The phone pealed sharply behind me. "A Good Yarn," I answered.

"Margaret Langley, please."

The crisp, professional male voice took me aback. It didn't matter what the words said, what I heard was trouble. "Could you tell me what this is about?" I asked as politely as my trembling voice would allow.

"I need to speak directly to Ms. Langley," the man told me.

"One minute, please." I set down the receiver and rushed to the front door.

Margaret swung around to face me almost as if she knew.

"There's a call for you."

"Julia?"

"No...you'd better take it."

"But Julia will be here any second."

"Take the call," I insisted.

I so rarely insist on anything with my sister that Margaret's brows rose abruptly. "Is everything all right?"

"I…I don't know."

She hurried into the shop and grabbed the receiver. "This is Margaret Langley."

She listened for a moment and then her eyes shot to mine. She gasped. Her knees literally went out from under her and she sank into the chair I kept behind the counter.

"Is she hurt?" Margaret asked shakily.

I bit my lip, awaiting the answer.

"Yes, yes, I'll be here." She replaced the receiver, looked at me and burst into tears.

"W-what is it?" I asked, starting to cry, too. "Has Julia been in an accident?"

"No… The police are coming to take me to the hospital."

"Julia's in the *hospital?*"

"Yes, yes, she's been hurt but they won't tell me how badly. The hospital needs me to sign the papers before they can take her into surgery."

"Surgery." I swallowed painfully. "What happened?" I cried, gripping my sister's arm. "Tell me what happened."

"She… Julia was on her way to pick me up, just like you said."

"Yes, yes." I knew Julia wouldn't have forgotten.

"She stopped at a red light and someone, a man, ran up to the driver's side and yanked open the door and—"

The picture that formed in my mind sent my nerves shrieking in protest. "Julia was carjacked?"

Margaret nodded. "He dragged her into the street and

when she tried to fight him off, he…he hit her again. Then he threw her into moving traffic so she had to scramble for her life."

I covered my mouth with both hands to stifle a scream. My beautiful niece had been attacked. I didn't know the extent of her injuries but apparently they were bad enough to require surgery.

The shock of this, the horror I felt, was more than I could take in.

Five

Colette Blake

Learning to knit might fill up some of the lonely hours, Colette reasoned. Susannah had convinced her to give it a try. To her surprise, Colette discovered she was actually looking forward to the first class next Wednesday. Perhaps that was because knitting suggested an image of peace and contentment. She could picture a heavily pregnant version of herself sitting in the comfortable chair Lydia had left behind, knitting something for her baby.

She hadn't told anyone yet. Within a few months, though, keeping her pregnancy a secret would be impossible. At this point, Colette didn't know what she'd do once the baby was born, where she'd live, or even whether she should tell Christian about his child. With no firm plan in mind, she decided to wait until she saw how the authorities responded to her anonymous letter. She assumed she'd find out from the news—or she could always call Jenny at the office. Jenny would be happy to hear from her, despite their lack of recent contact.

The flower shop had been frantic with activity this morning—not unexpected, this close to Valentine's Day. Susannah's daughter, Chrissie, who'd transferred from the University of Oregon to the University of Washington, had agreed to step in one afternoon a week in order to free up Susannah and Colette for the class. There were advantages for Chrissie, too. She wanted to learn the business and prove she was a responsible adult; not only that, she'd be making some extra money.

The class project was a prayer shawl, which Colette hoped to use as a blanket for her baby. Lydia had said the idea of knitting a prayer shawl was to make it for someone in need of prayer or healing. Colette certainly needed both.

At the shop the previous week, Colette had met Chrissie, who seemed like a typical undergraduate—alternately self-confident and insecure. She was ebullient with a natural charm she put to good use in the shop. Chrissie was close to her mother and Colette envied her that closeness. Her own relationship with her parents was fine, although there'd never been the kind of easy banter Chrissie enjoyed with Susannah. Still, she wished they weren't so far away, especially now. On the other hand, it could be awkward if they lived nearby. Colette hadn't told them about the baby; if she did, she knew they'd insist she tell Christian and she couldn't do that—at least, not yet. She felt suspended between her past and her future, unable to move ahead with the new life she'd begun.

She explained to her parents that she'd stayed because Seattle was familiar and comfortable and her home. That was true, but she also wanted to remain in town until she found out what would happen to Christian.

It wasn't dark as early in the afternoons now, but by four, the shadows started to lengthen. Colette liked watching the activity on Blossom Street as the streetlights came on, illuminating the sidewalk. She'd been assembling a funeral wreath, adding white carnations and filling the space between the flowers with salal, an evergreen that grew wild in the area, when Susannah returned from an appointment.

"How'd it go?" Colette asked, knowing her employer had been nervous about meeting with the director of one of the largest privately owned funeral homes in downtown Seattle. Susannah had recently tendered a proposal to provide floral arrangements for prearranged funerals, which included an allotment for flowers, and had been asked to stop by to discuss her bid with the director.

Susannah removed her jacket and hung it on the peg in the back room. "The meeting went really well," she said, looking hopeful. "I should know by the end of the week."

"That's great." Colette wanted Susannah to succeed. For the moment, of course, she hoped to keep her job, and the better her employer did financially, the better for her. That wasn't the entire reason, however. Colette liked Susannah, who'd hired her after a brief interview in which she'd asked a minimum of questions. Fortunately, she hadn't requested references. Afterward Susannah admitted Colette was the first person she'd ever interviewed and she was simply following her instincts.

Working side by side as they did every day, it was only natural that they'd develop a friendship, although

Colette hadn't shared anything very personal. Their conversations tended to be about Susannah's family, about books they'd loved and people on Blossom Street. Colette had, early on, described the external facts of her life—schooling, marriage, widowhood, and some vague details about her job. She held her memories of Derek close to her heart. They'd had a good marriage. The only real problem they'd encountered had been her inability to conceive. She'd loved her husband deeply and still grieved for him. At the same time, her feelings for Christian Dempsey confused her. During the past year she hadn't been honest enough to admit her growing attraction to him, which had culminated in their one night together. She wanted to believe their lovemaking had been more than physical hunger between two lonely people. That hope was dashed when she went back to work after Christmas. Without his ever saying a word, she knew he regretted that night, regretted everything about it. He seemed preoccupied and worried; foolishly, Colette had assumed this uncharacteristic behavior had to do with her. She didn't understand exactly what he'd gotten himself into or why he'd risk the business he'd worked so hard to build. All she could figure was that he'd found himself in financial trouble. Either that or he was being blackmailed. Whatever the reason, she wanted no part of it, or any association with him.

Susannah spoke, and Colette gratefully turned her thoughts away from Christian Dempsey.

"I'm not sure what I expected of Mr. Olson," Susannah said as she slipped the big apron around her neck and deftly tied it at her waist. "But then I don't normally hang around funeral parlors," she added. "He was so friendly. But not somber, you know? Just genuine and low-key. Later I saw him talking to a family who'd lost a loved one and he had such a gentle, reassuring manner." She gave a light shrug. "I was impressed with him—and I hope he felt the same way about me."

Colette knew that if Susannah received the funeral-home contract it would be a huge boost for the shop. Her only experience with funerals had been Derek's, which was a blur in her mind. His parents had flown in from Chicago and handled almost everything, making all the decisions about their son's interment. In her benumbed state, she'd been glad to let them do it. While sitting in the waiting room, Colette remembered glancing through a brochure about prepaid plans. She would never have guessed it might one day be part of her own job.

"I assured Mr. Olson that while I'm new to this business, I have every intention of being around for a long time. Joe helped me prepare what to say. He's been so wonderful."

Colette admired Susannah's husband, Joe, and the way he supported and encouraged his wife and her new venture. She envied them their loving partnership. She wondered if her own marriage would have deepened into that mature love. She liked to think it would have. But her husband was dead—and Colette was pregnant with another man's child.

The phone rang just then and Colette answered it. As she started entering the details of an order, the front door opened and someone came into the shop. Susannah stepped out front to deal with the customer.

Colette finished writing up the order—a bouquet to congratulate new parents on their baby. The flowers would be delivered to a local hospital that afternoon. Because the business was small, Susannah had hired a delivery service. The driver stopped by once a day to pick up the orders. Flower arrangements like this one, for joyous occasions, brought Susannah and Colette the most pleasure. Funeral wreaths and arrangements were a staple of the business, but Colette knew from her own experience that no quantity of flowers, regardless of how exotic or expensive, would ease the ache of having lost a family member. The point was to honor the person who'd died and to express condolences to the living.

Susannah returned to the back room. "There's a man out front who wants to speak to you."

"A man?" It could only be one person.

Susannah stared at the business card in her hand. "Christian Dempsey. Isn't he the man who left a phone message last week?"

Colette nodded jerkily. She hadn't called Christian back, which was probably stupid on her part. It was absurd to think he wouldn't be able to find her. Knowing him as well as she did, she should have realized her lack of response would only heighten his desire to confront her.

Squaring her shoulders, Colette moved slowly into the front of the shop and stood behind the counter. She would listen to whatever he had to say and pray that would be the end of it. However, nothing could have prepared her for the impact of seeing him again.

It wasn't that his appearance had changed. Christian looked just the same as he had last month. As soon as she entered the room, his eyes flew to hers.

"Mr. Dempsey," she said formally, which seemed a little ridiculous when she'd lain naked in his arms. But politeness offered her an emotional buffer she badly needed.

He frowned. "In light of…uh, recent events, calling me by my first name might be more appropriate."

She studied him, not sure if he was making fun of her. What would be appropriate, Colette felt like saying, was to avoid any mention of their encounter at the hotel. "All right. Christian."

"Did you get my message?"

"Yes. I did." She didn't offer any explanation as to why she hadn't returned his call.

His eyes narrowed ever so slightly. Anyone else might not have noticed. Colette did. After five years of working with him, she was all too aware of the nuances that relayed his mood and his thoughts. He wasn't pleased with her, and everything about him, his look, his stance, the set of his shoulders, told her so. She could only surmise that he'd discovered she was the one who'd written the letter. Coward that she was, Colette had no intention of bringing it up.

His gaze continued to hold hers. "I'd like to speak with you for a few minutes. Privately."

He knew. "That's…not possible. I'm working."

"Then I'll wait."

Nothing would intimidate walk-in customers faster than an irritated Christian Dempsey.

Colette hesitated and then reluctantly gave in. It wouldn't do any good to put this off, she decided; he'd only come back. "I'll see if my employer can spare me."

Christian responded with a curt nod and she hurried to ask Susannah if she could leave early.

"Who is that guy?" Susannah whispered the minute Colette reappeared.

"My former boss. Would it be okay if I left now?"

"With him?" Susannah frowned, clearly concerned.

"It isn't like we have a lot to say to each other." In Colette's opinion, this conversation should take about five seconds. Her biggest worry was how she'd feel afterward. The attraction was still there, despite everything she knew about him.

"Take all the time you need," Susannah told her. "Just promise me that speaking to this man is something you *want* to do."

It was, and it definitely wasn't. "I need to," she said, letting that explanation suffice.

Christian was waiting for her out front. Ever the gentleman, he held the door for her as they left the flower shop. She half expected some comment on the type of employment she'd taken after leaving Dempsey Imports. He said nothing.

"There's a café across the street," he said, gesturing toward the French Café with its striped awning. One of the windows displayed a multitude of baked delicacies and through the other they could see small tables and chairs.

"Why don't we go for a short walk instead?" She didn't want anyone from the café to listen in on their conversation.

Christian was agreeable. They spoke briefly, exchanging pleasantries as they strolled down Blossom Street. Christian walked with his hands behind his back, careful to keep pace with her shorter strides. What struck Colette was the way they both struggled to maintain a facade of unfamiliarity. They acted like strangers when they so obviously weren't.

"How are you?" Christian asked. He turned to look at her as if he possessed the uncanny ability to see straight through her, which in fact he did.

"I'm very well, thank you." She hoped her voice didn't reveal how on edge she really felt.

"I mean, how are you...physically?" he asked again.

"Physically?" she repeated.

"Do I need to spell it out for you?" His words were impatient. "If I remember correctly, neither of us took the time to employ any measures to prevent pregnancy."

"Oh." Embarrassment lit up her cheeks brighter than the red signal light at the intersection. "I'm fine. There's...nothing to worry about."

He didn't seem to believe her.

"If that's all," she said, ready to part company, "I should be getting back." Her mind was crowded with questions and accusations. She'd never taken Christian for a fool and yet she had proof that he was trafficking in Chinese aliens. Seeing him confused her. She didn't want to think about him or give him reasons to suspect she carried his child. The sooner they said their good-byes, the better.

"No, there's more," he countered sharply. He hesitated, as though he wasn't sure how to formulate the next question. After a brief pause, he blurted out, "I'd like you to return to Dempsey Imports."

His request shocked her, and Colette automatically shook her head. "I can't."

When the light changed, they crossed the street and continued walking, no real destination in mind.

Christian waited until they were on the other side. "Is it because of what happened?"

"Christian," she murmured and instantly knew he hadn't found out about the letter. "It wouldn't work. It's unfortunate and I feel bad, but that night will always stand between us."

"And day."

He seemed to be *trying* to add to her embarrassment.

"Fine, and that day," she admitted. "It doesn't matter. Working together is no longer an option."

"All right," he said regretfully. "I realize I made a mistake after the holidays. The relationship changed and I had no idea how to deal with it."

That wasn't the *only* thing that had changed, she thought sarcastically.

"I pretended nothing was different between us," he went on. "But it was…is. You've made your point. We need to discuss this like two mature adults and reach an understanding."

"I don't want to discuss it. And there's nothing to understand. We made a regrettable mistake. Blame it on too much champagne, too much Christmas spirit."

He raised his brows.

Colette stared down at the sidewalk. "I'm sorry," she whispered. "Everything's changed, Christian. I can't go back to being your assistant."

"Why can't we both consider what happened at the Christmas party a slip in judgment and let it go at that? You're a valuable employee. The company needs you."

"The company?" she asked.

He exhaled slowly. "I need you," he murmured. "I want you to come back."

Colette supposed she should be flattered, since Christian Dempsey rarely admitted to needing anyone or anything. "It isn't possible," she said and she meant it. "We can't undo what's already been done. Don't you see that?" He couldn't honestly expect her to resume managing his schedule, his travel arrangements and his *dates*. As soon as he learned she'd contacted the authorities, he'd fire her anyway.

He didn't answer.

"How did you find me?" she asked.

"Why? Were you hiding?"

"No…"

"It wasn't that difficult. I had Accounting contact your bank and get the new address—to mail your severance documents."

She shrugged, feeling a bit foolish. But she couldn't resist another question. "Did you hire a new assistant yet?" She could have asked any of the friends she'd made through the years. But the company must be rife with gossip and rumors as to why she'd quit so abruptly, and for that reason, Colette hadn't called anyone at Dempsey Imports. Getting in touch with them to ask for information like that was a last resort.

"Lloyd York," Christian said.

"Lloyd," she repeated. She tried unsuccessfully to remember a face to go with the name. "I don't know him." As much as possible, Christian made it a practice to promote and hire within the company.

"He's a temp."

Colette felt her eyes widen. Christian disliked using personnel from a temporary agency and until now he'd avoided it. The fact that he'd looked outside the company only underlined his guilt. What she didn't understand was his reason for wanting her back. Surely he knew she'd uncover his activities sooner or later.

"I hoped you'd come to your senses and return voluntarily. When I didn't hear from you, I had no choice but to contact you myself."

"Christian, I'm sorry, sorrier than you know. But I'm not going to change my mind."

"You're sure you won't reconsider?"

"No." She closed her eyes. Despite everything, she missed him, missed the demands and challenges of her position. Not a day passed that she didn't think of him. She wanted to tell him about the baby but knew she couldn't until everything had played out. Needless to say, she couldn't predict how or when that would take place.

"You *want* to come back, Colette. I can feel it. Tell me what's stopping you and I'll make it right. You want a raise, fine. I'll double whatever your salary was before. We know each other well and—"

Angry now, she whirled on him. "I beg to differ. After five years of working side by side, you know next to nothing about me."

"Really?"

"Yes, really," she flared.

"On the contrary, I know you *very* well, Colette Blake." The innuendo was so sharp, it felt like a carefully aimed needle pricking her vulnerable skin—and her pride.

"See what I mean?" she said as calmly as her hammering pulse would allow. "You just made my case. What happened…happened, and there's no going back. I suggest you hire a permanent replacement, Mr. Dempsey, because I can assure you I have no intention of working for you again…ever."

Conscious of the need to retain her dignity, Colette marched off, leaving him standing in the middle of the sidewalk.

Six

"The simple meditative act of knitting may not bring about world peace, but it certainly has made my world more peaceful."

—Ann Budd, Book Editor, Interweave Press.
Author of numerous knitting books, including *Lace Style,* coauthored with Pam Allen
(Spring 2007) and *Getting Started Knitting Socks,*
Fall 2007, Interweave Press

Lydia Goetz

If today wasn't the first knitting class for the prayer shawl, I would've closed the shop in order to be with Margaret and Julia. My niece was in bad shape. The hospital had kept her for two days after setting the pin in her arm, which was badly broken. Her face was swollen and bruised. I could barely look at her and not cry. It was beyond my imagination that anyone would do something like this to my beautiful Julia. More damag-

ing than the physical injuries was what this carjacking
had done to her emotionally.

To her and to my sister! I'd never seen Margaret
angrier. At the hospital she paced the waiting room
snarling like a wounded beast, snapping at the staff,
demanding answers and generally making a nuisance
of herself. I couldn't even talk to her. I don't know what
would've happened if not for Matt. My brother-in-law
handled the situation so tactfully. Again and again, he
reminded Margaret that Julia was *alive*. The loss of the
car was of no consequence as long as their daughter had
survived the attack. Insurance would replace the vehicle
but nothing could ever replace their child.

The door opened on this bleak Wednesday afternoon,
and Alix walked into the shop. I was pleased that she'd
decided to sign up for another class, although she didn't
really need one, since she's turned into an accomplished
knitter. Because Colette and Susannah were beginners,
I'd offered to teach two patterns, one a simple prayer
shawl, and the other, for Alix, a more elaborate, complicated lace pattern. She required a challenge, otherwise
she'd quickly grow bored. She also needed distraction,
and I figured this lace pattern would do the trick.

I was so grateful to see her I almost broke into tears.
I'd been so distraught by the assault on Julia that my
emotions were completely off-kilter.

"Did you hear?" I asked, struggling to keep my voice
from shaking.

Alix nodded. "How's Julia doing?"

"She came home after a couple of days in the hospital but she refuses to see anyone other than family."
With her face swollen and discolored, Julia was afraid
of what her friends would say. She'd immediately gone

into her bedroom and hadn't come out. I understood better than anyone might have guessed. After my first brain surgery, my head swathed in bandages, I'd been terribly self-conscious. Little did I realize this was just the beginning of my ordeal. I wouldn't allow my friends to see me, either, and later, when I was lonely and depressed, there were only a few who'd hung on. In retrospect, I knew I was responsible for sending them away; I hoped Julia didn't repeat my mistake.

All I could do was pray for my niece and give her my love and support. Her arm would mend and the bruises fade, but I doubted she'd ever be the same lighthearted girl she'd been a week ago.

The car thief had stolen more than their vehicle that day. He'd also taken Julia's innocent trust that the world was decent and safe. He'd blindsided my sister and Matt, too. Whoever he was, this man had a great deal to answer for.

"Did the boys in blue find the guy who did it?" Alix asked as she sauntered up to the table in the back room of the shop. That was where I held my classes. She set down her backpack and took out the yarn and needles she'd purchased earlier in the week.

"No word yet." Frankly, I didn't have much hope. The officer who'd talked to Margaret explained that the car was probably on a container ship in the Port of Seattle within a day of the attack. Apparently the new car my sister had chosen was one of the most desirable vehicles on the black market. The whole family had been so proud of their first brand-new car, and this only added to the burden of Margaret's guilt.

"If I were you, I wouldn't hold my breath," Alix muttered.

I knew Alix distrusted the police. I should've said something positive to counter her cynicism, but I didn't feel like arguing. Besides, it wasn't getting the car back that was important to my sister. It was justice she wanted. Justice she *demanded.* Margaret wasn't one to easily forgive and forget, and she was fiercely protective of her family, especially her daughters Julia and eleven-year-old Hailey.

The bell chimed a second time and in strolled Susannah and Colette. All three women had already bought the necessary needles and yarn and I'd supplied the pattern as part of the class fee. Because Colette and Susannah were new knitters, most of my time would be spent helping them.

"Susannah, Colette, this is my friend Alix," I said. "She works at the French Café, so you've probably seen her around the neighborhood."

Alix shrugged her shoulder in an unfriendly manner. Her attitude reminded me of the way she'd acted during my first knitting class, when she'd sat across from Jacqueline Donovan. I hadn't seen this side of Alix in a long while and knew something must be troubling her. Once more I bit my tongue.

"Colette, why don't you introduce yourself," I said, hoping to begin the class on a more optimistic note.

"Well, I obviously know Susannah and Lydia, and I've seen Alix at the café. I'm Colette Blake."

When she didn't offer any other information, I prompted her. "Tell us about yourself," I urged.

Colette looked at Alix. "What would you like to know?" she asked.

Again Alix answered with that halfhearted shrug.

"Nothing, unless it's some little fact you're dying to tell me."

I could no longer remain silent. "Alix!" I snapped, telling her I found her behavior downright rude.

She had the good grace to apologize. "I'm sorry, Colette, I've had a rotten day. Please, tell me about yourself."

Colette shook her head. "Actually, I don't have anything to say. I'd prefer it if we just started the class."

"Hey, everyone," Susannah inserted. "This is supposed to be a fun class. We're knitting a prayer shawl, for heaven's sake! Not a bulletproof vest."

That made me smile. "Okay, Susannah, why don't you take a turn?" I said. She, at least, seemed willing to chat.

"Well," she began, "as everyone here knows, I bought Susannah's Garden last September. It's a real change from my teaching position, which I had for over twenty-four years."

"What made you quit teaching?" Alix asked, sitting a bit straighter.

"I was in a rut," Susannah explained. "Burned out. Without realizing it, I'd lost my enthusiasm. When I started teaching, I loved every minute of it. Back then, I almost hated to see the school year end. The last year I taught, I couldn't wait for summer and I realized I was cheating my students—and myself."

Alix's question made me wonder if she wanted to have her own bakery one day, the way Susannah had opened a florist's business. I found that an exciting idea, but wasn't sure how Jordan would feel about it.

"Why a flower shop?" Colette asked, leaning forward. Susannah gestured expansively. "I've always had a beautiful garden and my mother did, too. I guess I inherited my love for flowers from her. Actually, I would never have thought of owning a flower shop if not for my husband. Joe knows me best." She paused and smiled. "I'll amend that. On a good day, he can be astonishingly intuitive about me and what I need. He's the one who checked out the For Sale sign at Fanny's Floral and talked to the previous owner. When he suggested I buy the shop, I knew right away that it was exactly what I should do."

"You like being your own boss?" Alix asked.

"I absolutely love it," Susannah said fervently. "Although I have to tell you I've never worked harder in my life."

Alix looked out the window at the French Café. I knew she'd once dreamed of working in such a place and her dream had become a reality, the same way mine had.

"Say, Alix, didn't someone tell me you're getting married in June?" Susannah asked.

Alix nodded, but not with much vigor. I feared her bad day was directly related to the wedding. I wish I knew what had set her off. But Alix isn't one to freely share her troubles; I suppose that kind of reserve comes from having only herself to rely on all those years. She'd been living on her own from the time she was sixteen.

"Have you ordered the wedding flowers yet?" Susannah asked.

Alix squirmed again. "I'm leaving that up to Jordan's mother."

"Don't you want a say in the matter?" Colette asked, glancing at Susannah and then at me.

"Not really." Alix reached for the knitting needles and yarn as if the subject bored her.

"But flowers are an important part of the wedding," Susannah said. "Shouldn't they—"

"I haven't made a single decision yet," Alix broke in. "Why would I start now?" She turned to me. "Are we going to talk all afternoon or are we going to knit?"

"Knit." Apparently the wedding was a subject best avoided. I picked up the needles and a skein of yarn. "There are various ways to cast on stitches," I explained as I inserted my index finger into each end of the rolled yarn. I've developed my own method of finding the end and pulling it through the skein. To be honest, I'm not always successful. Fortunately, this time I looked like a genius. I pulled out the end, then had Susannah and Colette do the same.

Finding the end of the yarn was a good ice-breaker and I was sorry I hadn't started with that. Alix clearly wasn't in a talkative mood, and Colette didn't seem interested in sharing a single piece of information about herself. I assumed she'd be willing to tell Alix that she was a recent widow. Or maybe she thought Alix had already heard. Then again, Colette might prefer to keep her grief about Derek's death private.

I continued by showing Colette and Susannah how to cast on stitches by knitting them onto the needle. It's not my favorite way of casting on; however, I find it one of the less complicated methods. It's also an effective prelude to learning the basic knitting stitch.

Alix had completed the first inch of the pattern before Colette had finished casting on and counting her stitches.

Colette frowned as she looked across the table. "You

know how to knit," she complained. "Why are you taking the class?"

Alix glanced up and made brief eye contact with me. "Jordan—my fiancé—suggested it might help calm my nerves."

"I'm not getting this," Susannah groaned and set the needles and yarn aside. "I thought this was supposed to be relaxing."

"Not necessarily at the beginning," I said.

"No kidding," Susannah muttered.

Alix burst out laughing. "You should've seen me when I was learning. Jacqueline turned three shades of purple when I dropped my first stitch."

"As I recall," I said, grinning at the memory, "it wasn't because you dropped a stitch but because of how you reacted—with a whole vocabulary of swearwords."

Alix's lips quivered with amusement. "I've toned down my language, so don't worry, ladies."

"You aren't going to say anything I haven't heard from my kids," Susannah told her.

"Don't be too sure."

Smiling, I raised my hand. "Are you two going to get into a swearing match?" I asked.

"Not me," Susannah said as she finished her first real stitch. The tension was so tight, it amazed me that she could actually transfer the yarn from one needle to the other. She heaved a sigh and turned to me for approval, as though she'd achieved something heroic.

"Good," I said as I leaned over to examine her work.

"I need some help," Colette moaned, the yarn a tangled mess on the table.

I couldn't tell exactly what she'd managed to do, but there was nothing I hadn't seen in the last three years.

I soon corrected her mistake and again showed her the basic stitch, standing behind her to make sure she understood. If I did the knitting for her, that would accomplish nothing. She had to do this on her own.

"I agree with Susannah," she said after a few minutes. "This has got to be the most nerve-racking activity I've ever tried. When does the relaxing part begin?"

"It just happens," Alix told them both. "All at once you'll be knitting and you won't even need to count the stitches. The first thing I made was a baby blanket, and after every single row I had to stop and make sure I hadn't accidentally increased or dropped a stitch. By comparison, the prayer shawl you're doing is easy."

I had to admit Alix was right. The baby blanket had been an ambitious project. I'd chosen it because it required about ten classes. If I'd started with anything smaller, like a cotton washcloth, I would've needed only one, possibly two, sessions. The blanket justified the number of classes I'd scheduled.

"Who are you knitting your prayer shawl for?" I asked Susannah.

"My mother," she answered without hesitation. "She's doing really well, better than I expected after we...after I moved her into an assisted-living complex in Colville."

"My own mother's in assisted living, as well," I said. "But it must be a worry living so far from her." Margaret and I shared the responsibility of checking up on Mom and spending time with her.

We hadn't told Mom what had happened to Julia. It would only have distressed her. I was afraid she might've guessed something was wrong because Margaret hadn't been by in several days. Mom, however, hadn't seemed to notice.

"It's not so bad," Susannah said, responding to my comment. "We talk every day, Mom and I." She paused, biting down on her tongue as she carefully wrapped the yarn around the needle. "I have a good friend who stops by periodically and lets me know how Mom's doing."

"What would we do without friends," I said, and saw how Alix instantly looked up. She seemed calmer now.

"What about you, Alix? Have you decided who you'll give the prayer shawl to?"

She nodded. "At first I thought I'd keep it for myself. I'm going to need plenty of prayers to get through this wedding, that's for sure." She grinned, shaking her head, and continued knitting. "But I'm going to give it to Jordan's grandmother. I think she'll really like the fact that I knit it for her."

"I'm sure she will," I said. "What about you, Colette?"

She didn't raise her head. "I might just keep it. Does that sound selfish?"

"Not at all," I assured her. I realized that the act of knitting had already worked its magic on all of us. Alix had come in stressed and ill-tempered, on edge about the wedding. Colette, too, had been nervous and unhappy, for reasons I didn't know. I was certainly upset, because of what had happened to my niece and to Margaret. Susannah had her own struggles, launching a new business. We were relaxed now, talking together, laughing, *knitting*.

Knitting had linked us all.

Seven

Alix Townsend

Finished for the day, Alix poured herself a cup of coffee, then sat down at the staff table in the bakery's back room and put her feet up on the chair across from her. The French Café did a thriving business and she liked to think she'd played a role in that success. Her muffins, coffee cakes, cookies, sweet rolls and cakes, baked fresh every morning, had attracted a following of regular customers.

Molly, one of the baristas, stuck her head into the kitchen. "Jordan's here," she announced in a tone that said Alix was lucky to have met a man like him. But Alix already knew that.

"Jordan? Here? Now?" she asked. They weren't supposed to meet for another hour.

"He looks like Jordan, talks like Jordan, walks like Jordan. My guess is, it *is* Jordan."

"Cute," Alix said, saluting Molly's wit with her coffee mug.

"Want me to send him back here?"

Alix nodded, even though she was a mess. If he'd waited an hour as they'd originally planned, she'd have showered and changed clothes. Seeing that he hadn't, he'd have to take her as she was, which at the moment was tired.

Jordan appeared, and she lowered her feet and motioned toward the vacant chair. He pulled it up to the table with one hand, holding a disposable container of coffee in the other. Leaning back in the chair, he smiled.

"Did I get the time wrong?" she asked, although she was sure she hadn't.

"No. I'm early."

"Any particular reason?"

He didn't meet her eyes. "Have you had a chance to look through the books yet?" he mumbled.

"Which books?" But she knew exactly what he meant. His mother had hand-delivered huge binders filled with sample wedding invitations; she was supposed to study them and make her selection. She'd *tried* to choose but every invitation she liked had been vetoed by Jacqueline or Susan. It had frustrated her so much she hadn't bothered to look again.

"Mom said we need to decide on the invitations right away so they can be ordered."

Alix did her best not to groan aloud. "Did *you* look at them?"

"No, I'm busy at the church and—"

"You think I'm any less busy?" she demanded, her anger firing to life.

Jordan met her eyes. "Alix, listen, I didn't come here to argue. We're both busy, that's a given, but we need to get serious about this wedding."

"I am serious." If she wasn't so tired, she would've had more control of her temper.

"I am, too," Jordan said. "Everyone's on my case about choosing the invitations."

"By everyone, you mean your mother."

"And Jacqueline," he added.

"Then let *them* choose," she cried, clenching her fists in frustration. Still, Jordan was right about Jacqueline. She was so consumed with wedding details that Alix had taken to avoiding her. Every conversation with her friend and mentor revolved around some aspect of the wedding or the reception. Jacqueline had actually hired a ten-piece orchestra! Then this morning, she'd said she was talking to someone about releasing doves at some meaningful point in the ceremony. Doves? As far as Alix was concerned, the idea of white birds flapping their wings, leaving droppings in their wake, was simply ridiculous. There'd even been talk of a horse-drawn buggy to transport "the bridal couple" from the church to the country club. The last she'd heard, it was still under consideration. A buggy! She could hardly bear to think about the flowers and the cake.

Alix didn't want to hurt anyone's feelings but this was *her* wedding and it seemed she should have at least a little say about the kind of event it was. Against her better judgment, she'd given in on this country club reception, because she knew a big reception would please Jordan's mother. Alix hoped to have a good relationship with her in-laws, especially Susan Turner, so she'd been willing to compromise. Except that it felt as if she was the *only* one doing any compromising.

"We can go through the sample books this evening," Alix finally said. It was pointless to argue.

"You don't seem too happy about it."

"I'm not." She might be conceding but she wasn't willing to pretend. "You know what I thought?" she asked, growing a bit sad that their wedding had slipped away from her.

"You were looking forward to some time for the two of us tonight. We'll have that, Alix, I promise, as soon as we pick out the invitations." Jordan sipped his coffee.

"It isn't just that," she said wistfully. "When you gave me the engagement ring and we started talking about the ceremony…" She paused. "I thought it would be a small service and I'd make the invitations myself."

"Really?" Jordan seemed impressed. "Maybe we could do it together."

She doubted it. "How many people on your mother's list?" she asked. Needless to say, her own would be considerably shorter.

"Three hundred at last count."

Alix's heart rate went into overdrive. "Three *hundred* people?"

"Invitations," he corrected, apparently unaware of what this news had done to her. "That means maybe five hundred people."

"You've got to be joking!"

"Alix, my father is a pastor. You wouldn't believe how many friends and associates my parents have. Mom's whittled the list down to three hundred invitations. If I told you how many she started out with, you'd have a panic attack."

"I'm having one now."

Jordan grinned, clearly thinking she'd made a joke; she hadn't. The idea of walking down the aisle in a church filled with hundreds of wedding guests—all of them strangers—was enough to make Alix sick to her stomach.

"I hope you realize how much I love you," she muttered.

Jordan grinned again as he reached for his coffee. "I sure do."

"Can we talk about something other than the wedding?" she asked. The inside of her elbow was beginning to itch and she suspected she was breaking out in hives. She hadn't experienced hives since she was a kid and assumed she'd outgrown the tendency, which she'd learned to associate with stress. Obviously not.

"Sure," he agreed readily. "What do you want to talk about?"

"Uh…" A few minutes ago she'd had a dozen different things she'd looked forward to discussing with Jordan. All of a sudden her mind was completely blank. "I went to the first knitting class for the prayer shawl."

"How'd it go?"

"All right, I guess."

"Tell me about the other people in the class," he said.

"There's only two other women. Susannah and Colette." Alix enjoyed having a smaller class. She'd helped Lydia teach Susannah, who'd had some of the same problems Alix did when she'd started knitting.

"Susannah, from Susannah's Garden?"

Alix stiffened. "I suppose your mother's upset because I haven't decided on the flowers yet?"

Jordan blew out an exasperated sigh. "Alix, we weren't going to talk about the wedding, remember?"

"Right." Actually that was a relief. It seemed there was always *something* she needed to be doing or should have done with regard to the wedding.

"Okay, so you're knitting a prayer shawl."

She nodded. "Lydia gave us a bit of the background on prayer shawls. Some church groups apparently take them to nursing homes and use them as part of their ministry. Lydia said the whole idea came about as a way of nurturing and caring for family or friends who've got health problems. I don't think the recipient necessarily has to be ill, though. The shawls are…small displays of love," she said on a burst of inspiration.

Jordan smiled in approval.

"I'm going to take your suggestion and knit mine for your grandma Turner." Right away she could see that Jordan was pleased.

"Alix, she'll adore you for that." His brown eyes were soft with appreciation. "You made quite an impression on her, you know."

Alix had begun to think of Sarah Turner as her honorary grandma. She couldn't remember having grandparents of her own, although she must have. At any rate, neither her maternal nor paternal grandparents had played a role in her life. If they had, she might not have ended up in foster care.

She'd never spent time around elderly people, so meeting Jordan's grandmother had been an experience. Grandma liked to talk and Alix had found her fascinating. Everyone in the family had heard Grandma's stories, but not Alix and she hung on every word. Grandma talked about the Depression and World War II, when she'd worked as a school secretary for twenty-five cents an hour. Later, when her husband was in the army overseas, Grandma Turner had gone to work at the shipyard in Portland, Oregon, as a welder and saved five thousand dollars. At the time, that amount of money was a fortune. With her savings they were able to purchase the property on Star Lake, near Seattle, where she lived to this very day. The Turners had raised their two sons there; she'd been a widow nearly twenty years.

Jordan reached for Alix's hand and entwined their fingers. "How about if we splurge and go to a movie?"

"Popcorn?"

"Why not?" He smiled and Alix leaned close to give him a lingering kiss.

They left soon afterward, stopping at Alix's place just long enough for her to change clothes. She'd been tired and cranky when Jordan arrived, but no more.

Date night with her fiancé was exactly what Alix needed to lift her spirits and take her mind off the fuss everyone was making over their wedding.

Her irritation was a symptom of nerves, she realized. By the time of the wedding, she'd be past all of that and eager to settle into married life. It would be a piece of cake. Wedding cake! And she was baking her own. On that, Alix wouldn't budge.

A few weeks ago, she'd tried to convince Jordan to elope. Now she understood how foolish that idea had been. Susan Turner would never forgive her if they got married in secrecy.

When they were back from the movie—a romantic comedy Alix had chosen—Jordan reminded her that they couldn't put the invitations off any longer. They sat side by side at her kitchen table in the Donovans' guesthouse and flipped through the huge three-ring binders, hoping to make a selection. Some of the invitations were elaborate and eye-catching, but those didn't suit Alix's taste in the least. She thought others were far too frilly and Jordan agreed. And some were just…silly. She couldn't imagine who'd want Donald and Daisy Duck on a wedding invitation. The simpler examples seemed too plain. In the end, after going through each binder twice, Alix couldn't find a single one she liked that would pass muster with Jacqueline and Susan Turner.

"What do you think?" Jordan asked.

"I wish I had time to make them myself." Alix had looked forward to that. Something elegant, individual…

"I wish you did, too," Jordan murmured, his head close to hers.

"You decide," she told him tiredly. "Just pick one."

"Me?"

"I can't."

"I can't, either." She didn't want Jordan to think she wasn't interested, because she was. But her choices weren't acceptable to Susan and Jacqueline— Wedding Planners run amok, she thought with a sudden grin.

"What am I going to tell my mother?" Jordan asked. He sounded a bit desperate.

Unable to stop herself, Alix grinned again. Apparently she wasn't the only one afraid to stand up to Susan Turner. Well, that wasn't entirely fair. Susan was his mother and wanted the best for them. The Turner family had put their very heart—and their bank account—into this wedding, and the Donovans had, as well.

"I know what we'll do," Alix said, feeling inspired. "I have a solution!"

"What?" Jordan asked eagerly.

Alix laughed and threw her arms around him. "Choose one," she insisted. "Any one will do. Close your eyes if you want."

Giving her a puzzled glance, he opened the first

binder and turned a few pages. He pointed to one of the more elaborate designs.

Alix wrinkled her nose.

"That one, then," he said, pointing to one on the opposite page.

"That's no better."

"Okay, *you* choose," he said.

She picked out an invitation with Disney characters.

Jordan grimaced. *"That* one?"

"How about this?" She purposely picked out one she knew Jordan would object to.

"No way."

"Good." She beamed him a smile. "We can't decide and we can't compromise, right?"

"Well...maybe we could?"

"Right?" she reiterated pointedly.

"Right," he echoed. "That means..."

"It means we'll have to let your mother and Jacqueline decide for us." The wedding was really for Susan and Jacqueline anyway, Alix reasoned. This way they'd be able to choose the invitations they wanted...and they could do it with Alix and Jordan's blessing.

Eight

Colette Blake

Colette woke from a warm and comfortable sleep, dreaming of Christian Dempsey. Alarmed, she opened her eyes, trying to banish his image from her mind. She'd worked hard to avoid any thought of him. And yet she'd forever be reminded of him through their child. Again, she felt torn, wanting to tell him about the baby, and realizing she couldn't....

Countless times, she'd gone over their last meeting, when he'd shocked her by coming to Susannah's Garden. The day she walked away from Dempsey Imports, she was convinced she'd never see Christian again. She'd never *wanted* to see him again. She'd been appalled and angry at what he'd done. But the weeks since then had blunted her outrage; unaccountably she found herself making excuses for him, trying to invent reasons for such immoral, illegal activities. Maybe he had a misguided sense of compassion, she told herself hopefully; maybe his intentions were actually good. Maybe he was helping people find a better way of life….

She shook her head, dispelling *that* idea, and got ready for work, dressing in loose jeans and a red cable-knit sweater. With her morning tea, she knit another row of the prayer shawl. The knitting was going well, and Colette was beginning to look at yarn in a different way. After only one lesson, she was already thinking about patterns she might one day attempt. Her next project, she decided, would be a sweater for the baby.

The day before, Lydia had shown her a new shipment of alpaca wool as expensive as it was lovely. Recalling it now, Colette immediately pictured that yarn in a cardigan, a man's sweater, and Christian Dempsey flashed into her mind. Irritated, she abruptly set aside her knitting. She had to stop thinking about him! He wasn't the man she'd believed he was, and the sooner she accepted that, the better. Again and again, she mentally reviewed the computer file she'd read. There could be no other explanation.

Susannah was at the flower shop when Colette got in and they worked together until noon. March had arrived the day before, and typical of late winter in the Pacific Northwest, one rainstorm had followed another all week long. Then—a thrilling surprise—the clouds parted and the sun peeked out, bathing Puget Sound in golden, glorious light. All at once, Colette felt an urgent need to get outside and breathe fresh air.

"I think I'll go for a walk," she said when Susannah returned from her lunch break. After nothing but drizzle for two weeks, Colette craved the sun on her face.

Taking her jacket in case the weather turned nasty again, she headed down the hill to the Seattle waterfront and the Pike Place Market. She loved the market and often used to shop there with Derek, although he'd never found the same pleasure in being downtown as she did.

With the sun out, the city had surged to life. There was a new sense of energy, of well-being, and Colette felt invigorated. People seemed to move more quickly, laugh more loudly. She giggled at the antics of a troop of uniformed schoolkids, whose teachers merely smiled in resignation. Purchasing a decaf latte she sipped it while she wandered toward the market.

"Colette!"

At the sound of her name, she turned but didn't see anyone familiar. After a moment, she gave up and continued into the market. Fishmongers tossed whole salmon back and forth, to the delight of tourists. She stopped to watch; it was a scene she'd witnessed any number of times but always enjoyed.

"Colette?"

Again she turned, and this time she caught sight of a man wearing a black overcoat. At first she didn't recognize him. When she did, she came to a halt, an astonished smile on her face. *"Steve?"* she said as he hurried toward her. "Steve Grisham!"

He stood directly in front of her and for a minute or two, all they did was stare at each other.

"What are you—"

"You moved and—"

They started speaking at once, then paused and laughed.

Steve motioned to Colette. "You first."

"Oh, my goodness, I can't believe it's you," she said, hardly knowing where to begin. Steve had been a good friend of Derek's, his first partner when Derek had joined the Seattle Police Department. The more experienced officer had been paired with her husband during Derek's initial two years on the force. Then Steve had been assigned elsewhere and eventually he'd made detective. Derek and Colette had attended a party his wife, Jeanine, had organized to celebrate his promotion.

"How are you?" Steve asked, his eyes serious as he studied her. His hands rested lightly on her upper arms, as if he wanted to hug her but wasn't sure how she'd respond.

"I'm fine," she told him, and at that moment it was true.

"What are you doing here in the market...now?" he asked.

When they realized they were holding up foot traffic in the narrow passageway between the stalls, they started walking together, leaving the market entirely and wandering down Post Alley.

"I'm on my lunch break," she explained, dumping her empty latte container in a trash can. "What about you?"

"Same thing. I came down to grab a quick bite. Join me," he said. "I'd like the company."

"I'd love to." He led her to a small hole-in-the-wall restaurant where the ambiance left much to be desired but the food was known to be exceptional. It was a police favorite, a place Colette had occasionally met Derek for lunch. Once or twice, Jeanine had come, too. Colette felt the predictable twinge of nostalgia but resolutely ignored it.

The last time she'd seen Steve was at Derek's funeral. With so many people in attendance, she hadn't been able to acknowledge and speak to everyone. She'd seen Steve and Jeanine but hadn't done anything more than thank them for their love and support.

"I tried to call you," Steve said after the waiter had taken their order. "You changed your phone number?"

"I moved and...well, there didn't seem to be any reason to get a phone. All I really need is my cell."

"You sold the house?" Steve asked in surprise.

"The very first day it was on the market. It went so fast I didn't have time for second thoughts." She suspected Steve had tried to contact her on the one-year anniversary of Derek's death.

He nodded as if he understood her need to move on.

"I tried to reach you at work, too," he said next.

"You did?" She was astonished he'd gone to such lengths to search for her.

But before she could question him further, their food arrived. Colette had ordered soup and Steve a hamburger and fries.

"I wanted to see how things were going," he said, squeezing a liberal amount of ketchup on the side of his plate. "It's been a year now, right?"

She didn't answer the question. "I'm doing okay," she assured him a second time.

He raised his head. "You look great," he said with an appreciative grin.

His scrutiny unsettled her and in an effort to hide her uneasiness, she picked up her spoon. The beef soup was homemade and full of vegetables and pieces of seasoned meat. It was so hot, steam rose from the bowl.

His expression sobered. "I didn't know if you'd heard about me and Jeanine," he said, grabbing the burger with both hands.

Colette hoped he wasn't about to tell her they'd split

up. Colette had always liked Steve's wife and saw them as a good match, with Steve's practical nature balanced by Jeanine's whimsy and sense of humor.

"Jeanine filed for divorce," he said abruptly. "She moved to Yakima before Christmas."

Saddened at the news, Colette set her spoon aside. "Oh, Steve, I'm so sorry." The couple had two little girls who were going to grow up without their dad.

His eyes revealed a depth of sadness as he finished chewing. "We both tried, but it didn't work out."

"How are the girls holding up?"

"They seem to be doing well—very well, considering," he said. After a brief hesitation he shrugged. "They're so young and with the crazy hours I work, I was hardly ever around anyway."

When he'd been with Derek, they'd worked swing shift, but she supposed a detective had to be available around the clock. Still, family should always come first. In her view, anyway. "Is there anything I can do?" she asked, thinking she might be able to help but with no idea how.

That sad look returned and he lowered his gaze. "I'm afraid it's too late for that."

"Too late?"

"The divorce is final this week. And like I said, Jeanine moved to Yakima—to be closer to her parents."

"But the girls?"

"I hated to see them leave Seattle but in the end it's probably for the best. Our parenting plan spells out my visitation rights and I have them for two weeks every summer, spring break and a week at Christmas. Jeanine's family really loves the girls, and all in all, it's a workable solution. Although I miss my family...."

Reaching across the booth, Colette touched his forearm. "I'm so sorry," she said again.

Steve nodded. "So am I. Being a cop's wife isn't easy. You know that. I always admired the open, honest relationship you had with Derek. That's one reason I was hoping to talk to you."

Not sure what to say, Colette glanced down. "Thank you," she murmured.

"You were a good wife."

Her throat thickened with grief—and guilt, because it was Christian who dominated her thoughts these days, not Derek.

"Colette?"

"Sorry," she said, plucking a napkin from the canister on the table.

"May I ask you a question?"

"Of course." She lifted her head in surprise.

"I know this must come out of the blue, but would it be all right if I phoned you sometime?" Steve said quickly.

"I…" Colette felt flustered and uncertain. "Sure, I… guess." This wasn't what she'd expected him to ask. It'd been years since she'd dated. That was obviously true for Steve, as well; he looked as uncomfortable as she did. If they were to start seeing each other, she'd have to tell him about the pregnancy. And yet, it seemed wrong for Steve to know and not Christian.

Suddenly he smiled and she saw him as the attractive man he was—not just Derek's friend and one of a social foursome. His features were classic with a square jaw that suggested he could be stubborn, as well as determined. His dark brown eyes were perhaps a bit small and slightly close together, but that didn't bother her. His hair was thick and well-groomed. He'd always looked good in a uniform and even more so in a suit. He exuded an authority that people instinctively respected. She remembered Derek's saying that Steve had spent time in the marines.

"Are you doing anything this evening?" he asked, then laughed gruffly. "I don't mean to rush you. It's just that I've been lonely, and I like the idea of having someone to talk to."

"Sorry, I've got a book club meeting this evening." She considered skipping it but Anne Marie, the bookstore manager, had asked her to attend. This was the first session, so Colette felt obliged to keep her word.

Steve seemed disappointed. "Okay, I understand."

"You could join us if you'd like," she added, not wanting to discourage him. "I doubt everyone's read the book, anyway."

"You think it'd be all right?"

"I'm sure it'd be fine," she said, warming to the idea. This wouldn't be a real date. They'd be around other people, and conversation would focus on the story, not on them.

"I don't remember you as a reader," he commented, going back to his burger. "Jeanine always had a book in her hand."

"I used to read quite a bit. After Derek died I couldn't for the longest time. No matter how gripping the story, my attention wandered. It was all I could do to scan the newspaper and do the crossword puzzle." In an entire year, she hadn't finished a single puzzle. "But now, thanks to this book, I'm reading again."

"What's different about it?"

"I guess the story strikes close to home for me. It's

about a widow adjusting to life without her husband. The title is *Good Grief,* and it's by a writer named Lolly Winston. It's very moving and surprisingly funny, and I really enjoyed it."

Colette had met the bookstore manager, who'd recommended the book, by accident. Anne Marie had been walking Baxter, her Yorkshire terrier, and the tiny dog had gotten his leash wrapped around Colette's ankles. When Anne Marie learned that Colette lived above the yarn store, she'd invited her over for tea. Her own apartment was above Blossom Street Books; in other words, they were neighbors. Colette liked Anne Marie and had agreed to join the discussion group, especially after she'd read the book.

"Good Grief," Steve repeated.

"I identified with how the widow felt. At one point she goes to work in her pajamas and housecoat. I laughed out loud and at the same time I was weeping because…well, there were days like that for me, too, especially at first."

Steve nodded and was about to speak when his cell phone rang. He automatically reached for it and snapped it open. "Grisham," he said in a terse voice, instantly the professional.

Colette ate a little more of her soup but after the latte her appetite was gone. She really should be getting back to the shop; she was already five minutes late and still had a brisk walk ahead of her.

Steve closed the cell and clipped it back to his waistband. "I have to go."

"Me, too." She picked up her purse.

"Listen, I'd better take a rain check on tonight," he

said and slid out of the booth. "Work intrudes." He scooped up the tab and headed over to the cashier.

Colette found a pen at the counter and wrote out her cell number on a napkin, then handed it to him.

He smiled and thanked her. Colette went back to Susannah's Garden in a good mood. The clouds had lifted in more ways than one and she felt as if her life was finally taking shape.

That euphoric sensation didn't last long, however. When she walked into the shop, the first person she saw was Christian Dempsey, drumming his fingers on the counter.

Colette felt her heart plummet. She could hear Susannah on the phone in the back room—which meant there was no one to rescue her. "What are you doing here?" she muttered.

"I've come to order flowers."

"A special occasion?"

"Not really. They're for a woman."

Colette should've guessed. "You couldn't do it by phone?"

"I prefer to order them in person."

She understood his intent. He wanted her to know he was seeing someone else now. Fine. Message received. In her opinion, he was acting both vindictive and immature.

"And while I was here, I thought I'd see how you were doing."

"I'm busy," she returned stiffly. "Actually, I have a date myself." She found herself stretching the truth, but Steve had asked her out, and even if it wasn't possible that evening, she would eventually be seeing him.

Her blatant attempt to discourage Christian didn't seem to be working. "With whom?"

"Not that it's any of your business, but he's an old friend of my husband's." She turned her back to him and removed her jacket.

His smile had vanished when she turned around. "Does this so-called friend have a name?"

"Of course he has a name. What's the matter, don't you believe me?"

"I believe you," he said, and looked away as Susannah stepped up to the counter and gave him back his credit card.

"Thank you for your order, Mr. Dempsey. I'll make sure the flowers are lovely."

She spoke with a little more enthusiasm than Colette deemed strictly necessary.

"Thank *you*," he said, and shot Colette an enigmatic smile that she puzzled over for days.

Nine

Lydia Goetz

Brad and I invited Matt and Margaret over for dinner on the first Sunday in March. It was my husband's suggestion and I'm grateful he thought of it. After Julia's attack, Margaret still wasn't the same. Julia herself was back in school but refused to talk about what had happened, even to her mother. It was as if a giant boulder had crashed through the roof; everyone had to walk around it and pretend it wasn't there. At any hint or mention of the carjacking, Julia disappeared into her room, plugged her iPod into her ears and zoned out for hours on end.

I knew this couldn't be healthy and I was afraid Margaret's response wasn't, either. My sister wanted revenge and she wanted it badly enough to hound the authorities day and night.

I'd hoped that an evening out with Brad and me would help my sister put aside her anger, at least for a few hours. Every day she arrived at work tense and angry, snapping at me without provocation. Just that week, I'd asked her a simple question about an order I'd had her place for circular knitting needles and she'd yelled at me, saying she was a responsible adult and I'd made her feel like a child. I hardly knew how to respond to the unreasonableness of her attack. Thankfully, no customers were in the shop at the time.

Brad and I spent the afternoon shopping and then cooking. We make a good team on the domestic front— and in every other way. My husband's a master at the barbecue, and we decided to grill chicken. I made a batch of potato salad, following a recipe Tammie Lee Donovan had given me. It has jalapeño in the mayonnaise, which provides a little kick. In addition to the potato salad, I doctored up baked beans with brown sugar and mustard and baked a carrot cake for dessert. It's Cody's favorite.

Unfortunately, it was still too early in the year to bring out the picnic table, so we planned to eat indoors. Our goal was a carefree, festive evening in the hope that Margaret and Matt would relax and enjoy themselves.

Brad had everything under control by the time my sister and her husband arrived. Although I see Margaret almost every day, I was shocked by her appearance when she stepped into the house that afternoon. Outside the familiar environment of A Good Yarn, I suddenly realized how haggard Margaret looked. She's physically bigger than I am, a good four to five inches taller than my five-foot-two height and sturdily built. Compared to this nightmare with Julia, so little has truly frightened her over the years. Even when Matt was unemployed for months she kept it hidden from me. For all I knew at the time, everything was perfectly fine at home. Only when they were about to lose their house did she reveal that anything was wrong.

That wasn't the case now. The dark circles under Margaret's eyes betrayed her inability to sleep. She'd lost weight, too, and her pants hung loose around her waist.

After hanging up their coats, I hugged Margaret. "I'm so glad you could make it."

Matt glanced in Margaret's direction, and I had the feeling that at the last minute, she'd wanted to cancel. I don't know how he managed to change her mind, but I was relieved he had.

"The chicken's on the grill," Brad said, shaking hands with Matt and hugging Margaret. I loved him all the more for the warm way he welcomed my family. "I'm not sure what Lydia's been making, but she's been in the kitchen most of the afternoon."

"You'll see," I teased and we shared a smile because he knew very well what I was making.

"How about a beer?" Brad offered Matt and the two men disappeared onto the back patio while I got a bottle of chardonnay from the refrigerator for Margaret and me. Cody was with a friend for the day and wouldn't be back until later. After investigating who was at the door, Chase, Cody's golden retriever, had returned to his bed in Cody's room.

"Is there anything I can do?" Margaret asked.

"You could set the table." I had the plates, napkins,

silverware and glasses ready. All Margaret had to do was carry them to the table and arrange each place setting.

"Would you mind if I called home first?"

"Of course not."

She excused herself and hurried into the other room. I could hear her talking to Julia, her tone anxious as she checked on her daughter's safety. Were the doors locked? she asked. The windows? Had she turned the oven off? Julia must've hated having her mother constantly standing guard over her, and yet I'm not sure I wouldn't have done exactly the same thing.

Margaret returned to the kitchen, where I was busy transferring everything to serving dishes and setting them in the middle of the table. "How's Mom?" she asked as she carefully folded the napkins. This was her attempt at avoiding questions about Julia.

Margaret had only seen our mother a couple of times since the attack. "She seems fine," I told her.

My sister gazed sightlessly into the living room. "I miss her."

Initially I didn't understand what she meant. How could Margaret miss our mother when all she had to do was drive over to the assisted-living complex? They'd always been close. Even now, they talked at least once a day. After we'd first moved Mom, Margaret stopped by the complex as often as twice daily.

"It's almost like we don't have a mother anymore, isn't it?" Margaret said sadly.

A sense of loss came over me. The role reversal had occurred so gradually, I was hardly aware of it while it was happening. All at once, Margaret and I were taking care of Mom. We had, in effect, become the parents, weighing decisions, dealing with financial matters and driving her to doctor's appointments. This situation had begun in earnest a year ago, when we discovered Mom was severely diabetic and needed to be on insulin. Lately, she'd slipped mentally. The medication she was on no longer seemed to be working.

"Mom will always be our mother."

"I *know* that," Margaret said and cast me an irritated glance. "It's just that I can't talk to her now."

"Of course you can," I challenged. Mom thrived on routinely hearing from us.

"Not about this."

This, of course, was the attack on Julia. I forgave Margaret for her hot-tempered response when I understood what she meant.

"I miss my mother," Margaret repeated.

I agreed. I missed Mom, too. Missed those special times we'd spent talking about anything and everything. I'd grown to rely on her insights about the store and my customers. But when I was a teenager, Mom had been so deathly afraid of my cancer that she'd forced my father to oversee all medical matters. My father was the one who'd chauffeured me to countless appointments and argued with doctors on my behalf. He'd sat by my bedside before and after my surgeries and whispered encouragement when the pain was more than I could bear. He was there when I suffered the debilitating effects of chemotherapy and buoyed my spirits every way he could. We grew exceptionally close, and in that, we'd excluded Margaret and our mother. True, Mom did her best for me, but my father was my anchor.

"I'd like to tell her about Julia," Margaret continued. "But...I can't."

What my sister wanted, of course, was our mother back the way she used to be. She wanted Mom to promise her that everything would be all right, that this nightmare would soon be over and life would return to normal. She sought assurance that the attack wouldn't have a lasting effect on her daughter. She wanted Mom to tell her that Julia would be able to sleep through the night again and smile and laugh as though she hadn't a care in the world. Margaret wanted *peace,* the kind of peace only a mother can give a hurting child, the peace she longed to offer her own daughter.

"Chicken's done," Brad said, coming in from the patio. It'd started to rain, which was no real surprise, since it'd been raining off and on all weekend. The chicken breasts smelled tangy and enticing. Brad had marinated them in a mixture of soy sauce, Italian salad dressing and herbs—a blend he could probably never duplicate again.

We all gathered around the table and after Brad had offered a simple grace, I passed the serving dishes around.

Matt dug into the meal with gusto. "This is great," he said between bites. He helped himself to a second scoop of potato salad before he'd finished his original serving.

"I haven't been doing much cooking lately," Margaret confessed, looking a little embarrassed at the way her husband kept commenting on the food.

"You've been busy," I said, dismissing her remark.

"She's driving the police nuts," Matt said.

Margaret glared across the table at him. I caught Brad's eye and we exchanged an exasperated grimace. We'd hoped to avoid exactly this conversation. Margaret had gone into the dining room twice during dinner to use her cell phone. I knew she was checking on Julia again. Most likely it wasn't only the police Margaret was annoying.

"I thought we weren't going to mention the attack," she said pointedly to her husband.

I noticed that Margaret had barely touched her meal.

Matt sighed, sounding genuinely regretful. "You're right. I apologize."

Now that Matt had brought it up, though, Margaret was loath to drop the subject. "The police don't even seem to be *trying*. To the authorities, it's not that big a deal. They aren't taking it seriously."

Matt raised his hand. "Now, Margaret—"

"Don't argue with me, Matt," she said, interrupting him. "*I'm* the one dealing with the police, and I'm telling you right now, what happened to Julia is being swept under the rug."

"Would anyone like coffee?" I asked in a blatant attempt to redirect the conversation.

"I'd love some," Brad said quickly.

"Coffee, Margaret?" I leaned over to touch her arm.

Margaret nodded impatiently. "I can't tell you the number of times I've talked with Detective Johnson," she muttered. "The man's an idiot."

"Margaret," Matt said softly, in an effort to deflect her.

My sister sighed deeply. I could tell she was trying not to ruin the evening. I also knew that Julia's ordeal was constantly on her mind.

Margaret had made it her mission to see justice done—more than justice, *vengeance*. The man responsible for hurting her daughter should be strung up, in her view, and left hanging in a public square. That sounds medieval, but it wasn't much of an exaggeration. If he was ever arrested and brought to court, she'd sit through every minute of his trial and cheer when a guilty verdict was read. I was just as outraged as she was, but I didn't have the same passion for revenge. Don't get me wrong; I wanted this man found and prosecuted to the fullest extent of the law. Margaret wanted that, too. But she also wanted him to suffer for what he'd done to Julia. She was obsessed with it.

I hurried to the kitchen to start a pot of decaf, and while it brewed, we managed to finish the meal without any further mention of the incident. It didn't come up again until we sat in the living room with our coffee and dessert.

"Does anyone know the name of a good private investigator?" Margaret asked unexpectedly.

"Whatever for?" Matt demanded.

"What do you think?" Margaret lashed out. "The police aren't doing a damn thing. I want to hire someone who will."

"Margaret…"

"Don't *Margaret* me," she cried, pinching her lips together in a way that told me she was determined to see this through. "Do you want this…this *bastard* to strike again? Next time, the victim might not be so fortunate. Julia's arm was broken, but if she hadn't rolled away, she could've been hit by an oncoming car. We're both aware that our daughter could have easily been maimed for life or killed."

"But she wasn't," Matt said gently, patiently.

"The next victim might not be so fortunate, did you think of that? This man needs to pay for his crimes and be prevented from ever doing it again. And if the police aren't going to see to that, then I am."

"It's the responsibility of the police to find him, not some investigator we hire. We're already paying taxes to support law enforcement. Give them a chance first."

Margaret's response was a derisive snort.

"More coffee anyone?" I asked, hoping to divert an argument.

Both Matt and Margaret shook their heads, and Brad and I shared another glance. Thankfully, Cody got home a few minutes later, bursting into the house with his usual enthusiasm. Chase bolted into the living room eager to greet his master, tail wagging madly.

"Can I have some cake?" Cody asked, looking at the empty dessert plates—and at Matt, who was eating a second piece.

"What did you have for dinner?" I asked.

Cody paused to think about it. "Roast beef with potatoes and gravy, peas and salad. Mrs. Martin's a good cook. Not as good as you, though."

That boy certainly had a way with words. "I'll see what I can do about that cake," I promised, not bothering to hide a smile.

Margaret stood and Matt finished off the last bite of his dessert before joining her.

"We should be getting home," Margaret said. "I don't like being away from the girls for so long."

Matt looked as though he wanted to comment but apparently changed his mind. "Lydia, Brad, we can't thank you enough for dinner. It was delicious."

My sister had already reached for her raincoat and purse and seemed anxious to be on her way. I'd lost count of the number of times she'd phoned home, and I wondered if she thought no one had noticed. Or maybe she simply didn't care.

Brad and I walked them to the door and stood on the front porch while they dashed through the rain to their car, which was parked at the curb. With the insurance money, Matt and Margaret had purchased a replacement car. This one was used and about as plain as they come. Margaret had no intention of risking a repeat of Julia's experience.

After they drove off, Brad heaved a sigh of relief. "How do you think it went?" he asked.

"Definitely not as well as I'd hoped," I admitted, leaning against him. He brought his arm around my waist.

"Matt said Margaret's up till all hours of the night, obsessing over this. She can't sleep."

"Neither can Julia." I wanted to hug my precious niece and reassure her. I only wished I had the words to comfort her and Margaret, too.

"Do you figure Margaret was serious about hiring a private investigator?" Brad asked as we went back inside. He closed the front door and turned the lock.

Before I could answer, Cody came into the living room, overhearing the end of our conversation. "What's a private investigator?"

"It's like a private detective," I explained.

"Can I be one when I grow up?"

"I don't see why not," I said, ruffling his hair. He wrapped his arms around my waist and grinned up at me. I hugged him back. I could hardly imagine how I'd feel if anyone hurt Cody. The thought filled me with such apprehension and sudden fear, I found myself holding on too tightly. I wanted to stand between him and the world, keep him safe from all harm.

Those were the same emotions my sister was feeling. After the attack on Julia, Margaret must have felt she'd somehow failed as a mother.

Ten

Alix Townsend

Alix stepped out from the bridal shop's dressing room and stood before Tammie Lee Donovan, waiting for her reaction.

She wasn't disappointed.

"Oh, Alix! It's perfect, just perfect," Tammie Lee sighed. She covered her mouth with both hands and when she looked up at Alix, her eyes were tender.

Alix loved this dress. She'd picked it out shortly after Jordan had given her the engagement ring. The minute she saw the white gown with its simple, elegant design, she'd known this was the dress for her.

"It's nothing to get mushy over," she said a bit more brusquely than she'd intended. Tammie Lee sometimes flustered her. Jacqueline's daughter-in-law was one of her best friends, which was why Alix had asked Tammie Lee to be her matron of honor. What unnerved her was how the other woman's emotions simmered so close to the surface. Tears came with the slightest provocation. Tammie Lee possessed an earthy kind of honesty, another reason Alix liked her so much. Besides, it was pure pleasure listening to her speak. Tammie Lee's words sounded like they'd been dipped in honey. Alix had read that somewhere, and it described her own feelings exactly. But while Tammie Lee had a genuine sweetness, there was nothing cloying or false about her.

Tammie Lee was someone she could trust. And because Alix didn't want Jacqueline anywhere near her wedding dress, she'd invited Tammie Lee to accompany her to this fitting.

"I hated the idea of a dress with a lot of lace and fancy detail," Alix said, finally daring to look at her reflection in the mirror. The white silk dress had cap sleeves, and a row of seed pearls sewn along the neckline and the hem. It cost more than she wanted to think about, but this was one expense she was picking up all on her own. From the moment she'd quit smoking, Alix had put her cigarette money aside for an extravagance, and this wedding dress was it.

"I can't get over the transformation—from tough girl to...to Audrey Hepburn," Tammie Lee said, wiping her eyes with a tissue. "You're going to be a beautiful, beautiful bride."

Despite herself Alix blushed. She hadn't thought there was any comment that could possibly bring a flush to her cheeks, least of all a compliment. Alix stared at her reflection. She *wanted* to be beautiful—for Jordan. And she wished with all her heart that she could be the virgin bride Jordan deserved. Her past was nothing she felt proud of. She'd never been in love before Jordan, and the sexual encounters she'd indulged in during her days on the street had been meaningless. Tawdry and desperate, without joy or affection. In fact, they'd meant so little to her, she couldn't even recall names or faces.

She'd told Jordan everything. She'd told him because he had a right to the truth. He'd listened and then assured her that everything she'd done was in the past and forgiven. Christ and His grace had made her whiter than snow—those were the words he'd used, and they'd given her great comfort. In confessing her sins to her husband-to-be, Alix had taken a tremendous risk. But he'd proved himself that day, proved his love.

As Tammie Lee continued to praise the dress, the seamstress arrived with a pin cushion attached to her wrist and a tape measure draped around her neck. She instructed Alix to stand on a raised platform, then quickly and expertly pinned the skirt hem.

Afterward, Alix was reluctant to change back into her T-shirt, jeans and combat boots. Wearing this wedding gown, she could believe that her wedding was going to be as perfect as the dress itself. She reminded herself that all the stress and worry associated with the ceremony—and the reception—would soon fade. It was just one day, as Jordan kept saying.

"Did I ever tell you about my cousin Savannah O'Brien-Jones?" Tammie Lee asked unexpectedly when Alix emerged from the dressing room.

"I can't remember if you did or not," Alix said. Tammie Lee was famous for her stories. Whenever she wanted to make a point, she did so in the form of a story.

"She's my aunt Frieda's youngest sister's girl. She grew up in New Orleans and was about as cherished as an only child can be. Then she went away to college and fell in love with a boy from Knoxville. It was as if her mother, my aunt Freida's—well, I already told you how we're related. Anyway, it was as if my aunt Dorothea had been waiting her whole life for this wedding."

Alix figured that sooner or later Tammie Lee would get to the reason for this particular story. She slipped her arms into her leather jacket and zipped it up.

"Big wedding, was it?" she asked.

"Oh, my goodness, Mama told me it cost as much as a new car and we're not talking a Ford, either." Tammie Lee paused to catch her breath. "Savannah had ten—count 'em, *ten*—wedding showers." She shuddered extravagantly. "Just think about writing all those thank-you notes! Her mama spent weeks planning every detail of that wedding, and I mean every single detail. She ordered orchids from Hawaii. She went to the city's top caterer for the reception dinner. She even chose the six bridesmaids."

"Six?"

"She wanted eight but Savannah put her foot down."

Alix and Tammie Lee left the bridal store. Shivering in the dreary March weather, they walked toward the parking garage. The wind was cold and the dark sky once again threatened rain.

"In my opinion, things would've gone better if Savannah had spoken up sooner."

"About what?" Alix was getting lost. "You mean the bridesmaids?"

"Uh-uh." She shook her head. "The wedding. It seems all *she* really wanted was a small wedding, and it was her mother who insisted on this huge affair that cost the earth. And her daddy. He wanted to show off his little girl." Tammie Lee paused for another breath. "The funny part is that while her parents were arranging an extravagant event, Savannah and Charlie, her fiancé, flew to Vegas and got married."

Alix gasped, and Tammie Lee broke into giggles. "I'd love to have been a fly on the wall when my aunt Dorothea got *that* phone call."

Tammie Lee wrapped her arm around Alix's. "Her daddy was fit to be tied. Her mama didn't know what to do. Eventually they went ahead with the big reception, and I have to say it was absolutely lovely. Savannah and Charlie were there greeting their guests as husband and wife, and they were *so* happy. Oh, I get goose bumps just remembering the way they looked at each other. They were so much in love."

"I know why she ran off to Vegas," Alix muttered. "Everyone was taking control of her wedding." And she couldn't blame Tammie Lee's cousin for eloping, either.

"Fortunately, no one was angry with Savannah for very long," Tammie Lee went on. "Everyone knew her mother had ridden roughshod over her. Of course, it helped that Savannah had her first child exactly nine months after the wedding."

"And they're still happy and everything?" Alix asked.

"Oh, yes. Savannah's had three children in the last five years and no one even remembers how her mother tried to take over her wedding."

Alix nodded slowly. Much as she appreciated Jacqueline's help, Jacqueline and Susan Turner had done exactly the same thing to her. It was as if her opinion no longer mattered and conferring with her was merely an afterthought. The wedding invitations were a good example. The order had been placed before Alix and Jordan had approved Jacqueline and Susan's decision.

Granted, that might be a formality at this stage, but Alix would've appreciated *seeing* their final choice.

Alix grinned at her friend. "Are you in the mood for one of those thick, juicy burgers we had the first time we went shopping?"

"You bet," Tammie Lee said enthusiastically and they drove to a fast-food restaurant. Sitting across from her friend and wolfing down a cheeseburger, Alix suddenly understood the point Tammie Lee was trying to make.

"Do you think I should be saying something to Jacqueline and Susan Turner?" she asked anxiously.

"Well," Tammie Lee drawled. "That's up to you. Do you feel they've taken over *your* wedding? Like Savannah's mama did?"

"Yes, they have and even though I don't like it, I haven't stopped it, either." Being on good terms with Jordan's mother was vital; arguing over the wedding could damage their future relationship. And Jacqueline and Reese had done so much for her already, how could she complain? Alix felt trapped, stuck in a quicksand of glittery invitations and unwieldy guest lists filled with strangers.

"Oh, Alix, I probably shouldn't have said a word…. But I was thinking about Savannah and Charlie and how happy they were after they got back from their Vegas wedding. Oh," she sighed. "I guess my mouth gets ahead of my brain sometimes. Jacqueline enjoys being part of this and she really believes she's doing a good thing. She just can't resist taking control. It's the way she is."

"I know."

"She and Reese love you like a daughter."

"I think the world of them, too." Love wasn't a word

that came easily to her, but Alix did love the Donovans. They'd done more for her than her own parents even knew how to do.

Tammie Lee took a delicate sip of her Diet Coke before she spoke again. "As I said, Jacqueline can get a bit carried away and while her intentions might be the best, I'm not sure she always makes the right choices for you."

"What now?" Alix asked wearily. "What did she do?"

Tammie Lee released a long breath. "You might want to check on your flower order," she said in a low voice.

Alix nodded. She'd chosen white daisies for her wedding bouquet. Daisies appealed to her in their utter simplicity and unpretentiousness. But when she'd mentioned her choice to Jacqueline, her friend had cringed visibly and stated that roses were more traditional. The bridesmaids' flowers had been discussed, too, and Jacqueline had overruled Alix's preference there, as well. Alix had tried to insist, but apparently Jacqueline hadn't been able to accept her decision, after all.

"Thanks for the heads-up," Alix said. As soon as she could, she'd go to Susannah's Garden and change the flower order back to white daisies.

An hour later, Alix met Jordan on the Seattle waterfront. He was standing near the ferry dock when she joined him for their afternoon date. Because of the wedding, neither of them had extra money for frivolous things like dinners out. A movie was a rare treat these days. Since the ferry was relatively cheap, they'd decided to ride it to Bremerton, where they'd explore the newly renovated waterfront.

"Hi," Jordan said, greeting her with a fervent hug.

They attracted a bit of attention. Alix was used to that. Jordan was clean-cut in crisp jeans and a shirt with a button-down collar and a light jacket. She hadn't altered her own dress style and wore mostly jeans, black leather and of course her combat boots. The two of them looked about as different as it was possible for any two people to look. It never bothered her and apparently her fashion choices hadn't distressed him, either.

They walked onto the ferry for the early-afternoon trip, moving inside when it began to rain. Jordan purchased them each a cup of coffee, which they drank gazing out at Seattle, rapidly disappearing into the foggy distance.

"How'd the fitting go?" Jordan asked. He put his coffee on the table in front of them and held her hand.

"All right, I guess." Alix noticed a seagull flying outside the ferry window. She longed to tell Jordan how beautiful the dress was and how pretty she felt wearing it, but she didn't. The thought of talking about this made her feel shy. Like a young, inexperienced girl—the virgin bride she wasn't. Instead, she drew his attention to the seagull that was keeping pace with the ferry.

"Would you like to start moving your stuff over to my place?" Jordan asked a moment later. They'd decided his tiny apartment would be their first home.

The question surprised her. "It's a little early, don't you think?" The wedding was three months away. They had plenty of time to arrange all that. Besides, everything she owned could be transported in a single load. Well, maybe two.

Jordan stared down at their clasped hands. "I can hardly wait to be married to you."

"Me, neither." Happiness like this was foreign to

Alix and sometimes it made her uncomfortable. For most of her life, happiness had been fleeting. She'd learned that the minute anything good came along, someone or something would take it away from her. She still believed that. It was a bad habit she was working hard to break, this attitude of waiting for the negative, expecting it.

Jordan slid his arm around her shoulders and she nestled against him. "You know, if we saved ten percent from each of our paychecks, within a couple of years we'd have enough to make a down payment on a house."

"You want to buy a house?" Alix asked, her head spinning at the very idea.

"Don't you?" He sounded surprised.

"I guess," she answered with a shrug. "I hadn't given it any thought."

"With our budget, the house'll have to be small. Seattle real estate's pretty pricey."

"I've never lived in a house I owned," she said breathlessly. The concept was an unfamiliar one. Living in a place without a landlord who'd be responsible for its care and upkeep. Not that any landlord *she'd* ever had came around to fix whatever went wrong. Except for the Donovans, but that wasn't really a landlord-tenant relationship.

"How does that seem to you?" Jordan asked.

"Good." Actually it was better than good. It was... thrilling. Never in her whole life had Alix thought she'd own a real home. Then again, she'd never dreamed she'd marry Jordan Turner, either.

His parents' place was provided by his father's church in the nearby town of Burien, but Jordan, as youth pastor at the Free Methodist Church off Blossom Street, only got a small housing allowance.

"Eventually, we're going to need more than two bedrooms," she said casually, thinking they'd be having children someday. She'd like two, maybe three, if Jordan agreed. She didn't have much confidence in her ability to be a mother, but she already knew that love could compensate for a lot.

Grinning, Jordan stared out over the dark green waters of Puget Sound. "I've been doing a lot of thinking about the bedroom myself."

"Jordan Turner, are you talking about…dare I say the word?"

Jordan chuckled. "Yeah, I am. *S-E-X.* I'm a healthy, normal male who's marrying the woman he's crazy about."

Alix snuggled closer to his side. "I'm looking forward to living with you, too."

"In the beginning I'll use one of the extra bedrooms for a study."

"What bedrooms?" Jordan seemed to forget that he lived in a bottom-level one-bedroom apartment two blocks off Blossom Street.

"In the house we're buying."

"Oh, yeah, that house," Alix said, joining in his game. "I'll need a big kitchen, though."

"Of course. Will you cook for me?"

"It will be my pleasure."

"Big meals on Sunday after church."

"Absolutely."

Jordan kissed her neck.

"There should be plenty of room in the backyard for the kids to run and play," she said.

"Kids?" he asked, eyebrows arching.

"Not right away."

Jordan closed his eyes and sighed. "I'm so happy, Alix. I've never been this happy."

"Me, too." Alix was beginning to trust that her happiness with Jordan wouldn't be snatched away by a cruel or indifferent fate. It was a heady and unusual feeling, but one she could easily get used to. *Wanted* to get used to.

She just had to survive the wedding first.

Eleven

Colette Blake

March was traditionally a slow month in the flower business; Colette remembered that from the time she'd worked in her mother's shop. The Valentine's rush was over, it was too early for Easter and Mother's Day, and school proms hadn't started.

Susannah worked hard at attracting customers to the store. She ran a weekly draw that anyone could enter and on slow days, she and Colette took turns standing on Blossom Street and giving away single flowers with a tag attached that advertised the store. This week, it was green carnations in honor of St. Patrick's Day.

Colette enjoyed the friendly working environment, but was often at loose ends, looking for things to do around the shop. If this continued much longer, she wondered how Susannah could justify keeping her on full-time.

It'd never been like that when she was with Dempsey Imports. If anything, she struggled to find enough hours for a personal life. It helped that Derek had worked swing shift; if he'd been home in the evenings he would've wanted her there, too. As it was, she often got home at eight or even later. She'd loved her job, thrived on it. She hadn't realized how much she'd miss it until the day she'd seen Christian again. She missed being involved in such a dynamic enterprise and the challenges that came with it —and she missed him. She didn't want to, hated herself for the attraction she felt, and yet no matter how hard she tried to ignore these feelings, they persisted.

Completely separate from their lovemaking was the fact that he'd gotten involved in something illegal. For that reason alone, she could never go back to work for him.

Susannah, who'd been in the back assembling a new-baby bouquet, joined Colette at the counter. "Seeing that it's so slow, I think I'll run a few errands."

"Is there anything you need me to do here?"

Susannah shrugged. "Unfortunately, no." Glancing down at her watch, she said, "I shouldn't be more than an hour, two at the most, but I'll have my cell with me."

"I'm sure everything will be fine."

"I'm sure it will, too."

Susannah left, using the exit that opened into the alleyway. As if they'd coordinated the event, as soon as the back door closed, the front door opened—and in stepped Christian Dempsey.

Again.

At the hard look in his eyes, Colette knew. The INS had acted on the letter she'd written. It was inevitable that sooner or later he'd find out who'd done this. Her stomach heaved with dread.

"It was you, wasn't it?" he said without greeting or preamble.

Colette's mouth went dry. Instinct told her to play dumb, to pretend she didn't understand what he was talking about. One glance told her he felt both angry and betrayed.

"You couldn't have come directly to me?" he demanded when she didn't respond.

Dredging up the courage to meet his eyes was difficult, but she managed. She clasped her hands behind her back to hide their trembling and shook her head.

"You got on my computer when I wasn't there." It wasn't a question but a statement of fact, a fact that obviously infuriated him.

Colette felt she had to explain. "I needed the service code for—" She wasn't allowed to finish.

"Who gave you my password?" His eyes were like burning coals. "My computer was off."

"I f-found it."

He didn't seem to believe her.

"Who other than me could figure out where to look?" she asked. "I know just about everything there is to know about you," she said and faltered because clearly she didn't.

"Who else did you tell?"

"No one…"

"Swear it."

"No," she cried, clenching her fists. "How *dare* you come at me like this! I'm not the one—"

Again he cut her off. "That's the real reason you resigned, isn't it?"

She refused to answer him.

"You led me to believe it was about us and what

happened at Christmas. That had nothing to do with it. That night was just a convenient excuse, wasn't it?"

For an instant Colette saw a flash of pain in his eyes. It was immediately replaced with resentment.

Colette had questions of her own. "Why would you risk everything like this?" she asked quietly.

This time he was the one who refused to answer.

"I've thought this through a hundred times, and it makes no sense." She gestured hopelessly, lifting both hands. "You have a profitable business in a growing market. You're respected. I can't understand what would compel you to take such a huge risk."

"I can't discuss this with you."

"If not with me, then who?" she muttered.

"You think I should trust *you?*" he said. "Because of you I spent an unpleasant morning with a roomful of attorneys."

"All I want to know is why," she pleaded, needing some excuse, some explanation. "Is it the money?"

"I said," he returned pointedly, "that I can't discuss this with you."

"Are you working for the INS?" That was the only possible reason that might explain his behavior. Or the only possible *legal* reason, anyway.

He didn't respond, just looked at her, his gaze impassive.

Colette had so desperately wanted to believe this was the answer that she felt like crying. Instead the anger broke through. "Unless you're here to place an order, I'm afraid I have to ask you to leave." Rather than let him see how upset she was, she stood with her back straight, her shoulders square and her feet firmly planted. Her arms hung loosely at her sides.

After an interminable moment, Christian released a deep sigh.

She thought he'd leave then, but he continued to stand there, studying her. He no longer seemed so angry, and the change in his demeanor confused her. Curious and at the same time afraid, she reached for her pad and pen as if preparing to take his order.

"I asked myself over and over why you left the way you did," he said at last. "Both of us made mistakes. Both of us reacted stupidly."

"Now you know," she said, doing her best not to be swayed by emotion. Colette had her answer. He'd gotten himself into a mess there was no getting out of. She couldn't be involved with him. "I think you should go. And please don't come here again."

"Not even to order flowers?" he challenged.

With business so slow, Colette didn't dare turn him down. "Perhaps you should deal with Susannah."

"I prefer to deal with you."

"Fine." She poised the pen above the pad.

"I'll take five dozen roses."

Five dozen? Colette wasn't sure she could even fill such a large order. "Where would you like these sent?" she asked as if it was perfectly normal to have a man walk in off the street and ask for five dozen roses.

"Make that ten dozen."

She found it difficult to hide her reaction.

"I'm ordering flowers. You just told me I had to, otherwise you'd have me evicted from the shop. I imagine you'd call on your detective friend to help you do that."

Colette remembered telling Christian about Steve Grisham but she didn't recall mentioning his name or his rank. Now she regretted any reference to Steve. In fact, she hadn't heard from him since their chance encounter on the waterfront. It was just as well; any relationship was sure to be complicated.

She bit her lip. "I *didn't* threaten to kick you out," she muttered wretchedly. "I just…suggested you leave."

He merely raised his eyebrows in an annoyingly superior way.

"Would you like roses of any particular color?" she asked, as though nothing else had been said.

"Red," he responded. "Blood-red. The best, most expensive roses available."

"I'll personally see that they're the best available." He was doing this purposely to hurt her. She'd hurt him and he was striking back, telling her there was someone else in his life. She'd been a one-night stand, and he was making sure she knew it.

He pulled a pen and pad from his briefcase and wrote something down. "Have the roses delivered to this address first thing tomorrow."

He handed her the slip of paper. *Ms. Elizabeth Susser,* she read. The address was on Capitol Hill.

Although Colette had worked for Christian for five years, she couldn't remember his ever dating a woman named Elizabeth. But she'd been gone for more than two months now.

"Would you like to sign a card?" she asked, keeping her voice devoid of emotion.

"Of course."

Colette's hand shook as she waited for him to write out the small card. He inserted it in the envelope, which he sealed, then scrawled *Elizabeth* across the front. Colette noticed that he'd chosen one of the more romantic cards.

"Will that be all?" she asked, struggling to maintain a professional facade.

"No, as a matter of fact, it won't. I'd like roses delivered to Elizabeth every week."

"Every week?"

"Yes."

"For what period of time?" Christian went through women so quickly, she couldn't imagine anyone lasting more than a few months, four or five on the outside.

"A year."

"A *year?*" she repeated, too stunned to keep her mouth shut. She couldn't have disguised her shock had she tried. So Christian was obviously in a serious relationship. He must be to go to this expense. As his personal assistant, Colette had ordered flowers for him dozens of times. She knew his routine; he generally ordered roses at the beginning of a relationship and again close to the end.

"Does that satisfy your demand that I do business or leave?" he asked.

"Yes," she said curtly. She didn't know whether to feel embarrassed at the way he'd outmaneuvered her— or sad about the connection that no longer existed.

"Is there anything else?" she asked after an awkward moment of silence.

"Nothing."

His voice was almost tender, and she had the feeling this would be the last time she ever saw him. "How would you like to pay for this?" she asked, working hard to keep the pain out of her voice.

He answered by withdrawing his credit card and handing it to her.

When the slip printed out, she tore it off and gave

it to Christian for his signature. He didn't so much as blink at the amount, which was substantial.

"Take my credit card number and bill me weekly for the roses. Make sure they're impressive."

"I'll see to them myself," she promised and wondered why she should care.

He stared at her, and she squirmed under the intensity of his gaze. "I wish you'd come to me before you wrote that letter," he said.

"I couldn't." Once she'd recognized what he was involved with, she had no option but to turn him in—even if she'd done it in the most cowardly possible way.

"I know," he said, sounding genuinely regretful.

"Can't you get out of it?" she pleaded.

Slowly he shook his head. "It's not that easy. I never meant it to go this far, and now there's no turning back."

"I'm sorry, Christian. Can I do anything to help?"

He hesitated, his eyes holding hers. "I know it's a ridiculous thing to ask, but would you have dinner with me?"

"Dinner?"

"Just once."

She couldn't understand why he'd ask. "Is there any particular reason?"

"No. It's just that I'd rather end our relationship on a positive note. I'll understand if you decline but I'm hoping you won't."

Colette saw the sincerity in his eyes. "I'm...not sure it would be a good idea."

"You're probably right," he said, his voice low and controlled. "But if you do agree, I'll give you my word of honor that I'll never trouble you again."

The silence between them crackled with tension. She

told herself she should run away from him, run in the opposite direction, and discovered she couldn't. Even knowing that he was involved in illegal activities and likely to be arrested, she couldn't refuse him this one request.

"All right," she said reluctantly.

Colette was terrified of spending an evening with him, because of what he might say—and because of what she couldn't.

Twelve

"If more people knitted and crocheted, the world would see fewer wars and a whole lot less road rage."

—Lily Chin, *www.lilychinsignaturecollection.com*

Lydia Goetz

The prayer shawl class was going well. Susannah, in particular, was learning quickly, full of enthusiasm for knitting. Before she'd even finished her first project, she'd already purchased a pattern and yarn for a sweater she planned to make for her daughter, Chrissie.

Alix was a great help to me in this class. And knitting, as usual, brought its calming effect. She was more relaxed, more optimistic and I hadn't heard her say anything negative about the wedding in at least a couple of weeks.

Colette managed to learn the basic stitches, although I have to admit she didn't take to it as easily as I'd hoped. It's like that sometimes with beginning knitters.

Almost always, a new knitter will catch on after a few simple instructions. Soon it's as if they've been knitting all their lives. Then there are others who struggle with each step and get discouraged when they see how slow they are compared to everyone else. In the previous class, I'd explained to Colette that each person learns at his or her own pace, reminding her that it isn't a competition. I felt confident that as she continued to knit she'd become more comfortable with the process.

Margaret joined the class, too. I'd hoped sitting down with the others and forming new friendships would help her. And I thought concentrating on the act of knitting would soothe her, especially since she'd stopped doing any handiwork at all. The attack on Julia had been more than a month ago, and my sister was still focused, to the exclusion of everything else, on finding the man responsible. I can't tell you how many times she called the police asking for an update on the case.

Some days there was no explaining her behavior. Out of the blue, she'd get restless and angry and reach for the phone. The way she talked to the police embarrassed me; no matter what she said about Detective Johnson, I couldn't believe the man was a slacker.

I'd tried hard to be patient with her and while I understood how she felt, I honestly thought it would be best for Julia if my sister let go of her anger. But Margaret refused to do that, refused to rest until the man who'd hurt her daughter was charged in a court of law.

The knitting class took place late on Wednesday afternoons, when Chrissie could fill in for Susannah and Colette at the flower shop. She'd visited A Good Yarn recently, and I'd enjoyed our conversation; Chrissie had a quick humor and wide-ranging interests. We'd spoken about the resurgence of traditional women's crafts. She'd chosen this as the subject for her Art History essay, and I found that exciting. Knitting was so many things, *could be* so many things. Including art.

That afternoon in late March, Susannah and Colette arrived together, toting their yarn and needles. They immediately sat down at the table, in the same chairs they used every class, and pulled out their projects. I noticed that Susannah was almost finished, while Colette had only about a third of hers done.

"We got the biggest flower order last week," Susannah told me, her voice shimmering with enthusiasm. "A man named Christian Dempsey placed a standing order—ten dozen roses, to go to the same address every Friday. For a *year!*"

"Now that's love," I said, joking. I have a wonderful husband, but I couldn't imagine Brad ordering me one dozen roses, let alone ten. Let alone for a *year*.

"It really helps," Susannah said. "Revenue was down for March and this new order makes a huge difference. Orders for wedding flowers are starting to come in, too."

"That's terrific!" I was genuinely pleased for Susannah and wanted her to know that.

During our conversation Colette had remained suspiciously quiet. I smiled at her and walked over to examine her knitting. I saw that the tension in her work had loosened in the past week and praised her effort. She returned my smile and made a small joke about relaxing more. I rarely saw her outside class these days and I missed our morning chats over tea. I understood her reluctance to join me, however. Margaret made it difficult, especially now that she was in a perpetual bad mood. Right now, she was helping a customer choose yarn for a baby sweater. I could only hope her demeanor wouldn't discourage the young woman, who was new to my store.

Alix was the last to arrive, breathless after racing across the street. "I was late getting out of the kitchen," she said as she sat down in her usual chair. She took her knitting out of her backpack and set it on the table.

Now that all my students were present, I checked their work and commented on the progress Susannah and Alix had made. Everyone was doing well and I took pleasure in complimenting their efforts. Actually, the pattern's relatively easy, even for a novice knitter, and Alix, of course, was equal to the challenge of her more complicated lace shawl.

I was interested in learning who would knit a prayer shawl and why. My little group of knitters was teaching me.

I pointed out that the border was knit in a seed pattern of knit three, purl three. "Does anyone have a comment on the pattern?" I asked, curious about what the women would say.

"I'll bet the three stitches are significant," Colette murmured as she switched the yarn from the back to the front in order to purl.

"Yes," I agreed. "Three is a significant number in our culture."

"Faith, hope, love," Alix stated in a thoughtful tone.

"Mind, body, spirit," Susannah said.

"Past, present, future," Colette threw in. I wondered again if living day to day was all she could handle.

"What about birth, life, death." This came from Margaret, who'd finished with her customer. Dressed in her dark sweater, she hovered in the doorway, a gloomy and forbidding presence. It figured, of course, that she'd be the one to bring up the subject of death.

I didn't meet her eyes as I circled the table. "All excellent observations," I murmured.

"Why knit a shawl?" Margaret went on. "I mean, we could be knitting anything for someone who needs a bit of TLC."

"True." I agreed with her there. A lap robe or any of a dozen other projects would do just as well.

"Why a shawl, then?" Alix asked.

I shrugged. "What do the rest of you think?"

Colette spoke first. "Wrapping a shawl around someone is a symbolic embrace. That's how it seems to me, anyway."

The others nodded.

"I like what Colette said—it's like a hug." Susannah sounded as if she was thinking out loud. "I can't be with my mother as much as I'd like, so when I mail her this shawl, it'll be like reaching out to her with an embrace, letting her know how much I love her and miss her."

"How's she doing?" I asked.

"She's more active than she's been in the last couple of years. Before the move, she spent hour after hour in her rocking chair, watching TV—mostly the Food Channel. Since she's lived at Altamira, she's interacting with other people more and taking small trips with them. Last week she went on a garden tour and loved every minute of it."

"Hey," Alix teased. "I guess this means your mother's off her rocker."

We all laughed. I wish I could say something that positive about my own mother. But I could see she was losing ground. Every time she had another health crisis, she deteriorated a little more. With Margaret consumed by the carjacking and Julia's emotional state, we hadn't really discussed Mom. I sometimes wondered if my sister had even noticed our mother's recent decline. Still, I decided I could deal with Mom for the moment; Margaret needed to focus on her daughter. Unfortunately, Julia had refused counseling, although the doctor had recommended it.

"I'm knitting my shawl for Jordan's grandmother," Alix said. "Grandma Turner is this really wonderful lady. I felt so *welcomed* by her. I felt like she understood me and, you know, she was just as interested in my stories as I was in hers." Alix smiled in wonder. "Jordan wanted me to meet her, and I was afraid she'd say something about how different we are."

"Why would she do that?" I demanded, ready and willing to defend my friend.

"Who could blame her?" Alix said calmly. "Think about it. Jordan's going to be a pastor in his own church one day, the same as his father and grandfather. You have to admit I'm not exactly a typical pastor's wife." She hesitated, biting her lip as she set her knitting in her lap. "I get the feeling that his mother would've preferred it if Jordan had fallen in love with someone else."

"I can't believe that!" I hated that Alix thought this, and I wasn't convinced it was even true. I'd met Susan Turner a couple of times. She was a knitter herself and had come by the shop for yarn and then later for a pattern book. We'd talked about Alix and Jordan, but I couldn't recall anything in her attitude that indicated uncertainty toward Alix.

"I shouldn't have brought up the subject," Alix said, splaying her fingers as if to release the tension.

"You've got the wedding bell blues," Susannah said with a laugh, but there was sympathy in her voice.

Alix picked up her knitting again. "Does anyone mind if we don't talk about the wedding?"

"Not at all," I assured her. I stepped behind Alix's chair and patted her shoulder.

"In case anyone's wondering, I've decided to give the shawl to my daughter Julia," Margaret said. She'd joined us at the table and had begun knitting, her fingers nervous. "I'm hoping this will bring her solace and comfort after what happened."

"How is she?" Colette asked.

"How do you expect she is?" Margaret snapped. "The poor kid doesn't sleep more than three or four hours at a time. Her grades have slipped and she doesn't leave the house except to go to school. Some days she can't even manage that. And," she said with a sigh, "she won't see a counselor."

I knew about Julia's reluctance to get psychological help, but the rest was news to me, and I felt dreadful. All Margaret had shared with me was her frustration with the police. My sister seemed to feel that everything would change once the perpetrator was behind bars. She seemed to believe that the situation would automatically revert to normal and Julia would be okay again. I didn't think it was going to be that simple.

"Furthermore," Margaret added, with a catch in her voice, "Julia won't talk about the carjacking. No one's allowed to mention anything about it. If we do, she gets up and walks out of the room. I wish now that Matt and

I hadn't bought her that iPod because all she does is use it to shut us out."

"The shawl will be Julia's shelter," I said quietly. "When she wraps it around her shoulders, she'll feel your love and prayers for her." This was my hope for my niece.

"I just want her to put all this behind her like it never happened," Margaret said.

That was what we all wanted, but I doubted it was possible.

"I wish I'd had a prayer shawl after Derek's death," Colette murmured, her concentration on her knitting and the pattern on the table in front of her. She kept her head lowered so it was difficult to hear her speak. "We had a good marriage. And then…he died."

No one knew what to say to that, and an awkward silence fell.

"Oh, Colette," Alix said, "I feel so bad that you went through such a horrible time." She shivered visibly. "I can't imagine what I'd do if anything happened to Jordan," she went on.

Colette nodded. "I hope you two will be very happy."

Alix smiled at her. "We have our future all planned. In two years we're hoping to buy a small house. Jordan wants to turn one of the bedrooms into a study until we start our family."

She positively glowed with happiness. It's a cliché, I know, but I couldn't have described this new serenity of hers in any other way. I remembered the first day I'd met her when she'd walked into the store, more than a little rough around the edges. At first she'd frightened me, but then I decided to treat her just as I would anyone else.

Susannah picked up the conversation by telling everyone about Joe's and her first home, a one-bedroom apartment that apparently had a ghost who flushed the toilet at odd times of the night. The mood immediately lightened as we laughed together.

I was always surprised by how quickly class time passed. It was the fastest hour of my day—of my week, in fact. Margaret needed to leave early, so I told her I'd close the shop alone. Brad was stopping by to pick me up on his way home. Normally we don't carpool because he has to be at work a couple of hours before I do, but he had a doctor's appointment this morning, so he drove me in.

I cuddled Whiskers before I locked up and then opened the door to Colette's apartment, knowing she enjoyed his company. For a while he traveled back and forth to the shop with me, but he's comfortable in the apartment, which was, after all, his home for nearly two years. After closing the door, I set the alarm. My fickle cat had divided his loyalties. Fortunately I'm not the jealous type, at least not when it comes to my cat's affections. But my husband—well, that's a different matter entirely.

"Hello, beautiful," he greeted me when I climbed into the front seat. "Have a good day?"

Every day with Brad and Cody was a good day, and I gave him a quick kiss—I had so much to thank him for. "I did. How was your physical?"

"Fine. The doctor says I'm a well man."

I smiled at his reply. "Make sure you stay that way."

"Yes, ma'am."

After a brief silence I told him, "I had my prayer shawl class this afternoon."

He nodded as he merged with the freeway traffic. We live only about fifteen minutes from my shop.

"Margaret's decided to knit her shawl for Julia," I continued. "She's so worried about her."

Brad glanced at me. "Is Julia sleeping any better?"

"I don't think so. I don't think Margaret is, either. She can't let go of this." My sister's always had an intense personality. It served her well in high school, when she excelled at sports. She's one of the most capable women I know; anything my sister set her mind to, she achieved.

Back when we were kids she was the top-rated female athlete in our school district and a star at every sport she tried. I was the sickly, puny sister everyone felt sorry for. It took Margaret and me a long time to start behaving like sisters. Sharing responsibility for our mother certainly brought us closer and so, of course, did the yarn store. I ached for Margaret now and badly wanted to help her. But Margaret was independent to a fault; in that way nothing had changed.

Last year, when Matt lost his job, she'd done everything possible to hide the fact that her family was about to lose their home. I'd been able to help them financially and was happy to do so, but Margaret—although certainly grateful—had difficulty accepting my gift.

"You're very quiet all of a sudden," Brad said as he exited the freeway. A few minutes later, we were driving into our neighborhood.

"I was just thinking about Margaret," I told him with a sigh.

"Anything you want to discuss?" he asked.

I thought about it, then shook my head. "How about

you? Anything *you* want to talk about?" I asked as we waited for the garage door to open.

"As a matter of fact, there is," Brad said. Cody dashed across the street—after carefully looking both ways, just like we'd taught him. One of our neighbors, a stay-at-home mother, babysat our son for an hour every afternoon after school.

Cody collected the mail, handing it to Brad as we entered the house. Chase bounded frantically around us, and Cody let him out, into our fenced backyard.

"You had something you wanted to discuss?" I reminded Brad.

He lifted his head from the mail he was sorting. "You bet I did. What's for dinner?" he asked with a grin. "I didn't have time for lunch and your husband's one hungry guy."

Thirteen

Alix Townsend

Saturday was one of those hectic days that sometimes overwhelmed Alix. She'd been with Jacqueline and Tammie Lee all morning, and by noon she was exhausted, although she still had a list of errands to run. Jordan would be away the entire day, taking the church youth group somewhere in eastern Washington to hear a Christian rock band. He wouldn't return until much later in the evening. Normally she accompanied him, but this time she'd begged off.

She'd picked up some dry cleaning for Jacqueline, bought herself toothpaste and shampoo, and dropped off her library books. Since she'd always been a voracious reader, she spent an hour at the library, checking out a couple of new mysteries, a historical novel set in the Puget Sound area and a travel book about Australia. With clenched teeth she added a wedding guide to the pile.

Anne Marie from Blossom Street Books was still

hosting the reading club she'd started earlier in the month. The book for April was the latest thriller by Brad Metzler. Colette, who'd also joined, had already finished it and offered to lend Alix her copy.

It was now midafternoon and she had yet to have lunch, so Alix decided to eat at the French Café, where she got an employee discount. By the time she arrived, most of the lunch crowd had left. She walked up to the counter, chatted with Julie for a minute, then ordered her favorite turkey sandwich and a cup of coffee.

As she surveyed the room, Alix caught sight of Colette Blake near the back of the café. Colette had brought her knitting and seemed intent on that. Alix debated whether she should say hello. During their knitting classes, Colette said very little. She seemed sad and vaguely troubled, although she was never rude or unfriendly. Alix hadn't really had much of a chance to know her; they'd sort of gotten off on the wrong foot and Alix blamed herself for that.

As she approached an empty table, Colette glanced up, saw her and smiled.

"Mind if I join you?" Alix asked impulsively.

"Please do." Colette put her knitting down with a sigh of abject frustration. "Tell me again that this is supposed to be relaxing."

"It will be, in time," Alix promised, sitting across the table from her. "Be patient with yourself. I lost count of how often I started my first project over. There were days I wanted to chuck the whole thing."

"But you stuck with it," Colette murmured.

"And I'm glad I did." Knitting had proved to be a turning point in her life. Back then, she'd had something to prove to herself. Refusing to quit had given Alix confidence in other areas, too. "It didn't come easy to me, either. I thought that was because I'm left-handed but Lydia kept telling me knitters use both hands, so that wasn't any excuse. She said it often enough, I finally believed her. After a while, I got the hang of it. I finished the baby blanket and even knit Jordan a sweater. Okay, so the neckline turned out a bit sloppy, but he still wears it." Alix smiled, thinking of her fiancé in that sweater. Now *there* was a real testament to Jordan's love. Alix had wanted to rip the whole thing out and start over, but he wouldn't let her. The yarn was ultraexpensive, too. Alix could never have afforded it on her own. Carol Girard from the class had given it to her. She'd refused any compensation for it, too. That kind of generosity had been a novel experience for Alix, and she'd never forgotten it.

"I'm not giving up, either," Colette said with what sounded like renewed determination.

After swallowing a mouthful of her coffee, Alix continued. "I found that if I had something on my mind, it helped to sit down and knit. If I could free my mind for even a few minutes, I could sometimes settle whatever was bothering me."

"Oh." Colette's shoulders slumped forward. "Knitting's not really helping," she said, staring down at her needles. "I might as well put it aside until after tomorrow. If I have to rip out this row again, I'm afraid the yarn will be completely frayed."

Alix studied Colette and saw the lines creasing her forehead. She'd picked up her cup of tea and nervously clutched the delicate handle. Alix was afraid it might snap off in Colette's hand.

"What's happening on Sunday?" Alix asked. She

didn't mean to pry, but perhaps if Colette talked about her problem, whatever it was, she'd feel better. Alix was a good listener. Jordan had taught her the importance of sharing one's troubles—and listening to those of others. Like Colette, she used to hold everything inside until it felt like she'd explode if she didn't do something to get rid of all those ugly emotions.

Perhaps surprisingly, Alix had also learned a few things from the pastor of the church that employed Jordan, the church she now attended. Pastor Downey used lots of homespun analogies and practical advice about living in the real world. Just last Sunday, he'd said that the grass wasn't greener on the other side of the fence; it was greener where it was watered. Alix liked that so much, she wrote it down on the inside flap of her Bible. She considered it good advice for a woman about to be married. It was advice she wanted to remember.

"I…I'm going out to dinner with my former employer," Colette explained haltingly.

"Is this your first date since you lost your husband?"

Colette shrugged and looked uneasy. "Sort of."

Alix wasn't sure what that meant but didn't press for an explanation.

"It's more a matter of *who* this date's with that's bothering me."

Alix nodded, encouraging her to continue.

"I agreed to go and now I wish I hadn't." Colette stared out the window for a moment. Alix let the silence build. She'd learned from Jordan not to be afraid of the silences in a conversation.

She thought Colette was about to speak when Julie, who worked weekends, delivered Alix's sandwich. Alix waited until Julie was out of earshot. She wondered why

Colette would have agreed to this date when she was so clearly reluctant.

"Can't you just cancel?" Alix asked. Problem solved. As far as she could see, there was no reason for Colette to be so worried about this. If she didn't want to go out with the guy, she didn't have to. Women changed their minds all the time. Men, too, for that matter.

"It's just that…I don't know what to expect from him."

"Why put yourself in this situation at all?" It didn't make sense to Alix.

Colette broke eye contact, lowering her head. "Christian said if I went to dinner with him this one time, he'd never bother me again." She spoke in a low, uninflected voice.

Alix was outraged. "That's blackmail!"

"I suppose it is."

"Suppose, nothing! You can't let a man manipulate you like that." Alix was getting worked up now. No way was a man taking advantage of Colette, not if *she* could help it. "You want me to deal with this loser?"

Colette smiled for the first time. "Thank you, but no. I'll be fine."

"How well do you know him?"

"I worked for the company for seven years, five of those as his personal assistant."

Alix frowned, a little confused by the inconsistency of Colette's reactions. "Is he the reason you left?"

Colette hesitated. "In a manner of speaking, yes, but it's…more complicated than that."

Alix wanted to say that *life* was complicated. She merely nodded, murmuring, "I understand," although she didn't really.

"I'll go out with him because there's something we should discuss… I'm just not sure I have the courage to do it."

"Would you like to discuss it with someone else beforehand?" she asked. If Colette needed a willing ear, Alix was happy to provide it.

Colette considered her offer for a long time before she replied. "I appreciate it, but no…" Her expression was sad, regretful, as if she badly needed a confidante but didn't feel ready to trust anyone just yet.

"So you haven't really dated since Derek died." Alix didn't know what else to say.

Colette shook her head. "I ran into a friend of his recently. He phoned a couple of times this past week and we've talked about getting together. Between his schedule and mine, it's difficult, though."

"By the way, I want to tell you again how sorry I am about your husband." Alix was afraid she might've been somewhat insensitive during their conversation last Wednesday, the way she'd been going on about how she couldn't bear the thought of losing Jordan when this woman's *husband* had died. "It's so tragic, and—"

"Don't say that!" Colette's mouth thinned and she bit her lower lip as if struggling not to cry.

Alix was completely confused now. "Why not? It's what people say when there's a death in the family."

"I know…." She grabbed her purse and scrabbled for a tissue, eventually finding one and dabbing her eyes with it. "It's hard to explain."

Alix remained silent.

"I…I don't know why I'm telling you this," Colette said, digging into her purse for a fresh tissue.

"Listen, it's all right," Alix said. "Whatever you tell

me goes no further. One thing I can do is keep my trap shut. That's a lesson I learned years ago."

"Okay." Colette gave her a watery smile. "I loved my husband and he was a good man. We were having fertility problems, and those problems affected our marriage. I wanted to see a specialist and Derek didn't. He said he wanted children, but if it didn't happen naturally, he was fine with letting it go. I wasn't." She paused and blew her nose. "The morning Derek fell from the roof, we'd had a huge argument. He should never have gotten on that roof. He probably wouldn't have if we hadn't been fighting."

"So now you feel responsible for what happened." Guilt manifested itself in so many different ways. Alix had dealt with it often enough to know the tricks it could play.

"I do and I don't. I begged him to call a roofing company. Derek wouldn't hear of it. I hoped that if he cooled off and thought everything over, he'd see my point about fertility treatments, so I didn't try very hard to stop him from doing the repair work himself." She shrugged in a dispirited way. "He had all these new tools he really wanted to use, too. Some of them were Christmas gifts from me…."

"You couldn't have known what would happen," Alix said in a reasonable tone.

Colette nodded. "That's true. But we had this…this issue between us. I wanted a family and Derek said he did, yet he wasn't willing to take the next step to make children a possibility. I'm over thirty and I didn't want to put it off any longer."

"That's understandable."

Colette nodded again. "What I told everyone at our last knitting class is a lie."

Alix tried to remember what Colette had said and couldn't recall.

"My marriage wasn't good anymore, even though I said it was. In fact, I was miserable and I suspect Derek was, too."

"I'm sure you would've worked things out," Alix said and reached for her sandwich, taking the first bite.

"I think we would have, too. Like I said, I loved my husband and I grieved for him when he died. I'm still grieving. But Derek's gone and he isn't ever coming back. Life goes on and I have to go on, too."

"Yes, you do," Alix said firmly. She took another bite of her lunch.

"It's just the one date," Colette said aloud, as if she needed to reassure herself. She'd obviously returned to the subject of her former boss.

"Do you really feel you need to go through with this?" Alix asked. Something had happened there, but Colette had dropped such obscure hints that Alix couldn't figure out exactly what it was. Probably an office romance gone wrong.

Colette nodded. "I'll have dinner with him, and then it'll be over, once and for all."

"I say almost the same thing about the wedding," Alix told her half-humorously. "It's just the one day and once it's over, Jordan and I can go on with our lives. My reward is that I'll have a husband I love who loves me. If I have to stand up in front of a bunch of people I don't know, if I have to pretend to be someone I'm not, then I can do that for one day." Alix had said these words to herself so many times, it sounded as if she was repeating a pledge.

When she'd finished, she discovered Colette studying her. "This wedding's freaked you out, hasn't it?"

"You have no clue."

Her friend laughed. "Wanna bet?"

They both smiled then.

"If you want, I can be at your place when the big bad wolf shows up," Alix offered.

Colette cringed. "He's not so bad. His name is Christian Dempsey."

"Dempsey. Well, let me be the one to tell this Mr. Dempsey that he isn't playing fair and that you refuse to be manipulated." She'd do it, too—in a heartbeat— and enjoy watching the man's expression.

"Listen, Alix, I can do this," Colette said with more confidence than she'd shown before. "You're right, you know. Talking helped. I don't feel comfortable burdening Susannah with my troubles. I like Lydia a lot, and for a while we had tea together every morning, but we haven't done that lately."

Alix knew the problem there. "Margaret's pretty needy these days." That was certainly an understatement.

"I can understand why." Colette smoothed out her knitting and smiled at Alix. "I'm so grateful you came in. I feel so much better."

Hearing that buoyed Alix's spirits. "I thought it was time we got to know each other." She sipped her coffee, which had grown cool.

"What kind of sandwich is that?" Colette asked.

"Turkey with cream cheese and cranberries."

Colette twisted around to read the menu board near

the counter. "I was so stressed about this dinner tomorrow that I skipped lunch and now I'm ravenous."

"Here," Alix said and slid the remaining half of her sandwich over to Colette. "Have the rest of mine."

"You're sure?"

"Positive."

Colette picked it up and took a bite. "Mmm. Delicious."

"My favorite. Hey, listen. Tell me how your date with Dempsey goes, okay?"

Colette raised her eyebrows. "It'll be fine."

"Good, because if he tries anything I'll break his kneecaps."

Colette laughed then, and the sound drifted through the almost-empty café.

Fourteen

Colette Blake

As Colette waited for Christian Dempsey on Sunday evening, she tried to calm her frayed nerves by reviewing her conversation with Alix Townsend the day before. She'd gotten to know Alix and to like her. After lunch, they'd chatted for nearly two hours.

Her conversation with Alix had clarified her own situation. She knew most of her comments had been cryptic and yet Alix hadn't pressed her for details Colette didn't want to disclose. She could only imagine what people would think once they learned she was pregnant. But Alix wasn't judgmental in the least. If anything, she was exactly the opposite—accepting, tolerant, *kind*.

During their conversation, Alix had opened up about her own life. Colette would never have guessed the trauma the young woman had endured, and she'd found it difficult not to reveal her shock. Hearing about Alix's struggles made Colette feel close to her in a way she hadn't with anyone in years.

Colette used to think she had good friends. For the past half-dozen years, her life had revolved around her job with Dempsey Imports, and most of her time was spent with colleagues, many of whom became friends. They'd replaced the friends she'd had in college. And when she and Derek socialized, it'd been with a completely separate group, primarily cops and their spouses. After Derek's death, their "couple friends" had eventually drifted away. Later, when she resigned from Dempsey Imports, she'd abandoned her work friends, afraid Christian would use them to contact her. It was a rude awakening now to realize her friends were so few.

Colette wasn't angry about it, or for that matter, upset. She viewed it all as rather enlightening. Examining herself, she was forced to admit she hadn't been much of a friend and was determined to change that. Jenny was a good example. Not once since leaving Dempsey Imports had she contacted Jenny, although she'd considered it from time to time—usually for the wrong reasons. Jenny must wonder why she'd left so abruptly and why she hadn't been in touch. That realization led her to a decision—two decisions. She'd give Jenny a call soon. And she'd be a friend to Alix. Following their chat, she believed Alix had felt a connection to her, too. They each had their troubles, and there was no need for pretense. If Alix wanted to talk about the wedding, Colette was determined to listen.

The knock at the door leading into the alley startled her. Colette drew a calming breath, and after climbing slowly down the stairs, opened the door. Christian Dempsey stood there, looking as confident as ever.

Colette managed a smile. "I see you're right on time," she said. It was a weak conversational gambit—especially since Christian had never been late in his life. His days were ruled by the clock.

"Are you ready?" he asked brusquely.

Colette nodded. "I'll get my purse and sweater." She went back up the stairs, gathered what she needed and when she came out of the bedroom, discovered that Christian had followed her up. He stood in the middle of her tiny apartment, looking curiously around. Whiskers wandered into the room and Christian bent down to pet the cat, who purred with delight, lifting his tail and arching his back.

"I didn't know you had a cat."

"Whiskers belongs to Lydia, the shop owner," Colette explained. "She used to live in this apartment. She left when she got married, but Whiskers considers this his home. I have the impression he's allowing me to live here."

Christian grinned as he straightened, and Whiskers wove his sleek body between Christian's legs, as if to say this man was welcome to visit anytime he pleased.

Naturally Colette chose to ignore Whiskers' warm welcome. She led Christian downstairs, and they walked through the alley to Blossom Street, where he'd parked. As she'd expected, he drove a fancy sports car that was low to the ground. She wasn't aware quite how low until he opened the passenger door and she tried to slip gracefully inside. Thankfully, he didn't so much as crack a smile at her less-than-elegant attempt.

He chatted amicably about Blossom Street as he got in next to her and started the engine. Never having been terribly interested in cars, Colette couldn't have identified what kind it was; all she could say was that it made lots of noise and seemed to speed up effortlessly between red lights, until they entered the freeway. From that point forward, they whizzed past every vehicle they encountered as if all the other cars were crawling along. He didn't seem worried about a speeding ticket.

It never occurred to her to ask where they'd be having dinner. When he mentioned a restaurant on the Everett waterfront, she was surprised. Everett was forty minutes to an hour from downtown Seattle, depending on traffic. They reached it in thirty-five minutes, with Christian carrying the conversation. Despite a determined effort, Colette couldn't make herself relax. She didn't understand why he'd insisted on this date. And yet she owed him the truth. He deserved to know she was pregnant, and that the baby was his. That she'd lied to him earlier when he'd asked. All she needed now was the courage to tell him.

She knew that sooner or later, he'd probably be arrested. The fact that she was responsible for alerting the law weighed heavily on her shoulders. A dozen times a day she wondered if she'd made a mistake. So far, though, everything said she shouldn't trust this man.... But no matter what, she had to tell him about the baby. That was a decision she'd reached during more than one sleepless night.

When they got to the restaurant in Everett, Christian parked in valet service and to her gratitude, helped her out of the car. They were escorted to a corner table for two that was both private and romantic. They were handed large leather-bound menus, and a bottle of French champagne arrived soon after that.

"I hope you like champagne."

"I do, but I only drink it when I have something to celebrate," she said. "I don't feel I do." She decided now was as good a time as any to bring up his legal position. "Christian," she said, looking intently across the table at him. "I'd like you to consider…" She faltered slightly.

"Yes."

She kept her voice low for fear of anyone listening. "If at all possible, I urge you to go to the police."

Christian leaned back in his chair. "I can't do that."

"Christian," she said, struggling not to plead with him. "You know what I did."

"I know about the letter."

"Then you have to realize it's only a matter of time before…there's an arrest."

He shrugged carelessly. "I have an excellent attorney."

"But—"

"I'd rather not discuss it."

Of course. She lowered her gaze, afraid that if she looked him in the eye he'd know how deeply she cared for him. Afraid he'd guess the secret she held so close to her heart. "If you aren't indicted now, you will be soon."

Again he shrugged. "Perhaps. Despite your letter, I seem to have passed INS scrutiny."

"Oh." But she wondered if the INS knew the whole story—or if he was even telling her the truth.

"So that's the reason you agreed to have dinner with me." His smile was amused. "You thought you might convince me to give myself up." He pressed his wrists together as if they'd been handcuffed. "Sorry to disappoint you."

It *was* a disappointment, but she refused to let him see that. "I'd hoped…I thought…" She couldn't finish.

"I'm sorry, Colette, but I can't do what you ask."

He wasn't sorry enough.

"Can we still enjoy our meal?"

Colette lifted her eyes to meet his and discovered a look of tenderness she hadn't expected. She wanted to believe Christian wasn't involved in smuggling other human beings, but the evidence said otherwise.

"I don't know," she said after a long moment. As far as she was concerned, the evening was already over. She'd go through the motions and even contribute to the conversation. But her desire to tell him about the baby had waned. There really wasn't any rush. He would learn about it eventually; she'd tell him when she had no other option.

Christian returned his gaze to the menu, sipping from his flute of champagne while Colette ignored hers. Then he set it aside and leaned closer. "Are you seeing Steve Grisham?" he asked bluntly.

The question took her aback. He'd said he wanted to take her to dinner so they could end their relationship on a positive note. Why would he ask about someone she'd only mentioned once? Perhaps his real intent this evening was to find out exactly how much she knew— and whether she'd said anything to Steve.

"That's none of your business." Colette quickly scanned the menu and decided on the grilled salmon with mango salsa.

"I beg to differ," he said. "Since this man's associated with law enforcement, you can imagine my concern."

She looked at him quickly, not sure whether he was laughing at her.

"I haven't breathed a word of this to anyone," she said stiffly.

"Other than the authorities," he interjected. He really did seem to consider it a joke.

"Do you think this is amusing?" she snapped. "Apparently so because..." She swallowed hard, tugging at the linen napkin on her lap. He'd committed a despicable crime and he found it funny? That disturbed her more than almost anything he'd done.

"I apologize," Christian murmured.

She nodded, slightly mollified. "I said nothing, I promise you. Not to *anyone.*"

He bowed his head. "Thank you for that."

She didn't want his thanks.

He hesitated, then added, "You really are a beautiful woman." His eyes were intense for a second or two, embarrassing her.

"Flattery isn't going to change my mind, Christian," she protested. This entire conversation was disconcerting. "I know the kind of man you are...now. I was fooled earlier but not anymore."

"Despite what you think of me, I meant that, Colette."

"Don't be absurd." Her cheeks filled with color and she glared at him.

"All right, all right." He raised one hand. "I believe I asked if you'd decided to date that friend of your husband's."

"And I believe I said it wasn't any of your business."

"You did," he concurred. "I'm asking again anyway, and not for the reason you assume."

"Why would you care?" She refused to look away. "And what legitimate reason could you possibly have for asking?"

He frowned. "Please, just answer my question. Yes or no?"

She could see he wouldn't drop it until she told him. "Steve and I have spoken a few times," she said.

"You haven't gone out with him, though, have you?"

"Not yet, but that's about to change. I'll be seeing him next week." She didn't understand why it should matter to him. Christian had gone out of his way to have roses delivered to another woman on a weekly basis, and he'd made sure they came from Susannah's Garden. More than that, he'd forced Colette to take the order. So he thought it was okay to flaunt his new girlfriend, but he somehow felt he could dictate who *she* was allowed to see!

"Don't do it," he said sharply. "Break the date."

"Can you give me one reason why I should?"

"I can't—"

Colette couldn't remain silent. "I happen to genuinely like Steve Grisham," she burst out. "He was a good friend to my husband and I've known him for years."

Christian set the menu aside. After the intense look he'd sent her earlier, he now gave the impression that it was of little concern. Talk about mixed messages! He'd been adamant only moments ago and now he seemed completely indifferent.

"I gather you've recently met someone yourself," she pressed, curiosity getting the better of her. "The woman you're sending all those roses."

He nodded. "I'll admit she's very special."

Colette's stomach twisted with what could only be jealousy. She didn't *want* to care and yet she did, more than she was willing to acknowledge. However, she kept her response light. "She must be special if you've ordered flowers for the entire year," Colette continued.

"As I recall, most of your liaisons didn't last nearly that long."

He arched his brows, and Colette grinned. "You forget I was the one who made the reservations for all your dinner dates—*and* ordered the flowers."

He cocked his head. "But you'll notice I didn't bring *you* to any of those restaurants."

Colette found it impossible not to smile. "So that's why we had to drive an hour outside of Seattle. You've gone through the entire roster of fine dining establishments in all of King County."

Christian was saved from having to answer when the waiter came for their dinner order. After he'd left, the subject changed and they discussed mutual acquaintances. It was common ground, and safe.

To say the meal was divine would be an understatement. Every course, from the roasted tomato soup with hot rosemary-scented rolls to the hearts-of-palm salad to her entrée was so delicious it practically dissolved on her tongue.

"You didn't drink your champagne," Christian said as the waiter carried off their dinner plates. He gestured at the full glass that had remained untouched throughout the meal.

"No, I didn't."

His expression sobered as he stared at her intently. "Why? Because being with me is nothing to celebrate? Or is there some other reason?"

That comment made her flinch, but it was the perfect lead-in for what she had to tell him—and she would have, had their conversation gone another way. Instead, she'd learned that he was relying on attorneys to rescue him from the law. Under the circumstances, Colette didn't feel she *could* let him know, not right now. She had to wait, see what the next few months would bring.

"Are you trying to ask me if I'm pregnant?" she asked, smiling as though the question was patently absurd. "I already gave you my answer, remember? I have no reason to lie."

The tension visibly eased from his shoulders.

"However, if I was," she said, purposely testing him, "I'd certainly know your feelings on the matter, wouldn't I?"

It was plain that talk of a pregnancy had unsettled him.

"Since it's a moot point, I don't think we need to belabor it."

Colette nodded vigorously. "My feelings exactly."

He sipped from his second glass of champagne as they read the dessert menu. Everything sounded delectable, and Colette was certainly tempted, but in the end declined and ordered tea instead. Christian did the same. Soon afterward, he settled the bill and they prepared to return to Seattle.

On the drive back, despite her best efforts to stay awake, Colette drifted off. The car was cozily warm, the ride smooth, the music soft. When he turned onto Blossom Street, she suddenly woke up, feeling disoriented for a moment. She glanced at his unyielding profile, then looked out at the familiar street.

Instead of parking on Blossom as he had earlier, Christian drove into the alley near the rear entrance to her apartment. He switched off the engine and they sat in the dark. There seemed little to say.

A feeling of sadness came over her, and she felt re-

gret that their relationship had dwindled down to this—
mutually kept secrets, mutually told lies.

"Christian, listen—" she began, but he cut her off.

"Before you say anything, I'd like to make a comment, if you don't mind."

"No, go ahead."

"We both agree that our...liaison, for lack of a better term, should never have happened," he said. He appeared to be choosing his words deliberately.

She nodded.

"It was a mistake," he said quietly, "and I apologize for my part in it."

"I do, too." Christian shouldn't assume all the responsibility for something in which she'd been a willing partner. "Please, Christian, I'd rather not talk about it."

"What I realize now is that by giving in to my—"

"Christian." She placed her hand on the door handle, ready to end this uncomfortable discussion. He couldn't say anything she hadn't said to herself a hundred times. "This isn't doing either of us any good. It happened. As you said, it shouldn't have, but it did. I don't blame you and I hope you don't blame me."

"Of course not."

"Fine. Then let's leave it. You said you wanted to end things on a positive note. We have. It's over. I wish it didn't have to end at all, but I can't be a party to what you're doing."

"And I accept that."

She opened the door. "Then this is goodbye."

"Yes." His voice was a hoarse whisper.

She started to climb out of the car.

"Colette," he said. Stopping her, he reached for her hand. "If you need anything, please contact me."

She shook her head. "Thank you, but no."

Even in the darkness she knew he was smiling. "Somehow I figured you'd say that."

"Take care of yourself, Christian."

"You, too."

"I'm sorry," she said. "I'm really sorry. About…everything."

Christian released her hand. "I meant what I said, Colette. I won't trouble you again."

She swallowed, nodding slowly, unable to speak.

"I want only the best for you," he added.

He opened the car door, and the interior light illuminated the alley with its concrete parking spaces and winter-bare tree. He walked around to the passenger side and helped her out, his hand clasping hers a little longer and a little harder than necessary.

It looked for a moment as if he intended to kiss her. Instead, he backed away and dropped her hand. Colette fumbled inside her purse for her keys; when she glanced up, she knew with certainty that this would be the last time she'd ever see Christian Dempsey.

He nodded once, then got back into the car, waiting long enough for her to unlock her door before he disappeared into the night.

Fifteen

Lydia Goetz

I was on my feet from the moment I walked into A Good Yarn until I flipped the lock and turned over the Closed sign at the end of a very long afternoon. We did a booming business, with thirty-eight sales. By anyone's standards, it was an excellent business day. I attributed this to the fact that it was now April, and spring had well and truly arrived.

Fortunately, Margaret seemed to be in a better mood. Although we didn't have a spare moment to discuss it, I had the feeling the police were closing in on a suspect. Margaret had said she'd heard there was promising news but that was all she was able to tell me.

Toward the end of the day, we'd had a couple of unexpected visitors—Carol Girard and her son, Cameron. I was eager to tell Brad about Carol's news.

When I got home, Brad had already started dinner, to my relief. I'd put three boneless chicken breasts in a marinade of buttermilk and ranch dressing spices that morning, and there was leftover coleslaw from the night before, plus Cody's favorite, Tater Tots.

Our son was in the backyard throwing balls around with a couple of neighborhood kids. As always, Chase was with him, barking and running after all the loose balls. The sound of Cody's excited young voice drifted toward me, and tired though I was, I felt a surge of happiness knowing that right outside this window was my son.

"Hi, sweetheart." I kissed Brad and he slipped an arm around me.

"How was your day?" I asked.

"Better, now that you're home." He smiled. "Aside from that, busy."

I set my purse on the kitchen counter. "Mine, too." Since Brad works for UPS, he has to meet a daily quota or "delivery expectation" every day, which means he's constantly on the go.

I took a tray of raw cut-up vegetables and dip from the refrigerator. It was difficult to get Cody to eat vegetables and he could be downright inventive at finding reasons he shouldn't have to. When he was eight, he'd announced in an earnest voice that God had personally spoken to him. When Brad asked him what divine message had been revealed, Cody had said that, according to God, he shouldn't eat any more green beans.

"What's so funny?" Brad asked, turning away from the stove.

"I was just thinking about God telling Cody he didn't have to eat green beans."

Brad laughed out loud. "Good thing the kid likes raw carrots and broccoli."

"I suspect that has more to do with the dip," I said, but at least he was putting something green and orange in his mouth that didn't contain sugar.

I opened the silverware drawer and extracted what we needed for the evening meal. "Carol Girard stopped in this afternoon," I said.

Carol was a good friend and one of my very first customers. When I met her, she and her husband, Doug, had been experiencing fertility problems. In an effort to reduce her stress and prepare for the IVF treatments, Carol had quit her job.

After working in a high-pressure position as an investment banker, she'd discovered that staying home wasn't as easy as she'd assumed. She'd grown restless and bored. Carol had wandered into the yarn store during one of the lengthy walks she'd started taking—and when she learned the class would be knitting a baby blanket, she felt it was a sign that she'd have her baby.

Their prayers were answered, but not in a way anyone had expected. She and Doug had adopted a baby boy they'd named Cameron.

"How is Carol?"

I looked my husband straight in the eye, grinning widely. "She's pregnant."

"Carol?" A smile broke out.

I nodded. I knew what he was thinking because that very thought had gone through my mind, too. Doug and Carol had spent thousands upon thousands of dollars trying to conceive. They'd finally given up on ever having a child—and then they'd adopted Cameron. And now…

"She's sure?"

"Three months sure," I told him.

As I recalled, there was no medical reason Carol couldn't conceive. It had just never happened, despite every test and procedure modern medicine could provide.

"I'll bet Doug's happy," Brad said. Like my own husband, Doug was one of those men who value family—a natural dad.

"Doug is *thrilled.* So's Cameron—they've told him he's going to be a big brother." The three-year-old was as excited as his parents. While they were in the yarn store, he'd wanted Carol to buy a plush lamb I had on display for what he called "Mama's baby."

"I'm glad for them," Brad told me. "Why don't we have them over sometime soon? We'll celebrate."

I nodded. I'd been on an emotional high ever since I'd heard the news. I knew Jacqueline and Alix would share my feelings. A new baby pattern book had arrived earlier in the week and I planned to knit a project out of it. Maybe another baby blanket. I could envision a reunion of that first knitting class in a few months. We'd present Carol with hand-knit gifts to welcome this new baby.

The high lasted until later that night as I got ready for bed. I was washing my face when it hit me. Carol's pregnancy had suddenly, cruelly reminded me: *I would never have a baby.* The emotional punch came out of nowhere and struck with such intensity that I closed my eyes and leaned against the bathroom counter. I held my breath until the pain began to subside.

Brad was already in bed, sitting up against the pillows, reading. Cody had been asleep for a couple of hours. I was grateful for that, because I didn't want him to see me like this.

Brad has always been sensitive to my moods. The moment I walked into the bedroom, he knew something was wrong. He lowered his book and looked at me.

With a huge lump in my throat, I lifted the covers and climbed silently into bed.

"Lydia, what is it?"

"I'm happy for Carol," I said in a shaking voice. "But it hit me just now…. I can't have children. I mean, I've known all along and it isn't like it's any surprise…so I don't understand why I should feel like this *now*."

"We'll never have a baby of our own," he said softly. "We have to accept that."

I was in my teens when I first underwent chemotherapy and radiation treatments. From the time I was sixteen, I knew my ability to conceive had been lost. I would never, under any circumstances, bear a child. Brad and I had discussed this at length before we married. I thought I *had* accepted it.

"We have Cody," Brad reminded me gently.

Cody was deeply important to me; I didn't need to tell Brad that. And yet, I still ached. My arms had never felt so empty. My heart hurt. For the first time, I understood with all my being the pain Carol had endured before Cameron came into her life.

"Cody is as much my son as if I'd given birth to him," I whispered.

"Yes, but you never knew him as an infant." Brad was telling me he understood what I was feeling. "Do you want a baby?" he asked, his voice low and soothing.

I nodded, deploring the tears that filled my eyes. "I want *your* baby."

Brad placed his arm around my shoulders and kissed the top of my head. I knew he was struggling to find the words to comfort me. Above all, I needed his assurance that he loved me despite my physical inadequacies. If he'd married just about anyone else, he could have fathered a second child. It was his bad luck that he fell in love with me.

I was aware of how ridiculous I was being. I didn't care. I wanted to feel a baby—our baby—stretching, kicking and growing within my womb. That was denied to me because of my cancer. It was unfair and wrong and I was miserable, swallowed up in self-pity.

"I would've been a good mother," I sobbed.

"You're already a great mother." Brad got out of bed and went into the bathroom, returning with several tissues.

"Let's adopt," Brad suggested as I mopped my face.

"Adopt?" I repeated the word as if I'd never heard it before. We'd talked about it, of course, but I suppose the option had never seemed real to me.

Brad stood there waiting for a response.

"Do you want to adopt?" I asked.

"I would if that would help you," he said. He made it sound as simple as snapping his fingers.

"Oh, Brad." In that moment I loved him so much. But the problem was, I didn't *know* what I wanted.

"We can start calling adoption agencies tomorrow morning." He seemed pleased with this solution. "I do have flashes of brilliance every now and then," he murmured, getting into bed again.

"You do," I said. With gratitude and love, I spread eager kisses over his cheeks and lips.

My husband took my face between his hands and kissed me back, each kiss growing in intensity. "This doesn't mean," he whispered between kisses, "that we should give up our efforts to…make a baby."

"Absolutely," I agreed, sliding my arms around his neck and pulling him to me.

My husband is an appreciative lover, and I felt his tenderness and his love in every cell of my body as we moved together, whispering encouragement.

Afterward, we lay spent in each other's arms. Earlier I'd felt bereft, lacking as a woman. Brad had showed me I was woman enough to satisfy him, and knowing that brought me intense pleasure and pride.

"I'm hungry," he whispered close to my ear.

"Brad! How can you think about food at a time like this?"

"Sorry, I can't help it. I'm famished."

"There aren't any cookies left." I'd baked peanut butter cookies Sunday afternoon for Cody. But Brad liked them as much as Cody did and had eaten more than his share.

"I'll have a peanut butter and jelly sandwich," he said, tossing aside the covers. He shrugged into his robe. "Want one?"

My first reaction was to decline, but then I changed my mind. "Yeah, that sounds good," I said, folding back the blankets. I found my nightgown and slipped it over my head.

By the time I joined Brad, he had the bread laid out on the countertop and was searching the cupboard for a jar of peanut butter.

"Next to the stove, right-hand side," I instructed him.

While he made the sandwiches, I got out milk and poured us each a glass.

"So, should I check into adoption agencies tomorrow?" Brad asked.

"I…I'm not sure yet."

"You don't seem convinced." He turned to look at me. "We need to be very sure about this before we apply."

"Let me think about it some more, all right?"

"Of course."

"There are a lot of questions we'll have to ask ourselves," I pointed out.

"Such as?"

"Well, we both work. What about day care?"

Brad unscrewed the lid on the jelly jar. "My mother watched Cody after he was born so Janice could work," he said. "I can approach her about that so we won't have to worry about child care."

"Okay." Still, there were plenty of other questions. Like: Would we be willing to maintain a relationship with the birth mother if she wanted one? And what if the child had some inherited disease or condition—could we cope with that?

"I could pick her up after work," Brad was saying.

"Her?" I teased.

"Did I say her?" he asked, sounding surprised. "I guess I just assumed you'd want a girl."

"How about you?" I asked.

"I'd be happy either way."

"Me, too."

"On the other hand, if we have a choice, I think I'd like a little girl." Brad slapped two slices of bread together and handed me the first sandwich. I reached for a plate and cut my sandwich in two. Brad ate his standing over the kitchen sink.

"Cody will be good with an infant," I said, picturing my stepson with a baby. "Boy *or* girl."

Brad agreed with a quick nod. He'd gobbled down his whole sandwich before I'd had the chance to eat half of mine. I put the second half in the fridge and we went back to bed.

We cuddled close and I felt the even rhythm of his breathing a few minutes later and realized he'd fallen asleep. It took me a while longer as I reviewed our discussion. *Adoption.*

Brad and I could bring an infant into our lives. I thought about how my family was likely to react. I knew it would please my mother; she'd always wanted more grandchildren.

I could say with certainty that Margaret, however, would insist adoption was a mistake. After making sure I knew she disapproved, she'd list ten excellent reasons why Brad and I shouldn't adopt a child. But it wasn't Margaret's life, was it? I reminded myself that the decision was ours, not my sister's.

What seemed like minutes later, the alarm on our clock radio was buzzing. The morning news followed. Brad was already out of bed and in the shower. Although I don't have to be at work until ten, I make it a habit to get up with my husband.

Yawning, I went into the kitchen, started the coffee and dropped slices of bread in the toaster. Cody, lucky boy, could sleep for another hour before he had to wake up.

"Have you done any more thinking about what we

discussed last night?" Brad asked me as he took his first sip of coffee.

"A little. What about you?"

"I'll do whatever you want, Lydia."

"Let's talk about it again in a few weeks."

He nodded. Before he left for work, Brad kissed me with extra fervor, and I took comfort in what he told me so effectively without words. I stepped outside with him, into a spring morning soft with promise. Standing on the deck, I watched him pull out of the garage.

I must've done something very good in my life to deserve Brad Goetz.

Sixteen

Alix Townsend

With Jacqueline and Colette's encouragement, Alix joined Go Figure, an exercise gym for women, which had recently opened on Blossom Street.

Exercise, Alix heard from a variety of sources, was a good tension reliever. As the wedding date grew closer, Alix was in desperate need of something to calm her increasingly frazzled nerves. Knitting just wasn't doing it anymore, not when this farce of a wedding got more ridiculous with each passing day.

As an added inducement, Colette had signed up with her. Go Figure wasn't like any gym Alix had ever seen. It had equipment but no mirrors, except in the changing stalls, and no men.

The exercise program was predesigned and set to music. You went around the circle of exercise equipment, spending forty-five seconds on each machine, then you spent another forty-five seconds dancing or running in place on a small platform. After that, it was on to the next piece of equipment, and so on. The goal was to do thirty minutes of exercise, which meant completing the circle twice. Forty-five seconds? Anyone could manage that.

When Colette suggested they try this out, Alix had scoffed. She didn't want to brag, but she was in good shape. She hoisted twenty-five-pound bags of flour nearly every day. Mixing all that bread dough and lifting it onto a floured board wasn't for weaklings. Still, the first time she completed the cycle at Go Figure she discovered muscles she didn't know she had.

After their initial week, during which they were allowed to visit as often as they wanted for free, Colette and Alix had decided to sign up. The gym recommended three to four sessions in a seven-day period. Having an exercise partner was great encouragement. Alix felt the workout had reduced her stress and Colette appeared to be enjoying the benefits, as well.

One drawback was that they couldn't really chat. Not with the music blaring and the beat urging them on. But Alix and Colette usually found a few minutes before or after their sessions to talk.

"Did he call?" Alix asked when they'd finished the latest round of exercise. She didn't have to explain who *he* was.

"No," Colette muttered. Her face was red from exertion. She draped a small towel around her neck as she moved toward the dressing room. Pushing aside the curtain, she glanced at Alix. "I already told you he wouldn't. That's the way we both want it."

When Colette had first mentioned Christian, Alix had serious doubts about him. Who wouldn't? He seemed to be virtually blackmailing her into that dinner date. Something was going on between those two, something Colette hadn't told her. Based on what she'd said earlier, there'd obviously been an incident, maybe a disturbing one. Alix wouldn't pressure her, though.

After her dinner date with Christian Dempsey, Colette had told her a bit more. From the way she talked, Alix could only assume that Colette had fallen in love with him. But if that was the case, she didn't understand why Colette chose to avoid him.

"Do you feel like walking down to Pike Place Market with me?" Colette asked as Alix pulled on her jeans.

"Sure." Alix's Saturday was mostly free. Her future mother-in-law wanted to meet with her later in the day to go over the menu for the rehearsal dinner. Alix felt her stomach knot at the prospect of dealing with one more wedding detail.

Jordan's mother meant well, and Alix tried hard not to say or do anything that would have a negative effect on their relationship. She did her best not to feel resentful. *It's just one day* had become a mantra that she repeated incessantly. The problem was that Alix wasn't willing to surrender *everything*. So far the only battle she'd really won had been over her wedding dress. Every other decision had gone to Jacqueline and Susan, and most of the time Alix's wishes were ignored.

In her ongoing effort to keep the peace, Alix felt she'd swallowed her pride far too often. Worse, Susan and Jacqueline hardly seemed aware of her mounting frustration. So any excuse to delay the meeting with Susan was a welcome reprieve.

The morning had brightened, which improved Alix's mood. But although the sun was out now, that didn't guarantee it would stay out. Above all, April weather was unpredictable and today could end with a storm.

As they walked, Alix saw that Colette seemed more subdued than usual. She guessed that her friend was mulling over their earlier conversation.

"Are you seeing Steve anytime soon?" Alix asked, leading indirectly to the subject of Christian Dempsey. Colette had mentioned the Seattle policeman last week and for some reason, seemed reluctant to accept his invitation. She'd talked it over with Alix. Although not generally a fan of cops, Alix couldn't see any harm in it and had urged her to go. The evening had turned out to be a success; according to Colette, Steve had been both attentive and charming. Alix wasn't fooled, though. Colette was still hung up on her old boss, regardless of how she tried to convince Alix otherwise.

"I told Steve I'd go to the movies with him this afternoon," she said without enthusiasm. "We'll probably have dinner afterward."

"So that relationship's going well?" In contrast to the one with Christian Dempsey.

"Yes, if it's any of your business." Colette grinned. "Steve's a lot of fun."

Alix studied her friend. "Then why aren't you jumping for joy? No, don't tell me—let me guess."

"Would you cut it out." Colette rolled her eyes.

"Why are you dating this guy?" Alix asked abruptly. "You like Christian."

Colette shrugged her shoulders helplessly as they waited at a red light.

"Colette, you have to do what will make you happy." Alix nudged her as the light changed and they crossed the street, heading to the Hill Climb that connected the market to the Seattle waterfront.

"It would never work with Christian and me." Colette held up one hand. "Before you ask, let me say I can't tell you any more than that."

"He's not married, is he?"

"No," Colette muttered as they continued walking.

"Was he abusive?"

"Of course not!"

"You should call him, you know." Alix couldn't see what was standing in their way.

"Oh, Alix, it's much too complicated to explain. I wish things were different, but they aren't."

Colette picked up her speed and Alix had to work to keep pace with her. "Trust me, you can't possibly say anything that's going to shock me."

Colette's steps slowed then, and she looked at Alix with questioning eyes. "What if I told you—" She didn't finish.

"Told me what?"

"That I drank too much and spent nearly twenty-four hours in bed with him," she blurted out.

Alix waited, knowing there had to be more to this story.

"Aren't you going to say anything?" Colette demanded, sounding angry now.

"If you're looking for someone to judge you, it won't be me," Alix returned promptly. "If you want to talk about what happened, fine, but if you expect me to beat you up over it, you've come to the wrong person."

Colette thanked her with a solemn nod. "It was the night of the company Christmas party." Misery and guilt suffused her face. "We'd both had too much to drink."

Alix gently placed her hand on Colette's elbow. "You don't have to tell me any of this."

"I want to," Colette said, but she avoided meeting Alix's eyes. "You'll probably understand better than anyone else. Until then, I didn't realize how much I'd come to love Christian. He was so wonderful to me after Derek died, so compassionate and generous. And working so closely together, well…I suppose it was only natural that I'd fall for him. I hate to admit it. Falling for the boss is such a cliché."

"Does he share your feelings?"

She shook her head. "I don't think so. He's dating someone else."

"How do you know?"

"He ordered flowers for her at the shop. Roses— every week for a year."

"Oh."

A short silence ensued.

"Everyone makes mistakes," Alix told her. "I certainly made my share. Jordan knows." It practically killed her to tell him, but she had to do it. Laying out the sordid details of her past had been the most humiliating experience of Alix's life. She felt deep shame, remorse, self-reproach and about ten other emotions too painful to name.

"You told him…*everything* about your past?" Colette asked. Immediately she seemed to regret posing the question. "You don't have to answer that if you'd rather not."

"I don't mind answering. And yeah, I did tell him the whole story." Alix lifted one shoulder in a shrug.

"But I don't make a habit of revisiting that time in my life. I'm an entirely different person now."

"Of course you are."

"Until Jordan, I didn't know what to do with all the ugly baggage from my past. It dragged me down. Every time something good happened, like when Jacqueline and Reese invited me to live in their guesthouse, I kept thinking I didn't deserve it."

"But Alix…"

"Yes, I know. Jordan was great." She paused, running one hand through her short, spiky hair. "He told me something I'll never forget."

Colette was staring at her intently. "What was that?"

"He said that sometimes the hardest part of forgiveness is forgiving ourselves."

Colette nodded thoughtfully. "I'm not the kind of woman who does one-night stands. Or at least, that's what I used to think. I always had contempt for women who did."

"I never thought I'd sink as low as I did, either," Alix said and swallowed the bile that rose in the back of her throat. The ugliness of the things she'd done had tainted her view of life until she'd made her peace with God—and with herself. "All I can say is I'm not going back there again."

"You won't," Colette said with utter confidence. "Like you said earlier, you aren't the same person you were then."

"The point I'm trying to make," Alix said, eager to turn the mirror away from herself, "is that you're doing the same thing I was. The person you can't forgive is you."

Colette agreed with a quick smile. "It isn't easy, is it?"

"Tell me about it." This had been the most difficult aspect of her new life, and Alix wasn't sure how to explain it to her friend. "These negative reactions? You know, when you expect the worst 'cause it's all you deserve?" When Colette nodded, she said, "I call it stinking thinking."

Colette frowned. "You mean when you start rehashing the past?"

"Yeah." Alix closed her eyes. "But it's more than that. Let me give you an example. Once, Tammie Lee, Jacqueline's daughter-in-law, told me how pretty I looked in red. At the time I had on a black shirt with jeans."

"So? She gave you a compliment."

"She *intended* it as a compliment," Alix explained, "only I didn't hear it as one. Instead I convinced myself that Tammie Lee had purposely insulted me."

"I'm sure she didn't mean it that way!"

"She didn't," Alix concurred. "I don't know if this'll make sense to you, but it all goes back to those old messages I'd gotten as a child."

"I think I understand," Colette said slowly.

"Tammie Lee made a casual comment and what she intended as a compliment I turned into an insult. That's because those messages told me I'd never been pretty so I couldn't be beautiful, no matter what color I wore. Not only that, I assumed she was saying I *wasn't* pretty the way I was." She took a deep breath. "My mother used to call me horrible names. For years I heard her voice in my head—sometimes I still do, but now I know how to drown it out. Whenever I remembered her saying things like 'You ugly little bitch' I'd sink into this dark pit of depression."

"Oh, Alix…"

"That's one of the effects of not being able to forgive yourself—or to cut yourself loose from those hateful insults and accusations. No matter what wonderful things people say, you don't believe them."

Colette seemed to understand.

"Why should anyone love me?" Alix asked rhetorically. "If I don't care about myself, then how can Jordan or anyone else?"

"Yes, but… In my case, it's best to leave matters between Christian and me as they are," Colette said, her voice low. "There's more I can't explain—stuff that's not directly related to Christian and me. I care about him, but I can't go down the path he's chosen. I…want to help him, but I can't. I have to simply walk away."

"Can you?" Alix pressed. "Can you really do that?"

A long time passed before Colette answered. "I really don't have any choice and yet…"

"Yet…" Alix pushed gently, knowing there was something else her friend wasn't telling her.

"I don't think we can ever get past what happened that…night."

"Everything seems to go back to that," Alix murmured.

Colette stopped walking for a moment, looking out toward the Sound. "We didn't use birth control," she whispered and Alix watched as she swallowed hard.

"You're pregnant?"

Colette nodded, her eyes brimming with tears. "I haven't told anyone… I don't think I've really taken it in myself. Why is life like this?" she groaned. "Derek and

I couldn't get pregnant and then...then one night with Christian and—" She left the rest unsaid. "I haven't figured out what I'm going to do. I'll keep the baby, of course. Christian doesn't know... Every time I try to tell him, I realize I can't. For now, that's for the best."

"But, Colette, he has a right to know!"

"I'll tell him," she promised and wiped the moisture from her cheeks. "Just not yet."

"The prayer shawl?" Instinctively Alix knew it wasn't a shawl Colette had been knitting, but a baby blanket.

"It's for the baby," Colette said. "Christian's and mine."

Seventeen

Colette Blake

Colette prayed she'd done the right thing in telling Alix about the pregnancy. She hadn't intended to, but it had seemed so natural…. Every day it became more difficult to conceal the news. Her instinct was still to keep the baby a secret for fear Christian would somehow discover her condition before she was ready to let him know.

Embarrassment had kept her from revealing the pregnancy to her family and her in-laws. What could she possibly say to Derek's parents? Thank goodness they lived in Chicago! At least they wouldn't find out until she chose to tell them—which she would. Eventually. They were wonderful people who loved their son and loved her. Colette was their last link to Derek and they kept in touch with her. Sooner or later she'd need to tell them the truth.

Then, of course, there was Christian. She expelled him forcefully from her mind. He'd made his choice and she'd made hers. When the time came, whenever that might be, she'd break the news to him. It seemed wrong to tell others and not the baby's father; that, however, couldn't be helped.

Discussing her pregnancy with Alix had given her a sense of exhilaration and relief. That old saying about confession being good for the soul—she'd certainly found it to be true.

Her high spirits had continued during her afternoon with Steve Grisham. She'd enjoyed their date, yet she felt something was missing in their relationship. In the beginning she'd assumed it had to do with her and the secret she kept. But after Saturday she realized there was a lack of connection between them. She liked Steve and was grateful for his company, which was pleasant and undemanding. And yet...

It surprised her that he didn't notice anything amiss. At the end of the evening he'd kissed her tenderly and seemed disappointed when she didn't invite him into her apartment. He'd asked to see her again and they were meeting for dinner on Friday evening.

"That's lovely," Susannah said, nodding at the arrangement of roses Christian had ordered for Elizabeth Sasser. As if to prove he meant absolutely nothing to her, she'd worked doubly hard to make the arrangement as attractive as possible. Roses didn't need much to enhance their beauty, but she'd carefully chosen a gleaming copper tub and interspersed ferns and baby's breath among the deep-red blooms.

"Would you mind if I delivered this personally?" Colette asked. She couldn't explain why she felt the need to meet the new woman in Christian's life. Elizabeth had apparently made quite an impression on him. Christian's past relationships had never lasted more than a few months, and yet he'd left his credit card number and instructions for a full year of weekly flower deliveries.

Susannah blinked at the unusual request. "We have a service."

"I'll do it on my own time." That would save Susannah the delivery fee.

"I don't see why you couldn't," Susannah returned, not bothering to conceal her surprise. "If you want to…"

"Thank you." Colette wasn't so convinced she'd be thankful after she'd made the delivery, though. Elizabeth was probably beautiful beyond description, talented and rich to boot. Colette's own shortcomings overwhelmed her. All she could think was that she was setting herself up to feel like a pathetic little waif, insecure and ridiculous. And yet her curiosity overrode common sense.

Then she remembered her most recent conversation with Alix. Her friend had talked about the ugly voices that shouted at her and dragged her into despair. Voices that told her she was worthless. She'd referred to it as "stinking thinking." Colette was hearing voices like that now. They were just as destructive as the voices Alix had mentioned. Everyone heard them at one time or another, Colette decided. She was determined not to listen.

Before she left Susannah's Garden, Colette refreshed her makeup and ran a comb through her hair. The other woman might be Hollywood beautiful, but Colette wouldn't allow that to influence her own feelings about her appearance or self-worth. Or so she repeatedly told herself as she sought out the Capitol Hill address.

When she pulled up in front of the huge three-story house—actually, mansion better described the residence—her confidence deflated faster than a balloon in a sticker bush. The lawn and yard were meticulously groomed. The sidewalk leading to the entrance was lined with blooming roses; their scent readily identified them as antique varieties and not hybrids. How like a man to send dozens of roses to a woman who had a yardful!

It took Colette several moments to find the courage to ring the bell. A full minute passed. Then an elderly woman, dressed in a black uniform with a white apron, opened the massive front door.

"Hello," Colette said with a friendly smile. "I have a flower delivery for Ms. Elizabeth Sasser." In all her life, she'd never known anyone rich enough to employ a maid.

The other woman unlatched the screen door and pushed it open, accepting the arrangement with both hands. "They're especially beautiful this week."

"Is Ms. Sasser at home?" Colette asked, while she still had the courage.

"Doris? Who's at the door?" The voice was that of an older woman.

"Flowers, Miss Elizabeth."

"Again?" A woman in her seventies or early eighties made her way into the entry, walking slowly but without a cane. Her silver hair was piled on top of her head and she wore a light pink pantsuit with a diamond brooch pinned at the collar.

"You're Elizabeth Sasser?" Colette blurted out.

The older woman's eyes narrowed as she studied Colette. "Doris, invite the young woman in for tea."

"Yes, Miss Elizabeth."

"We'll take our tea in the library," she said, before turning away from the door and disappearing.

The other woman nodded. She set the copper tub of roses on a round marble-topped table that stood in the entryway.

Colette stepped inside the house and immediately noticed the scents of lemon and polished wood—and roses. The floors gleamed and a wide, sweeping stairway curved toward the second floor. There were two doors off the entry, one to the left and the other to the right. She could see that the one on the right led to a formal dining room with tables and chairs and a huge sideboard.

The door on the left apparently led to the library. Built-in mahogany bookcases stretched from floor to ceiling on three sides. A marble fireplace dominated the fourth wall. Two leather chairs, creased with age, sat facing the fireplace. The room enchanted Colette, who suppressed the urge to run over and examine the leather-bound volumes that filled the bookcases.

"You may have a seat." Elizabeth Sasser gestured toward the leather chair next to her own.

"Thank you." Colette self-consciously sat and placed her hands in her lap. She had no idea what to say. But since Ms. Sasser had invited her, Colette decided to let the older woman ask the questions.

"We'll have tea presently."

"That sounds very nice." Colette glanced down at her hands, which were clenched in her lap like those of a schoolgirl called to task. With a determined effort she forced herself to relax.

"Christian sent you?" the woman asked.

"No... I mean, yes, in a manner of speaking. He ordered the flowers and I delivered them."

"I see."

They were briefly interrupted by Doris, who carried in a tray with a china teapot, creamer and sugar, two ornate teacups with saucers and a plate of delicate French cookies. "Madelines," Elizabeth pointed out when Doris had left. "I'm sure you recall your Proust."

"Remembrance of Things Past," Colette said dutifully. She didn't add that she'd always *meant* to read the books.

Elizabeth smiled faintly. "I'll ask you to pour. My hands aren't as steady as they once were."

"I'd be happy to," Colette said. She went over to the library table and carefully followed the other woman's instructions about sugar and lemon. After both cups were ready, she set a cookie on each saucer and brought the first to Elizabeth. She took the second for herself and reclaimed her seat.

"You know my great-nephew?" Elizabeth quickly returned to her questions.

"Yes." Colette didn't elaborate, but she was pleased that the mystery of the older woman's relationship to Christian had been revealed.

Elizabeth raised the cup to her lips and sipped her tea. "It's my understanding that in previous weeks the flowers have been brought to the house by a delivery service."

"That's correct."

"Was the service unable to make the delivery this week?"

The moment of truth had arrived. Colette could easily lie and save face. Admitting that she'd been curious about the woman in Christian's life would tell Elizabeth more than Colette was comfortable sharing. If she lied, she'd be on her way in a matter of minutes and out of this embarrassing situation.

"Actually I asked to deliver the flowers," Colette murmured, deciding on the truth. "I work for Susannah's Garden, the flower shop on Blossom Street."

"Was there any particular reason you felt it necessary to bring them yourself?"

"I...I wanted to meet the woman Christian loved."

A smile spread across the older woman's face. "How clever of you. Now that you recognize it's an old woman, you must be amused—or disappointed? I'm his great-aunt and one of his only surviving relatives."

Colette wasn't disappointed at all. If anything she was baffled. As Christian's former assistant, she was shocked to discover he had family she knew nothing about. "He's never mentioned you."

"That doesn't surprise me," Elizabeth commented drily. "I'm afraid he prefers to forget he has family."

Colette frowned.

With a dismissive wave of her hand, the older woman said, "It's a long story and one better saved for another day."

"I worked with Christian for five years. I never knew he had family."

"Five years?" Elizabeth repeated. "And in all that time he never mentioned me. I find that insulting." She made a soft huffing sound. "There are times I'd like to box that young man's ears." She muttered something under her breath Colette couldn't hear.

"What about his mother?" Colette asked. She didn't want to appear inquisitive or nosy, but she hungered for information. For the sake of her child it might prove important, even necessary. She'd assumed his mother was dead but now she no longer knew.

"The dear girl died in childbirth when Christian was eight. A terrible loss. One doesn't hear of that often these days. Still, it happens. Elliott lost both his wife and his infant daughter. And Christian lost more than his mother, I'm afraid. He lost his security."

Colette's heart ached for the little boy Christian had been.

"For a year afterward, Elliott buried himself in the bottom of a whiskey bottle, too immersed in his own grief to help Christian deal with his." Elizabeth set her cup back in the saucer with a sharp clink. "My husband, God rest his soul, brought young Christian to me. Charles and I had never been blessed with a family. Unfortunately, we were of an age at which we didn't have the foggiest idea what to do with a youngster. We kept him until Elliott had straightened himself out and then sent him home to live with his father." She paused, shaking her head. "I regret that to this day."

Colette tried to picture Christian as a hurting, motherless little boy but couldn't. He seemed too self-possessed, too confident, too remote. Perhaps his childhood explained the unyielding exterior he presented to the world.

Only three times in all the years she'd known him had Christian revealed a different facet of his personality. The day of Derek's funeral, the night of the Christmas party and just recently, when they'd gone to dinner.

"Did his father ever remarry?" she asked, wanting to know more details of Christian's young life.

"Unfortunately, no. When he finished with alcohol,

Elliott buried himself in his work. He traded one addiction for another, although arguably a less destructive one. Christian was raised by a series of housekeepers. I sent for him every summer and at Christmas, but as you can imagine, neither Charles nor I knew how to entertain a young boy."

Colette smiled, picturing Christian sitting at that huge dining table for a formal meal.

"I did teach him to play bridge, and I'll admit he's quite good."

Colette had never heard that he played any form of cards.

"Unfortunately, his relationship with Elliott is strained. My nephew decided long ago that Christian would one day take over his investment firm. Christian's never shown the slightest interest in stocks and bonds. From the time he was a child, he loved to travel. Christian spent hours in this very library, studying maps and reading about faraway lands. He started the import business with an inheritance he collected from his mother's side of the family."

"He's very successful at the business," Colette said, and wondered anew why he'd put so much at risk.

"And an utter failure at personal relationships, much like his father. Elliott blamed the world for his loss and instead of getting on with life, he held his bitterness inside. I'm afraid Christian is more like his father than he realizes. He, too, keeps everything hidden. He refuses to get close to anyone." Elizabeth shook her head sadly.

"He…he seems to have plenty of women friends."

"Pieces of fluff," Elizabeth said scornfully. "They never last long, do they? He woos them and then grows bored with them. Am I correct?"

Colette felt as if she was telling tales out of school. "Uh, that was his pattern when I worked with him. But I haven't been with Dempsey Imports for the last four months, so I can't say about more recent…relationships."

The other woman put down her tea cup and studied Colette. "You're in love with him, aren't you?"

Colette felt the blood rush to her face. "I wouldn't say that…."

The old woman gestured with one elegant hand. "Don't bother to deny it. You wouldn't have come here otherwise. Stand up," she demanded. "I want to get a good look at you."

Haltingly, Colette complied, thankful for her loose-fitting clothes.

"Straighten your shoulders," Elizabeth snapped. "What's the problem with young people these days? It's a wonder you don't all come down with back problems."

Colette managed to restrain a smile.

"I like you," Elizabeth announced abruptly.

This time Colette did smile. "I like you, too. Do you mind if I sit?"

"Go ahead." Elizabeth nodded. "All I can say is that it's high time my great-nephew settled down. I was beginning to wonder if he had the brains God gave a goose."

Colette wanted to laugh at Elizabeth's disgusted tone.

"Can you stay for dinner?"

"That isn't necessary. I—"

Elizabeth cut her off with an imperious wave. Before Colette could stop her, she'd called for Doris, instructing the housekeeper to set another place at the table.

"Over dinner, tell me *everything* you know about

Christian. I haven't seen the boy in months and I'm starving for news of him."

"I—"

"Elliott and Christian are my only living relatives," Elizabeth said before Colette could attempt an answer. "One day this house will be his." As she looked around, her gaze fell lovingly on the things in the room—the books, the antique desk, the rich Oriental carpet. "I'll tell you right now, if he marries one of those…those girls he's been dallying with for the last few years, I'd rather donate my home to the zoo. As I said, it's time he settled down and married a lady."

"I…I'm not sure I qualify as one," she murmured.

The older woman's gaze narrowed and she appeared to carefully choose her words. "You'll do. Now, tell me about yourself."

Colette paused and was about to describe her own family when Elizabeth raised a hand.

"Before you get started, I'd like you to answer one question. It might be an uncomfortable one and I apologize for that in advance. Nevertheless, I insist on the truth."

"All right." Colette hoped it wasn't the question she feared most.

Elizabeth leaned forward and stared at Colette intently. "It's obvious you love the boy. Something's gone wrong. What?"

"I…"

"The truth," she demanded.

Colette clasped her hands and nodded. "It's complicated."

The older woman sighed. "My dear, dear girl, love is *always* complicated. It wouldn't be love unless it was."

Colette agreed with a silent nod.

"You're pregnant, aren't you?"

Colette's eyes widened and then instantly flooded with tears.

Eighteen

"I love capturing the beauty and movement of a dog in intarsia knitting. It's fun to use a colorful palette of yarns, to knit a sweater that shows not only the splendor of the breed but its owner's love and pride."

—Peggy Gaffney, *www.kanineknits.com*

Lydia Goetz

Friday started off well. Sales were steady, and I saw some of my favorite customers.

At home the night before, Brad and I had spent hours discussing adoption, weighing the pros and cons.

My biggest fear, and one I shared with Brad, was the future. It was one thing to open a yarn store; if the cancer returned, I could always sell out. Bringing a child into our lives was another story entirely. As much as I lived in hope and health, the threat of the disease always hung over me and I couldn't ignore that and neither could Brad.

By the end of the evening, we were still of two minds, but I felt closer to him than ever. We decided to set the question of adoption aside for the moment.

Friday morning, I noticed an improvement in Margaret's attitude. I assumed this had come about because of Thursday's conversation with Detective Johnson. It seemed likely that the suspect they'd been watching would soon be picked up. Margaret was in a state of excitement all day, and I felt so pleased for her. Pleased and relieved. Yes, by all means, I wanted this lunatic found, charged and sent to jail. Even more, I wanted this matter shelved for Julia's sake. And my sister's.

The yarn store was doing well financially and I felt such a strong connection with my customers, especially the women in my prayer shawl class. I'd noticed that Colette and Alix had become friends. That shouldn't have surprised me, and yet it did. I wouldn't have thought they had much in common. But then, Alix is probably one of the most complex people I've ever met. She's able to adjust to people and situations easily—except for that out-of-control wedding. Still, she was doing her best to cope because she loves Jacqueline.

Who would've believed Jacqueline Donovan and Alix would become so close? That was a shocker. I think the world of Jacqueline and Reese for the way they helped Alix, helped and encouraged her through her schooling and as a bride-to-be.

When Paul, their only son, married Tammie Lee, Jacqueline wasn't involved in the wedding. At one time there were hard feelings because of this. Now, of course, that's all water under the proverbial bridge. With Alix's wedding, however, it was as if Jacqueline was making up for lost time—and lost opportunities. She was planning the social event of the year. I had to hand it to Alix; she'd been patient and good-natured about the whole thing.

At about four o'clock, the phone rang, and because I was standing closest to the cash register I automatically reached for it. "A Good Yarn," I said into the receiver.

"Aunt Lydia?" It was Hailey, my niece and Margaret's youngest daughter.

"Oh, hi—"

"Don't say my name," Hailey pleaded. She was whispering. "Is my mother there?"

"Well, yes."

"Is my mom watching you? She doesn't know it's me on the phone, does she?"

This was a very odd conversation, and it was beginning to alarm me. "She's with a customer," I said, lowering my own voice. Margaret apparently wasn't listening, since she didn't acknowledge the comment. "Is something wrong?"

"I...I don't know what to do. Julia's crying."

"What happened?"

"I...I don't know," Hailey said, and she seemed close to tears herself. "No one's here and...and Julia's talking crazy."

"What do you mean, crazy?" I asked urgently.

"I...I don't want to tell you."

"All right." I hesitated for a moment. "Let me talk to Julia."

"Okay." The relief in Hailey's voice was evident. "I'll take the phone to her."

"She's in her room?"

"No, she's on the kitchen floor," Hailey said.

As soon as she walked into the kitchen, chatting as

she went, I could hear Julia's heart-wrenching sobs. Crying like this wasn't normal, and the sound sent shivers through me.

The customer left and Margaret looked at me. I tried not to reveal that I was talking to her daughter.

"Hold on a minute," I said to Hailey.

"Okay."

I held the phone away from my ear and glanced at Margaret, who'd gone into the office to retrieve her purse.

"I'm going to run over to the French Café for a latte," my sister told me. "Can I get you anything?"

I shook my head. "Thanks anyway."

"I shouldn't be more than ten minutes," Margaret said on her way out the door, blissfully unaware of what was happening in her own home.

"Okay."

The bell above the door jingled as she left and Whiskers, my lazy cat, raised his head, then stretched his well-fed body in the warm afternoon sun.

As soon as Margaret was gone, I went back to the conversation. "Okay," I said to Hailey, "put your sister on the line."

"Here. Julia, talk to Aunt Lydia," Hailey said.

"Julia," I said softly, trying to encourage her. "Sweetie, tell me what's wrong."

She hiccuped a couple of sobs. "I…I don't know. I can't stop crying."

"Are you frightened?" I asked, thinking something must have happened to trigger this emotional breakdown.

"Yes…I can't sleep. I try and try."

Margaret had told me how poorly Julia had been

sleeping after the incident. The carjacking had taken place more than two months ago and I'd thought Julia was doing better. Apparently not.

"Have you talked to anyone?" I asked.

"No." The word was accompanied by a sob.

"Are you ready to talk?"

"No!" she screamed, anger taking control. "I want to *forget*. Why did he have to pick me? I hate him... I hate him." She sobbed again, harder this time, almost wailing. "Why won't everyone just leave me alone? It's all anyone wants to talk about. I can't stand my life.... I don't want to live anymore."

Now I understood why Hailey was so frightened. "Sweetheart, don't say that."

Julia must have tossed the phone away, because I heard a loud clang and soon afterward Hailey was on the line again. "She's still crying, only now she's got her face on the floor."

Julia screamed an obscenity that made me blink a couple of times.

Hailey gasped. "What should I do, Aunt Lydia?"

"I'd better tell your mother about this."

"Can she come home?"

"Of course." Julia might not want to see Margaret, but it was evident to me that she needed to talk to someone, perhaps a counselor or her doctor.

A few minutes later, after I'd reassured Hailey as well as I could, Margaret returned. "Alix was working as the barista," Margaret told me, grinning. It'd been such a long time since I'd seen my sister this carefree that I hated having to tell her about Julia.

"That was Hailey on the phone," I said.

The animation immediately left her face. "Is everything all right with Julia?"

I shook my head. "I think she's having some kind of breakdown."

The color drained out of Margaret's face. The reprieve was over. She tensed and for a moment seemed rooted to the spot, frozen with indecision about what she should do.

"She needs you," I told her. "She's talking nonsense." I couldn't tell her Julia was talking about not wanting to live anymore. It terrified me that she'd even suggested…

Margaret stared into the distance.

"Go home and call me once you're there so I know everything's okay. Leave now, Margaret."

My sister nodded.

I went to her then and hugged her. "Everything's going to be fine," I assured her and I prayed that was true.

Margaret left. As soon as I saw her drive away, I wished I'd closed the shop and gone with her. I wasn't sure it was a good idea to let her deal with this by herself.

An eternity passed before the phone rang again. When I picked up, it was Hailey. I didn't recognize her voice at first because she was crying so hard. "My mom and dad are here," she sobbed into the phone. "They decided to take Julia to the hospital. Daddy thinks Julia needs professional help."

A hard lump formed in my throat.

"I'm coming over," I told Hailey.

"They don't want me to go with them and I don't want to be here by myself."

"I'm on my way." I'd never just left the shop like this.

Even when Margaret and I learned that our mother had been found unconscious at home, Jacqueline had been here to take over.

After reassuring Hailey, I called Brad on his cell and told him what had happened. He confirmed that I should put a note on the door, lock up and leave right away. I promised to phone him as soon as I had any news.

I don't even remember getting in my car and driving to Matt and Margaret's house. The minute I pulled up in front and parked, the door banged open and Hailey raced down the steps and hurled herself into my arms, sobbing.

Holding her tightly, I stroked her hair. I noticed two neighbors watching us, and knowing what a private person my sister is, I kissed the top of Hailey's head and steered her back toward the house.

Once inside, she got herself a tissue and blew her nose loudly.

"Do you know what set Julia off?" I asked, wondering why this had happened now.

Hailey shook her head.

I put on water to make tea. Tea always seemed to calm me and I hoped it would help my niece, too.

"Mom tried to talk to Julia. She said the man's going to be caught and the police are making an arrest soon."

That was the same news Margaret had given me. "Did that make any difference?" I asked.

"No." Hailey stared up at me with tearful eyes. "Julia just kept crying. She tried to stop. I could tell she wanted to, but she couldn't do it. It's like…like she's kept everything inside and then it all just broke loose." She bit her lip and looked as if she might start weeping again herself.

The tea kettle whistled and I immediately tended to it. I poured the boiling water into a ceramic pot that had once belonged to our mother and added plenty of sugar to our cups, thinking the events of the afternoon warranted it.

"Tell me exactly what happened," I said, carrying our tea to the table and sitting down next to Hailey.

My niece frowned, as though trying to remember the details. "Julia was home before me and I could see she'd been crying." She gestured at the tissues scattered about the kitchen. "I asked her if everything was okay, and she said...she said she wanted to die."

I couldn't help it; I swallowed a gasp just hearing those words again.

"Julia said...she said everyone looks at her. That's not true, Aunt Lydia! No one looks at her any different than they did before—she just *thinks* they do."

"I know." I wondered if there'd been any other signs of trouble since the carjacking.

"When Mom got here, Julia started talking about dying again and Mom phoned Dad. When he got here, he said we had to get Julia to a hospital." She sipped her tea and sucked in a wobbly breath as she made a determined effort to hold in her emotions. "Julia *scared* me."

"How?" I asked.

"I think she might've done it... She might've actually killed herself. She looked so desperate and I think...I think she really meant it. That's why I called the shop. I was so glad when you answered. I...I—" She shook her head, unable to go on.

"You did the right thing," I said, trying to comfort her.

"I know." She held the mug with both hands. "It isn't right that a strange man could hurt Julia like this."

"No, it isn't," I agreed.

"He broke her arm, but he did more than that. He broke her spirit, too—that's what my dad says," she told me in a solemn voice. "Julia isn't the same person she used to be. I hardly know her anymore."

I'd seen a change in Julia, too, and I was with her a whole lot less than her family. When it happened, the attack had seemed terrible enough. But I'd had no idea how far-reaching the impact on my niece and my sister would be.

Another two hours passed before the phone rang. Hailey nearly threw herself against the wall in her eagerness to answer it. As soon as she did, her gaze flew to me.

"Aunt Lydia's here with me," she said into the receiver. Following that, she nodded a couple of times. A minute later, she said, "Okay," and hung up. Then she burst into tears. "The hospital's going to keep Julia overnight—they have her on suicide watch."

Nineteen

Alix Townsend

"**I** want to bake my own wedding cake," Alix said. She looked at her future mother-in-law and Jacqueline, who both sat across the table from her. They were in Jacqueline's home, and this meeting was one Alix had delayed as long as she dared. The last time she'd been involved in a wedding discussion had been the Saturday she'd gone to the gym with Colette. Susan had already determined the entire menu for the rehearsal dinner. Why, Alix wondered, had Susan even gone through the facade of soliciting her opinion?

Instinctively she knew these two women she loved would try to thwart her on the issue of the cake. Alix had done her best to be amenable, biting her tongue, sweeping aside her natural inclinations. The wedding cake, however, was a different matter. Her professional pride was on the line.

"Alix," Jacqueline said, sounding sympathetic and conciliatory. "It's perfectly understandable that you'd

want to make your own wedding cake. You're a baker—
it's what you do." She gestured vaguely. "But, darling,
you've got so many other things to worry about."

"Actually, I'm looking forward to it," Alix insisted.
She practically needed diplomatic training to prepare
for this wedding. With tolerance and patience (Jordan's
words, not hers), hoping to inspire unity (again from
Jordan), Alix had all but given Jacqueline and Susan
Turner free rein. However, with the wedding cake, she
was determined to get her own way. She had a very
distinct idea of what she wanted.

"You're going to be far too busy to spend time on
the cake," Susan chimed in, agreeing with Jacqueline.

The two older women had become friends during all
of this. Alix was pleased for them both—and alarmed
that neither seemed to realize how much they'd alien-
ated her in the process. They had a vision of what they
wanted this wedding to be and as far as Alix could
figure, she and Jordan were just props. Alix tried to
remember that they loved her and were doing this for
her and for Jordan.

"Actually, I'd like something to take my mind off
things," Alix said. Every time she had to deal with another aspect of this stupid wedding, her skin started
to itch.

"Alix," Jacqueline said in the same tone of voice
she used when speaking to three-year-old Amelia. "I
don't think you recognize the pressure you're putting
on yourself." She shook her head. "Susan and I aren't
saying you can't bake your cake."

"Thank you." Alix felt some of the tension leave her
shoulders. She reached for her coffee and sipped from
the edge of the cup. She didn't usually drink coffee

from anything other than a mug, but Jacqueline didn't own one. Everything was top-of-the-line china for her.

Now that her friend was a grandmother twice over, she'd compromised her standards—to a degree. The kitchen was a good example; the cupboards were still stacked with the finest dinnerware, while the bottom drawers contained an assortment of toys and children's eating utensils.

"That's not a good plan," Susan challenged, sitting back and regarding the two of them.

"Why don't we discuss the cake itself," Alix said, hurriedly changing the subject. She might still end up attending those diplomacy classes at the rate this was going.

"All right," Susan reluctantly agreed.

"I was at a wedding a couple of years ago," Jacqueline piped up enthusiastically. "And the wedding cake was in-cred-ib-le." Eyes closed, she enunciated each syllable. "I was surprised to find out it was cheesecake."

"Cheesecake?" Susan repeated.

"I don't think—"

Jacqueline broke in. "Cheesecake would be perfect for the wedding dinner at the country club. It would be such an elegant finishing touch."

Susan shook her head, dismissing the idea. "Since my husband's a pastor, we've had the opportunity to attend a *large* number of weddings. So I can tell you that the huge wedding cake isn't how it's done anymore."

"Really?" This came from Jacqueline, who looked somewhat taken aback.

"Oh, there's a formal cake, but not one of those three-tiered monstrosities that so often dominated a reception table. My heavens," she said, warming to the subject, "I remember a wedding where there was a larger cake—" she held her hands a distance apart to indicate the size "—and then five or six smaller ones surrounding it. I must say it was all cleverly done. I learned later that the cakes cost—well," she said, mildly embarrassed. "None of that's important."

"I want the very best for Alix," Jacqueline insisted proudly.

"I was thinking of baking a traditional white cake," Alix inserted, seeing that the conversation was rapidly getting away from her.

The room went silent as both women stared at her. Her suggestions seemed to be neither wanted nor appreciated.

Susan picked up her coffee, and after clearing her throat, said, "What I started to explain is that a lot of brides are opting for a variety of flavors. Not everyone enjoys white cake."

"It's *my* favorite," Alix said, although it was plain no one heard her.

"The last wedding I attended served carrot cake and lemon cake and the most delicious chocolate one with a mousse filling," Susan continued. "I meant to ask what bakery they used but I got sidetracked."

"Carrot cake," Jacqueline repeated, sounding astonished. "How…unique."

"It was wonderful with the cream cheese frosting."

Jacqueline nodded excitedly. "The cheesecake I mentioned was beautifully decorated. I remember wondering what they'd used for frosting and it was a sweetened cream cheese, too. It would be *perfect* for Alix and Jordan."

"How about a traditional white cake?" Alix asked.

Both women frowned at her as if they'd grown irritated with her interruptions.

"We want this to be a wedding everyone remembers," Jacqueline said kindly. "I'm afraid white cake is just so—" She paused, apparently searching for the right word.

"Ordinary," Susan supplied.

"Yes, ordinary," Jacqueline echoed.

"Jordan and I would prefer an 'ordinary' wedding and an 'ordinary' cake baked by me." The only way to get either woman to listen was to speak loudly. She didn't want to be rude but Alix had taken about all she could stand.

Not entirely to her surprise, their immediate reaction was silence. Her words seemed to fall like large stones onto the table, startling Jacqueline and Susan.

"I see," Jacqueline murmured, looking crestfallen.

Despite her exasperation with them, Alix felt contrite. She didn't want to hurt Jacqueline's feelings, or Susan's, either. She just wanted them to *hear* her. "I don't mean to sound unappreciative," she said earnestly, "but—"

"Maybe we should ask Jordan," his mother suggested as if it was necessary to bring in reinforcements.

Alix hated to drag her fiancé into this, and yet it might be the only way to settle the matter once and for all. Jordan knew how badly Alix wanted to bake her own cake. They'd discussed that very subject the night before. True, Jordan had seemed distracted and tired, but he'd agreed she should be able to do this. Alix knew he couldn't care less if the cake was white, yellow or purple. Like her, he just wanted this affair over with.

"He's at the church," Susan pulled her cell phone

from her purse and hit speed dial. "Jordan Turner, please," she said, smiling over at Alix.

Alix crossed her arms and waited impatiently, wishing now that she'd taken the initiative and called him herself.

"Hello, Jordan," Susan said, her voice brightening now that her son was on the line. "We're all here discussing the wedding and we seem to be at a stalemate."

After a moment she laughed.

Alix frowned and wondered what Jordan had said that his mother found so amusing.

"No, no, nothing like that," Susan said next. She glanced at Alix. "Now, about the wedding cake…"

After a few seconds, Susan sighed audibly and handed the phone to Alix. "Jordan wants to talk to you."

Alix took it. "It's me," she said unnecessarily.

"Hi, sweetie," he said.

"Hi." Alix kept her voice devoid of emotion, suddenly uncertain whether he even remembered their discussion the night before. Her stomach tensed as a familiar ache came over her. "What's this about the wedding cake?" Jordan asked.

"Jacqueline wants cheesecake, frosted with sweetened cream cheese."

He made a noncommittal reply. She supposed that was so she'd know he was listening.

"Your mother suggested a selection of cakes in a variety of flavors."

"That's okay, too," he murmured vaguely.

"Jordan, are you *listening?*"

"Sorry," he mumbled. "I was reading an e-mail."

"This is important," she snapped. She stood up and walked over to the window, presenting her back to Jacqueline and Susan. "We're talking about our wedding cake, Jordan. Yours and mine." In other words, the cake celebrating the beginning of their marriage should be one chosen by them, not anyone else.

"Of course it's important," he said. "Listen, can you wait a minute? I've got a call coming in."

Before she could answer, Jordan put her on hold. It was fast becoming clear that her fiancé was less than interested in the details of their wedding.

"Sorry," he said, switching back after an irritating two minutes.

"No problem," she lied. It *was* a problem. This whole wedding was. The inside of her elbow started to itch, and Alix scratched at it through the sleeve of her jean jacket.

"What were you saying?"

"We're discussing the wedding cake," she reminded him, trying not to sound as annoyed as she actually felt. "You and I, Jordan," she said, speaking slowly and distinctly, "discussed this very subject last night and we reached a decision."

"Yes, we did."

"Do you remember what that decision was?" she asked pointedly.

Jordan laughed. "You didn't tell me there'd be a test."

"Yes, and this happens to be a *big* test," Alix said evenly. "Call it the final exam."

The amusement was gone when he spoke again. "You're really upset about this, aren't you?"

"You could say that."

"What *did* we decide last night?" Jordan asked.

"You don't remember, do you?" Knowing beforehand that there'd be a showdown with Susan and Jacqueline, Alix had pleaded her case with Jordan. She'd explained how much she wanted to make a personal contribution to their wedding. The cake was perfect for her. She'd baked several wedding cakes already and this was something she could do and do well. Despite what Jacqueline and Susan seemed to think, she was more than capable of making that cake a showpiece.

"I'm asking you to tell your mother what we decided," Alix repeated, a cold chill running down her spine.

"I'm sorry, Alix, I was tired last night. I had other things on my mind."

"I...see."

"Is it really that important?"

"Apparently not," she returned. She realized how flippant that sounded—and didn't care.

Jordan sighed. "Come on, Alix," he pleaded.

She reacted with stone-cold silence.

"I assumed you could make at least one decision on your own. Do what you want. Bake the damn cake if it's that important to you."

Jordan was angry now and not bothering to hide it.

"I will, then."

"I've got another call," he said and without asking, put her on hold again.

She clicked off the phone. Taking a moment to allow her nerves to settle, Alix turned back to face the two women. "We've reached a decision," she told them.

"That's a relief," Susan said.

"Cheesecake?" Jacqueline asked, her eyes wide with hope.

Alix nodded. "For one of the cakes."

"You're going to do what I suggested?" Like a little

girl who'd been promised a special treat, Susan clapped her hands cheerfully. "We'll have several smaller cakes, right?"

Alix nodded again.

"Each of the cakes will be a different flavor?" Susan turned to Alix for confirmation. "One a cheesecake, of course."

"That'll be fine." Alix walked across the kitchen and gave Susan back her cell.

"I hope Jordan talked you out of baking it yourself." Susan dropped the phone in her purse, watching Alix.

"He did."

"Good." Jacqueline looked pleased. "You'll thank us later, Alix. Just wait and see."

Alix's cell phone rang and she knew without checking that it was Jordan. She turned it off.

"You made the right decision," Susan assured her. "You'll have enough to think about on your wedding day without worrying about the cake."

Alix murmured agreement. Only she was seriously beginning to wonder if there'd *be* a wedding day.

Twenty

Colette Blake

Colette glanced at her watch. She was meeting Steve Grisham for dinner at seven-thirty; it was only ten after now. She'd arrived at the restaurant early. This Italian place was new to her and because she'd walked, Colette had given herself an extra fifteen minutes.

Actually, it'd been her idea to meet Steve here rather than have him pick her up. Susannah's husband, Joe, had recommended the restaurant. It was romantic with small, intimate enclaves, dim lighting and flickering candles. The pungent scent of garlic drifted from the kitchen. If the food was half as good as it smelled, she'd be in epicurean heaven.

Colette wasn't sure why she hadn't wanted Steve to come to her apartment. He had before, several times. It just seemed more convenient to meet him here, she told herself.

The waiter brought her iced tea and she thanked him and paid for it. This was the fourth time she'd gone out with Steve. She enjoyed his company but didn't feel any real attraction to him or any strong sense of connection beyond friendship, and a fairly casual friendship at that. He'd been Derek's friend more than hers. She didn't know if anything had happened between them, but the men had begun to grow apart, although the two couples had still socialized fairly often. Derek and Steve were partners for a few years and then Derek had started a new assignment. Colette had assumed the reassignment came from headquarters. She was no longer so sure of that.

She felt uneasy with Steve but couldn't explain precisely why; to some extent, she blamed the fact that she was keeping such an important secret. If they continued to see each other, she'd have to tell him. However, she couldn't really imagine doing that and wondered if it was such a good idea to go on seeing him. Although Steve hadn't said anything overt, he'd made it plain that he'd like to deepen their relationship. Colette didn't want that. Thinking about it, she decided the main reason she'd accepted his invitations was his link with Derek. Her husband was their most consistent topic of conversation. They'd exchanged memories of Derek as a rookie and laughed about the day Steve had helped them move; it'd been midwinter and the men had accidentally killed most of Colette's houseplants, leaving them in the cold truck for hours. They'd recalled happy times, like the New Year's Eve after Steve's first daughter was born and the four of them had stayed up all night, delirious with exhaustion. Steve sometimes talked about the end of his marriage, too.

What she and Steve had in common besides their

memories was their pain. But was this a solid basis for the kind of relationship he seemed to want?

Colette forced herself not to consider these uncomfortable thoughts for the moment. Since she had a few minutes to wait, she decided to check her mail, which she'd slipped into her purse on the way out. The first two envelopes contained bills. The following three or four pieces were junk mail and the last was a card, addressed to her. She immediately recognized the handwriting as Christian's.

The night before, Colette had dreamed of him. She'd awakened around three that morning and hadn't been able to get back to sleep. Those dreams shouldn't have surprised her, though. Christian constantly turned up in her thoughts. She was in love with him and she worried about his future. She hadn't told his great-aunt any of what she knew. How could she disillusion this woman who loved him so much?

It annoyed and perplexed Colette that she was always looking for him. A man would walk past Susannah's Garden and for a split second she'd think it was Christian. Her heart would race with excitement—and then she'd recognize that she'd made a mistake.

Reading the handwritten return address on the card, she frowned. In all the years she'd worked for Christian, she couldn't remember him ever sending a card. But then she wouldn't, would she? He could mail out a thousand such cards and she'd never know it.

Feeling nervous, she delayed opening the envelope. Then she couldn't stand to wait another second. Steve wouldn't be there for five or ten minutes; she had plenty of time. Eagerly she tore open the envelope and withdrew a small card, a single sheet of heavy deckle-edged paper.

She read the short note he'd written. *I wish you only happiness, Colette. But I'm not sure Steve Grisham is the man who will give it to you.*

A comment like this was so unlike Christian that Colette just stared at the card. As he'd promised, Christian had stayed out of her life—until now, until this.

She still believed Christian Dempsey was a man of his word. Once she'd told him she didn't want to see him again, he'd made no attempt to contact her. That he'd done so now meant he knew something about Steve, something he felt *she* needed to know. Otherwise he would never have broken his word; Colette was positive of that.

"You seem very absorbed," Steve murmured, standing beside the table. He kissed her cheek before pulling out a chair to join her.

Colette quickly slipped the mail back inside her handbag.

"I see you got a head start on me," Steve said and nodded toward her glass of tea, apparently believing it was the Long Island variety. He raised his hand to get the waiter's attention and motioned that he wanted a glass for himself and another for Colette. She smiled, thinking how shocked he'd be when plain iced tea was delivered.

Their dinner was enjoyable. Steven had quickly switched to wine and he ordered port following the meal. She declined, choosing decaf coffee instead. As always, her date was charming and personable. They shared the usual reminiscences of Derek, and Steve regaled her with stories about his job and the investigation he'd just wrapped up. He seemed to know people wherever they went. Apparently, not everyone had heard about his divorce, and Colette received several curious looks. They lingered over their drinks and talked until Colette yawned and said she really did need to get home. After collecting his car from a nearby parking garage, Steve drove her the short distance to her apartment.

"I had a lovely evening," she told him. And it was true, although Christian's warning was never far from her mind.

"I did, too," Steve said, leaning close.

They kissed, his mouth moving fervently over hers until she squirmed away. When they broke apart, Steve whispered, "Are you sure you don't want to invite me in for coffee?"

"Not tonight."

"Soon?" he asked.

She smiled and gently kissed his cheek. "Perhaps."

Steve released a sigh. "Colette, Derek's been gone over a year now."

"Yes, I know," she said in a small voice.

"It seems longer than that." He pressed his thumb against her chin and inclined her face toward his. "It's time you moved on with your life," he urged, his eyes warm. "Derek wouldn't have wanted you to hide yourself away, working in this—" he hesitated, apparently searching for the right word "—obscure little flower shop. He'd want you to be happy." Once more he lowered his lips to hers. "I can do that for you, Colette," he promised in a husky voice. "I can help you remember what it means to be loved and cherished."

"I...I—" The words clogged her throat.

"I'm not pressuring you," Steve said, kissing the side

of her neck. "Just know that I'll be here when you're ready."

In her rush to escape, Colette reached blindly for the door handle and nearly fell out of the car.

"Thank you again for dinner," she said. She couldn't get inside the apartment fast enough. Without looking back, she scrabbled for her keys and let herself in. Her heart pounded as she leaned breathlessly against the closed door. A moment later, she secured the dead bolt. She stood there motionless, her hand on her forehead. What was wrong with her? It was more than Christian's message. More than her own sense of caution. Only Colette didn't know what.

Sunday afternoon, Colette picked up the phone, put it down and paced her tiny living room, wondering if she was doing the right thing. Then determination took hold and she picked up the phone. She called directory assistance; half a minute later, she had Jeanine Grisham's number.

Jeanine answered on the third ring.

"Hello, Jeanine," Colette said, hoping she sounded cheerful, when in fact her hands trembled with a combination of anxiety and fear. "This is Colette Blake."

"Colette! Oh, my goodness, how are you?"

"I'm fine." She hesitated and then decided to plunge into the reason for her call. "I heard about you and Steve. I'm so sorry."

"I'm sorry, too, but the girls and I are doing well." Jeanine paused. "I heard via the grapevine that you sold the house and moved. Are you still in Seattle?"

"Yes...yes." Colette explained the changes—some of the changes—in her own life since they'd last talked.

"It's been ages! I meant to keep in touch after Derek's funeral, but you know what they say about good intentions. By then, Steve and I were having major problems—and well, I was pretty consumed by all of that. How did you find me?"

"Steve told me you'd moved to Yakima to be closer to your parents."

"For that and other reasons," Jeanine confirmed. "So you've been in touch with Steve?"

"Yes… Actually, he's why I phoned."

"He asked you out?" Jeanine's voice cooled considerably. "That doesn't surprise me."

"It isn't like that…."

"Listen," Jeanine said without emotion. "Steve and I are no longer married. If you want to date him, you don't need my permission."

"That's not why I called."

"Okay."

Colette looked out the window to the alley below. The conversation had grown uncomfortable, but she'd come this far and wouldn't turn back now. "Steve…he never really explained why you got a divorce."

"No, he probably wouldn't," Jeanine murmured.

"I've just started to date again," Colette said. "Derek and I were married for a long time, and the whole dating scene's changed so much."

"You're telling me?" Jeanine laughed lightly, the tension in her voice gone.

"Since it's a whole new world for both of us, I was hoping you wouldn't mind if I asked you a few questions."

"Me?" Jeanine said. "Hey, I'm no expert."

"What I mean is, can I ask you a few questions about Steve?"

"Oh, I see..." The wariness was back. "Colette, I like you. I've always liked you, but I don't think I'm the right person to talk to about my ex-husband."

"Who else would know Steve the way you do?" she asked.

Jeanine's laugh lacked any pretense of humor. "Oh, about fifty other women."

"What?"

"Colette, I'll be blunt here. Steve couldn't keep his fly zipped."

Colette sank onto the edge of the sofa. "Steve... cheated on you?"

"It was more than that. He screwed anything in a skirt." She snorted in disgust. "He was indiscriminate. Any woman who was available—and some who weren't."

Colette felt like she was going to be sick.

"You know this for a fact?" she finally managed to say.

"Oh, yes. It started even before we were married. I heard from a friend, a good friend, that she'd seen Steve with another woman about a week before our wedding."

"Did you ask him about it?"

"Of course I did. He made up this completely credible story about this other girl being a cousin of his. When I mentioned this to my friend, she said they were obviously kissing cousins."

"I'm so sorry." Colette hated opening old wounds like this.

"The only one to blame is me. I was gullible enough to believe him. The man is a consummate liar. He'll lie even when it's more convenient to tell the truth. It's his nature."

"But…he's a detective."

"Astonishing, isn't it?"

"But…"

"You can't say anything I haven't asked myself a dozen times," Jeanine told her. "Steve can be the most devoted, wonderful man in the world—when he feels like it. The girls adore him, even now, and yet he practically ignores their existence."

"They're his *children*." Colette found herself getting angry on Jeanine's behalf.

"Out of sight, out of mind," Jeanine muttered.

"But you stuck it out for so many years. Why did you divorce him now?"

Jeanine's sigh came in a long rush. "My parents asked me the same question and I wish I knew the answer. I think Steve was more shocked than anyone. I didn't even ask him if he was seeing someone else. He probably was, but I didn't really care anymore and that frightened me. My emotions had become paralyzed, and that made me realize what I was doing. Over the years, Steve had become blatant in his affairs. I'd turned a blind eye for so long I literally couldn't see anymore."

Colette heard the pain in her friend's voice.

"One morning I woke up," Jeanine continued, "and I knew that if I didn't get out of this marriage I'd lose my sanity. Steve left for work and I phoned my parents and asked if I could move in with them until I found an apartment in Yakima. They agreed."

"You went that day?"

"That same day," Jeanine said. "I knew with absolute certainty that I wouldn't change my mind. It wasn't just my pride at stake, or my children's future. I know this might sound melodramatic…but my very soul was at risk."

"Did Steve ask you to reconsider?"

Jeanine snickered softly. "He was convinced I'd come back and God knows he tried to talk me into it. He can be persuasive when he wants. What he didn't understand was that he'd killed whatever love I'd felt for him. To be fair, I'd threatened to leave him any number of times."

"Did you ever do it?"

"No, more fool me," she said. "It took him six months to figure out I wasn't moving back to Seattle."

"You never let on, all the times we saw you. I would never have believed Steve was that kind of man."

"That's the sad part. I couldn't believe it even when I had the evidence right in front of me."

"I'm not going to see him again." Colette's mind was made up about that. Christian's note and her own instinctive reaction to Steve were all she needed to know that Jeanine had told her the truth. Deep down she'd felt something was wrong, but she couldn't identify it. Because she hadn't trusted her instincts, it was Christian's note that had prompted her to contact Steve's ex-wife. How Christian had learned this about Steve, she had no idea.

"You're smart," Jeanine said. "I don't think many women ever talk to the ex-wife before getting involved with a guy."

Colette didn't enlighten her, but she wasn't nearly as smart as Jeanine thought. Without Christian Dempsey, she probably would've let her relationship with Steve drift on, a relationship that could only have brought her heartbreak.

Twenty-One

"No matter how much skill, passion and creativity one brings to knitting, you can't make something better than the quality of the yarn you use."

—Rebecca Deeprose,
www.arizonaknittingandneedlepoint.com

Lydia Goetz

Margaret and I talked it over yet again, and decided not to tell our mother about the carjacking. Her physical and emotional health was fragile and growing more so all the time. It would've been too much for her.

The problem neither of us foresaw was her intuitive awareness of her children. Neither of us said a word, but somehow Mom sensed that something was wrong. She asked repeatedly if everything was all right. Again and again I assured her it was.

"Lydia," she said the minute I stepped into her room. "Where's Margaret?"

This wasn't exactly the greeting I'd hoped to receive,

and not only because it reminded me that Margaret had always been closer to her than I was. "She's at the shop," I explained, coming into Mom's room. "Business was a bit slow this afternoon, so I thought I'd take some time and come for a visit." I didn't mention that Margaret had purposely stayed behind.

Mom sat in her favorite chair in front of the television, which had become her main source of entertainment. She used to rarely turn it on. These days the set was constantly tuned to one program or another. I sometimes wondered if Mom actually turned it off when she slept.

Mom pursed her lips. "I haven't seen Margaret in days."

"Wasn't she here on Sunday?" I asked, although I already knew the answer. Margaret and Matt had come by early in the afternoon, the first time they'd left Julia alone since she was released from the hospital. Margaret had fretted the entire time and they'd gone home after only the briefest of visits.

Mom picked up the remote and lowered the volume on her television. She was watching one of those courtroom programs with ordinary people appearing before a judge. "When are you going to tell me what's wrong?" she asked anxiously.

I sighed. At that moment I wanted to tell her everything. I couldn't, though. If she learned about the carjacking it should be from my sister, not me.

"What did you have for lunch?" I asked instead.

Mom's eyes returned to the television. "I don't think I went in for lunch this afternoon."

One of the advantages provided by the assisted-living complex was that they served three balanced meals a day. Margaret and I had carefully evaluated a number of places before selecting this one. For us, the meals had been a selling feature, and so were the many social events.

Mom had her own apartment and even a tiny kitchen with a microwave and refrigerator. Best of all, she was surrounded by her own things. Margaret and I had gone through the house before it was sold, choosing pieces we knew she particularly loved. Mom was pleased that we were able to get so much of her furniture into her new home; it was a comfort to have familiar things after so many unnerving changes.

I was immediately alarmed to learn she'd skipped lunch. "Mom, you're diabetic. You need to eat!"

"Yes, honey, I know. I had some tuna on a cracker." She sent me a weary look that pleaded for understanding. "I don't seem to have much of an appetite."

It was more than skipping a meal that concerned me. She also needed the social contact. I hated the thought of Mom sitting alone in her room for days on end. When she'd first moved into the complex, Margaret and I were ecstatic at how quickly she'd made friends with her tablemates. But Helen Hamilton had moved to Indiana a month ago to be closer to her children. And Joyce Corwin had died of a stroke. Both losses had been blows to my mother. She'd been far more reclusive ever since.

"Margaret's fine, Mom," I said, trying to reassure her. "Everyone is." I wouldn't have said that if I didn't believe it to be true. Julia had given us all a scare, but the counselors had been wonderful, helping my niece deal with the tumble of emotions that sometimes overwhelmed crime victims. Julia met regularly with a group of other people who'd undergone similar ordeals.

They'd helped her cope with her anger, and perhaps more profound, the sense of vulnerability.

Personally, I felt the sessions might help Margaret, too. I happen to like my head, however, and I knew my sister would've bitten it off had I suggested she meet with a support group herself.

Mom reached for my hand. "Tell me about the yarn store. You say business is down?"

"Not down. In fact, we're doing better than ever. This afternoon was a bit slow, that's all."

"Oh."

"Would you like me to tell you about my classes?" I asked. Mom used to enjoy hearing about them. I've run classes for beginning knitters; I also taught sock-knitting on circular needles and held a workshop on Thursday mornings for anyone who had a knitting problem. The charity knitting class on Friday afternoons continued, too.

Mom stared blankly at me. "Perhaps some other day," she murmured. "I didn't know you taught." She smiled rather proudly at me.

I decided to try something else. "You remember Alix Townsend, don't you?"

Mom frowned.

I couldn't believe she could possibly have forgotten Alix. "She was in my original class." Mom had met her dozens of times over the past three years.

"Oh, yes, yes, the one with the baby."

I didn't correct her. "Alix is taking my prayer shawl class. She hopes that knitting will get her through the wedding jitters."

Mom's face lit up. "Alix is getting married. That's wonderful news."

I swallowed hard and realized Mom didn't remember Alix at all. I didn't know when she'd slid so far downhill mentally, and it worried me. I should've noticed this long before now. I wondered if she'd become adept at disguising what she understood and what she didn't.

"It's going to be a lovely wedding," I went on in a bright voice. "Brad and I are invited."

Mom frowned again.

"You remember Brad, don't you?"

Mom nodded, but I knew she didn't. A sick feeling settled in the pit of my stomach. In my recent concerns over Margaret and my own busy life, I hadn't been sufficiently aware of Mom's decline.

"You know who I'm looking for?" Mom asked, twisting around as she spoke.

I turned, too, assuming she'd misplaced something and needed me to find it.

"Spunky," Mom said. "I haven't seen him all day."

Spunky had been our family dog when I was a child, a self-assured little terrier who'd adored my mother. He'd been dead for years. The last thing I wanted to do was tell my mother that the dog she'd loved had died— even if it happened decades ago.

"I'm sure he'll be back soon," I said.

"I'm afraid he's lost and can't find his way home," she worried.

We'd had a fenced yard and Spunky had never escaped or run away from it. But I needed to tell Mom something that would reassure her and give her peace. "Just wait. He never goes far," I said.

"He's a good dog." Mom smiled. "Do you see his mouse anywhere?"

"Spunky had a mouse?" I didn't remember any such toy.

"It's a little stuffed animal," she reminded me, staring down at the floor.

Then it came to me. I *did* remember the mouse, which wasn't a mouse at all, but a small stuffed poodle that Spunky carried from room to room and had with him almost constantly. The fact that my mother remembered that and not my husband astonished me.

"I can't imagine where he's gone."

Spunky died at about the time of my first cancer diagnosis when I was sixteen. Margaret had wanted to get another dog right away. Dad said no, and it wasn't because he didn't want another family pet. Just then, taking care of me was all he could handle. My sister knew that and added one more resentment to the pile she was accumulating. One more resentment against me.

"Can I get you anything before I leave?" I asked Mom. Instantly I could tell she didn't want me to go.

"You just got here," she said accusingly.

Actually, I'd been with her for over an hour. "I need to get back to the shop and then home to Brad and Cody," I told her as gently as I could. From the blank look in her eyes, I knew she didn't recognize either.

"Will you come tomorrow?"

I nodded. I'd make the time and if I couldn't, I'd ask Margaret to visit. Before I left, I hugged her and made sure she was comfortable. I handed her the remote and Mom flipped up the volume on yet another judge show, one with a woman on the bench.

As I stepped into the hallway, Rosalie Mullin, the staff nurse who gave Mom her insulin injections, passed me. I stopped her. "How have Mom's blood sugars been?" I asked, remembering that she said she'd skipped lunch. A cracker with a bit of tuna could hardly be considered a meal.

"Her sugars have been good." She paused, then said, "The diabetes is under control." Her eyes held mine.

Rosalie's hesitation told me she had other concerns. "There's another problem, isn't there?"

She nodded. "Perhaps we should talk in my office. I can be there in five minutes."

I took the elevator to the bottom floor, where I waited outside Rosalie's office. She seemed to be away far longer than a few minutes, but that might have been due to my nervousness. Each minute felt like at least ten.

Without a word, Rosalie ushered me into her office. She sat behind her desk and motioned to the chair on the other side. With a lump in my throat, I perched stiffly on the edge of the cushion.

Already I could feel the beginnings of a headache. Probably because of the brain tumors, I'm prone to migraine headaches. They're crippling, and they can last for days. It'd been months since I had one and I chose to believe that this was a simple tension headache and forced myself to ignore the nausea and dizziness.

"I'd been planning to call you and your sister," Rosalie said. She reached for a file from the stack on her desk and opened it. "I've asked the assistants to keep tabs on your mother."

"Why?"

"She's been missing a lot of meals, growing less social and showing signs of paranoia. She was reacting badly to the Aricept, so the doctor took her off. He warned me she might lose ground quickly and she has.

Unfortunately, one of the symptoms of this sort of decline is lack of appetite."

My first inclination was to defend Mom, to make excuses for her. "I'm sure that has something to do with losing both Helen and Joyce in such a short time. I don't think I'd want to eat, either."

Rosalie agreed with me. "To a point, that's true. However, I've started to notice other signs."

"What do you mean?"

"I'm afraid your mother's showing early symptoms of Alzheimer's."

That had been my worry, as well, although I couldn't verbalize it, even to myself.

"As far as meals go, what about bringing them to her?" I said.

"We can do that, of course," Rosalie assured me. "There's an additional charge after a certain number of delivered meals. But what I'm trying to say isn't about your mother's eating or her diabetes." Her eyes were sympathetic. "I'm thinking the time is fast approaching when her needs will exceed what we have to offer her."

My mouth was dry. The light from the lamp on her desk was bothering my eyes. "You're not suggesting a nursing home, are you?" The thought of placing my mother in one was more than I could bear.

"Not a nursing home," Rosalie told me. "A memory care facility."

"Memory care?" I repeated. I'd never heard of such a thing.

"They're wonderful for people like your mother. There's a greater level of individual care, and the environment is more controlled. I'd recommend that you and your sister visit a few, talk to the staff, get a feel for each place. I can give you information on three of them." She opened a drawer, removed a file and handed me a sheet with names and addresses. "I'm familiar with all of these, and I can guarantee that Mrs. Hoffman would be well looked after."

"Thank you," I said shakily as I stood. My eyes had started to water and I wasn't sure if it was because of the light or my emotions. Probably both.

By then I knew I needed to get home as quickly as possible. I don't usually talk on my cell phone while I'm driving, but this was an emergency. At least it felt like one. My first call was to my husband, who was just getting off work.

"Hi, sweetheart," he said as he answered. "Where are you?"

"Driving. I probably shouldn't be," I said, hardly able to function now as my head throbbed painfully. "I'm on my way home. I have a migraine."

"Your medication's at the house?"

"Yes." At one time I carried it with me, but after all these months I'd become careless. "I'll be all right once I'm home," I said. "I should have asked the nurse for a painkiller, but it didn't enter my mind."

"How far are you?"

"Five minutes from the house." That was true on a good day, but it was rush hour and the traffic would slow me down.

"What can I do?"

"Call Margaret for me," I said. "Ask her to close the store. She'll know what to do."

"Okay. Anything else?" I heard the concern in his voice.

I swallowed a sob and when I spoke my voice was

hoarse with emotion. "It's Mom, Brad. She's not doing well."

"I'll be home as soon as I can."

"Thank you." I clicked off the phone and exited the freeway. By the time I'd pulled into the garage and made my way into the house, the pain in my head was blinding me. I stumbled down the hallway to the bathroom, where we kept the medications. Turning on the light wasn't an option. I found the bottle in the cabinet more by luck than intent, nearly ripped off the cap and swallowed the pill without water.

Keeping my eyes closed I braced my hand against the wall and dragged myself into our bedroom. The first thing I did was close the shades. Once the room was dark, I undressed and climbed into bed. Soon the medication would kick in and the pain would subside. Tears crept from my eyes, sliding down my cheeks.

"Mom," I sobbed. "Oh, Mom." She wasn't there to comfort me and would never be again. Nor, it seemed, could I comfort her.

The tragedy of this disease was that it took away so much of who my mother was. She'd become completely dependent on Margaret and me to make decisions for her. As her mental capacities diminished, we'd be assuming all responsibility for her care. Most painful, perhaps, was her growing inability to remember her own life. My sister and I would have to be the keepers of her memories, for her and for ourselves.

Margaret had talked about how much she missed our mother, and I knew now that we'd be missing her more and more.

Twenty-Two

Alix Townsend

When Colette met her at Go Figure, Alix could tell that she was worried about something. For that matter, so was Alix. They completed their workout routine and then went for a drink at a nearby restaurant.

"You're looking very thoughtful," Colette said, sipping her herbal iced tea.

"You are, too," Alix said. She wasn't about to let Colette's uncharacteristic silence that morning slip past without comment.

"Is everything all right between you and Jordan?" Colette asked.

Alix shrugged, dismissing the comment. Her relationship with Jordan was strained at the moment; it'd all started with the wedding cake and escalated from there. She'd avoided him since then and he seemed to be avoiding her, which only complicated matters. "We had a…difference of opinion. It's no big deal."

Colette studied her. "What about?"

Alix reached for her iced coffee and took a deep swallow before answering. "What else? The wedding."

Okay, so it was an actual argument, not merely what you'd call a friendly difference of opinion. Alix had been good and angry, and she hadn't been afraid to let Jordan know how badly he'd disappointed her. Now, though, their disagreement was about more than the wedding.

Alix didn't doubt that Jordan loved her. That wasn't the point. The problem was he hadn't listened; worse, he hadn't heard *anything* she'd said. Because of that, Alix had been forced to surrender herself one more time at the altar of this blasted wedding.

"What about you?" Alix asked. She wasn't spilling her guts if Colette wasn't willing to do the same. That was what friends did.

Colette sipped her tea. "I won't be dating Steve Grisham again."

Alix sat up. This was news. "That's the detective, right?"

"Right."

Alix had no time for what she sarcastically called the boys in blue. She didn't know even one who didn't lie through his teeth. Not only that, they saw what they wanted to see. She'd gone down on a bogus drug charge because of her roommate. The cop had been ready to believe the lie as long as it added to his arrest record. Alix didn't plan to forgive either him or her onetime friend.

She knew Colette had recently met Steve for a fancy dinner. Alix didn't have that much experience with detectives, but she figured they weren't any better than the cops on the street. Out of respect for Colette's dead husband, Alix hadn't shared her opinion of the police. "Did Columbo put the moves on you?"

Colette grinned. "No, but I talked to his ex-wife and learned a few things that…I didn't know and, well, it was obvious this was never going to work out, anyway."

Alix wasn't convinced Colette should listen to the ex. Still, she tended to believe it was a mistake for Colette to date any man other than Christian Dempsey when she was so clearly in love with him.

"Don't you think the ex-wife might have her own agenda?" Alix asked.

Colette shrugged. "If it was someone else, I might think so, but not Jeanine. We were good friends once, the four of us, and then Derek got transferred and we didn't see as much of them. Now I wonder… Jeanine was always friendly but there were times she seemed distant. I thought it might've been me. She never talked about it. But it turns out Steve's been unfaithful for years, so it all sort of makes sense now. Besides, he's just a little too smooth, a little too…practiced, especially around women."

"Does Columbo know you don't plan to see him again?"

Colette shook her head. "He'll get the message soon enough." She sipped her iced tea again. "Enough about me. You've been in a bad mood all day. Are you going to tell me what's really going on?"

After a moment's hesitation, Alix explained her on-going disagreement with Jordan, and described the incident the previous week.

"You can't let Jacqueline and Susan treat you like this," Colette exclaimed.

"Easy for you to say," Alix muttered. It wasn't as if she hadn't tried.

There was a brief silence, then Colette asked, "You're close to Jacqueline, aren't you?"

Alix nodded. She used to be, but lately she wasn't so sure. Jacqueline was protective and a real advocate in ways Alix treasured, but when it came to this wedding, she had a will of iron. She made very clear that she was the social expert, and her ideas were not to be ignored.

"Talk to her one-on-one," Colette suggested. "Remind her that it's *your* wedding. Tell her you appreciate everything she's done but you feel like the wedding's not about you anymore."

Colette was right; any reference to the wedding these days was enough to make her cringe. This couldn't go on. Alix was at odds with Jordan and just about everyone else involved with this wedding. It was time to mend some fences....

When they finished their drinks, Colette went out to do errands and Alix took the bus home. Since the guesthouse was behind the main house and next to the garage, Alix saw right away that both cars were there. Reese's golf clubs were leaning against his trunk.

Alix knew she had to talk to Jacqueline *today*. This wedding belonged to her, and as much as she valued everything the Donovans and Turners were doing, she could no longer remain silent.

She knocked at the back door and then entered. Reese was sitting at the table, a cup of coffee in hand, his newspaper propped up against the floral centerpiece. He smiled at Alix.

"How's the bride-to-be?" he asked with his usual cheer.

Alix shrugged and gave him a wry grin in response. "Reese, I need to talk to Jacqueline."

"She's on the phone in my office," he said.

Typical. Jacqueline had more friends and acquaintances than anyone Alix knew. "Is it okay if I wait?"

"Of course." Reese glanced at his watch. "I've got a golf game in half an hour. Do you mind if I leave you here?"

"Not at all."

Reese stood and retrieved his sweater. "Grab a coffee if you want," he offered.

"Thanks. Already had one."

Reese left with a jaunty wave, and Alix wished him a good game.

Having once worked as the Donovans' housekeeper, Alix automatically folded the newspaper and placed Reese's cup in the dishwasher. She wiped down the counter as she waited for Jacqueline to finish her call. Then she decided she should probably let her know she was in the house. Not that she wanted to rush her or anything; Jacqueline could talk as long as she liked. In fact, the more time she spent on the phone, the longer Alix had to prepare for their conversation. She tried not to think of it as a showdown—just a congenial but necessary discussion with a friend.

Walking down the hall to the office, Alix heard Jacqueline speaking and stopped when her name was mentioned.

"I can't believe you'd suggest something like that," Jacqueline said, sounding irate.

Alix froze. She hadn't come to listen in on a private conversation and yet, when she heard her own name, she couldn't make herself leave.

A few minutes later, she realized that the person on the other end of the line was none other than Susan Turner.

"Jordan doesn't have any such concerns, does he?" Jacqueline asked, obviously dismayed.

A pause.

"I should think not." Jacqueline seemed satisfied with the response, whatever it was.

Alix breathed a bit easier.

"You don't need to tell me Alix is unconventional," Jacqueline said next. "That doesn't mean she won't make Jordan a good wife."

It felt as if the floor had just dropped. *So that was it.* Susan didn't think she was the right wife for her son. Alix had suspected as much and now her suspicions were confirmed.

"Of course, Jordan will be a senior pastor one day," Jacqueline said. "And Alix will—"

Whatever Jacqueline intended to say was abruptly cut off.

Alix didn't want to hear any more of this conversation. She knew what Susan was saying and to be fair, it was a question she'd asked herself a dozen times since the engagement.

What kind of pastor's wife would she be?

Apparently, her future mother-in-law had her doubts. Alix didn't blame Susan Turner; she had concerns of her own in that department. Jordan was the only one who seemed convinced that she was perfect for him and his ministry.

In light of her current feelings, that was a real laugh. What had she been thinking when she agreed to marry Jordan? What *was* she thinking? For the past couple of

years, everything had been going so well. Jacqueline
and Reese had given her a step up in life. They'd provided a home and part-time employment. Not only that,
Reese had helped her with tuition to culinary school.
Then she'd been hired by the French Café. During that
whole time, she'd been dating Jordan. And—during that
whole time—she'd been blinded to the truth.

Good things don't last. Not for women like her.

Alix had been riding a wave, but that wave had
crested and she was about to be swept into shark-
infested waters. Women like her, girls with her background and her past, weren't destined for a decent life.
They ended up on the street, society throwaways, refuse. No better than garbage headed for a dump.

Alix hurried into her small guesthouse and placed
her hands over her ears to block out the voices that
were shouting at her. This was "stinking thinking" at its
worst. Those ugly, frightening demons of hate seemed
relentless, determined to push her into the gutter. To
punish her.

Damn, she needed a cigarette. The craving was
worse than ever and she *deserved* one. She wanted one,
she needed one, and she didn't care if anyone saw her
with it, either.

She walked down to the corner store and bought
a pack, shocked at how expensive they'd gotten since
she'd quit. She wasn't even out of the store before she
tore open the pack and pulled out a cigarette.

Her hands shook as she struck the match. Already
she could feel a sense of calm and anticipation. Lighting the cigarette, she inhaled deeply and nearly choked.
It tasted like shit.

"Damn." She tossed it on the ground and stomped it

out as if she were Smoky the Bear wiping out the first forest fire of the season.

Her cell chirped. She removed it from her purse to see who it was, frowning when Jordan's name showed up on caller ID. She wasn't in the mood to talk to him. Or anybody else, either. They'd parted on shaky ground and had ignored each other ever since. Feeling the way she did just then, Alix didn't know what she might say.

She was tempted to turn off her cell; she didn't but she waited a few extra minutes before she listened to her messages. There was only the one.

"Alix, it's Jordan. Call me, all right?"

She didn't.

He phoned again an hour later as she sat alone in her dimly lit room. And again she waited for his message.

"Alix," he said, his voice more than a little exasperated. "I know you're screening your calls. This is crazy. We need to talk. I'm going over to my parents' and Mom's invited you to dinner, too. She said there's something she wants to talk over with us. Call me."

Alix nearly threw the phone across the room. She knew what Susan wanted to discuss. *Her*. The question being raised was whether Alix would be an appropriate wife for Susan Turner's son, the minister. The good boy who was about to marry the bad girl. Well, screw them all.

Alix fell on the bed, staring up at the ceiling. What she ought to do was pack her bags and leave. That was it. She'd walk away. Let them think what they wanted. She didn't care anymore.

To her surprise, she fell asleep and when she woke it was dark outside. It took her a moment to recognize the sound of someone knocking. Disoriented, she sat up and let her eyes adjust to the dark before she stumbled over to the door. She turned on the light and saw Jacqueline, hands cupped around her face as she peered in through the small window.

Alix opened the door.

"Alix?" Jacqueline asked, looking worried. "Is everything all right?"

"Sure," she said. She pushed the disheveled hair out of her face. "Why wouldn't it be?"

"You weren't answering your phone."

She didn't tell Jacqueline she'd turned off her cell. "I was asleep." That was the truth, after all.

"Jordan called me to see if you were home."

"Oh." Jordan again. Good, let him worry. "What time is it anyway?"

"Nine."

"At night?" Alix couldn't believe it. She'd been asleep for hours.

Jacqueline nodded. "Come on over to the house and let's talk. You must be starved. When did you last eat?"

Alix couldn't remember; still, she wasn't sure she was in the mood to deal with Jacqueline's concern. "What've you got?"

Her friend laughed. "Your favorite."

"Macaroni and cheese?"

"That, too."

Alix hesitated. The voices weren't shouting at her as loudly as before, but they were still there, reminding her that she'd never be good enough for Jordan. She refused to listen. Jacqueline was right, though; she *was* hungry.

Stepping outside, she closed the door and followed her to the house.

"Reese said you stopped by to talk to me this afternoon."

"Yeah." Alix yawned before dismissing the need to have the conversation she'd planned hours earlier. "Nothing important."

"You didn't stay long," Jacqueline commented as she led the way into the main house.

"No… I waited for a few minutes and you were still on the phone. Like I said, it wasn't all that important, so I went out for a while."

Jacqueline stopped, lean closed and sniffed the air. "Do I smell cigarette smoke?"

"Ah…"

"I suppose you were with a smoker?"

Alix shrugged. She couldn't lie but she was willing to stretch the truth when necessary.

"Smoking's such a disgusting habit. I'm so grateful you gave it up."

"Yup," Alix agreed. "Me, too."

Twenty-Three

Colette Blake

Colette read the simple handwritten invitation a second time. The gold-embossed card had arrived in the mail that afternoon. It was a request for Colette to join Elizabeth Sasser for dinner on Friday night. Elizabeth wrote with a fountain pen and her handwriting was much like the woman herself: blunt and forthright. Although it was technically an invitation, the card read more like a summons.

Despite her reservations, which had to do with her knowledge of Christian's recent activities, Colette was eager to visit the older woman. She'd liked Elizabeth immensely and felt she'd developed a sense of Christian as a motherless boy, then a disillusioned teenager and an angry young adult. Christian was confident enough to stand up to his father and fight for his own choices in life. Colette appreciated the courage that must have taken and it made her wonder why he was risking everything now, why he was violating the principles he believed in for foolish gain. Colette could hardly imagine what his great-aunt would think when Christian was arrested. He would be sooner or later, and it would devastate her.

As Colette climbed the stairs to her apartment, she found herself smiling, anticipating an evening with the woman she'd come to admire on so brief an introduction. At this point, Elizabeth and Alix were the only people who knew about the baby. The other day, she'd felt movement for the first time and was looking forward to sharing this news with Elizabeth.

Yesterday, Steve had phoned and left a message on her cell. Coward that she was, Colette hadn't returned his call. She would, though, and now, thanks to Elizabeth, she had a legitimate excuse to turn him down. She hoped he'd figure out that she was no longer interested in seeing him. If she needed to spell it out, she would, but she'd rather avoid a confrontation. It wasn't as if they'd been dating seriously.

As she entered her apartment, Colette turned on the local news, a habit she'd gotten into. The television was company in the evenings. Putting aside the mail as the news reader described a four-car pileup, she rummaged through the refrigerator, seeking inspiration for dinner. While she decided, she opened a container of yogurt and ate that, half listening to the news story. No fatalities in that highway accident, she was glad to hear.

When her phone rang, she assumed it was Steve again. But caller ID didn't indicate a number and after hesitating only a moment, she reached for the receiver. "Hello," she said, half expecting some form of sales pitch.

"It's Christian."

The immediate joy, mingled with dread, utterly confused her. He'd promised not to have any contact with her and so far—other than his note about Steve—he'd kept his word. He hadn't called or come to the shop in more than a month.

She'd been relieved.

She'd been disappointed.

She didn't know what she felt for him anymore. She didn't *want* him in her life, and at the same time she dreamed about him nearly every night.

"Hello." She tried to sound disinterested and wondered if she'd succeeded. She'd rather Christian didn't suspect she was so thrilled to hear his voice. Yet that was the feeling that quickly overwhelmed every other reaction.

"Your card came…."

"I wanted you to know," he said with reluctance. "But that wasn't part of our agreement, was it?"

"No, it wasn't." If he was guilty of breaking his word, she was equally guilty for being so pleased to hear from him. She'd never admit that, though. "How did you learn about Steve?" she asked. "Did you have him investigated?" The real question was: Why would he?

"No," he replied tersely. "I know someone who used to be a friend of his."

"Oh." Colette wasn't convinced she should believe him.

"Are you still seeing Grisham?" Christian demanded.

It was none of his business, and yet he might have saved her untold heartache. "No." She didn't offer any more explanation than that.

"Good."

The silence between them made her nervous. Finally, Christian asked, "How are you, Colette?"

"I'm very well." She wondered if he'd called to find out about her and Steve. No, more likely something had happened. "Have you…are you—you know?" She couldn't say it. She was afraid he was about to be arrested and had turned to her for some kind of help or perhaps comfort.

"You don't need to worry," he said. "I'm not in jail yet."

She was annoyed that he could joke about it, although he'd provided the information she'd been trying to find out. "Is there a reason for your call?" she asked curtly. Keeping an emotional distance was the only way she had of protecting herself.

"As a matter of fact, there is. I understand you recently met my aunt Elizabeth."

Colette was instantly defensive, not wanting him to know she'd sought out the other woman. She probably should've realized that Elizabeth would talk to Christian about her visit.

"I delivered one of the weekly floral arrangements you ordered for her," Colette told him. She wasn't going to admit anything beyond that.

"I see."

Her shoulders were so tense, they ached.

"My aunt Elizabeth is pretty special, isn't she?"

"I really liked her." There was no point in denying it.

"So my suspicions were right."

"I beg your pardon?" Colette said. "What suspicions?"

"You received a dinner invitation from her, didn't you?"

"How did you know?" Had Elizabeth told him about that, too?

"Because I also got one."

It had never occurred to Colette that Elizabeth had invited anyone else, least of all Christian.

"I should've guessed," he murmured.

"Guessed?" she repeated irritably. "Guessed *what?*"

"I hope you realize that my sweet, old-fashioned aunt is playing matchmaker," he explained. "I received an invitation from her and she says she won't take no for an answer."

"What made you assume I was involved?" Colette asked.

"Because my dear aunt has never insisted I come to dinner before."

"So you knew something was up." He was far more perceptive than she'd been and she felt a bit foolish, considering how easily Elizabeth had recognized her feelings for Christian.

"She made it fairly obvious," he said wryly.

"Have you asked her about it?"

"Yes, and my aunt was uncharacteristically quiet. She did admit she'd invited a 'special guest' and it was someone I already knew...very well."

Colette's face burned with embarrassment. His aunt had probably suggested Christian knew his dinner companion *intimately.* "I see," she mumbled.

"Don't worry," he told her. "I'll come up with some excuse to decline."

Instantly contrite, Colette felt she couldn't let him do that. "No, no. I'll decline."

"I appreciate the offer, but it's not necessary."

"She's *your* aunt," Colette said. "She loves you. She's

only doing this because she wants…well, she wants to see you—" Colette searched for the right word "—happy," she finished.

"That's interesting," Christian commented.

"What is?" She hated that the defensiveness was back in her voice.

"That you'd learn this much from a simple flower delivery."

"Oh." Colette's throat was suddenly dry. "Yes… She, uh, invited me in for tea."

"And you accepted?"

"Yes."

"Is there anything else you told her?" he asked pointedly.

"If you're referring to the ongoing investigation regarding your illegal activities," she said stiffly, "then the answer is no. I didn't breathe a word."

"Thank you," he said.

"How could I? How could I break this lovely woman's heart?" she blurted out. "Christian, if for no other reason than your aunt, you need to get out of this."

His hesitation was brief, and when he spoke he sounded regretful. "Don't you think I would if it were possible? I'm sorry, Colette. I'd give just about anything to turn back the clock. But it's too late now."

"Christian—"

He cut her off as if he'd lost interest in the conversation. "I suppose my dear aunt told you the story of my less-than-happy childhood?" he asked.

It wouldn't do any good to press the subject of his pending troubles, so she dropped it. "Some," Colette admitted, instinctively realizing that he'd hate her knowing about that part of his life.

"I was afraid of that."

Colette thought about the deep affection his aunt had for him. She yearned to tell him how grateful she was for that hour with Elizabeth. During their visit, she felt she'd come to understand Christian in ways that would never have been possible otherwise.

"No doubt she bored you to death with stories of my love of maps."

"She mentioned it."

"Just how long were you there?"

"Oh, not that long."

"Apparently, long enough to let her think you and I were involved."

"I didn't! I promise." Colette had told his aunt about their one-night stand and the result. She'd also said that they weren't seeing each other anymore; she'd claimed—convincingly, she'd felt—that it was for the best. Apparently, Aunt Elizabeth didn't believe her.

"*You* go to dinner with her," Christian said. "I assure you, she'll enjoy visiting with you far more than she would me."

"That's not true," Colette countered. She could see that this was quickly becoming a clash of wills. "Arguing is ridiculous. You're the one who's related to her, not me, so you should accept her invitation."

He chuckled. "Yes, I suppose it is ridiculous. Nevertheless, I gave you my word."

"I absolve you from it for that one evening," she told him. She refused to be responsible for disappointing the older woman. "We'll both go to dinner and be done with it."

He considered her suggestion. "I don't think that's a good idea. It would only encourage her. Unless you've had a change of heart." At her hesitation, he laughed. "That's what I thought. No, it's better that we not have anything to do with each other."

"Yes, I suppose it is," she answered sadly. Her instincts about Christian were accurate; it would've been a mistake to tell him she was pregnant with his baby. A painful mistake.

"Go to dinner with your aunt," she reiterated.

"Perhaps I will."

They left it at that, and a few minutes later, Colette closed her phone. Nothing had been decided. Not until the night of the dinner would she know whether or not Christian planned to go.

The next morning Colette woke feeling depressed. The baby fluttered within her womb and she pressed her hand against the slight bulge. She loved this child with a swell of emotion that produced unstoppable tears. For her own sake and the sake of the baby, she'd keep her secret, but eventually Christian would need to know. She dreaded the day she'd have to tell him and decided to wait as long as she could.

Tuesday afternoon after work, when Colette met Alix at Go Figure, she casually brought up the conversation.

"Christian phoned," she said as she stepped out of the dressing room. She'd noticed a pack of cigarettes in Alix's open purse and wondered when her friend had taken up smoking. Maybe the cigarettes belonged to someone else, she told herself. She hoped so, anyway.

Alix stared at her with an intensity that made her squirm.

"We both heard from his aunt," Colette explained. The music pounded, fast-paced and energetic. She wanted to get started on their routine, but Alix wasn't budging. Colette regretted saying anything.

"He wants to see you again, doesn't he?" Alix said triumphantly.

"No." Colette shook her head. "Like I told you, we both received invitations to his aunt's for dinner."

"Are you going?"

When Colette nodded, Alix immediately smiled. "Good answer."

The music had a hypnotic effect on Colette as she threw herself into her exercise routine. All the while, she could feel Alix watching her, silently encouraging her to give Christian another chance—give *herself* another chance. But Alix couldn't possibly understand that the situation was hopeless. And Colette couldn't tell her.

Once they'd finished, changed clothes and walked outside, Alix pulled out the pack of cigarettes and lit one up.

"When did you start smoking?" Colette asked, making an effort not to sound as disapproving as she felt.

"Saturday." She inhaled deeply. "I don't want to talk about it, all right?"

"But—"

"I need to smoke until after this wedding business is done. I'll quit then."

"If you say so." Colette sighed. Then she realized she'd been oblivious to Alix's problems. "You want a cup of coffee to go with that?"

"Don't have time," Alix answered with a shrug, blowing out a stream of smoke.

"Is everything okay?" she asked. "I've been so absorbed in my own life that I wasn't paying attention to what's happening in yours."

With a shake of her head, Alix dismissed her concern. "Don't worry about it. It's not a big deal."

"It's big enough for you to take up smoking, so clearly *something's* happened."

"Not yet it hasn't," Alix said cryptically, then tossed the half-smoked cigarette on the sidewalk and squashed it with the toe of her boot. "Listen, if you don't mind, I'd rather not discuss it."

"Whatever you say."

Alix actually grinned then. "Thanks. I appreciate it."

"Are you going to be okay?" Colette asked.

Alix didn't look nearly as confident now. "I don't know," she said. "Ask me again next week."

Twenty-Four

Alix Townsend

Alix woke feeling miserable, itchy and vaguely unwell. Scratching the inside of her elbow, she sat upright and switched on the bedside lamp. The alarm would go off in another ten minutes anyway, so there was no point in delaying the inevitable. The instant she turned on the light Alix knew her suspicions were correct.

Hives.

She'd broken out in a full-blown case of hives. No one needed to tell her why, either. Stress over this damned wedding. Nothing had helped. Cigarettes certainly hadn't. Neither had avoiding the issue with Jordan. Or pretending she hadn't overheard Jacqueline talking to Susan. In fact, she couldn't think of any solution—except one.

In eighteen months on the job, not once had Alix phoned in sick. Even now, with her arms swollen and her face blotchy, she hated doing it. Not showing up, especially at the last minute like this, was a hardship on everyone. Alix took her responsibilities seriously.

Reluctantly she picked up her phone. After making the call she swallowed two antihistamine tablets and went back to bed.

Thankfully, they made her sleepy, and when she woke again, she felt a little better. She took a shower, slathered on some calamine lotion and put on loose jeans and an old T-shirt. Then she caught the bus to Blossom Street. Only she didn't stop at the French Café. Instead, she walked over to the Free Methodist Church, where she knew she'd find Jordan.

When she arrived, he was on the phone in his office. His eyes widened when she came into view. Alix couldn't tell if his reaction was simply one of surprise or of shock at her appearance—the swollen face with its red blotches and the calamine-pink streaks on her throat and arms. Cute, very cute.

He ended the conversation quickly and Alix made herself comfortable. Or as comfortable as someone with hives could be. She slouched in the chair across from his desk, trying not to move any more than necessary.

"Alix, what are you doing here?" Before she could answer, he asked anxiously, "Are you all right?"

"Does it *look* like I'm all right?" she fired back. "I've got hives."

His concern was immediate. "Have you made a doctor's appointment?"

She knew from past experience that medical help could only address the symptoms. "No doctor can do anything for me." Even with her jacket on, she couldn't resist scratching. With a determined effort she stopped.

"Nerves?" he asked gently.

Alix tried hard not to let him know how close to the edge she was but didn't quite succeed. "Something like that," she snapped.

"You need to relax." He reached absently for his coffee mug, which stood by the telephone. "Anything I can do?"

"As a matter of fact, there is."

Apparently her answer surprised him, because his gaze shot to hers. "Name it."

This was the opening she'd been waiting for. "Cancel the big fancy wedding," she pleaded. "Let's go away and just get married. It wouldn't be an elopement, but it wouldn't involve all these strangers. The only people we need are family and a few friends. Can we do that, Jordan? Can we end this craziness and have a simple, private wedding? Please?" she added, staring intently at him.

Jordan frowned. "You want to cancel the wedding?"

"The big fancy affair and replace it with a small *sane* one." The itch was too severe to ignore and she tore into her thigh, scratching relentlessly through her jeans.

Her fiancé's shoulders sagged with what could only be described as disappointment. "Alix, we've already had this discussion, remember? We can't change everything at the last minute. It'd be too difficult and cause a lot of hard feelings."

"Don't you think I *know* it's the last minute?" she cried. Today was May first; the wedding was in exactly four weeks and one day. She was well aware of what backing out would mean. The invitations had been mailed; people had started sending gifts. Alix hadn't seen any of them yet, but Jordan had told her about the pile accumulating at his parents' home.

"I know you're feeling nervous," he began.

"*Look* at me," she cried, holding out her arms, although her jean jacket prevented him from seeing much. "I've got hives from head to foot. And there's something else I didn't tell you about earlier, because you'd get mad."

"Something else? What?" he asked, frowning.

"I started smoking again."

Jordan's eyes widened, but to his credit he held his tongue. "Did it help?"

She held out her arms again for his inspection; her sleeves slid up, revealing the red welts and the streaks of pink lotion. "You tell me."

He nodded. "Guess not."

"I threw away that pack of cigarettes this morning, which probably wasn't the best idea." Still, Alix figured she might as well quit now. With the price of cigarettes, she couldn't afford them anyway.

"Alix, it's going to be all right," Jordan murmured. "The wedding will be fine, I promise you."

Unfortunately, she knew otherwise. But the problem wasn't just the wedding and everyone else taking control. It was also the man she was about to marry. He hadn't listened. He kept pushing her away, putting her off, discounting her concerns. Much as Alix loved him, much as she wanted to be part of his life, she was beginning to realize that marrying him was a mistake.

"This isn't our wedding anymore. It never has been. Your mother and Jacqueline have turned it into a…a circus. I know they mean well and I appreciate their efforts, I really do." She struggled to explain how trapped she felt. "I've tried to pretend everything would be fine. I wanted to do this for you and your family and for Jacqueline and Reese, too. But I can't go through with the wedding as it stands. I just can't."

"You don't mean that!"

Her throat tightened and her eyes stung with tears. She swallowed painfully. Her voice was choked, hoarse, when she spoke again. "It's far too important to you to make everyone else happy, Jordan."

"That's not true!"

"Yes, I'm afraid it is." She looked sadly down at her hands and then removed the diamond from her finger. For an instant she closed her hand around it, wanting to hold on to it a moment longer.

"You can't be serious," Jordan said, and he sounded almost as if he were laughing, as if he thought this was all some practical joke.

Alix set the diamond ring on the corner of his desk.

"Alix, listen to me. Every bride goes through these prewedding jitters. It's normal."

"These hives aren't normal. Jordan…" She took a deep breath. "There's nothing I want more in this world than to be your wife, but I can't become someone I'm not. I can't marry a man who's so willing to ignore me and listen to what everyone else wants."

Jordan frowned at the ring. "You're actually calling it off?"

Her throat constricted again; unable to speak, she simply nodded.

"Just like that?"

She gave another nod.

He stood and leaned forward, placing his hands on the edge of his desk. "Fine. You want out. That's wonderful news. Just what am I supposed to tell everyone?"

That was all Jordan cared about? What other people

thought? Alix would have answered him but the pain in her throat made speaking impossible. When she turned to walk away, Jordan stretched out his hand. "Don't do it," he pleaded. "We need to talk this out."

"There's nothing more to say," she whispered, watching as he reached across his desk for the ring. He held it between his thumb and finger and stared down at it in disbelief, as if the diamond could explain what had gone wrong.

"Your mother had me pegged from the first," Alix said. She wanted Jordan to know she was aware of Susan's feelings toward her. "I'm not the right kind of woman for you. I never have been and I was a fool to believe otherwise."

Jordan gaped at her.

"Apparently *you* hadn't noticed, but your family did," Alix continued. "I'm really not good church material, either."

"That's…that's absurd," he stammered.

Alix felt he was the absurd one, thinking she could change who she was, wipe out her past and play the role of pastor's wife. "I'm sorry. More than anything, I wish I could be the woman you and everyone else want me to be. I tried, but it's not going to work."

"You're serious, then? It isn't just the wedding you're calling off, it's the whole marriage?"

This wasn't a ploy or a trick to get him to change his mind about the wedding and do it her way. He'd summarized the situation clearly. She *couldn't* marry him. She'd let her love cloud her feelings, confuse her actions. She'd realized, while scratching the skin off her arms, that Jordan hadn't listened to her. He *thought* he had, assumed he'd allayed her fears. Because she'd wanted to believe him, she'd allowed his confidence to momentarily reassure her.

"What do we do now?" he asked. He gestured weakly, then let his arms fall to his sides.

Alix shook her head and shoved her hands in her pockets for fear she'd start scratching again. "Your mother will know the proper protocol," she told him.

His mouth thinned, and Alix could tell that the prospect of facing his mother displeased him.

"I don't think canceling the wedding's going to be that much of a problem. Don't worry. Your family will smooth everything over." With these words, she walked out of his office.

Jordan didn't come after her.

Alix got on the bus and rode around for a long time, lost in her misery. On impulse she changed buses and went out to Sea-Tac Airport, then walked to nearby Star Lake, where Jordan's grandmother, Sarah Turner, lived. With the wedding officially canceled, Alix didn't know if she'd ever see her again. The prayer shawl was finished and she wanted to give it to Sarah. Unfortunately she didn't have it with her.

It was quite a hike from the road to the residential area around the lake, but the physical exertion made Alix feel better.

She recognized the house from her visit at Christmas and the time she and Jordan had gone in January. She walked down the dusty driveway and discovered Grandma Turner busy working in her yard. The old woman held a large watering can and wore coveralls and rubber boots, her thick white hair tied back with a red-and-blue bandanna. She straightened when she saw Alix.

"Hello, Grandma," Alix said, although she knew it was presumptuous to address Pastor Turner's mother as Grandma, since Alix was no longer going to be part of the family.

"Alix? Is that you?"

She nodded.

"Where's Jordan?"

Alix shrugged. "Work, I guess."

Grandma set the watering can aside and clumped over to the house to turn off the faucet. "Well, come inside and have a glass of iced tea. I'm glad you're here." Her welcome was so warm, it almost brought Alix to tears.

Obediently Alix followed her to the house.

"I was watering my garden and tending the rhododendrons," Sarah said as she removed her boots, lining them up on the back steps. "They're gorgeous this year. Did you notice?"

Alix barely heard her. She stood in the doorway, hands in her pockets, and knew she had to say something, had to explain. "I shouldn't have come," she mumbled.

"Nonsense," Grandma Turner said briskly. As if to prove her point, she took two glasses from the kitchen cupboard.

Alix stepped inside and breathed in the simple beauty around her—the scarred oak table, scrubbed clean, the pots of herbs, the handwoven curtains and braided rug. She loved this house and she loved Jordan's grandmother. To her horror, she began to cry.

Sniffling, she ran her sleeve under her nose. "I... wanted to tell you I knit you a shawl." Somehow she managed to get the words out but she didn't know if they were even intelligible.

Jordan's grandmother turned to squint at her. "Where'd I put my eyeglasses?" She started moving things on the table in a fruitless search. "I hear better with my glasses on."

Despite her misery, Alix grinned. Seeing them on the counter, she walked farther into the kitchen and handed them to the old woman. Grandma Turner slid them on, then looked at her and frowned.

Alix wiped her nose again. "I didn't know if I was ever going to see you again," she said. "I came to say thank you and to tell you goodbye."

"Goodbye? Aren't you marrying—" Grandma stopped abruptly, her eyes narrowed.

"There isn't going to be a wedding," Alix told her, refusing to lay blame or offer elaborate explanations. Grandma Turner would hear all about it soon enough.

The old woman pulled out a kitchen chair, sat down and sighed. "No wedding. Now, that's a crying shame. I like you, Alix. You're exactly what this family needs."

Alix desperately wished that was true.

"Talk about a bunch of stuffed shirts."

"Grandma!"

Sarah Turner sipped her iced tea, then patted Alix's hand.

"I didn't…know where else to go." Even now, Alix wasn't sure what had drawn her to the old woman. Telling her about the shawl was only an excuse.

"You came to exactly the right place," Grandma Turner assured her.

Alix choked on a sob. "I gotta leave." The old lady didn't need her blubbering all over the kitchen. Besides,

Alix wasn't in the mood to sit around and exchange polite chitchat.

"Did I ever tell you about Jordan's grandfather and me?" Grandma Turner asked. "Before we got married?"

"No."

Grandma passed her a box of tissues.

"The Turner family didn't think I was the girl for him."

Alix found that hard to believe.

"As you know, I worked back in the days when it was rare for a woman to hold a job outside the home. The Turner family was in the ministry and disapproved of that."

"But you did marry him," Alix said, dabbing at her eyes. She hated showing any kind of weakness.

"Yes, I did—because Lawrence stood up to his family and insisted he loved me. I remember him talking to his parents as firm as could be. He said he was well past the age of consent, well past letting them make his decisions for him. If they couldn't see the blessings I brought to the family, then they needed to open their eyes."

Grandma Turner thought she was helping, but the old woman didn't realize how badly her words hurt. Jordan would never do that for Alix. In fact, he seemed almost relieved about canceling the wedding. What worried him most was facing his mother and telling her the whole thing was off. Alix loved Jordan, but it had become obvious that she wasn't the right woman for him—and that he wasn't the right man for her.

Twenty-Five

"Why do people who love to knit complain about knitting a row with 1200 stitches and not about knitting 20 rows with 60 stitches?"

—Candace Eisner Strick, author of
Sweaters From a New England Village
(Down East Books, 1996), *Beyond Wool*
(Martingale Books, 2004)
and *Knit One, Stripe Too* (Martingale Books, 2007)

Lydia Goetz

I was now standing guard over Margaret, and that was a real switch. From my teen years onward, I was the coddled one, fragile and sickly, and as a result, I developed the troubling habit of waiting for others to step in and take care of me. That didn't change until my life finally stopped revolving around my needs, my desires—which happened when I opened the yarn store three years ago.

I've learned such valuable lessons about running a

business and coping with people and making decisions. And that included everything going on in our family. I'd become my sister's protector, and one manifestation of that was shielding her as much as possible from what was going on with Mom. Margaret had enough to deal with in taking care of Julia—and herself.

Because of this, Margaret was taking a lot of time off work. I let her go as often as she felt necessary, which wasn't easy for me. Some days I didn't even get a lunch break. It was one customer after another until the end of the day. Thankfully, I loved what I was doing! I still love it.

This Wednesday morning in early May was un-usual—because Margaret had nothing to say. My sis-ter's always been quick to share her opinions, wanted or not. She showed up for work and hardly said a word. Questions hovered on the tip of my tongue. I knew Julia had joined a support group for crime victims—which I'd learned from Hailey.

At first it irritated me that my own sister hadn't given me this latest update. But vocal as she is, especially about other people's actions, Margaret can be intensely private about her own life and affairs. I supposed she would eventually have mentioned this counseling group of Julia's; at least I hoped so.

As if she'd been reading my thoughts, Margaret ap-proached me where I was taking inventory. This par-ticular wool was one of my favorite brands and it felted beautifully. I could hardly keep it on the shelves. The key is choosing the right colors and with hundreds of choices from which to select, I'd been experimenting, bringing in new shades.

"I'm going to need time off this afternoon," Margaret announced bluntly. "That isn't a problem, is it?"

"It's the shawl class," I reminded her. I counted on my sister to be there in case customers stopped by.

"Yes, I know, but this is important." I heard the defensiveness in her voice.

I bit off the words asking my sister how much longer she'd be requiring time away from work. "I'll manage," I told her, although I didn't look forward to running the class while waiting on customers.

Margaret's reluctance to explain worried me. At one point she'd talked about hiring a private detective, but if she'd done so, I wasn't aware of it. I hoped—trusted— that Matt had talked her out of it.

After an interminable pause, Margaret answered my unspoken question. "Julia's going into police headquarters at three to identify the defendant in a lineup," she said.

"The police caught him?" You'd think Margaret would've said something!

"Detective Johnson believes this is the one," she muttered. "He's in a lineup so Julia can get a good look at him."

My immediate concern was for my niece and how she'd react to seeing her attacker again. "How's she handling that?"

Margaret didn't betray her feelings easily; nevertheless, I could see she was nervous. "Matt and I talked to her this morning. We told her the *suspect*—" she spat out the word "—can't hurt her again. I assume he's already behind bars."

I didn't tell my sister that just because he'd been brought in for a lineup didn't necessarily mean he was

in jail. Of course, everything I knew about police procedure I'd learned on *Law & Order*. I did realize that a lot
depended on Julia's ability to make a positive identifica-
tion. Then and only then would the suspect be charged.

"Julia's stronger now than at any time since the attack," Margaret went on. "Matt and I are going with
her."

"Is there anything I can do?" I asked, grateful that
my sister and brother-in-law would be with my niece.
I wanted to help Margaret through this crisis, but felt
powerless to do anything more than give her the time
off she needed.

She shook her head. "I appreciate your being so understanding about all of this," she said brusquely.

I didn't let on how perturbed I'd been earlier. I certainly would've liked more notice but guessed she
hadn't been given much herself. And her acknowledgement, her thanks, meant a great deal to me. "You'll call
and tell me what happened, won't you?"

Margaret nodded. "I'll call you from the police sta-
tion."

By the time the members of my class started to arrive, Margaret was gone for the day. Alix didn't show
up, which surprised me. I'd never known her to miss a
class. I was sorry she wouldn't be joining us; her presence always made our knitting sessions livelier.

"I haven't talked to Alix since last week," Colette
told me.

"Me, neither," Susannah said. "But last time we met,
Alix was almost finished with her shawl."

I remembered that, too. In fact, she'd purchased yarn
for another project, a felted purse. Still, it wasn't like
Alix to stay away, even if she'd completed a project.

My guess was that wedding plans were keeping her extra busy.

"I read an article about people knitting with wire," Susannah commented as she sat down at the table and brought out her knitting. After a slow start, she'd done well with the shawl.

I'd heard of wire-knitting, too. "I guess some people get desperate to knit," I said, trying to be funny. "Some poor knitter was probably stuck somewhere without a yarn store and broke into her husband's tool kit."

Colette didn't laugh the way I'd expected.

"Seriously, though, I've seen some lovely jewelry made with gold wire," I said.

"Really?" Colette finally looked up from her knitting. Her own shawl was coming along, though not at any great speed. I'd hoped she'd be nearly finished by now. Next week was our final class and she had more than half the shawl yet to knit.

"Anyone heard from Alix in the last few days?" Colette asked a moment later.

She seemed concerned suddenly, although when I'd first mentioned Alix I hadn't sensed any uneasiness in her.

"Come to think of it, I haven't seen her in a while," I said slowly. Alix usually dropped in two or three times a week. She'd long been more than a customer; we were friends.

Friends. And then it hit me. "You know what we need to do, don't you?" I said in a rush, wondering why I hadn't thought of it earlier. "We should hold a wedding shower for Alix."

"Great idea," Colette agreed. "Just us—her knitting friends."

"How about next Wednesday, since that's our last class," Susannah suggested.

I nodded. "That would be perfect. We'll make it a surprise."

Everyone agreed enthusiastically. We discussed knitting-related gifts—pattern books, yarn in a color we knew she liked, a gift certificate for the shop.

"We could order a cake from the French Café," Susannah said. "Alix might even end up decorating her own cake."

We all found that amusing, especially in light of the problems she'd had over her wedding cake. She'd talked about it one afternoon when she'd come by for yarn. She'd sounded depressed about the decision Jacqueline and Susan had made regarding it. I tended to side with Alix, but not wanting to cause any discord, I said nothing to her or to Jacqueline.

"Has anyone else planned a shower for her?" I asked, certain there must be others.

"Tammie Lee Donovan," Colette said. "Alix brought it up the last time we worked out at Go Figure."

That made sense. Jacqueline's daughter-in-law was a good friend of Alix's. And I recalled that Jacqueline had, in fact, mentioned the shower. Tammie Lee had invited all their friends from the country club, where both couples were prominent members.

"She didn't seem that excited about it," Colette added.

"I don't think she knows a lot of the women who frequent the country club," I said. "She's probably feeling a bit apprehensive."

Colette's mouth turned down in a sympathetic grimace. "Yeah. She's afraid she'll be out of her element."

"There's another shower being held by the ladies at the Free Methodist Church the week before the wedding," Susannah said.

"That's nice," I murmured.

"It would be if it were someone other than Alix," Colette said.

"Is she uncomfortable about this one, too?" Susannah asked.

Colette hesitated. "That might be an overstatement. But she seemed kind of shocked people would do that for her. I think she's afraid she might forget someone's name."

That was a problem I could easily identify with. A lot of people come to my shop, and while I make an effort to remember all their names, I sometimes forget. It's embarrassing to admit, especially when they've been to A Good Yarn a few times.

"It isn't like Alix to miss our workout sessions," Colette said. "But we haven't gone together since last week. She's not answering her phone and she wasn't at work today."

I was beginning to feel worried, even a little scared.

The bell above the door chimed then, and in walked Jacqueline Donovan. She marched purposefully toward the back of the store, where the rest of the class had gathered. And she looked…unlike Jacqueline. Her hair was actually disheveled, her mascara smudged and her raincoat badly wrinkled. Appearances are important to Jacqueline, and I'd never seen her like this before.

She glanced at the table and her shoulders sagged. "Oh, dear."

"What is it?" I asked, but I could guess. She was searching for Alix.

Her next words confirmed it. "When's the last time any of you saw Alix?" she asked.

We all looked at one another. "Last week for me," Colette admitted. "We were talking about her just now, wondering where she is."

"Have you heard from her?" Jacqueline demanded, turning to me.

"No—not recently. Has anything happened?" I was convinced there must be something seriously wrong for Jacqueline to leave her house with less than a full application of cosmetics and several pieces of expensive jewelry, not to mention a perfectly pressed coat.

Jacqueline seemed indecisive, then shook her head. "I don't know yet," was all she'd tell me. She remained stubbornly tight-lipped. If anyone had an opportunity to talk to Alix, it would be Jacqueline, since Alix lived in the Donovans' guesthouse. Surely Jacqueline needed only to cross the lawn and knock on the door. This told me Alix hadn't been home. And that meant trouble.

"If you see her," Jacqueline said urgently, "*promise* you'll get her to phone me."

"Of course." That would be an easy promise to keep. I was truly worried now, without knowing exactly why.

Jacqueline left and as soon as the door closed, the three of us exchanged anxious looks.

"Now I'm *really* wondering what's wrong," Susannah muttered, stopping long enough to count the stitches on her needle.

"Maybe holding a wedding shower isn't such a good idea, after all," Colette began.

Before I could respond, the phone rang. I hurried over to the counter, hoping the caller would be either Margaret or Alix. It was Margaret.

"How'd it go?" I asked.

"His name is Danny Chesterfield," my sister said.

It sounded like a nice name, the name of someone pleasant, an upstanding citizen, not a hardened criminal.

"Danny Chesterfield," I repeated slowly. "Did Julia recognize him?"

"Right away," Margaret told me with a hint of pride. "As soon as they marched the men into the room, Julia grabbed my hand."

I wish I could've been there to reassure Julia, too.

"She called out Danny's number even before all the men turned to face us." Margaret snickered derisively. "And guess what—first thing he did was get a lawyer."

Of course he would.

"Detective Johnson says he belongs to a gang of car thieves that target certain cars. Apparently, Danny's been in enough trouble through the years that there's no chance he'll get off lightly."

"Good." Like my sister, I wanted this criminal behind bars, the sooner, the better.

"I can already see a difference in Julia," my sister told me. Margaret sounded more carefree than she had in weeks.

"Where is she now?" I asked, hoping to talk to her, if only for a minute. It couldn't have been easy to confront this felon. Even though he couldn't see her behind the glass, Julia saw *him* and with his face in full view, she would've felt the terror and helplessness all over again. I was proud of what she'd done and wanted her to know it.

"She went over to a friend's house," Margaret announced triumphantly.

I wondered why my sister's tone held such a note of

pride—and then it came to me. Since the carjacking, Julia had refused to get behind the wheel of a car.

"Julia *drove?*" I asked breathlessly.

Margaret, who so rarely laughs, did. "Yes. By herself."

"Oh, Margaret, that's fabulous!"

"It's over," she said soberly. "At last this nightmare is over."

I prayed my sister was right.

Twenty-Six

Colette Blake

Susannah had a doctor's appointment, so Colette was opening the flower shop on her own Friday morning. As she approached the alley doorway, she noticed someone squatting there, puffing away on a cigarette. A plume of smoke rose from the hunched figure.

"Alix?" Colette couldn't keep the relief out of her voice. "Is that you?"

Slowly Alix Townsend rose to a standing position, then dropped the cigarette and ground it out. Colette was filled with questions. Everyone had been talking about Alix and no one seemed to know where she'd been for the past four days.

"What are you doing here in the alley?" Colette asked, unlocking the door.

"I need to talk to you," Alix said gruffly and followed Colette into the back of the shop.

"It's so good to see you," Colette told her, ignoring her rudeness. She flipped on the lights and punched in the code to shut off the alarm. Walking to the front of the shop, she turned over the Closed sign. Susannah liked to prop open the door, which she saw as an invitation for customers to come in and browse. Her "open-door policy" had been successful, too; equally enticing were the buckets of fresh flowers she arranged along the sidewalk.

Colette left the door open; she would set everything up when she'd finished talking to Alix. This was going to be a busy day for her. After work, she'd be joining Christian and his aunt for dinner. Although she was reluctant to admit it, Colette was looking forward to the evening. It'd been more than a month since she'd seen Christian and despite everything, she craved the sight of him.

"What's up? Is there anything I can do for you?" Colette asked, but what she really wanted to know was where Alix had been and why. Her friend looked as if she hadn't slept in a week. The smudges under her eyes spoke of misery and exhaustion.

"I came to cancel the wedding flowers," Alix said abruptly.

This was a shock, but Colette tried not to show it. "Are you changing the order?" she asked. "Or canceling it altogether?"

Alix's eyes were shadowed. "Canceling."

Susannah would be disappointed. The Turner wedding was a huge order and had come with a substantial down payment. Although she'd hold a certain amount back, it would still be a loss.

"So you and Jordan have decided to call off the wedding?" Colette asked, finding this hard to believe. Colette knew how much Alix loved him. In fact, Colette envied her friend the close relationship she had with her fiancé.

"As of last Tuesday, the wedding's officially off," Alix said blandly. Colette stared at her. Despite Alix's no-big-deal attitude, this must be ripping her heart out. It also explained why no one had seen her all week. Colette noticed that Alix's hands were shaking, although she tried to hide it by shoving them in her pockets.

"The paperwork's in the office," Colette said in a noncommittal tone. She led Alix there, out of view of anyone who might be looking in the shop windows. As soon as they were alone, she breathed, "What *happened?*"

Alix tried unsuccessfully to pretend it was a small thing. "Jordan and I agreed it was for the best, that's all."

"Oh, Alix, I'm so sorry."

"Don't be," she said, rejecting Colette's sympathy. "Anyone looking at the two of us could see it was a mistake."

Colette didn't buy that for a minute.

"I was living in a fool's paradise," Alix went on. She climbed up on a stool while Colette prepared a pot of coffee. After a few minutes, the rich, tantalizing scent drifted through the small office.

"I'm not the right woman to be a pastor's wife," Alix said. "Thank goodness I recognized that before it was too late."

Colette was stunned. "But…"

"I didn't mean to disappear," Alix was saying.

"Where *were* you?"

Alix stared down at the hardwood floor. "I took a few vacation days and went to see a…family friend.

Then, yesterday afternoon, I started looking for someplace to move. I applied for a few other jobs, as well."

"But why?"

When Alix glanced up again, Colette winced at the
pain in her eyes. "I can't stay around this neighborhood
with Jordan here. It would hurt too much to see him
nearly every day and I would, you know."

That was true enough. Colette had run into Jordan
at the French Café a number of times. Even if he and
Alix made an effort to avoid each other, it would be almost impossible.

"I figure I need to get away from here," Alix con-
cluded.

Colette felt like weeping. Alix was her *friend,* one of
the best she'd ever had, and couldn't stand the thought
of losing her. Trying to remain calm—or at least appear
that way—Colette leaned casually against the side of
the desk, hands behind her, ankles crossed. "You and
Christian's aunt are the only people I've told about the
baby," she said. "And do you know why that is?"

Alix met her gaze and after a moment shrugged.
"You and I work out together—or we used to."

"No," Colette said flatly. "I knew you wouldn't judge
me. In fact, you told me that yourself, and you were
right. I could talk to you when I couldn't talk to anyone else. You listened to me. You cared and you didn't
make me feel guilty or stupid."

Alix bowed her head. "Thank you," she whispered
and her voice cracked with pain. "That means a lot to
me. But the wedding is off. Jordan and I agreed a few
days ago to cancel everything. The only reason I'm here
now is to take care of business before I find a new job
and someplace else to move."

"Does Jacqueline know about this?"

"I haven't talked to the Donovans yet."

"Have you decided where you're going?"

"No," she said, "but that's not a problem. As a kid I changed neighborhoods more often than a moving van."

Colette dredged up the energy to smile. So Alix was going to run away. Well, she'd been on the run, too. And what she'd learned in the last months was that the person she was running from was herself. Not Christian, not her circumstances, but herself.

Alix was quiet for several minutes. "Susan doesn't think I'd make Jordan a good wife and she should know." Alix tried to make it sound like a joke, but Colette wasn't amused. "You have to admit she's more of an expert on this than either Jordan or me."

"I don't agree." Colette rested her hands on her hips, struggling not to reveal her irritation. "Don't you understand how *comfortable* you make people feel?" she asked. She turned around and grabbed two mugs from the shelf. She filled them with coffee, handing one to Alix. "You're the *perfect* wife for Jordan and if he hasn't figured that out, he isn't half the man I thought he was."

Tears glistened in Alix's eyes as she cradled the steaming mug. "You're a good friend."

"I'll be shocked if Jordan lets you leave the neighborhood. He's smart enough to know what he has."

Alix put her coffee down on a nearby worktable and sniffed. "I wish that was true."

"Alix, are you here?"

The sound of Jordan's voice obviously shocked Alix and she slipped off the stool. Eyes wide, she cast a pleading look at Colette.

"Alix!" he repeated.

When she didn't respond, Colette stepped out of the office. "She's in here." If Alix looked unkempt, it was nothing compared to Jordan. He must've slept in his clothes, because everything he had on was a mass of wrinkles. He hadn't shaved in days, and his hair stood on end.

Jordan entered the small office, standing squarely in the doorway. Alix realized she was trapped and Colette saw the panic cross her face.

"How'd you know I was here?" Alix demanded, her voice angry and defensive.

"A friend of mine saw you. He came to get me," Jordan told her.

Alix had backed all the way up against the wall.

"Alix!" Jordan's entire body sagged in relief. "Alix, for the love of heaven, where did you go? I've been sick with worry. I called everyone I could think of…. I didn't know what to do when I couldn't find you. No one—not even Jacqueline or the people at the café— knew where you were."

"I spent a few days at your grandma Turner's."

"Grandma's?" He seemed bewildered; clearly it had never occurred to him to call his own grandmother.

Colette felt like an unwanted third party and would gladly have left the room if Jordan hadn't blocked the entrance.

"That's where you went?" Jordan shook his head. "Why?"

"I love your grandmother," Alix said.

"I love *you*," Jordan told her. "Alix, I can't let you walk out of my life. I'd be the biggest fool who ever lived if I did. You tried to tell me how unhappy you were, only I wasn't listening. I thought… Oh, I don't know what I thought. The wedding's nothing," he said. "Nothing. You're all that matters. You don't want the big wedding, then it's out. Done with, canceled, forgotten. If you want a small ceremony with family and a few friends, that's what we'll have. But please marry me. I need you."

Alix remained rigid, frowning as if she didn't believe him.

Colette wanted to give her a shove in Jordan's direction. But Alix stood exactly where she was.

Jordan removed the diamond ring from his pocket and held it out to her. "Let me put this back where it belongs—on your finger. Just like you belong with me, and I belong with you."

Colette could feel Alix weakening as she looked down at her left hand. "You need to listen to me," she said in a low voice.

"I will, as God is my witness," he vowed.

"Then I'd like to be married by the lake on your grandmother's property."

"That can be arranged," Jordan said immediately.

"With your family and a few of our friends."

"Done."

Alix frowned again, as though she felt he'd given in too easily and she wasn't sure she could trust him.

"Nothing's more important to me than being with you," Jordan whispered.

Tears flowed down Alix's cheeks then, and she moved slowly toward Jordan. A second later they were locked in a fervent embrace.

Colette wanted to give them some privacy. Making her way past Jordan and Alix, she tiptoed out of the office, closing the door. She felt happier just knowing they were back together. However, Colette didn't envy them the task of breaking the news to Jacqueline and Susan Turner. She was certain they'd be delighted the wedding was on, but less pleased about the kind of event it was going to be.

That morning's encounter left Colette in a melancholy mood for the rest of the day. The satisfaction she felt for them seemed to emphasize the bleakness of her own life. She was eager to see Elizabeth—and to be with Christian, although there was virtually no chance of a happy resolution there.

The dinner invitation said she should arrive at six. Colette was ready much earlier than that, but she trotted down the stairs to her car with only ten minutes to spare. She drove to the house on Capitol Hill and was struck again by the beauty of the stately home with its white pillars and sweeping grounds. She noticed immediately that Christian's car was nowhere in sight. She'd hoped to time her arrival so he'd already be there.

The same woman, Doris, who'd answered the door previously did so this evening. "Miss Elizabeth is waiting in the library," she told Colette.

It all sounded very formal. Colette was led to the other room and sure enough, Christian's aunt was sipping tea by the fireplace. "I'm so glad you decided to accept my invitation," Elizabeth Sasser said, rising awkwardly to her feet.

"You also invited Christian," Colette said in a gently chiding voice.

"I did," his aunt agreed. Her eyebrows rose in an expression Colette couldn't quite decipher.

"You decided to play the role of matchmaker."

"Yes, I'd thought… Well, it's neither here nor there. Christian declined."

He'd said he would but Colette had hoped he'd change his mind. She was overcome by a deep sense of disappointment, which she tried to conceal. She assumed she'd succeeded until she caught a look in the old woman's clear blue eyes.

"I'll try again on another occasion," Elizabeth said matter-of-factly. "And next time I'll be more clever about it."

Colette laughed and slipped her arm through the other woman's. Together they walked slowly into the formal dining room, where the table was set with the finest china and crystal. Everything looked flawless and yet to Colette it seemed incomplete without Christian.

"Sit down, my dear," Elizabeth said.

Colette took her seat.

"I brought out some photographs you might like to see."

"Of your travels?" Colette asked.

Elizabeth smiled as Doris came into the room, carrying two lovely salads, heaped with fresh scallops, shrimp and large chunks of Dungeness crab. "No, not my travels, although Charles and I did enjoy seeing the world. We had wonderful adventures…." Her face softened for a moment, as if she'd forgotten where she was. Then she roused herself. "These pictures are of Christian as a youngster."

Colette rested her hands in her lap and it took her pulse a moment to return to normal. Even then, she couldn't entirely trust her voice. "I'd enjoy that very much."

Elizabeth raised her eyes to Colette's. "I thought

you would." With a mischievous smile, she continued. "Now, tell me a bit more about yourself. You said your family lived in Colorado?"

Colette nodded and the conversation flowed from then on.

The evening was pleasant; the meal was superb and the conversation over coffee afterward was stimulating. Later, studying photographs of Christian as a child and a teenager, Colette felt his absence with a sharp longing that was very different from the way she still missed Derek. That grief was like a dull, familiar ache. This new sensation was...pain.

"Next week," Elizabeth murmured as Colette prepared to leave.

"I—"

"Next week," Elizabeth reiterated. "And I'll make sure Christian comes." She pinned Colette with narrowed eyes. "You'd like that, wouldn't you?"

Colette was well aware that Elizabeth already knew the answer to her own question, but she didn't respond immediately. And when she did, she simply told the truth. "Yes," she whispered. "Yes, I'd like that."

Twenty-Seven

Alix Townsend

The weekend was hectic for Alix and Jordan as they quietly went about changing their wedding plans. The first person they talked to was Grandma Turner, who didn't disguise her pleasure or excitement.

"I'd *love* it if you had the wedding here," she said, beaming with pride. "Didn't I tell you?" she whispered in Alix's ear as she hugged her. "My grandson's much too smart to let you go. He knows he has a winner."

Alix felt a sense of pure joy at Grandma Turner's words. In the time she'd stayed with Sarah, they'd grown even closer. Alix hadn't realized how great the physical and emotional toll had been these last few months. She'd slept twelve hours both nights she was at Sarah's.

Jordan had spent those days thinking. He confided in Alix that he hadn't mentioned the broken engagement to anyone. Instead, he'd thought long and hard about what really mattered in his life. After that, he came to find her, to tell her how much he loved her and needed her. His declaration of love in the back room at Susannah's Garden had been the most beautiful thing Alix had ever heard.

While they were separated, Alix had sat by the lake for hours. Being there had calmed her and revived her spirits and it had given her the courage to return to Blossom Street and face her future, with or without Jordan. She felt giddy with relief at the outcome, which his grandmother had never once doubted. It was Sarah who'd suggested the lake house as the perfect place for their wedding. At the time, Alix had been convinced there'd be no wedding.

The most difficult part would be breaking the news to Jacqueline and Susan. Jordan had asked them both to meet him and Alix at his church office, at nine o'clock Monday morning. As they waited, Alix paced nervously; she couldn't sit or remain standing. This was going to be horrible; she just knew it. She could feel it in the pit of her stomach. Susan would hate her after this, and Jacqueline would think she was an ingrate.

"Your mother's never going to forgive me," she murmured, pacing the rug in front of Jordan's desk.

"Alix, will you relax?"

"But all the money Jacqueline and Reese have put into this reception…"

"They should never have booked the country club before they discussed it with us. We were trapped."

"Yes, I know," she concurred, but while that was true, it didn't ease the ache in her stomach.

"This is *our* wedding, Alix," he reminded her, and it seemed deliciously ironic to have her own words quoted back to her. "I'm as much to blame as anyone. I didn't listen to you, either. It embarrasses me that I failed you so completely." He shook his head. "It's a wonder you're still willing to marry me."

His love washed over her, bringing peace to Alix's heart. But her sense of peace didn't last. Susan Turner arrived first, bursting into Jordan's office as if she had a dozen other places she needed to be. She frowned at her watch. "I hope this isn't going to take long," she said impatiently.

"We're waiting for Jacqueline," Alix said, finally sitting down.

"Okay, fine, but I have a meeting and I can't be late."

"I'm sure Jacqueline will be here soon," Alix said, although her friend would probably show up a fashionable five minutes late, if not ten or fifteen.

Jordan came around his desk and stood next to Alix's chair, placing his arm around her shoulder.

Fortunately for Susan's schedule and Alix's nerves, Jacqueline got there almost right away. She looked exquisite, beautifully made up and wearing an elegant pantsuit. "You asked to see us?" she said, turning to Jordan and Alix with a smile of expectation.

"Mom, Mrs. Donovan, it might be best if you both sat down for this." Jordan gestured to the sofa, which was positioned against the wall.

The two women exchanged a puzzled glance, as if the other should be able to provide an explanation.

Jordan waited until his mother sighed and sank onto the sofa beside Jacqueline. He reached for Alix's hand and said, "Alix and I want you to know how much we appreciate everything you've done for us."

His mother checked her watch a second time. "I'm glad you're grateful, Jordan, but Jacqueline and I are meeting with the caterers in fifteen minutes."

Ah, so that was it, Alix thought. They were seeing the caterers for her wedding, and she hadn't even been informed. That said it all, as far as she was concerned.

"Really?" Jordan shared a knowing look with Alix.

Alix felt vindicated; Jordan could now see for himself what had been happening all along.

"What is it?" Susan Turner demanded, glaring at them. "We have that meeting…"

Jordan returned his mother's gaze. "Then this will be the perfect time to tell the caterers that the big, fancy wedding you two have arranged has been canceled."

His mother's jaw dropped and she leaped to her feet. Jacqueline gasped. "You're canceling the wedding?"

Jordan brought Alix's hand up and tucked it in the crook of his elbow. "Not entirely. We—" He wasn't allowed to complete his sentence.

"You can't *do* this! Jordan, what are you thinking?" His mother could barely get the words out fast enough.

"Mother, if you'd allow me to finish."

Jacqueline just sat there quietly. When she caught Alix's eye, she winked. Alix wasn't sure what that meant, but she had the distinct feeling Jacqueline understood more than she'd let on.

Jordan took advantage of the brief silence to say, "We're still having a wedding. A different kind of wedding, that's all."

"Do you realize how much work, effort and money have already gone into the preparations for this event?" Susan shrieked.

"Yes, but—"

Jacqueline stopped her. "Susan, it's only right to hear them out."

"Mrs. Turner," Alix said, speaking quickly in order to be heard. "I know this must be a shock."

"A shock," Susan repeated and sank down onto the sofa again. "Shock doesn't *begin* to describe what I'm feeling right now."

"I actually felt we'd gone too far," Jacqueline said to the other woman.

"But—"

Jacqueline interrupted her again, nodding at Alix and Jordan. "Tell us what you've decided."

"We want a small, private wedding," Alix explained, forever grateful to her friend. "I've spoken with Grandma Turner and she—"

"The invitations have already been mailed," Susan argued. "The wedding's scheduled to take place right here in the downtown church. Our friends..." His mother paused and raked her fingers through her shoulder-length hair. "Oh, my goodness, we have friends driving all the way from California to attend our son's wedding."

"Then apparently you're going to have houseguests for a while," Jacqueline said. "We'll go to the country club afterward."

"But...but..." Susan sputtered.

"It's Alix's wedding, too," Jordan told his mother. "She tried very hard to be the kind of bride you wanted, but unfortunately that isn't going to happen."

"This is the reason you disappeared, isn't it?" Jacqueline asked.

Alix nodded.

Jordan brought her closer to his side. "Alix has been uncomfortable with this from the first and she did everything she could to let us know her feelings. But like you, I didn't listen."

"You *can't* cancel," his mother insisted. "Not at this late date. Everything's been arranged!"

"Susan," Jacqueline barked. "Get a grip here. This is their wedding."

"I apologize that all of this is last-minute," Jordan said.

"You want a small intimate wedding?" Jacqueline continued. "Then that's what you'll have. The people who are owed an apology are the two of you. Susan and I need to apologize for taking over the way we did."

Jordan's mother was speechless.

"A small wedding is what Alix has always wanted," Jacqueline pointed out to Susan. "We were the ones who let things get out of hand. Reese told me that the other night. When Alix disappeared, he said I'd run roughshod over her, and he was right."

Alix bit her lip to hold back tears. How privileged she was to have these two wonderful friends.

"I've had more time to adjust to this since Alix left," Jacqueline said kindly. "Susan, once you've had a chance to think about it, you'll see this is the best thing all around."

In her effort to build a positive relationship with her future mother-in-law, Alix had repeatedly given in to Susan's demands. The hives had taught her a valuable lesson—denying her emotions didn't mean they'd disappear.

"I'm so sorry for causing all these problems," Alix whispered, feeling guilty about the expectations she'd thwarted.

"There's no reason for you to apologize," Jordan

said, bringing her clenched hand to his lips and kissing her fingers. "You told us what you wanted and your wishes have been consistently ignored. That won't happen again."

"You're actually calling off the big wedding and planning some little gathering by the lake?" Susan obviously remained incredulous.

Jordan nodded. "Yes, Mom."

"But I told you—the invitations have been mailed. The country club's been booked, the dinner ordered. Everything's in motion. I don't know if it can be stopped."

"It can and it will," Jordan said with complete confidence. "Alix and I are prepared to send out a second mailing."

"And say what?" she snapped. "How can you possibly explain what you're doing?"

"We have everything ready to mail. The notice states that we've decided on a private ceremony with only our family and a few friends in attendance."

His mother shook her head vehemently. "You can't do that. Jordan, don't you see what's going to happen?" Her eyes widened with alarm. "If you cancel a church wedding at the last minute in favor of a private ceremony, people are going to talk…. It'll hurt you. Alix," she said, changing tactics. She turned to face her. "Is *that* how you want to start your married life, with speculation and…idle gossip as to why you and Jordan are marrying in…in secret?"

"Susan," Jacqueline urged a second time. "Let it go, will you?"

"People can talk all they want," Jordan said, discounting his mother's concern. "Alix and I have nothing to hide. If there are rumors, they'll go away soon enough."

"Does your father know about this?" she asked next.

Jordan shook his head. "Alix and I plan to talk to Dad this afternoon."

"What about the reception?" Jacqueline inserted.

The thing that bothered Alix most was the expense her friends had gone to on her behalf. "I'll reimburse you, Jacqueline," Alix promised. She had no idea how long it would take, but she was determined to pay back every dime the Donovans had invested in this wedding.

"Nonsense," Jacqueline said emphatically. "It's my own fault. You didn't ask me to set this up at the country club. As Reese was more than happy to remind me, I brought it on myself." She leaned back against the sofa. "Do you remember the time I decided to give you a makeover?" she asked, and the memory brought with it a look of sheer amusement. "I took you to my French hairdresser and it was a catastrophe."

Alix rolled her eyes. Jacqueline had made a serious attempt to turn her into a beauty queen, with disastrous results. It'd all started when Jordan had asked her out to dinner; it was their first date and Alix had so badly wanted to look pretty for him. In her inimitable way, Jacqueline had decided to help. Not only was the hairstylist deeply offended by Alix's lack of appreciation, but being forced to try on designer outfits of Jacqueline's choosing had been a nightmare. Thankfully, Tammie Lee had come to the rescue.

"Jordan," Susan Turner said, turning to her son as if Alix wasn't there. "Despite what Jacqueline says, I can't allow you to do this. I *can't*. I know you love Alix and so do I. We all do." She spoke as if this was a fore-gone conclusion.

But if that was the case, Alix found it odd that Jordan's mother had shut her out of the conversation.

"I just can't let you throw away all our hard work. Don't you realize Jacqueline and I have slaved on this wedding for weeks?"

"If only you'd asked me," Alix implored, answering for Jordan, "then none of this would be necessary."

"Okay," Susan said, throwing her hands in the air. "I should've listened. Now that I think about it, I do re-call your objections to certain aspects of the wedding. I agree we didn't listen as well as we should have, but Alix, that isn't any reason to flush all our hard work down the toilet."

Alix was grateful Jordan's mother remembered her small protesting voice, although she'd ignored all her wishes at the time.

"The only reason I went ahead with our plans," Susan went on, "is that I have a lot of experience with weddings and I hoped...I *believed* you'd be interested in what I had to say."

"I was interested, but we didn't want the same things," Alix said.

His mother released a deep sigh. "All right, then, I apologize. Nevertheless, it's been done and while we can certainly make some changes, a lot of what's al-ready been decided will need to stay as it is."

"No, Mother, it doesn't," Jordan broke in. "Alix and I have made new arrangements. We spent the weekend creating our own wedding invitations. There are about twenty and each is handmade." Jordan walked around the desk and passed one to his mother, who stared down at it stupefied.

She looked it over, then glanced up, her expression carefully neutral.

Jacqueline took it out of her hand and studied it. "You made these?" she asked.

Jordan nodded. "Actually, Alix did most of the work. I helped where I could."

"They're exceptional... Alix, I had no idea you were capable of something like this. I love the way you've incorporated the hand-knitted lace. What a lot of work!"

"She's baking the wedding cake, too." Jordan looked pointedly at his mother. "It'll be a three-tier traditional white cake, decorated with real flowers."

"Okay, fine." Susan Turner pronounced the words slowly and distinctly as if dragging them through her teeth. "Since you're so set on this, the only thing left to do is compromise."

"Mother," Jordan said, more sternly this time. "Alix and I have made our decision. I'm sorry it isn't one you like or approve of, but—" He shrugged. "That's the way it's going to be."

"It doesn't mean we can't compromise," Susan tried again.

Jordan shook his head. "Mom, I'm sorry, but there's nothing more to discuss. Alix and I are going to be married at Grandma's place on Star Lake."

Susan looked helplessly at Jacqueline; Alix read her look and felt terrible. This wasn't how she wanted her marriage to begin—with disappointments and regrets. For just an instant she wavered.

Jordan's hand tightened around hers. Alix knew he

understood her need to please others and was forestalling any tendency to surrender.

"Alix and I will be working on Grandma's yard, getting it ready. It's going to be a lovely wedding, *our* wedding, just the way Alix and I want it."

"Yes, I know, but…" All at once, her argument seemed to die. Susan's shoulders sagged with defeat and she nodded glumly. "Is there anything you'd like me to do?" she asked.

"Oh, yes," Alix assured her. "I'm going to need all kinds of help."

"What about me?" Jacqueline asked, eager not to be excluded.

"You'll both be vital to the success of our wedding."

Susan's loud sigh reverberated in the small office. "I just hate letting all that food go to waste," she murmured.

"It won't," Alix promised. "We can talk to the caterer and reduce the order. We're changing the menu a bit, but it's still going to be exceptional. We'll have tables set up outside and—"

"You want an *outside* wedding?" Susan made it sound as if Alix had declared she wanted the ceremony performed underwater with Elvis as minister.

"Yes," Jordan answered for her. "Alix and I plan to be married in a place of beauty and peace, surrounded by those we love and not a group of strangers."

"But—" Whatever she'd intended to say was broken off. "It could rain," Susan said, and seemed almost hopeful that it would.

"No, it won't," Jordan said.

"You don't know that."

"Ah, but I do," he retorted. "I've already asked God to bless our day with sunshine."

Twenty-Eight

"Sometimes in the chaos of everyday life, knitting represents the one thing over which I seem to have any control...and that is sometimes just an illusion."

—Joan Schrouder, well-traveled knitting teacher and tech answer guru on many knitting lists

Lydia Goetz

I couldn't believe the change in Margaret after Julia had positively identified Danny Chesterfield. She actually looked taller to me. I told Brad while I was making dinner one night and he lowered the paper and stared at me. He seemed to think it was a silly comment. If he'd seen her at the store recently, he would've noticed the difference himself, especially after this past weekend. Margaret, the girls and I participated in the Relay for Life cancer walk. As it turned out, it was a positive and very emotional experience not only for us but for Amanda Jennings, a teenage cancer survivor I'd come to know. Julia, Amanda and I took part in the survivors' walk. Margaret and Hailey walked later, taking the early morning shift in the twenty-four-hour event. I met Amanda through Annie Hamlin, daughter of my friend Bethanne. Two years ago, Annie came to me when Amanda was diagnosed with her second bout of cancer. I used to visit Amanda in the hospital back then, and we still keep in touch. Annie marched with us, too. Our conversation was lighthearted, and Amanda sounded like the teenager she is. She'd been in remission for fifteen months, and was doing well.

We all were.

I actually heard Margaret whistling one morning when she arrived for work. *Whistling.* I didn't even know Margaret *could* whistle. Oh, she can do the kind of whistling where you insert two fingers in your mouth and let it rip. Even as a kid she was known for those earsplitting blasts. This, however, was like a sweet song. Margaret! I hardly knew what to say—although not commenting was probably for the best.

She was extra helpful, too. The minute a customer walked in, she was right there, offering service and advice or instructions as needed. She couldn't do enough, which was a strong contrast to the previous weeks, when she'd glared at anyone who had the temerity to walk into the shop.

This change in attitude was welcome for more reasons than the obvious. I'd missed her, missed our discussions and I'd especially missed her perspective concerning the changes in our mother's life.

Without burdening Margaret with a lot of details, Brad and I had started looking for a facility capable of dealing with Mom's diminishing mental capabilities.

Watching our mother decline was heart-wrenching. Several times I'd had to stop myself from telling my sister about Mom's troubles. Until recently, we'd talked over every decision.

In the beginning, Margaret balked and said I was exaggerating. She claimed I was worrying too much about one brief conversation with a nurse. I wished that was true, but I knew otherwise. Still, I realized Margaret had all she could cope with just then and I'd accepted that I should be the one to look after our mother.

When I'd finished my lunch in the back office, there was a lull between customers. "Do you have a minute?" I asked as I joined my sister in the shop, thinking now would be a good time to discuss Mom.

Margaret looked up from her crocheting. "Sure. What do you need?" I couldn't remember Margaret ever being this agreeable.

I sat down on the stool by the cash register. Anything to do with our mother drains me physically and I discovered I think better when I'm sitting. Everyone else needs to stand; it's the opposite for me.

"When's the last time you were by to see her?" I asked.

Margaret's smile disappeared. "Sunday afternoon I went over and I took her out for a while."

Mom's symptoms appeared more pronounced to me after the nurse had pointed them out. "How was she?"

Margaret considered the question and lifted one shoulder in a halfhearted shrug. "In a word—confused. We walked around a bit, because I thought the fresh air would do her good. I said you'd been checking out a few new facilities. Afterward she seemed to think *I* was looking at these places." Margaret hesitated.

"When I brought her back to her room, she gave me the biggest smile and said, 'Look, this place has furniture just like mine.'"

If it wasn't so sad I might have laughed.

"I saw Mom on Tuesday, and she didn't remember Dad had died," I told my sister. I'd had to fight back tears. It'd nearly broken my heart to tell my mother that our father had died four years ago. At first she refused to believe me and then, after a few minutes, she'd started asking about other people. Like her sister, who was gone, too. She and Mom had always been close. Then she wanted to know about a favorite neighbor. After a while, Mom just sat and stared at the wall. I had no idea how to comfort her, so I left, my stomach in one giant knot.

"This memory loss isn't all that recent," Margaret commented. "I can't say I see *that* much difference."

I frowned. Before Dad died, Mom was as mentally fit as anyone I knew.

"Dad was aware that she was losing her memory, but he didn't say anything to you."

I stared at her in shock. And yet, I suppose it made sense that my father would share his concerns with my sister and not me. I'd been recovering from my second brain tumor and undergoing an ordeal that would forever mark me. It was just like my father to spare me any additional worry. Naturally, he would've discussed his apprehensions with Margaret.

"In the beginning, after Dad died, the decline in Mom wasn't all that noticeable," I said. "To me, anyway." I was still living at home. She seemed lost and grieving but that was to be expected after the death of her husband.

"Dad was her brain," Margaret said matter-of-factly. "For a while, after you opened the yarn shop, Matt and I thought about having her move in with us so I could keep an eye on her."

"You talked to Mom about this?"

Margaret nodded. "She wouldn't hear of it. Nevertheless, we didn't like the idea of her living alone."

That caught my attention. Since I'd lived with my mother until I started my business, it was no wonder Margaret had felt so angry with me. My sister saw the fact that I'd launched my own life as an abandonment of our mother. I longed to explain the situation from my point of view so Margaret would appreciate my need for independence. But I couldn't think of any way to do that without sounding defensive. Or selfish...

"Last year, her health took a turn for the worse," I said, returning to the subject of Mom's condition. "And everything started to fall apart for her."

"Now the doctor's taken her off the medication, too," Margaret said.

"The one that helped her memory," I murmured.

Margaret shrugged, not looking at me. She straightened the yarn on the worsted weight shelves, making busy work, I realized, because she didn't really want to talk about this. Then, bluntly and to my complete surprise, she said, "Mom's ready to die, you know."

An immediate protest came to my lips but I managed to swallow it, although I couldn't hold back the tears.

"I don't think it'll be much longer."

"No!" Every adult faces the loss of his or her parents sooner or later. It comes with the territory, as Brad once put it. But I didn't feel ready to deal with Mom's death four years after Dad. Not so soon, I prayed, pleading silently with God, willing to bargain. Dad had been gone nearly four years; sometimes it seemed like only yesterday and at other times it felt like eons ago.

"Did you find a new place for Mom yet?" Margaret asked. "Because I want to talk to the administrator when you do."

I nodded. "I meant to tell you. A memory care facility. It's one the nurse at the assisted-living center recommended." Brad and I had gone there late Monday afternoon and were impressed with how kind the staff was. We had an appointment later in the week to meet with the administrator.

"Matt and I can help with the move," Margaret assured me. "We'll rent a truck. There isn't much furniture anymore…."

It went without saying that this would likely be our mother's last home.

The bell above the door chimed and I looked hurriedly away, wiping the tears from my cheeks. The last thing my customers needed was to find the store's proprietor weeping.

Before I could turn back, Margaret let out a bellow of welcome. "Detective Johnson! This is a pleasant surprise."

My sister was nearly animated with delight. I'd heard her mention Detective Johnson many times. Before Danny Chesterfield had been brought in for the lineup, Johnson's name had been followed by murmurs of disgust and an occasional swearword. Ever since Julia had identified her attacker, the detective walked on water. Margaret believed in the system again, believed that justice would be served. Soon the world would be made right once more.

"Hello, Mrs. Langley," the detective said with a cursory glance around the shop. He seemed uncomfortable in an environment generally reserved for women—although plenty of men enjoy knitting and crocheting, too.

"Have you met my sister?" Margaret asked and all but dragged me forward to meet her hero. "This is Lydia Goetz."

"Nice to meet you." He was a nice-looking man in his forties, wearing a well-cut suit, his hair slightly on the long side. I vaguely remembered Colette saying she'd heard of the man assigned to investigate the carjacking. Apparently, her husband had known him.

"Can I do anything for you?" Margaret asked. "Would you like some coffee? Tea? Knitting lessons?" This might have been confused with flirting had it come from anyone else. My sister is far too abrupt to flirt; I doubt she even knows how.

"Nothing, thanks." The detective stood there awkwardly, gazing down at the floor for a moment. He raised his head. "I felt I should let you know we took everything we had on Chesterfield to the prosecutor."

"You're going to arrest him now, right? That's how it works, doesn't it?" Margaret asked.

I detected a change in her voice. It was almost as if the anger was back, just below the surface, ready to explode given any provocation.

"Normally, yes, but Chesterfield came up with a valid alibi."

"It's a lie!" she burst out.

Detective Johnson nodded. "We think so, too. However, we can't prove it."

"But Julia identified him."

"It isn't enough," the detective said. "The prosecutor

said he can't make a case. I'm sorry. We can't charge Chesterfield."

"So you *aren't* making an arrest?"

He shook his head sadly. "I know you're upset."

Margaret didn't bother to acknowledge his statement. Instead she wanted the details. "How did this happen?" Her voice was nearly devoid of emotion, which told me how dangerously furious she was.

"I'm sorry...."

Margaret was too angry to hold still and started pacing. "I can't believe this!"

"Mrs. Langley."

I walked over to my sister and put my hand on her shoulder, trying to offer comfort where there was none to be had.

"You mean to say Danny Chesterfield's free to hurt someone else's daughter?" she demanded, not giving the detective a chance to answer her previous question.

He nodded, his expression grim. "We did everything we could."

Margaret stared straight ahead. "I see."

"He'll be caught sooner or later," the detective told Margaret. "It's only a matter of time. Again, I can't tell you how sorry I am."

Margaret looked at him coldly.

"The problem is that Danny Chesterfield's all too familiar with the legal system. He knows how to work it. He's a career criminal with a rap sheet that looks like a spoiled kid's Christmas list."

"That's supposed to reassure me?"

"No. I feel bad about this, Mrs. Langley." I had the definite impression that he'd rather be anyplace than here.

I admired his courage in coming to talk to Margaret personally rather than telling her this over the phone. Facing my sister couldn't have been easy, especially when he had to deliver such distressing news.

My inclination was to console Margaret as best I could. One glance at the hardness that stole over her face told me I'd do well to keep my distance. My sister wasn't in the mood for consolation.

"I appreciate your stopping by," I said politely when it became apparent that she had nothing more to say.

Detective Johnson had walked to the door when he noticed Whiskers, warming himself in the shop window. He paused, then went over to my cat and scratched his ears, forever endearing himself. Whiskers stretched his lean body to its full length and yawned loudly. With a final nod over his shoulder, the detective left.

Margaret's confidence that Julia's ordeal was almost over had been destroyed. "What now?" she asked in a hoarse whisper. "How am I supposed to tell Julia?"

"Do you have to mention it?" I asked.

"She'll know." Margaret still hadn't moved. "She'll find out."

I had the urge to take her by the hand and lead her to the office, where I'd force her to drink a cup of heavily sugared coffee. She seemed to be in some form of shock, an anger-induced torment that frightened me. I'd seen Margaret angry before but never like this.

"I want another detective assigned to the case."

"Don't be ridiculous," I said sharply.

"A woman this time," she added, ignoring my outburst.

"The prosecutor could be a woman," I said in an attempt to reason with her.

"I doubt it," Margaret said contemptuously. "Only a man would do something this stupid."

"Margaret!" She didn't seem to recognize how outlandish she sounded.

She grew quiet again. An unnatural quiet that made chills race down my spine. "This isn't over yet," she said.

"Margaret." I tried again, beginning to feel a little desperate. "What are you going to do?" I wasn't letting her out of my sight until I knew her intentions.

She stared at me, frowning. I wasn't sure she even saw me because she seemed to look right through me.

"Margaret," I repeated, lightly touching her arm. "What are you going to do?"

She turned to meet my gaze with eyes so cold and fierce they made me shudder. "It's better for you not to know." Then she calmly retrieved her purse from the office and walked out of the store.

Twenty-Nine

Colette Blake

Colette had looked forward to her dinner with Elizabeth—and Christian—all week. She wondered how his aunt planned to coerce him into making an appearance; she could only hope Elizabeth succeeded. Colette felt an overwhelming urge, a *need,* to see him…and talk to him. Five months into the pregnancy she couldn't keep it a secret much longer. It was time Christian knew. Time she found the courage to tell him. Perhaps this evening… Maybe if she told him about this new life, it would convince him to step forward and confess—do whatever was required.

His aunt Elizabeth had opened Colette's eyes to so many things about Christian and, surprisingly, about herself. Hiding from him—and hiding the pregnancy—had been foolish, a mistake she wanted to rectify.

It wasn't Doris who answered the door this time, but Elizabeth herself.

Pursing her lips, she announced, "Christian won't

come." She shook her head. "I tried everything I could to persuade him, but he saw through my ploys."

"It's fine," Colette assured her quickly, putting on a brave smile. She was determined to look past her own disappointment and enjoy dinner and Elizabeth's company.

"No, this just won't do," Elizabeth muttered. "My nephew is such a stubborn young man. He refuses to listen to reason." She clasped Colette's arm, drawing her into the house.

They sat in the formal dining room and despite the crisp, vivid-green asparagus, the wild rice and tender broiled salmon, neither had much of an appetite.

"You must go to him," the old woman said halfway through the meal. That thought had apparently just occurred to her because she brightened instantly. "If he won't come to us, then we'll take action ourselves. We'll simply make it impossible for him to ignore us." She reached for her fork with renewed vigor.

"I…I'm not sure that's a good idea."

"Nonsense," Elizabeth countered. "It's brilliant. Why didn't I think of it earlier? You *will* go, won't you?"

Colette noticed the less-than-subtle shift from *us* and *we* to *you*.

Justifications and excuses tumbled through her mind. She offered the first one she thought of, weak as it was. "I don't know where he is."

Elizabeth Sasser scoffed. "He's at home." She rattled off his address, which of course Colette already knew, although she'd certainly never been there.

"He doesn't want to see me." That was a far more valid reason.

The old woman laughed outright. "Contrary to what

you think, I'm very sure he does. I know Christian. Go to him, Colette, and it will change everything."

Colette *wanted* to believe her. Before she could actually accept or reject the idea, she found herself standing on Elizabeth's porch with Christian's address clutched in her hand.

"Go now," Elizabeth said, waving her away as if she were an unwanted salesman. "What is it those commercials say? Just do it! What are you waiting for?"

Good question. She had to tell him about the baby; she knew that. It wouldn't be easy, though, especially after she'd lied—and lied more than once. She'd refused to have anything to do with him for fear of getting dragged into the mess he'd created. And now she was supposed to show up at his front door and gleefully announce that she was pregnant with his child?

He'd be furious. She couldn't even begin to imagine what he'd say.

"Colette." His aunt sighed. "You're being as difficult as my nephew."

"I'm not sure…" she whispered, unable to hide her dread.

"Go to him," Elizabeth encouraged.

His aunt made it sound so simple. It wasn't, but she couldn't possibly understand that, because she only knew half of what was at stake. And under no circumstances could Colette tell her the rest.

She suddenly had a mortifying thought. "He's dating again, isn't he?" What if she got there and Christian was with another woman? Based on his history, she wouldn't be surprised to discover him seeking solace elsewhere.

Elizabeth glared at her. "Does it matter?"

It shouldn't. Not really. And yet Elizabeth's response didn't exactly reassure her.

Still…

She would go to him, and the two of them would talk. Whatever happened, happened. If he went to the police and turned himself in as she hoped, she'd stand by his side. If not, if not…she didn't know what she'd do.

In an unexpected display of affection, Elizabeth stepped forward and hugged Colette. "Everything will work out," she whispered.

"You promise?" Colette joked.

His aunt grinned. "Have him take you to dinner, my dear. You barely touched a bite."

Colette walked down the steps and climbed into her car. Elizabeth remained outside until Colette had pulled onto the street. Through the rearview mirror, Colette saw her raise one hand and wave.

The drive took less than fifteen minutes. Colette's heart pounded so hard she didn't hear anything else— not the car radio, not the music that played, not the siren of the fire truck that blared and honked as it roared past. Only when she saw other vehicles pull over did Colette realize she had to move to the side of the road.

Once she arrived at his house, she sat in her car and stared up at it. Built of slate, it featured large picture windows that overlooked a bluff on Puget Sound. She could envision the panoramic view his home offered of the water and the Olympic Mountains.

Her nerve was about to desert her, but she remembered his aunt and the encouragement Elizabeth had given her. Fortified with new determination, Colette got out of the car, ignoring the other vehicles parked on the street.

After ringing the doorbell, she waited for what might have been ten minutes or a few seconds; she could no longer tell.

When Christian opened the door, he stared at her, as if uncertain who she was.

"Colette?"

"Surprise," she said. Her voice rose like a little girl's, embarrassing her even more.

After an uncomfortable moment during which neither of them spoke, he narrowed his eyes, obviously questioning her presence. He made no move to invite her in. "What are you doing here?" he asked.

This wasn't the warm greeting she'd hoped to receive. "I need to talk to you." Because this was so difficult for her—and no doubt for him—she added, "If you'd rather I left, I'll understand."

"Then leave." He glanced quickly over his shoulder.

"You have a...guest?" So he *was* involved and this other woman was with him. Colette felt her cheeks burning; coming here had brought her nothing but anguish.

"I'll come back another time," she said hastily, about to turn away.

He leaned forward to take her shoulders. "It's not what you think."

"You don't owe me any explanations."

"You're right. I don't."

They continued to stare at each other. When she could stand it no longer, Colette lowered her gaze. "Like I said, we need to talk."

"Not now."

"Fine," she whispered. "We can do it later."

His face remained unyielding. "Go now and—"

There was a noise behind him and he threw another irritated glance over his shoulder. He seemed on edge and eager to have her leave and yet he still held on to her.

"Forgive me for interrupting your meeting…your privacy," she said.

He nodded.

"Could we set up a time to talk, maybe tomorrow?"

He shook his head. "I leave for China in the morning." She had trouble identifying his tone—regret? Wariness? Resolve?

"Oh."

"I'll phone you when I get back," he said as he released her.

She backed away and he did, too.

The urge to touch him, to kiss him was overpowering.

As if reading her thoughts, he reached for her again, and pressed his mouth to hers. His lips were moist and fervent.

In the distance someone—a man—called his name and Christian pushed her gently away. "Go," he said. "Just go."

Confused, she stumbled to her car. That was when she saw the black sedan with a couple of muscular-looking Chinese men, obviously bodyguards, watching her. This could only mean that Christian was meeting with the people involved in the smuggling operation.

Shaking with fear, Colette drove back to Blossom Street. The first thing she did when she got into her apartment was lock the door. Then she made herself a cup of tea, sipping it slowly. Finally she called Alix. Her friend was expecting to hear how the evening had gone. So, of course, was Elizabeth, but Colette didn't know what she could say to Christian's aunt.

Alix answered on the first ring. "Did he show up?" she demanded before Colette could say a word.

During their lunch hour, they'd gone to Go Figure, and Alix had offered Colette a complete exercise circle's worth of advice about tonight's dinner.

"He wasn't there."

"You mean to say he *didn't* come?"

"No…he had a meeting." Colette swallowed against the dryness in her throat.

"And?"

"His aunt suggested I should go to him."

"Good idea," Alix said approvingly.

But neither Elizabeth nor Alix understood that this was the worst idea of all. Swallowing again, Colette continued. "He had…guests. He said he's leaving for China tomorrow morning." And whatever he intended to do there, Colette didn't want to know.

Thirty

Alix Townsend

Monday was Jordan's day off from his work at the Free Methodist Church. With so much to do before the wedding, which was two weeks from this coming Saturday, they'd decided to spend the afternoon cleaning up Grandma Turner's yard.

Alix had brought the completed prayer shawl and looked forward to giving it to the woman who'd come to mean so much to her. She could hardly put into words the solace she'd found with Jordan's grandmother after she'd broken off the engagement. Sarah had sat with her and listened while Alix spilled out her frustration and pain. Then she'd insisted Alix eat. She'd had her stay in the spare bedroom, looking after her like a cherished guest. It was just the pampering Alix had needed.

On Monday afternoon, Jordan waited for Alix to finish her shift at the French Café. The day had turned out to be gloriously sunny and warm, an exception to the cool weather May had brought so far. Although

her fiancé had assured his mother the sun would shine
for their wedding, Alix was pragmatic enough to suggest they rent a large white tent. There was always the
chance, she'd joked, that someone else with a connection to the Guy Upstairs had asked for rain to water
his crops.

"Hi," Alix said as she got into the car beside Jordan.

"Hi, yourself." He leaned over and touched his lips
to hers in a casual kiss.

Like her, Jordan seemed a lot more relaxed since
their confrontation.

"Grandma's really excited that we're coming to
visit," he said as he checked his sideview mirror and
merged with the Blossom Street traffic.

"You didn't tell her we're doing yard work, did you?"
Once Grandma Turner heard that, Alix was afraid she'd
be out digging in the flower beds herself.

"I didn't say a word." He headed for the entrance to
the Interstate.

"Good." Alix laid her head back and closed her eyes.
She'd been awake since three that morning, with the
same questions chasing around and around in her mind.
She'd tried to ignore them, especially those having to
do with his mother. "I love you, Jordan," she said, her
eyes still closed.

"Any particular reason?" he asked, as if her statement amused him.

"Lots. Mostly, I love you for loving me enough to
cancel the big wedding."

"Oh. That." His voice fell, and Alix opened her eyes
to look at him.

"Is it bad?" she asked, biting her lip. It couldn't be
easy for any of his family. Susan was the one on the

front lines. The curious questions from relatives and friends would all be directed at her. She was stuck canceling the arrangements, too, since she'd booked most of them.

"Mom will survive," Jordan assured her.

"Does she hate me?"

"Alix, of course not! She understands."

That comment produced an involuntary smile. The one thing Alix had gleaned from their meeting the week before was that Susan Turner most definitely did *not* understand.

When they arrived at Grandma Turner's house on Star Lake, the sun gleamed on the water and the afternoon was about as lovely as Alix could have hoped for. After greeting them, Jordan's grandmother insisted on serving them iced tea out by the lake.

"I thought that while I was here I'd mow the lawn," Jordan told her.

"You don't need to do that. I have a service that comes in every two weeks. I've already asked them to make a special trip right before your wedding."

"Grandma, we don't want you to do that," Alix said. "We'd like to do it for you."

"Nonsense," she said, refusing their offer with an airy wave. "Getting the lawn mowed is the least I can do." She urged Alix and Jordan to eat more of the oatmeal cookies she'd brought out with the tea. "I can't tell you how happy I am that you're holding the wedding here." She gazed wistfully out at the lake. "I've always loved this house. It'll be wonderful to have all my children and grandchildren together."

"I'm happy about it, too," Jordan said, linking his fingers with Alix's.

Jordan had described his visits to the lake when he was a child but Alix didn't know how much he'd loved his grandmother's home until she'd suggested getting married here. An elated expression had come over him and he'd immediately agreed it was the perfect place, a perfect solution.

This close to the lake, Alix could feel a light breeze. She set her iced tea on the round patio table and saw Jordan's grandmother glancing over her shoulder.

"Jordan, would you mind bringing me my sweater?" Sarah asked. "It's hanging on the peg just inside the kitchen."

Alix nodded to Jordan and instead of heading for the house, he went to his car and came back with a white box, tied with a red bow.

"What's this?" Grandma Turner asked when he returned.

"A little something for you from Alix."

"Alix?" Wearing a puzzled look, Grandma Turner turned to her.

"Just open it."

"Why would you be bringing me gifts?"

The answer to that was simple. "Because I love you."

"Oh, Alix," the old woman said, sighing. "You're the best gift I could ever have." Shaking her head, she added, "I couldn't ask for a better match for my grandson. I'm so happy for you both." Her eyes filled with tears, which she blinked rapidly away.

Alix struggled not to cry herself.

"Open the box before we all start to boo hoo," Jordan teased, pretending to wipe tears from his face.

Alix elbowed him in the ribs as his grandmother removed the lid and peeled back the tissue paper.

"Alix knit it herself," Jordan explained even before his grandmother had the opportunity to lift the lacy shawl from its box.

"It's the prayer shawl I mentioned earlier," Alix said. "People knit them for other people who are special in their lives or in need of prayer or healing. You listened when I needed a friend and loved me when I didn't think anyone in this family ever would again." Alix looked at Jordan, who leaned forward and kissed her forehead. "Those days with you meant a lot to me. I realize you're not sick or in need of extra prayers, but I did want you to know how much I love you."

"Oh, Alix." Grandma Turner breathed her name softly, reverently. "I remember you telling me about the shawl. I don't believe I've ever received anything more precious. All the effort that went into this… I will treasure it for the rest of my life."

Alix gently, almost ceremoniously, arranged the shawl around the old woman's shoulders, and they hugged.

After they'd finished their tea, Jordan mowed the lawn over Sarah's objections and clipped the hedge, while Alix tackled the flower beds, weeding and cultivating the soil. When they were done, she planned to spread beauty bark over the freshly tilled beds.

"This garden used to be the pride of the neighborhood," Grandma Turner said as she stood beside Alix. "I do what I can now, but it isn't enough."

"We never had flowers at our house when I was growing up." Alix kept her voice matter-of-fact. She remembered that the house had gone without more than flowers. Several times it lacked a window and once, the front door. Her mother had thrown a beer bottle at her father, who'd ducked; the bottle had broken the living-room window. Another time, when Alix was around six, her father had kicked in the front door.

Alix had always envied people who had yards with flowers. Her own yard was an embarrassment, not that Alix spent much time worrying about grass and stuff like that. It was a much higher priority to stay out of range of both her parents when they drank. That was the reason she'd found a safe haven in her bedroom closet, where she'd created her fantasy family.

"I want you and Jordan to stay for dinner," Grandma Turner said.

"I don't think Jordan has any plans. Let me ask."

Jordan, done with clipping the hedge, drank a second glass of iced tea and then joined Alix in weeding the flower beds. She told him about Sarah's invitation.

"Knowing my grandmother, she's already inside fixing a meal," he said, moving close enough to kiss Alix's sweaty neck.

"Jordan!"

"Would you like to stay?" he asked.

She nodded.

It'd been so long since they'd spent time together like this. Alix hadn't fully understood how much strain the wedding had placed on their relationship. Once they'd made the decision to take control of it, the stress was gone.

Dinner was a simple affair of soup and sandwiches, which they ate on the patio facing the lake. Grandma Turner fell asleep soon after Alix had carried the dishes inside. Jordan saw his grandmother into the bedroom and then helped Alix clean up the kitchen.

"Not every girl enjoys spending time with a guy's

grandmother," he said as he took a dish towel from the rack.

"You know what I was thinking?" Alix murmured, washing by hand the few dishes they'd used.

"That you're crazy in love with me," Jordan responded quickly. "In fact, you can't wait to drag me into your bed and have your way with me."

Alix grinned. "Well, other than that."

"Tell me." He stood behind her and wrapped his arms around her middle.

"I was just thinking how peaceful it is, being here with you."

"Mmm." He dropped a kiss on the curve of her neck. "Well, this place isn't going to be so peaceful on June second."

Alix leaned against him. "Tell me the truth—has it been a problem for you at church?" She guessed that Susan's concerns about what this might do to Jordan's career were valid. Changing the wedding to a small, private affair so close to the date was likely to cause speculation.

"Some," Jordan admitted.

"Like what?"

He hesitated. "Pastor Downey, my dad and I had a heart-to-heart."

Alix wasn't sure what that entailed nor was she sure it was her business to ask. She waited for Jordan to volunteer the information.

After a brief silence he sighed and released her, then rested against the kitchen counter. "Dad asked me if I'd gotten you pregnant."

"What?" she exploded, and watched as a grin spread

slowly across Jordan's face. "Did he really ask you that?"

"Yup." Jordan nodded. "And I enjoyed telling him I looked forward to doing exactly that."

They'd talked about starting a family but not for several years. "Your mother put him up to it, didn't she?"

Jordan shrugged. "I assume so."

Alix knew she faced some damage control with Susan Turner. As soon as the wedding was over, she'd begin to repair their relationship.

"Actually, it's a good thing Pastor Downey, Dad and I talked," Jordan went on to tell her. "We don't do that enough. Male bonding." He pounded his chest in a Tarzan imitation. "Me like bonding."

She rolled her eyes, loving him all the more for making a joke of it.

"We all felt better afterward," Jordan said in his normal voice, "and I have you to thank for that."

Alix hoped it was true.

"What about Jacqueline and Reese?" Jordan asked her.

Alix assured him they were fine. The funny part was, neither Jacqueline nor Reese seemed especially upset about the wedding plans being overturned. If anything, Reese found his wife's wedding fixation rather comical.

As Alix had suspected, it all went back to Paul and Tammie Lee's wedding. To Jacqueline's horror, not only hadn't she been included, she hadn't even been invited. She'd felt cheated, and as a result, she'd turned Alix and Jordan's wedding into a substitute—and then some.

"You know what?" Jordan murmured. "I'm much happier with what we're doing now."

They hugged and Alix closed her eyes. In a little more than two weeks she would be Jordan Turner's bride. June second couldn't come fast enough.

Thirty-One

"Knitting a prayer shawl is 'putting legs to your prayers.' It is an outward reminder that some-one cares."

—Cheryl Gunnells, Executive Director
of Publications, Leisure Arts, Inc.

Lydia Goetz

Apparently, Alix hadn't guessed that this last get-together of the shawl-knitting class was a surprise wedding shower for her. Once the word was out, I was delighted by how many people wanted to be part of it.

The first person to contact me was Carol Girard. She still had trouble believing she was actually pregnant. Every time we talked about it, Carol started to giggle. A pregnancy was never supposed to happen for her and Doug.

I told her I'd once read a scientific report that stated there was no logical reason a bumblebee should fly. The aerodynamics were all wrong, but apparently someone forgot to tell the bumblebee.

Carol's pregnancy did give me pause. I wondered if such a miracle would be possible for me. Unfortunately, chemotherapy and radiation play havoc with the reproductive system.

A part of me longed for a child, an infant to hold and nurture and love. I'd assumed that in time this resurgence of baby hunger would go away, but it hadn't yet. I lay awake at night thinking about a baby. Brad and I continued to discuss adoption, but we'd decided to think it over for a few months. There was no need to make a decision yet.

Back to Alix's party... Bethanne Hamlin was supplying the decorations. Her party business had become a notable success, and there was even talk of franchising the company. Whenever I thought back to the first time I met her, I was astonished that this was the same woman. In those days, Bethanne had lacked the initiative to do something as simple as sign up for a knitting class; her daughter Annie was the one who'd phoned. To be fair, Bethanne was still staggering from the pain and shock of her divorce, and her self-esteem was in ashes.

Well, talk about *rising* from the ashes! The woman who was convinced she had no skills, no talents and no prospects, now headed a huge party business. The last I heard, she had thirty employees. Thirty!

Annie was in her first year of college and planned on getting a business degree so she could join her mother. Two years ago who would've believed something like this could happen?

Courtney, who'd also been in my sock-knitting class, mailed a gift for Alix when Annie Hamlin told her about the surprise shower. Courtney was away at the University of Illinois at Chicago; she hoped to eventually become a nutritionist. Bethanne's son, Andrew, and Courtney were still in touch, too, which pleased me. I knew they'd maintained their long-distance relationship, because Courtney had recently e-mailed me about shipping her some yarn. She was knitting Andrew a sweater for his birthday in his school colors. Alix would love knowing that Courtney hadn't forgotten her.

Naturally, Jacqueline and Tammie Lee planned to attend, even though they'd already been part of another shower for Alix at the country club. They were bringing all kinds of treats for the party, everything from small quiches to a selection of cheeses. Tammie Lee told me she was also preparing a southern delicacy—pickled hard-boiled eggs. Jacqueline said I should count my blessings that Tammie Lee hadn't decided to cart in a Crock-Pot full of boiled peanuts.

It warmed my heart to see the two of them getting along so well.

Margaret would be here, too. I'd hoped Julia and Hailey could come, but unfortunately, they both had after-school events. Margaret hadn't said much about Julia lately. When I asked, she changed the subject, evaded the issue or glared defiantly. Clearly, this wasn't something she wanted to discuss, especially now that Danny Chesterfield had been released. My sister's anger and her frustration with the police had returned tenfold.

I tried not to worry about Julia or Margaret, but it was hard. Hailey and I talked every once in a while, and I got more news from her than I did from my own sister, whom I saw five days a week.

The door opened and Bethanne Hamlin breezed into

the store, hauling a huge box. Her hair was shorter than I remembered, and her sleeveless summer dress revealed a golden tan. I could tell she felt embarrassed when I told her how gorgeous she looked, but it was the truth.

"Thanks for doing all this," I said and would've hugged her if not for the large carton she held.

"I wouldn't miss it for the world." Bethanne set the box on the table and started to unpack. She had ties for the back of each chair, which resembled wedding veils, and silk flower bouquets that she attached to the veils, each one in a pastel shade. She draped the table with a decorated cloth and then brought out a silver tray with minisandwiches and sugar cookies shaped like champagne glasses.

Even before she'd finished, Jacqueline and Tammie Lee came in with their bounty, followed by Elise and Maverick Beaumont. I immediately pulled out a chair for Maverick, who seemed thinner than the last time I'd seen him. His complexion was pale, too, and he seemed weak and tired. He was losing his battle with cancer. No one needed to tell me that; I could see it for myself.

Elise stayed close to his side, as she had for the past two years. They were devoted to each other. Watching them together, so tender and loving, brought tears to my eyes. I hoped Brad and I would be like them in our old age.

Elise used to be an embittered woman who resented her ex-husband, Maverick, for his many supposed transgressions, including the fact that he was a professional gambler. Her life had become more and more rigid in her retirement, not less, as you might expect. But reconciling with Maverick had completely changed her.

In addition to being my friend, Elise was one of my

very best customers. When it came to knitting, there wasn't any project Elise couldn't tackle. The most complicated patterns didn't daunt her.

As the time neared for Alix's arrival, everyone dispersed.

"I see her," I called from where I stood by the window. I watched Alix leave the French Café, carrying a basket of what I suspected were warm croissants. "Hide, everyone," I instructed, and all my friends scrambled. I hurried over to the counter.

The three customers in the shop had been told what was happening and been invited to join the festivities.

The bell chimed as Alix stepped inside, then paused, glancing around. I'm no actress, but I did my best to look as if this was an ordinary afternoon.

"What's going on?" she asked, frowning.

I stood behind the cash register, trying to keep our little secret as long as possible. The plan was to wait until Alix approached the table before everyone leaped out and shouted, "Surprise!"

I shrugged. "What do you mean?"

"No one's here," Alix said in a puzzled voice.

"Colette and Susannah will be here in a few minutes." In reality, they'd been among the first to show up. They had a large order to get out that night and it was a sacrifice for them to be here at all, but neither was willing to miss it.

Alix still didn't move.

"Go on back." I gestured to the rear of the shop.

Alix sent me an odd look, and I was sure that despite my efforts I'd given the surprise away. She moved past the yarn—and then everyone rushed forward to shout.

To my utter satisfaction, Alix was stunned. Her

mouth fell open and she slowly turned and studied each face. The table was piled high with gifts and food, and everyone crowded around to offer her their best wishes.

Alix always claimed she wasn't any good in social situations, but after I saw her at this wedding shower, I begged to differ. She charmed her friends and thanked them for their gifts with unquestionable sincerity. The gifts were mostly thoughtful with a few comical ones tossed in. My sister's present, a toaster, was as practical as Margaret herself. Mine was a gift card for $100 worth of yarn. My favorite present was an oversize T-shirt with an image of Shakespeare knitting a sleeve. "That's the 'raveled sleeve of care,'" Elise the ex-librarian explained. "Sleep knits it up again. Isn't that a lovely metaphor? It's from *Macbeth*."

"In other words, knitting puts you to sleep," Maverick teased.

Alix laughed and hugged them both.

At closing time, the party broke up and people started drifting away. Bethanne had to leave early because of an "appointment"; I was willing to bet she was going out on a date, but I didn't question her. I knew she'd met someone, and I was eager to hear the details. I could've asked Annie, who'd stayed to clear away the decorations, but I figured Bethanne would tell me when she was ready. I could wait.

At one point I saw Margaret talking intently to Alix and wondered what that was about. My sister didn't look happy, nor did she seem to be congratulating Alix on her marriage. A while later, Alix moved off to visit with someone else. Then, before I knew it, Margaret had left for the day without even a word of farewell.

Colette and Susannah had to get back to the store to

work on the arrangements for a funeral home, which was a new account Susannah had recently won.

Elise and Maverick didn't last long after the gifts had been opened and the food served. I walked them to the car, which Elise drove. I could see the sadness in her eyes and felt an almost maternal urge to comfort her. These next few months were going to be difficult. Maverick, however, didn't show any concern for himself.

I understood that, too. He'd received far more love and care in these last few years of his life than he'd ever dared to hope. I knew he was as content and happy as possible, happier than he'd been in all the years he was a champion poker player. He'd been a fairy godfather to us all and we loved him deeply, each and every one of us.

When I returned to the store, the only person left was Alix.

"I phoned Jordan," she said as she gathered up her gifts. "He's going to come by in a few minutes to drive me home."

"Oh, that's good."

Alix helped me clean up and I saw her glance my way a couple of times.

"Were you surprised?" I asked as I dumped paper plates in the garbage.

"Totally." She looked up at me, her eyes shining. "It was *wonderful,* Lydia. Thank you so much!"

"We were happy to do it for you, Alix," I murmured, moved by the fervency of her response.

"Did you see me talking to Margaret?" Alix asked a few minutes later as she wrapped the leftover croissants in a plastic bag.

I nodded. Naturally, I was curious and hoped Alix

would elaborate. Margaret shared so little with me these days.

"Margaret came to me," Alix began. "She asked if we could talk privately." Alix frowned, presumably at whatever Margaret had said. "I told her I'd talk to her, but it'd have to wait until after the shower. I couldn't very well leave everyone," she said.

I agreed, and couldn't figure out what my sister had to say that was so confidential.

"When the party was winding down, she pulled me into a corner," Alix went on. "It was about what happened to Julia. I thought things were sort of back to normal, but I guess not."

"I don't know if you heard or not," I told her, "but the police felt they were close to an arrest. Then the prosecutor decided they didn't have enough evidence to charge him."

"Yeah, that's what she said. And why she asked..."

"Asked *what?*" I had the feeling I wasn't going to like this.

"Margaret wanted me to...help her."

"How?"

"She thinks I might have a contact." Alix's eyes didn't meet mine. "Apparently, Margaret thinks I might know someone who'd be willing to hurt Danny Chesterfield."

Despite my effort to remain calm, I gasped and brought my hand to my mouth.

"She didn't want him killed or anything," Alix rushed to explain. "She wants him hurt. Badly. At least one broken bone—his right arm's what she suggested, but if the leg was easier, she'd settle for that."

I hardly knew how to respond other than with absolute horror. My sister was prepared to go to any lengths to see that Danny Chesterfield was punished for his crime.

"She said she was willing to pay, and she wanted to be sure that whoever I found let Danny know this was payback for what he'd done to Julia."

Reaching for the back of a chair, I yanked it out and sat down. I felt as if my legs would no longer hold me upright. Never in all my life had I believed my sister capable of such an action.

"She wasn't very pleased with me," Alix said.

"You told her you wouldn't do it, didn't you?"

"Of course! What do you think I am?" She paused, giving me a wry smile. "I might've considered doing it as a favor three or four years ago, but I don't do things like that anymore."

I couldn't speak. I simply couldn't speak. I vacillated between pity and anger. I considered having Brad contact Matt, since they got along well and I figured my brother-in-law would know how to handle the situation. Or should I talk to Matt myself?

"She didn't like what I had to say," Alix continued. "I told her that hurting Danny, breaking his leg or anything else, wouldn't fix the way she felt."

No, Margaret wouldn't like hearing that.

"I said Danny Chesterfield was a despicable human being who deserved to be in prison. I told her I thought it was only a matter of time before he ended up there. If not for what he did to Julia, then for some other crime. It's a shame someone else has to suffer—I feel bad about that."

Alix wasn't the only one. Margaret had ranted about it for days until I thought I'd scream.

"Hard as it is, I suggested she try to forgive the creep," Alix said. "It's what I had to do with my mother. For a long time I was angry with her for not being the kind of mother I needed. Her addictions to drugs and alcohol made my childhood…difficult. I mean, I know she was a product of her own weakness and her own background. But her problems could weigh me down for the rest of my life if I let them." Alix's face brightened with the intensity of her feelings. "Instead of letting that happen, I followed Jordan's advice and…*forgave* her."

My admiration for Alix, already high, rose about a thousand percent. I wanted to tell her that, but the lump in my throat prevented me from speaking.

"About two years ago I wrote her a letter," Alix told me. "Jordan helped me with it."

"What did you say?"

Alix shrugged. "Not much really. Just that I supposed she did the best she knew how and that I forgave her."

"How did she respond?" It wasn't any of my business but I was understandably curious.

"She didn't," Alix told me with a tinge of sadness. "I didn't hear from her for about six months, and then she wrote and said that since I got religion I probably wouldn't be any good to her." Her eyes glazed over for a moment.

"Did you tell my sister any of this?" I asked.

"I tried, but…" Alix shook her head. "Margaret wasn't in the mood to hear it."

That figured. Once again I wondered what—if anything—I could do to help my sister. And once again, no real solution presented itself.

Thirty-Two

Colette Blake

Christian had left for China a week ago. Colette could only speculate on his business there. During her years as his assistant, she'd booked any number of flights for him and knew he frequently traveled to Asian countries, particularly China. The thought of him dealing in human cargo turned her stomach. How long had it been going on, she wondered. And the question she asked over and over: *Why?* Still, she had difficulty equating the man she knew and loved—yes, loved—the man whose child she carried, with a man who'd do something so criminal. And beyond criminal, so cynically cruel.

Regardless, and in the face of her dangerous knowledge, Colette waited patiently for word from him. He hadn't said exactly how long he'd be away. His trips lasted anywhere from one to three weeks, and more often than not, he experienced delays, but she expected to hear from him soon. Now that she'd made the decision to tell him about the baby, the news burned within her.

For the first time since she'd left Dempsey Imports, she felt a real sense of hope. The thing about hope, she discovered, was that it was like a powerful painkilling drug. Despite her fears, her mood remained optimistic. Even the weather cooperated, and the days were bright with sunshine.

Fridays were usually busy at Susannah's Garden and this particular Friday was no exception. All morning, Colette was occupied with walk-ins, who were quickly becoming twenty to thirty percent of their business.

One of the local high schools was having their Junior/Senior prom that evening. Susannah and Chrissie spent the afternoon assembling boutonnieres and corsages as fast as they could in their crowded workspace.

Colette admired the way Susannah constantly came up with inventive ideas to make her little shop known in the area. If that meant offering a large floral arrangement as a raffle gift to one of the service organizations, then she did so willingly. She visited hospitals, wedding planners and funeral homes and outlined her services. Business continued to flow into the shop at an increasing rate. Some days the two of them could barely keep up; more and more often, Chrissie was coming by after her classes to help out.

Colette appreciated her assistance and calm, cheerful demeanor, but what impressed her most was Chrissie's devotion to her grandma Leary, who lived in eastern Washington. Every two or three days Chrissie made a point of phoning her grandmother. Colette knew Susannah was close to her mother, too, and called her often.

Fortunately, she had a good friend who kept in touch with Mrs. Leary and reported back.

The phone rang and Susannah answered it. She glanced at Colette, and thinking it might be a private conversation, Colette walked outside to check on the flowers in their buckets. She rearranged them, adding irises to the lilies to create an appealing array of colors.

After several minutes she returned to find that Susannah was still on the phone. She removed it from her ear, held her hand over the receiver and said, "Actually, this is for you."

"Me?" Colette's first thought was that it must be Christian, although she recognized that this was more hope than expectation. She couldn't understand why Susannah would be talking for so long with someone who'd asked to speak to *her*. She hurried over and Susannah passed her the phone.

"This is Colette Blake," she said in her most professional voice.

She heard a sob and then in crisp tones, "Colette, it's Elizabeth Sasser."

Alarm filled her instantly. "Elizabeth, is everything all right?"

"No, my dear, I'm afraid…it isn't." Her words faltered, and Colette could tell that Christian's aunt was struggling to keep her composure.

"Is it…Christian?"

"I'm afraid I have bad news." The old woman paused, then exhaled sharply. "When it's convenient, would you mind stopping by the house?"

"Of course." Colette's pulse hammered violently. *Bad news?* Something had happened to Christian; that was the only thing it could be. All her fears came together at once and for a moment she felt as if she might throw up.

"Thank you," Elizabeth whispered. Almost in afterthought, she added, "Come as soon as you can."

The line was disconnected before Colette could question her further.

Slowly she replaced the receiver. Susannah came to stand next to her and slipped an arm around Colette's shoulders.

"Did she tell you what happened?" Colette asked her, needing to know, no matter how bad the news.

"No. She couldn't. She was so upset, the housekeeper had to talk to me. But she was pretty distraught, too, and I had trouble understanding her."

"Doris," Colette said. "Her name is Doris."

Susannah nodded. "Doris explained that Elizabeth received a phone call about half an hour ago and that she'd nearly collapsed."

"He's dead." It was the same feeling Colette had experienced when she'd followed the aid car to the hospital after Derek's fall.

"Colette, there's no need to believe the worst." Susannah gave her a reassuring squeeze. "Do you want Chrissie or me to drive you?"

She shook her head. "No, I'll be fine." She was surprisingly calm, but then she had been after Derek's accident, too. The initial rush of panic had subsided and in its place had come this numb sensation, this chilling certainty. "I don't mean to leave you in the lurch," she told her employer.

"Go, don't worry. Chrissie will be here in an hour and in the meantime I have everything under control."

Not feeling any need to rush, Colette washed her

hands, collected her purse, then walked to the alley where she kept her car. The numbness started to fade, and she felt a tightness instead, gripping her chest. If she'd been older, she might have feared that this pain signaled the beginning of a heart attack. But she knew it wasn't that. This was what loss felt like.

The identical sensation had accompanied the E.R. physician's words when he'd led Colette into a private office and told her there was nothing left to do but wait for death. Derek would never recover from his coma, he'd said. Nothing could change that outcome.

Even in the heavy Friday-afternoon traffic, Colette didn't lose her composure. Because Christian would still be dead, whether she got to Elizabeth's house in ten minutes or in forty.

When she arrived at the old woman's picturesque home, she carefully parked the car. In that instant her grief felt too much to bear and she pressed her forehead against the steering wheel and silently prayed for strength.

She loved Christian. If she'd ever doubted it before, there was no question now. He would never know. Never learn the truth. Never hold their baby. She'd have to accept that the same way she'd accepted everything else in the last two years.

Drawing a deep breath, Colette climbed out of her car. She'd barely rung the bell when Doris flung open the massive door, and with red-rimmed eyes, led Colette into the library.

"I'm so glad you're here," Doris told her, wringing a white handkerchief between her hands. "Miss Elizabeth needs you."

Colette entered the library and sat down on the ottoman at the older woman's feet. "Can you tell me what happened?" she asked softly.

Elizabeth shook her head. "No one knows. Christian is missing, lost somewhere inside China. No one's seen him." She swallowed hard. "For the past week, no one's heard from him. *A whole week.*"

"He got on the plane in Seattle, correct?"

Elizabeth nodded. "According to the airline, Christian landed in Beijing. That's where the trail stops. As far as his office is aware, he was scheduled to change to a connecting plane there, but he never arrived in the other city. I've forgotten its name," she added fretfully.

"How did you hear about this?" she asked.

"My nephew Elliott phoned. Christian's father. Someone at Dempsey Imports called him. He phoned me right afterward."

"What's being done to find him?" Colette asked, her mind darting in several different directions. Surely there were ways of locating someone inside a foreign country.

"Elliott asked if anyone had contacted the U.S. embassy, and apparently that's been done. The hospitals have all been checked, jails, hotels. Other places, as well. Nothing."

"Do you know the name of the person your nephew talked to at Dempsey Imports?" Colette hated to be drilling some poor staffer, but she needed as many facts as she could get.

"I...don't."

"Do you mind if I use your phone?"

"Of course not. Anything. I just have to know Christian's alive."

It'd been almost five months since Colette had talked

to anyone at Dempsey Imports. In fact, she'd gone out of her way to avoid contact with her former friends. But none of that mattered now.

Elizabeth pointed to the hallway. "There's a phone in there." For the first time the old woman's expression was hopeful, as if Colette might discover something no one else had.

Colette found the phone and turned on the hallway light. She didn't need to look up the number or the extension. Even after all these months, it was still as familiar as her own.

Two short rings. "Jenny Hilton."

"Jenny, it's Colette Blake."

"Colette! Oh, my goodness, Colette!" Jenny exploded with surprise. "What *happened?* It's like you disappeared off the face of the earth. Everyone's been asking about you and I didn't know what to tell them."

"I got another job," Colette said. She wanted to keep explanations to a minimum.

"Oh, my goodness, have you heard about Mr. Dempsey?"

Before Colette could respond, Jenny continued. "He's somewhere in China. At least that's what we think—no one knows for sure. It's all kind of crazy around here at the moment."

"I heard," Colette said, hoping for more information. "What can you tell me?"

"Not much," murmured Jenny. "His assistant's been on the phone for three solid days. Apparently Mr. Dempsey's father is flying to China to start a private search. From what I understand, Mr. Dempsey was making one of his routine trips to Zhongshan, the same one he's made at least a dozen times."

"Anything else?"

"Just that no one's heard from him, either here or in China. Most of the time it's perfectly safe for tourists there… But the strange part is that he was supposed to visit the manufacturer in Zhongshan and they had no record of him coming."

"They weren't expecting him, then?" she asked in confusion.

"Right. But *we* thought that's where he was. Anyway, Mr. Dempsey's father checked into his flight plans and discovered he landed in Beijing but had never made a reservation to continue on to Zhongshan."

If Colette was frightened before, it couldn't compare to what she felt now. Wherever Christian was inside China, she had to believe it was connected to the mess he'd become involved in. She'd pleaded with him to get out; unless he did, there could be no future for them. Colette had begun to suspect that Christian had heeded her words. He'd *tried* to get out—and his disappearance was her fault. He'd done this for her…

Colette bit her lip. Christian had gotten in deeper than he'd ever intended and now he was trapped. The men involved in operations like this weren't the forgiving kind. Maybe it was too late to get out; maybe he knew too much. That seemed the only logical explanation.

"It's weird, you know," Jenny was saying.

"What do you mean?" Colette asked. "Weird, how?"

"There've been all kinds of government agents here the last couple of days."

Colette closed her eyes and swallowed hard. "Do you have any idea what they were looking for?" Another thought hit her. Maybe Christian didn't *want* to be found. Maybe his disappearance was all part of some escape plan to avoid prosecution in the States. It made sense, and yet Colette couldn't make herself accept it. He'd told her he was coming back, asked her to wait. He would never have done that if he'd *planned* to disappear.

Jenny sighed. "The agents talked to several people but not to anyone I know well, otherwise I would've asked what it's all about. As you can imagine, the office has been buzzing, but it's hard to tell which rumors have any basis in truth and which don't."

"Would you phone me if you hear anything new?" Colette asked.

"I would if I had your number," Jenny said tartly. "You never answered my question. How come you disappeared like that?"

"I…needed a change."

"Of friends, too, it seems."

"I'm sorry, Jenny, it was just…too much. Do you understand?"

"Why are you so interested in what happened to Mr. Dempsey?"

"I worked for him for five years. Why wouldn't I be?"

"Okay, okay. Give me a number where I can reach you."

Colette rattled off her cell phone number. After thanking Jenny and agreeing to get together when this was all over, she replaced the receiver.

Elizabeth stood in the hallway, leaning against the wall. "What did you learn?" she asked.

Colette told her what little she knew, but she kept her own suspicions—and the part about the government agents—to herself.

Christian's great-aunt seemed to be more in control of her emotions now. "I don't suppose there's anything we can do other than pray," she said. She looked older and frailer.

"Let's have a cup of tea," Colette suggested. "My mother told me everything seems better after tea."

Elizabeth favored her with a smile. "Your mother is a wise woman."

"Yes, she is," Colette said. "I've missed her very much since my parents moved to Colorado."

Elizabeth headed back into the library. "I'd be honored if you'd consider me family," she murmured after slowly lowering herself into her chair.

"Then I will," Colette told her.

"Will you stay?" Elizabeth asked.

"Of course."

"Until we know?" she added. "I don't think my heart can deal with more bad news."

"I'll stay with you," Colette promised. Her own heart couldn't take any more bad news, either.

Thirty-Three

Alix Townsend

Jordan's parents had invited Alix and Jordan to a barbecue at their home on Sunday afternoon. Hoping to patch things up with her future mother-in-law, Alix had readily accepted. She made a bowl of potato salad and baked a rhubarb cake, one of Jordan's favorites.

Alix looked forward to being part of the Turner family, which she'd always seen as a delightful bonus to marrying Jordan. It was invitations such as this backyard barbecue that she'd longed for as a child. If her parents had friends over it was so they could drink together. What food there was on those occasions came from a fast-food joint.

When the kids at school talked about camping trips and picnics, Alix had nothing to say. Not once in the entire time she was growing up had she walked through the woods or experienced a family outing.

Her fantasy family in the closet did all those things,

though, and that was where Alix laughed and played and escaped.

Jordan picked her up before church and placed the salad in a cooler he'd brought in his trunk.

"That cake doesn't happen to be rhubarb, does it?" he asked, eyeing the glass dish hopefully.

"It might."

Grinning, he settled his arm around her shoulders. "You love me, don't you?"

"I must," she returned. He'd been teasing but she was entirely serious. She'd never been this happy, never known she could be. It still astonished her that this very special man could see past the gruff exterior she'd maintained a few years ago, when she was working at the video store. That was where they'd reconnected. She would be forever thankful for his persistence and his ability to recognize the *real* Alix Townsend beneath the spike-haired, leather-jacketed tough girl she'd been back then. Come to think of it, though, her *appearance* hadn't changed that much….

Today, however, in deference to his parents, she wore a straight khaki skirt, plain white blouse and ballet-style flats.

After church, Jordan drove to his parents' house in south Seattle. His father, Larry, was a pastor at the Free Methodist Church there. The parsonage was next door, a brick, single-family home built in the 1950s, long before either Jordan or Alix was born. The front lawn had recently been mowed and Alix could see a thin line of smoke spiraling from the backyard.

"Looks like Dad's already got the barbecue going," Jordan said as he led the way into the house. "Less work for me." He didn't knock, but opened the front door and walked in, calling out as he did. "Mom, Dad! We're here."

Susan came out of the kitchen, her face wreathed in a smile. She hugged each in turn, and Alix could tell that her welcome held nothing back.

"I brought a cake and a salad," she told her, setting the cake on the table. Jordan put the cooler on the kitchen counter.

"Alix," Susan said, "that wasn't necessary. My heavens, your wedding's next week! You must have a hundred things to do."

"Oh, no, everything's under control." Or it was now that the wedding had been scaled down to just Jordan's family and their own close friends. Alix loved the simplicity of it—especially compared to the five-act play, complete with sets, props and a cast of thousands that Jacqueline and Susan had tried to produce.

Jordan's father came inside, and father and son exchanged hugs.

Alix liked the fact that her fiancé and his father had such a good relationship. When it came time to start their family, she knew Jordan would be a wonderful dad and his parents would be ideal grandparents. That was a comfort—although the thought of motherhood still scared her. She told herself repeatedly that it was something she didn't need to worry about yet.

Susan had prebaked the spareribs and while Alix set the outdoor table, Larry and Jordan stood on the lawn by the barbecue. They chatted as Larry slathered the ribs in sauce, and their laughter floated over to her. Alix enjoyed their easy camaraderie.

"I talked with Grandma Turner," Susan said, joining Alix on the patio, carrying two glasses of lemonade.

"She's very pleased that you and Jordan are using the lake house for your wedding."

"She's been so good to us." Alix didn't know what she would've done without the love and support of Jordan's grandmother.

Susan handed Alix her lemonade. "I invited her to join us today, but she called this morning and said she was feeling a bit under the weather."

"The wedding isn't too much for her, is it?" she asked anxiously. Although she and Jordan had done everything they could to ensure that none of the burden fell on his grandmother, Alix was still concerned. Sarah was eighty-six, after all.

"No, no." Susan dismissed her question. "Grandma would be terribly disappointed if you and Jordan were married anywhere else. Besides, your wedding will be like a family reunion for her."

Alix took a small sip of her lemonade.

"What's going on with Colette's friend?" Susan asked next as they sat at the picnic table across from each other. "I was at the flower shop and Susannah said Colette's been off work because someone she knows— her former boss, apparently—has gone missing."

"Yeah." She nodded. "His name's Christian Dempsey."

The word was out to the media now, and there was plenty of speculation. "Isn't it bizarre?" Christian Dempsey's disappearance in China had made all the local newscasts.

"There's a front-page article in this morning's paper," Susan told her. "No one seems to know what's happened to him. When's the last time you talked to Colette?"

"Yesterday." Alix remembered their lengthy conversation. "She's staying with Christian's great-aunt Elizabeth. He's like a son to her and she's taking the news badly."

"I'm so sorry," Susan murmured. "We'll keep all of them in our prayers."

Alix mumbled her thanks. Extra prayers certainly couldn't hurt, and she'd given it a try herself, as well.

There was a pause as Susan leaned forward, tension in every line of her body.

"Uh, Alix." She cleared her throat. "I hear that Margaret Langley asked a favor of you." Susan seemed to be making an effort to sound casual.

Alix hid her frown behind the glass, sipping while she composed a response. She'd told Jordan about Margaret's request and while she hadn't explicitly asked him to keep their conversation to himself, she hadn't expected him to run tattling to his parents, either.

"Apparently she wanted some...help from you?" Susan elaborated.

Setting her glass on the picnic table, Alix wrapped her hand around it. "Jordan talked to you about that, did he?"

"I hope you aren't upset, but he did mention it to his father, and Larry told me." Susan seemed surprised by her reaction. "I would never have brought it up if I'd known...well, actually I would have. Do you mind if we talk frankly?"

Alix pushed the glass aside and nodded. "Sure, go ahead."

"I've come to love you, Alix. I want you to know that. I remember you as a child, attending Sunday school classes. You were always a sweet little girl, so eager to please and learn. When my husband started the bus ministry, we were so happy that both you and your brother were part of it."

It was difficult to hold back a snicker. "My parents were willing to send us anywhere as long as we were away from the house for a couple of hours on Sunday morning." She stared right into Susan's eyes. "You know, so they could sleep off their hangover."

Susan ignored that. "I remember how hard you tried to fit in with the other girls," she went on.

Alix remembered, too. She hadn't owned any clothes other than what she wore to school. There were no pretty dresses for her at Easter or Christmas. She felt fortunate if she got a piece of clothing that didn't come out of a secondhand store.

"I really stuck out, didn't I?" she said. She recalled how badly she'd wanted to win the Bible that was a prize for the kid who could recite the most verses from memory. She'd been willing to memorize a hundred of them. She'd won it, too, although she'd lost that Bible somewhere along the way. Her Bible and just about everything it stood for.

"Well, you weren't typical of the children in Sunday School," Susan confirmed.

"I still stick out, don't I?" Alix asked, getting to the essence of the conversation. "That's what you want to say, right?" Alix tried to make this as straightforward as possible. "Speaking plainly, you don't think I'll be a good wife for Jordan."

"No, no, that's not it at all," Susan rushed to explain. "It's just the church where you don't fit in." She sighed. "That sounds so unkind and I don't mean it to, Alix, I really don't. I'm thinking of Jordan a few years down the road when he's a senior pastor."

"In other words, you're afraid I'll be a hindrance to him."

"Being a pastor's wife takes a special kind of woman."

Alix took a moment to consider that. "You're saying I need to be more like you."

Susan shook her head. "It isn't easy working in a church, that's what I'm trying to say. People have no idea they're being so critical. The congregation will judge Jordan when they look at you."

"I see." Alix hadn't thought of it in those terms.

Susan glanced over her shoulder at her husband and son. "Larry doesn't know we're having this conversation," she said in a low voice.

"Does Jordan?" If he did, Alix swore she'd get up and walk out right this minute.

"Heavens, no!" Susan said. "I wanted this to be woman to woman."

Jordan's mother didn't need to say it; Alix already knew. She knew because she'd heard that one-sided conversation at the Donovans'. "Last month, a few days before I called off the big wedding," Alix said, staring down at her lemonade, "I was over at Jacqueline's. The two of you were talking on the phone and Jacqueline didn't realize I was in the house. I wasn't intentionally eavesdropping and should've left, but I heard my name mentioned. I got the gist of the conversation in about two seconds. You'd rather I didn't marry Jordan."

A flush of embarrassment rose to the other woman's cheeks. "No, that's not it at all! Oh, dear, I'm making a mess of this."

"Then explain it to me," Alix said, struggling not to sound defensive or angry.

"It's just that…" Susan paused. "I'll admit I've had some concerns and," she added quickly, "it's occurred to me that my son's ready to marry a woman with connections to a hit man."

"I know a few whores, too," Alix said as if this were all a joke. "Actually, they were pretty decent people. I'll bet that surprises you."

Susan blinked a couple of times.

"Did Jordan ever tell you about when I was living on the street? Or how often I ran away from foster homes?"

"Alix, I'm sorry," Susan whispered.

"Don't be. You're probably right. You expected your son to marry a pretty blond church girl. You certainly didn't expect him to choose someone with a mother in prison and a father who walked out and never looked back. I've committed my share of sins, done drugs, lived on the edge. I'm a long way from that skinny little girl working so hard to earn a Bible in Sunday School."

Jordan's mother paled.

"That isn't the worst of it," Alix told her coldly.

"Please, this isn't necessary," Susan pleaded. "Jordan loves you and—"

"Listen. What you need to understand is that I'm not the person I used to be," Alix said, swallowing the lump in her throat. She refused to allow Susan to see her cry. "Jordan knows that, but I don't think you do."

"Perhaps not," Susan admitted. "But what am I supposed to believe when I hear about people coming to you asking to have someone killed?"

"Not killed, injured," Alix corrected—as if that really made a difference. "Margaret wanted the man who attacked her daughter to hurt the same way he'd hurt her." She must have raised her voice because Jordan glanced at them.

"Did Dad tell you about that?" he asked his mother, hurrying over to where they sat.

Susan met Alix's eyes and silently pleaded with her not to divulge the rest of their conversation. "Yes, he did say something about it," she said tightly. "Alix and I were discussing…the incident."

Stepping up behind Alix, Jordan rested his hands on her shoulders. "Did Alix tell you what she told Margaret?" His voice was impassive but Alix could feel the intensity of his emotion.

His mother shook her head. "We hadn't gotten to that."

"She talked to Margaret about forgiveness," Jordan said. "What a marvelous response, don't you think? I'm pretty sure Margaret listened, too."

"I hope she did," Alix murmured, but she couldn't know for sure.

"She listened because Alix has experienced that kind of anger and pain herself. She doesn't like me to mention it, I know. It takes a pretty incredible woman to rise above the life Alix was forced into. Every day she amazes me more." He reached down to squeeze her hand. "Only someone who's learned to forgive great pain can help someone else who's still hurting."

Clasping his hand, Alix twisted around and shot him a warning glance, which Jordan ignored.

"That's one of the reasons Alix is going to be such an asset to me, in church and outside of it," Jordan continued. "People aren't afraid to talk to her about anything. That's the gift she brings to my ministry." His eyes met hers and he smiled. "Having been raised in the church, I have a hard time reaching street kids. They don't think I can identify with their problems and they're right, I can't. I've never spent a night sleeping in some alley. But Alix has and she's risen above it. They'll listen to her far more than they ever will me."

"Does a street ministry interest you?" his mother asked, sounding surprised.

Jordan nodded enthusiastically. "Mom, I don't want to preach to the choir for the rest of my life. A doctor goes to people who are sick. These kids need God's love. But I can tell them all about it and what they need to do and they'll yawn in my face. Then they look at Alix and see someone who's changed her life. Who do you think they're going to listen to? Me, who's lived a comfortable life, or Alix who's been where they are?"

Susan turned to Alix, her expression unreadable.

"It isn't just street kids, either. It's *everyone*. I couldn't have chosen a woman with a kinder heart. She cares about people and they see that and love her back." He paused. "I see the way kids gravitate toward her. She doesn't judge them, she listens with love and understanding and tells them there's a better way."

Once more Susan's eyes locked with Alix's.

"Jordan, would you bring me the plate?" his father called out from his position at the barbecue. "These ribs are done to perfection."

"Sure thing!" Jordan disappeared into the kitchen.

Susan hung her head. "I feel like such a fool, Alix."

"Why?" she asked. After his little speech about forgiveness, Alix couldn't possibly be angry. It hurt, what his mother had said, and it would take a while for that pain to go away; nevertheless, this was an important relationship to both her and Jordan. "You love your son and you want the best wife for him. I can't be upset about that."

"It's just... Oh, I feel so foolish. Jordan's right. You're going to make him a wonderful wife, and you're going to be a good pastor's wife, too."

She shrugged. "I plan to try."

"Please," Susan whispered and her voice cracked as tears filled her eyes. "Don't hate me."

Alix took the other woman's hand. "I don't."

"I've given you every reason to dislike me and despite that you've been nothing but kind. I'm so sorry. Can we put this behind us?"

"Isn't that what the Lord's Prayer is all about?" Alix asked. "Asking God to forgive us our trespasses as we forgive others'?"

Susan smiled through her tears. "I've been married to Larry for thirty-eight years and been a pastor's wife all that time, yet it seems I have much to learn from you." She stood, and came around the table.

Alix met her halfway and they held each other fiercely.

This was a new beginning—the beginning Alix had been hoping for.

Thirty-Four

Colette Blake

Colette couldn't sleep. It might as well be noon instead of three o'clock in the middle of a moonless night.

Every time she closed her eyes, all Colette could think about was Christian. The scenarios that ran through her tortured mind were so terrifying, she had to force herself not to scream or cry. Every day without news intensified her fear that Christian would never be found. China was a huge country and no one seemed to have any idea where Christian might be. No one was saying anything, at any rate.

Elizabeth had asked Colette to stay with her until this was resolved, one way or another. But how much longer should they continue to hold out hope?

Elliott Dempsey had landed in Beijing and phoned to tell them he'd spoken to the U.S. embassy. He'd hired an investigative team and was awaiting word. He phoned at least once a day with an update. So far every lead had come to an abrupt dead end. Christian had never arrived in Zhongshan—but this was information Colette already had. His trail began and ended in Beijing.

Climbing silently out of bed, Colette crept down the stairs. A glass of milk might help relax her enough to sleep.

When she came into the kitchen, Colette was surprised to find Elizabeth sitting at the table, dressed in a long robe. Her white hair hung down around her shoulders.

Elizabeth gave her a tired smile. "You couldn't sleep, either?" she asked.

Colette shook her head. "I came down for a glass of milk."

"I did, too, but it hasn't done me any good," the old woman said. "I doubt it'll help you, either."

"Give it time." It wasn't like Elizabeth to be so negative.

"Time! I've been sitting here for an hour and I don't feel the slightest bit tired yet."

"You haven't slept in days."

Elizabeth grimaced. "Neither have you."

That was true. Ever since she'd gotten word, Colette hadn't been able to rest for more than an hour or two. She couldn't release the tension—and the fear—that held her in its grip.

"Sit down," Elizabeth said. "We should talk."

Colette poured the milk, then sat at the wooden table, wondering what Elizabeth could possibly say that hadn't already been said a hundred times.

"Christian and I spoke the night before he left," the old woman began. "I wasn't going to tell you, but I think now…now that it's been nearly ten days without word… Well, I've decided you have a right to know."

She paused and Colette waited for her to go on, hardly daring to breathe.

"He came to me after I tried to play matchmaker." She revealed a hint of a smile and motioned with her hands, as if to say that entire scheme had been a failure. "I'm no good at subterfuge."

"It was sweet of you to try."

Elizabeth's eyebrows shot up. "That's a compliment compared to what Christian had to say on the subject."

"I can imagine." As long as she'd worked for him, Christian had never refrained from expressing his feelings.

"He told me it was better for both of you if he stayed away." Elizabeth scowled in disapproval. "I argued with him but it got me nowhere. Men! I never met one with a lick of sense. Even Charles…" Sighing, she lifted her shoulders in a resigned shrug. "Never mind, this is about Christian and not Charles, although they're more alike than I realized."

She sighed again. "Christian also said there were things he couldn't discuss. Why he'd say that to me, I have no idea. I tried to get him to talk but he refused. He said it was safer if I didn't know." Elizabeth seemed perturbed at his reticence. "He did tell me something significant, though. Perhaps he had a premonition that he wouldn't return, but…"

"Tell me!" Colette pleaded.

"It should come as no surprise. My nephew loves you."

Colette brought her hand to her throat. "He actually *told* you that?"

Elizabeth snorted. "Do you think I'm making it up?"

"No, but…" Tears filled her eyes.

"He's in some kind of trouble," his great-aunt said thoughtfully. "He wouldn't tell me, no matter how hard I pressed."

Colette lowered her head. "I know what it is."

Elizabeth stared at her, incredulous. "You *know* and you haven't said anything to me?"

"It's something you won't want to hear."

"You'd best tell me right this minute, young woman."

And so Colette did, describing what she'd found on his computer and her own reaction to it. She told Elizabeth about everything, including the anonymous letter she'd written to the INS, her suspicions about where he was now and why.

The old woman didn't ask a single question until Colette had finished. "You don't seriously believe my nephew's involved in human trafficking?" she said, incredulous.

"I...I'm not sure what to believe."

"My dear girl. Christian would no more sink to that level than I would. If you had a single active brain cell, you'd know that." Then, more sympathetically, she asked, "Have you been carrying this burden all these months?"

"I know what I saw," she said defensively.

"Or what you *thought* you saw," the old woman countered.

"He didn't deny it."

This gave Elizabeth pause, but only for a moment. "I refuse to believe it."

The baby moved, reminding Colette how much she had at stake. "The only thing we can do is ask Christian himself—once he's back," she said, unwilling to accept that he wouldn't return. Hope was all they had to live on, and for now it was enough to see her through another day.

They were silent for a long time after that.

"I have contacts in the government," Elizabeth eventually said. "I'll get to the bottom of this."

"But—"

"You should never have kept this information to yourself, Colette."

"But…"

"Had I known, I could have acted sooner."

"Who will you ask?"

She straightened. "Charles and I were good friends with the parents of our state senator."

"A…senator?"

"He'll get me the information I need. I wish you'd had the common sense to tell me all this before now," she complained again.

"Me, too, but I didn't want to distress you."

"Never mind." Elizabeth patted her hand. "At least you've told me. I'll deal with it, and we'll find out the truth, no matter how uncomfortable it is."

"Thank you," Colette said. "And you might've said something about what Christian told *you*."

Elizabeth had the grace to smile. "Yes, my dear, I suppose I should have." She gazed at Colette with somber eyes. "Let me tell you this. You hold his heart in the palm of your hand."

Colette felt a warmth that spread through her whole body. "And he has mine. All I hope is that he knows it."

Christian's great-aunt relaxed in her chair. "He visited me late that night—the night before he left. It was well past the time I generally retire, but I'd been reading. I'd just headed up to bed when he came unexpectedly to the house. I spoke to him about his manners, but I let him in." She shook her head in some amusement. "Men, especially the younger ones, have no sense of propriety."

Christian's visit had occurred the same night she'd gone to him. The night he'd kissed her.

"We had tea in the library," Elizabeth said, "and it was the best visit I've had with him in years. It reminded me of when he was a boy...." Her voice grew soft with affection.

Colette closed her eyes, picturing Christian with his aunt in this room she'd come to love, with its marble fireplace and row upon row of books. She could so easily see him there, leaning forward intently as he spoke.

"He told me about your...night together," Elizabeth continued, eyebrows raised. "Naturally, I didn't let on that I knew all about it—and its consequences."

"Thank you," was all Colette could say.

"It wasn't just for your sake, my dear girl. My nephew was making his grand confession. He was in a wretched state, certain that his impulsiveness had ruined everything. I wasn't about to admit that you'd already shared your secret with me."

"I'm...glad."

"He told me, as you had, that you'd worked for him for five years and that he'd never looked upon you as anything more than a valued assistant—until after your husband's death. He was also sure you'd seen him only as your employer. Until then..."

"I had."

"Afterward he said he'd behaved badly. He was afraid he'd destroyed your relationship. Apparently, you had the same reservations."

"Yes." Everything Christian had told his aunt was true. But two unexpected events had altered the situation. The first was the fact that she was pregnant and the second was what she'd discovered on his computer. She understood now that at least part of his reserve after the holidays could be attributed to his illegal activities.

Colette saw that Elizabeth was smiling now. "I've known Christian his entire life," the old woman said. "I know that young man better than his own father does. He can be stubborn and unreasonable. When he came to me that night, I saw him as a man in love, a man who feared he'd risked too much."

Tears clouded Colette's eyes as something else occurred to her. "It's like you said earlier—he suspected he might not come back. That's why he told you."

Elizabeth grabbed Colette's hand with surprising strength. "We have to trust he'll come home."

"I want him to know we love him," Colette whispered.

"He knows," Elizabeth said, her voice confident. "I have to believe he does."

Colette had to believe that, too.

"Now," Elizabeth said. "I'd suggest we try again to sleep."

Colette finished her milk, rinsed the glass and set it in the sink. Together, the two women climbed the wide sweeping staircase to the second floor. They parted there, Elizabeth going to her own room at the end of the hall, while Colette walked to the opposite end, to the guest bedroom.

For the first time since she'd arrived, Colette slept for four hours straight. When she woke, the sun was high and light spilled into the room.

Seconds later, she realized what had awakened her—the sharp ring of a phone. With a burst of hope, she tossed aside her covers and ran out of the room. She stood at the top of the stairs and listened as Elizabeth answered the phone. After the initial greeting, the other woman was silent for a long moment.

"Thank God!" she cried suddenly, but her exclamation of joy was immediately followed by a cry of frustration.

Colette moved down to the top step.

"Yes, yes, of course," Elizabeth was saying. "Don't spare any expense," she said. "Find him, Elliott, and don't come home until you do."

So Christian hadn't been rescued. Overcome by discouragement and frustration, Colette sank onto the step and buried her face in her hands. She didn't know how Elizabeth was holding up when Colette's own sense of hope was all but shredded.

Colette returned to her room and quickly pulled on slacks and a light sweater. She'd shower later. Right now, it was more important to learn what Elizabeth had been told by Christian's father.

Colette found her in the garden, watering her plants.

"I heard the phone," Colette said, stepping onto the back patio.

Elizabeth gasped. "Didn't anyone ever tell you to announce yourself properly instead of scaring people half to death?"

Taken aback, Colette froze. Then she saw that Elizabeth's cheeks were stained with tears. "Tell me," she whispered.

"We know where he went," Elizabeth said hoarsely. She took a moment to compose herself. When she spoke again, her voice was clear. "The investigator Elliott hired discovered that Christian ended up in a completely different city. A town actually. In Shanxi province."

"But...why?"

"That I can't answer."

Colette frowned. "Has Elliott tracked him down in this other place?"

"No." Elizabeth sighed heavily. "Not yet. He's making arrangements to search for him now. I trust he'll find Christian soon."

Colette did, too. She was counting on it.

Thirty-Five

"In knitting, as in life, there are usually two ways to go: The easy way and the hard way. Often we find out about the easy way only when we are three-quarters of the way through with the hard way."

—Ann Shayne and Kay Gardiner,
Mason-Dixon Knitting (Potter Craft, 2006)

Lydia Goetz

I was very concerned about Margaret. I couldn't ignore what Alix had told me about her wanting to pay someone to injure Danny Chesterfield. I waited, mulling over the situation before I approached Brad. When he heard my news, a dark frown crept slowly across his face.

"Do you think Matt knows about this?" he asked, bringing me a cup of coffee after dinner on Tuesday evening.

"I doubt it." I gratefully accepted the coffee. It had become our habit to sit down and talk after the evening meal. We took turns making coffee or tea, and now that it was springtime, we often sat on the patio behind the house. I treasured these hours with my husband, even when we just sat in companionable silence.

Brad lounged on the deck chair next to me and cradled his mug with both hands. "We should tell him," he finally said.

"I think so, too. Only…" I wasn't sure how to say this. "You know how private Margaret can be."

Brad looked over at me. "You don't want to offend your sister by going behind her back."

I nodded, feeling relieved at his understanding. "It might be best if we talked to the two of them together," I said.

"How do you figure Margaret will react to being confronted with this?"

"Probably not well," I admitted. "But I hope she'll realize I couldn't ignore this. I want her to know that I know." My worst fear was that my sister would end up in jail while Danny Chesterfield roamed free. But Margaret was already in a prison of her own making, confined by her hate and her unwillingness to come to terms with what had happened.

Brad stood abruptly and set his mug aside. "Let's go."

"Now?" I should've known he wouldn't want to delay doing something about this. Brad is a man of action.

I don't think the same way Brad does, which is one reason I hadn't mentioned it immediately. I needed to consider the problem from all angles, examine various options. Not Brad. He wanted to move forward, talk to Matt right away. A part of me was grateful not to carry this burden alone anymore, and yet I wasn't sure that marching over to Matt and Margaret's was the best course of action.

Brad settled the matter with one incisive question. "Do you want your sister to follow through with this?"

"No, but…"

"She will, Lydia."

I knew he was right and the longer we waited, the more likely it was that Margaret would find someone to commit this crime on her behalf.

Fortunately, Cody had gone to his friend Zack's down the street, and Mrs. Miller was happy to keep him there for another hour.

On the drive over to my sister's, I asked Brad to do the talking once we arrived. I was nervous. Margaret can take offense so easily and she'd be furious with me for involving myself in affairs she considered none of my concern.

I pictured her blowing up at me, quitting her job and cutting off our relationship. That would devastate me. My mind always seemed to gravitate to the worst possible scenarios. It's a tendency I've had for most of my life, even before the cancer. I find it frightening, unproductive and disconcerting—and I couldn't quite suppress a sigh as I thought about this. I was about to confront my sister and risk the very relationship I treasured most, outside of the one I shared with my husband and son. And yet I had no choice. All at once I felt like weeping.

As the cliché has it, Brad could read me like a book. When we parked in front of my sister's house, he gently took my hand. "Everything's going to work out," he assured me. "Don't worry, okay?"

I hoped he was right.

Matt opened the screen door for us even before we made it to the top step. He's a big man, tall and thick-waisted now that he'd reached middle age. I remember when my sister first started dating him in high school. I'd been half in love with him myself. My sister had chosen well; I liked and admired Matt.

"This is a nice surprise," Matt said, leading us into the house. He kissed me on the cheek, and he and Brad exchanged handshakes.

Margaret stepped out of the kitchen, a dish towel tossed carelessly over one shoulder. She looked instantly suspicious. "What's this about?" she asked.

"Sit down." My brother-in-law gestured toward the sofa, ignoring Margaret's lack of welcome. He turned off the television and, with his usual hospitality, offered us a drink.

We declined. Brad and I sat close to each other on the sofa. I folded my hands over my knees and waited for my husband to speak.

"I hope you'll excuse our coming without any advance warning," he began.

"Of course," Matt said, glancing toward Margaret. "You're welcome anytime."

Reluctantly, my sister sat down on the oversize chair beside Matt's recliner. A wicker basket next to the chair was filled with her knitting. I recognized the pattern; it was the prayer shawl the class had knit together. Everyone, even Colette, had finished by now. Everyone except Margaret.

"Lydia told me something this evening that worries her, and it involves you," Brad said. "I'll let her explain."

Both Matt and Margaret turned their attention to me. I looked at Brad, wanting him to do it. But apparently it was up to me. I leaned toward my sister, silently pleading for her forgiveness.

"Alix came to me the other day," I said after an awkward moment.

As soon as I mentioned Alix's name, Margaret crossed her arms and averted her eyes.

"You know what she told me, don't you?" I asked softly.

Matt looked over at his wife, who remained stubbornly silent, her lips pursed, her eyes flashing lightning bolts at me.

This was exactly what I'd feared. "Do you think I care what happens to Danny Chesterfield?" I blurted out, which I'm sure confused my brother-in-law even more.

"What's that creep got to do with anything?" Matt demanded of his wife.

Margaret ignored him and continued to hold my gaze.

"Don't you realize you're putting your entire family at risk?" I cried. "You could end up in prison!"

Matt stormed to his feet. "Would someone tell me what the hell's going on here?"

Brad stood, too. "Margaret's trying to hire a hit man to injure Danny Chesterfield."

The room went completely still as Matt digested those words. Then, as if the weight of this was more than he could carry, he sank into his chair, leaned his head back and closed his eyes.

Margaret had yet to utter a single word.

Finally, Matt straightened and turned to his wife. "What are you *thinking?*" he asked, his voice weary and discouraged. There was no anger in his question, only pain and confusion. "Why can't you let this go?"

For the first time since I'd started speaking, Margaret's gaze left mine. "I refuse to rest while that man walks around free to hurt someone else's daughter. Since our justice system has seen fit to release him, I don't have any choice but to take matters in my own hands."

"Have you hired someone?" Matt asked, raising his voice, something I was sure he rarely did.

"No."

"Tell me the truth."

"I haven't," Margaret snapped. "Alix wouldn't help and I didn't know anyone else to ask."

"Did you plan to stop there?" Matt pressed.

Her brief hesitation was followed by a muffled response. It sounded like "no."

This didn't surprise me. When Margaret wants something done, she finds a way to make it happen.

Shocking us all, Julia stepped out of the hallway. "Mom! What have you done?"

I'd hardly seen Julia since the attack and noticed the changes in her right away. She'd lost weight and cut her long blond hair. While the physical injuries had healed, I knew she still struggled with the emotional damage.

Margaret responded defensively, a typical reaction when she was caught. "Were you eavesdropping?"

"Yes." Julia didn't bother to deny it. "I couldn't help it. I heard Aunt Lydia and Brad stop by and I was coming to say hello when I heard what you'd done."

"This doesn't concern you," Margaret said resolutely.

Julia almost laughed. "How can you say that? I'm the one who was attacked. I'm the one who was dragged out of that car and thrown down on the road." She paused to glare at her parents. "I watched cars all around me slam on their brakes. They were trying to avoid running over me. That's what I dream about, being unable to move, paralyzed with fear on the street. The cars are all racing toward me, and they can't stop in time."

"Oh, baby." Matt stood and put his arms around his daughter.

Julia stifled a sob. "Mom, I can't deal with your anger anymore," she cried. "It wasn't *you* who went through this. It was *me*."

"I can't stand to see you hurt," Margaret said, pleading her case. "I hate the man who did this to you."

"You hate him enough to destroy all our lives?" Julia spun away from her father, hands tightened into fists at her sides. "Your anger isn't helping me, Mom. Don't you see that? It's hurting me. Each and every day I have to deal with my own pain and yours and Dad's, too. It can't go on…it can't." She covered her face with both hands and broke into heart-wrenching sobs.

Unable to bear seeing my niece weep like that, I joined her parents, putting my arms around the three of them. When we finally broke apart, Julia sat on the ottoman next to her mother. She reached for Margaret's hand and clasped it in her own.

"It's time we talked," Julia said, sounding more adult than any of us.

"I made a mistake," Margaret admitted in a voice that was barely audible.

"No," Julia said and shook her head dramatically. "I'm glad you did this, Mom, because it's brought everything to a head. That's what had to happen and so far it just hasn't. Everyone's so afraid of talking about the… accident and I need that. You and Dad need it, too. We all do," she said, looking toward the hallway.

Hailey came out from the shadows, her sweet face

streaked with tears. Slowly she walked into the room and sat on the sofa with Brad and me. I drew her close and she leaned against me.

"Everyone's so *angry*," Julia continued. "We all pretend there's nothing wrong, but there is. We can't go on ignoring the fact that I was attacked. I could easily have been killed—but I wasn't."

"I thank God you survived," Margaret whispered. Matt nodded.

"Afterward I didn't feel like I wanted to live, and you and Dad got me help. The counselor and I talked a lot. I learned that the feelings I had aren't uncommon. The counselor said lots of victims feel like I did." She took a deep breath. "I'm getting better now, and I've learned so much. I want everyone to know that."

Tears spilled down Margaret's cheeks.

"Mom," Julia said, looking up at her mother. "I was angry, too, so angry I actually wanted to die. I hated Danny Chesterfield the same way you do, but I've seen what that anger's done to you. I've seen what it's done to me."

Margaret nodded, wiping her face with one sleeve.

"Anger takes too much energy, too much effort," Julia said.

I wondered when my niece had got so smart and realized this wisdom was a by-product of her pain.

"After I was released from the hospital, I was obsessed with hurting him back. Thinking of ways to make him suffer was how I got through those first few weeks. I'd go to sleep at night and dream about throwing him into moving traffic and watching him scramble for his life like I did. I'd dream about standing there, watching him cry for help and then walking away and listening to his screams when he was hit by a car."

My sister bowed her head and instinctively I recognized that her daughter's words had struck a deep chord in Margaret.

"Then one day I was with some friends," Julia said, her voice dropping. "They asked me to do Relay for Life."

She smiled at me and I nodded, remembering the wonderful time we'd had together.

"My friends were raising money to save lives," Julia went on, "and while they were making a positive difference, I was plotting, dreaming, thinking about vengeance." She lowered her eyes as though ashamed. "I understood then that I didn't like the person I was becoming."

Tears filled my eyes and I tried to hide how intensely Julia's words had affected me. I saw that everyone else was equally touched. Julia's wisdom moved me, impressed me, and again I understood that this wisdom had come at a terrible price.

"Mom." Julia brought her mother's hand close to her own heart. "I probably won't ever be the same person I was before the carjacking and in some ways, that's good. But the one I'm worried about now is you."

Margaret lowered her head, unable to look her daughter in the eye.

"I need you to let go of your anger because I'm afraid I might never completely heal if you don't. Can you do that, Mom? Can you do it for me?"

Slowly Margaret raised her head. "I can try," she whispered.

"That's all I ask," Julia said.

Mom and daughter hugged.

Hailey excused herself and briefly left the room, returning with a box of tissues, which we all needed. Soon we were laughing and crying at the same time. That's how it is sometimes. The laughter can be as healing as tears.

Brad and I went home soon afterward and Margaret walked us to the door.

"Thank you," she whispered. It came as a surprise when she hugged me. Before she stepped back, she said close to my ear, "I'm going to be all right now."

I knew it was true. We all would.

Thirty-Six

Alix Townsend

The morning of June second, Alix woke up and remembered that this was her wedding day. She felt a sense of profound joy—but it was a joy mingled with sheer terror. Standing up in front of all those people, even though there'd be far fewer than the number originally invited, terrified her. But despite her fears, she wanted to do this, more than anything in her life. She loved Jordan and knew he loved her, but she wasn't unrealistic about marriage; love didn't mean there wouldn't be conflicts and problems. The difference was that if you loved each other, the way she and Jordan did, you could resolve those conflicts and find solutions to the problems.

Alix was too nervous and excited to have breakfast. At nine, Tammie Lee drove her to Grandma Turner's house, which was already stirring with activity.

Reese and Jacqueline had canceled the orchestra they'd hired for the country club reception; with Alix and Jordan's permission, they'd arranged for a five-piece band instead. The sound system people were getting everything set up.

The tent was raised, and the folding chairs stood inside in neat rows. Jacqueline had insisted on white wooden chairs with padded seats at a cost Alix didn't even want to think about. The caterers had arrived and were preparing the food. The French Café had delivered the wedding cake, a traditional cake Alix had baked and decorated herself. As a surprise for Jacqueline, she'd used a sweetened cream cheese frosting.

Susannah and Colette were there, too, working on the flower arrangements. They were filling large baskets with white roses, yellow daisies and sprigs of fern. Smaller bouquets of the same flowers were attached at the end of every row. The effect was simple, springlike and elegant.

The minute Alix caught sight of Colette, she flew across the grounds. "I can't believe you're here," Alix murmured, throwing both arms around her. The last Alix had heard, Christian still hadn't been located. Colette had kept a vigil with Christian's aunt since his disappearance became known, and Alix hadn't expected her to come to the wedding.

"I wouldn't miss it," Colette assured her, hugging her back.

"Christian?" Alix whispered.

Colette shook her head. "Nothing new." She looked tired but seemed to have found some measure of peace.

"I'm so glad you came," Alix said. "It means a lot to me."

Colette smiled at her. "Oh, Alix, you're going to be a beautiful bride."

"I'm about to be *married*." Alix giggled with happiness and headed toward the house, where Jacqueline and Reese were waiting for her. Family drifted in and out; someone had brought a large coffee urn and Jordan's relatives came in to help themselves to cups of coffee. Someone mentioned that Grandma Turner had decided to rest for a while. Alix didn't want to disturb her.

"The hairdresser's here," Jacqueline announced, ushering Alix into the house.

Alix glanced at her warily.

"Don't worry." Jacqueline must have read the look in her eyes. "It's not Desiree." Early in their friendship, Jacqueline had taken her to an expensive hairstylist named Desiree; this was the famous makeover disaster they still laughed about. "Desiree said I couldn't pay her enough to work on your hair again."

Alix grinned. Desiree wouldn't want to hear what she thought of her, either. "Just as long as I have final approval." She wasn't about to go through her wedding looking like one of the boys from that 1970s TV series, *The Brady Bunch.*

Jacqueline nodded and led her to the bathroom. In short order her hair was washed and blow-dried, curled and sprayed. Alix stared at her reflection and decided she rather liked this more mature version of herself.

"Is Grandma Turner still resting?" she asked. Any number of people had been in and out of the house all morning.

No one seemed to know. Her bedroom door remained shut. Alix had brought over her wedding dress earlier in the week and Grandma had insisted on hanging it on the back of her door.

Still in her housecoat and slippers, Alix approached

the bedroom. Her knock went unanswered. If Grandma Turner was sleeping, it was time to wake her. The photographer would be there soon and Alix wanted Grandma in the pictures.

After knocking a second time, Alix quietly opened the door, to see Jordan's grandmother sitting in the rocking chair by her bed, her Bible in her lap. The shawl Alix had knit was draped around her shoulders. It looked as if the old woman had been reading her Bible and fallen asleep.

"Grandma," Alix whispered, trying not to startle her.

Sarah Turner didn't respond.

Kneeling in front of her, Alix reached for Sarah's hand and swallowed hard when she discovered the fingers were stone-cold.

Alix knew that Grandma wasn't asleep.

She was dead.

She'd died that morning, reading her Bible and wearing her prayer shawl.

Sobs filled Alix's chest and she laid her face against Grandma's lap as she struggled for composure. When she could breathe evenly again, she lifted her face, gently touched the old woman's cheek and rose to her feet.

Alix stepped quietly out of the bedroom, closing the door behind her. The first person she saw was Jacqueline.

"Please find Jordan for me," she whispered brokenly.

"What's the matter?" Jacqueline asked.

"Just get Jordan. Please."

Jacqueline started to tell her it was bad luck for the groom to see his bride before the wedding, but Alix's expression obviously stopped her. "I saw him a little while ago. I'll look around."

She left, returning with him a few minutes later. Jordan frowned when he saw Alix still wearing her housecoat and slippers. He was in his tuxedo. "Is something wrong?"

Alix nodded and took his hand. Together they entered his grandmother's bedroom. Jordan knew instantly.

"I think she's been dead a couple of hours," Alix told him. Her voice faltered, and when she could speak again, she asked in a hoarse whisper, "What should we do?"

Jordan sat on the edge of his grandmother's bed and lowered his head as the realization hit him. "My grandmother loved you, Alix. I don't know why the Lord chose to take her home this morning, but He did. Everyone's here. It seems to me that this was exactly what Grandma was waiting for—to see us happy and to have all her family around her. We're getting married today. Grandma would want us to. Her love is here."

Jordan stood and wrapped his arms around Alix, then briefly buried his face in her shoulder. "I'll tell my parents."

While Jordan went in search of his family, Alix removed her wedding dress from his grandmother's door and slipped into it. She went out into the kitchen, beckoning to Jacqueline and Tammie Lee. They found a private corner, and while she explained the circumstances, Tammie Lee fastened the buttons in the back of Alix's dress.

Larry and Susan Turner rushed into the house and Jordan brought them to the bedroom, where Alix joined them a few minutes later. Jordan's mother had dissolved into tears.

Jordan placed his hand on his father's shoulder as Larry slumped on the bed.

"What about the wedding?" Susan jerked up her head. "We can't cancel it at the last second like this. We've already canceled it once and—"

"Mom, it's all right. Alix and I have decided to go through with the ceremony."

His mother sniffled loudly and nodded.

"She went so peacefully," Larry whispered. He looked down at his mother, her Bible open on her lap, and a fleeting smile touched his lips. "When my time comes, I want to leave this earth just the way she did."

"Oh, Larry," Susan cried. "How can you say that? You'd think your mother could have timed it better, wouldn't you?"

"We don't make those decisions, Susan," her husband reminded her. "It was God's timing."

"I don't care whose timing it was, it was bad."

Larry simply shook his head.

"Are you up to performing the ceremony?" Jordan asked him.

Larry nodded.

"We can't have the wedding with your mother's body in the bedroom!" Susan dabbed at her eyes with a tissue she'd extracted from her purse.

"I'll contact the sheriff," Alix said, taking control. She could tell that Jordan's family had all they could do to deal with their shock and grief. "The sheriff will send the coroner."

As Alix talked to the sheriff's office, Jordan's family—his older brother, Bret, his uncles, aunts and cousins—came to bid their grandmother farewell. How ironic that a day meant for joy should be so full of sorrow...and then joy.

The sheriff's patrol car arrived at the same time as the musicians. The rows of chairs had started to fill up with wedding guests.

Alix met the sheriff, whose badge identified him as Lyle Carson, and led him inside the house. The bedroom was crowded with weeping family members. She could only imagine what it must look like, a bride in her dress and gown leading him to the body.

He removed his hat and asked Alix a few questions, as she seemed to be the only one capable of answering. The coroner came shortly afterward and it was Alix who answered his questions, too.

While he examined the body, Alix ushered everyone out of the bedroom and directed them to join the other guests.

"Larry," she said to her soon-to-be father-in-law, "you need to go to the tent now with Jordan and Bret." Bret had flown in from California and was standing up as Jordan's best man. "I suggest you tell our guests what's happened. Perhaps you should call for a moment of silence and then say a prayer."

Larry nodded and followed her instructions.

Taking Susan's hand, Alix guided her out of the room, whispering reassurances as she went. Jacqueline came to their side, and Alix asked her to help Susan repair her makeup.

The rest of the family moved slowly toward the tent.

The photographer wandered aimlessly around, looking confused and uncertain. "Take a bunch of random shots of the wedding," Alix told him. "As much as possible, avoid getting any of the emergency vehicles."

He nodded.

Colette approached her. "Is there anything I can do?"

"Thank you for asking, but I can't think of a thing."

The musicians began to play the wedding march and Colette gave her a swift hug. "Go," she said with a warm smile. "You're about to become a bride."

"Your guests have been apprised of the circumstances," Reese whispered when he met Alix outside the tent. "It was handled beautifully by Jordan's father." He offered her his arm as he prepared to escort her down the aisle. His smile revealed his pride. "I have to say, Alix Townsend, you're really something. I don't know of anyone who could've dealt with this crisis as well as you have."

Alix smiled shakily. The music continued and with her head held high, she walked toward her groom.

On her side of the aisle were all the people Alix loved. Lydia, Brad and Cody, who squirmed until he saw her and then waved frantically. Carol, Doug and Cameron sat in the second row. This was the first time Alix had seen her friend in a maternity dress. Elise and Maverick were there, and Bethanne and Annie, along with Susannah, Joe, Chrissie and Colette. She saw her friends from the French Café, too.

Alix could hardly believe how many friends she'd made these last few years. It'd all begun the day she'd impulsively crossed Blossom Street and signed up for a knitting class. Who would've guessed that such a simple decision would forever change her life?

As she stood beside Jordan and they exchanged their vows, Alix saw the love in her husband's eyes and knew it was a reflection of her own. As soon as the ceremony was over, Jordan kissed her. His father announced them as Mr. and Mrs. Jordan Turner, and there was a moment of sustained applause.

Everyone made an effort to celebrate, despite the sadness of that morning. They enjoyed the meal, the music, the conversation with family and friends. At around 7:00 p.m. Alix and Jordan were leaving for Victoria, British Columbia, where they'd have a two-day honeymoon.

"Are you sure we should go?" Alix asked after they'd cut the cake and made a final round of their guests.

"We should," he insisted. "Dad and I talked it over, and we decided to hold Grandma's funeral on Tuesday, the day after we get back."

"Okay." Under no circumstances did Alix want to miss it.

As she changed out of her wedding dress and into comfortable traveling clothes, Susan Turner joined her.

"Oh, Alix," she whispered and snapped open her purse to search for another tissue. "I don't know what we would've done without you today."

Alix was uncomfortable with the praise.

"You took care of everything."

"I didn't do—"

"Yes, you did." Susan touched her arm. "You kept your head, you held the family together, you and Jordan made crucial, on-the-spot decisions."

Alix shifted from one foot to the other. "Speaking of Jordan, I'd better go find my husband." Calling Jordan her husband for the first time seemed momentous to Alix. Until now, the meaning of that word had been abstract, impersonal, describing a role, not a man.

Now it meant Jordan.

Husband.

Alix had never realized how intimate it sounded. Intimate and yet public—a declaration of love and belonging.

"I won't keep you." Susan hugged her tightly. "I hope we can be very good friends, Alix."

Alix hugged her in return. "It'll be nice to have a mother," she whispered.

Thirty-Seven

Colette Blake

After Alix and Jordan's wedding, Colette returned exhausted to Elizabeth's home. They had a quiet dinner of shrimp salad later that evening. Neither of them spoke much. With every day that passed, their hope diminished. It was only a little after nine when Colette excused herself and climbed up the stairs to bed.

Surprisingly, she fell asleep almost right away, only to be awakened abruptly by Elizabeth at around ten. "Colette," the older woman said excitedly, coming into the bedroom and turning on the overhead light. "Christian's been found! He's alive!"

Colette immediately sat up and blinked against the bright light and the shock.

"He's on the phone," Elizabeth told her.

"You mean *now?*" Colette cried, thinking this must be part of some wonderful dream.

"Yes, yes! He's waiting to talk to you."

"Oh, thank God, thank God." Tearing aside the

sheets, Colette leaped out of bed and raced down the stairs so fast her bare feet slipped on the carpeted steps. Breathlessly, she grabbed the hallway phone.

"Christian? Christian!"

"Colette?" He sounded as if he was phoning from the moon. She heard an echo, and his voice seemed tinny and distant.

"Yes, yes, it's me! Are you all right? Where are you?" She dashed away tears of relief and joy.

"I'm okay," he said, "and anxious to get home. I'll land tomorrow night. Will you be there? I have so much to tell you."

"Yes, yes, I'll come to the airport. What time?"

He gave her the airline and flight number while she frantically searched for a pen and paper to write it down. When she had all the details, she repeated them back to him.

"I'll be there, Christian. I'll see you tomorrow...."
She was so excited now she doubted she'd sleep again.

"Colette, listen," he said, speaking quickly. "I know I'm throwing this at you out of the blue, but I need to tell you something important. I'm not involved in smuggling. I couldn't tell you before, but the INS sent me to China. We were cooperating with the Chinese government. I was supposed to make contact with some smugglers. Get evidence."

"Christian, tell me later. As long as you're safe..."

"I can't spend another second having you believe I'm a criminal! Colette, I—"

There was a burst of static on the line, cutting him off.

Colette wanted to scream with frustration. "Repeat

that," she pleaded when he came back on. "I couldn't hear you."

"I have to go. I love you, Colette. I love you."

"I love you, too," she cried. The connection was completely broken then, but she held the receiver against her ear, letting his parting words settle over her. *He loved her.*

After a few minutes, she reluctantly hung up the phone and turned to find Elizabeth standing at the top of the stairs.

"Christian's coming home!" she shouted. "He's safe!" That was by far the most important news. Christian who'd been lost had now been found, and even better, he'd soon be on a plane and flying home. "He told me he's working with the INS—"

"I learned that, too," his great-aunt interrupted.

"Your sources…"

"I couldn't get a thing out of them," she muttered, shaking her head as if to say it was a sad state of affairs when the government didn't trust her with its business.

"He's safe," Colette repeated simply to hear the words again. "He's safe."

"I certainly hope he realizes he's put us both through hell," Elizabeth said briskly.

"Well, it was hardly his fault," Colette murmured. Then she smiled, and because it was impossible to hold back the words any longer, she cried, "He loves me."

Elizabeth sighed impatiently. "I already told you that."

"I know, but he said it to me himself." That made all the difference.

The old woman nodded and a slow smile creased her face. She looked more than a little pleased with herself. "Perhaps international intrigue has its uses, after all." She raised her eyebrows. "An experience like that would make a person appreciate what—or should I say whom—he's got at home."

Twenty hours later, Colette and Elizabeth were at Sea-Tac Airport, waiting outside the secure area for Christian and his father to clear customs. Their flight had landed on time and without incident, according to the monitors. Colette should know; she'd checked them often enough.

Colette paced while Elizabeth sat restlessly. "What could be taking them so long?" his great-aunt complained. "I'm an old woman and these seats are a form of torture."

"He's with his father, you said." Colette remembered Elizabeth's telling her that their relationship had been strained for years.

"I assume so," Elizabeth said irritably. "How am I supposed to know all this? I *assume* they're flying back on the same flight. If so, that's no guarantee they're speaking. Both of them are stubborn fools."

All Colette could do was pray that this misadventure had torn down the walls between father and son. She knew only a little about their history but enough to gather that their estrangement had hurt them both.

People started to emerge from the customs area a few at a time and then finally the door opened and Elliott Dempsey stepped out, followed by his son. Christian looked thin and tired and badly in need of a shave.

Christian immediately searched for Colette. She hurried forward, and the biggest smile she'd ever seen appeared on his face. He held out his arms.

Without a pause, Colette walked into his embrace.

For the longest moment all they did was cling to each other. Then he kissed her, his hands cradling her face, his mouth moving over hers. Soon she was crying, her relief overwhelming even her joy. Christian kissed her cheeks, her tears, his unshaven face scraping her skin as they rocked back and forth in each other's arms.

"Hello, Aunt Elizabeth," he said after a few minutes, speaking over Colette's shoulder, still holding her against him.

"Glad to see you, too, young man," she said with her customary curtness. "I hope you know this nonsense of yours cost me ten years of my life. I'm too old to worry like that."

"Sorry, Aunt Betty."

"My name is Elizabeth and you well know it."

With her arm around Christian's waist, Colette turned to find Elizabeth glaring at him with tears in her eyes.

Christian released Colette and wrapped his aunt in a fierce embrace, lifting her off the ground.

"Put me down this minute," she insisted.

"Yes, Aunt Betty."

"Stop calling me that!"

"Yes, ma'am. Anything else I can do for you?"

Elizabeth glanced at Colette and then back at her great-nephew. "As a matter of fact, you can. Marry this woman." Her gaze shifted to meet Colette's. "Soon, if you know what's good for you."

"Elizabeth," Colette chided, flushing with embarrassment.

"I'll take it under advisement," Christian said, smiling down at Colette.

Elliott approached them, dragging a small suitcase.

Introductions were quickly made, and Colette studied the older man. So this was Christian's father. Despite his rumpled clothes and unshaven appearance, he had a dignity that impressed her.

Somehow, the news had gotten out to the press, and as soon as they walked into the main part of the terminal, the small group was bombarded with reporters. The flashes from a dozen cameras nearly blinded Colette, who put her hands in front of her face. Questions were fired at Christian, one after another. He answered a few, then authoritatively steered Colette, his aunt and father toward the car that awaited them.

Elizabeth and Elliott sat on one side of the stretch limo; Christian and Colette sat opposite them.

While his great-aunt and father spoke quietly, Christian whispered in her ear. "Come home with me." His hand gripped hers. "I need you."

She nodded. She needed him, too.

When the vehicle stopped at his great-aunt's home, Colette ran in to collect her things. Elizabeth watched her climb back into the car, a disapproving glint in her eyes. "Make sure there's a ring on your finger before you give him what he wants," she said loudly enough for Christian to hear.

"Yes, Aunt Betty," she teased, and when the older woman frowned, Colette gave her a big hug.

During the short drive from his aunt's house to his father's, it became apparent that Christian and Elliott's relationship had come a long way. They spoke to each other with affection and familiarity, laughing more than once. Christian walked his father to the front door and she watched as the two men exchanged first handshakes and then hugs.

Christian was silent when he returned to the vehicle. "I didn't know if I'd survive this, Colette. All I could think about was getting back to you." He reached for her hand again, entwining their fingers. "It wasn't supposed to be dangerous, you know. The government's occasionally used other businessmen to do this sort of thing in the past. All I had to do was meet with the smugglers—pretend to work with them. A setup, in other words. Then two of them kidnapped me in Beijing and took me to a small rural town in Shanxi province. I still don't know how they found out. But somehow they were on to me—" He shuddered visibly.

"Tell me the rest later," Colette said. "The only thing that matters right now is that you're here."

They arrived at the house and Christian let them inside. Closing the door, he gathered her in his arms and kissed her until she thought she'd faint with longing and need.

Christian rested his chin on the top of her head. "I'm exhausted. I feel like I could sleep for a month."

"I know." Colette nodded. "Go to bed now."

Christian leaned back, looking directly into her eyes. "Come with me."

The temptation was as strong as a riptide. But she shook her head, slowly, regretfully. "We have to talk first."

His disappointment was obvious.

"Sleep," she suggested, "and when you wake, I'll be here."

He seemed about to argue with her. Instead, he murmured "Good night," and disappeared into a room at the end of the hallway. She checked on him an hour later and discovered he was dead to the world. He lay stretched out on the covers, still wearing his clothes.

Colette opened windows to let in the mild June air and disperse the stuffiness of a house that had been shut up for more than three weeks. She found a can of soup in the kitchen, heated that for dinner and phoned Elizabeth to assure the old woman that her morals were safe.

"You tell him he *has* to marry you," Elizabeth insisted.

Colette planned to do no such thing.

She slept in a spare room and woke at about seven the next morning, when she heard Christian rummaging in the kitchen. After dressing, she joined him. "Good morning," she said cheerfully.

She was glad to see that he looked rested. His hair was damp, he'd shaved and wore black slacks and a teal sweater, which highlighted his blue eyes.

"You must be starved," she said.

"I am," he agreed, "but before I do anything—other than have a coffee—I want us to talk."

Colette hadn't expected it to happen this soon and she wasn't ready for it. "Let's sit down," she said. He'd made a pot of coffee and carried his mug over to the table. She located tea bags and heated water in his microwave.

"I love you, Colette," he said, just as she took the chair opposite his.

Her lips trembled as she savored his words. "I love you, too."

"A lot of things happened before I left for China," he said. He took her hand in his.

"Who were those men that night?"

She didn't need to clarify her question. "The evening

before I flew into China," he said, "I met with a group of government agents."

"Those men were with the government?" Colette remembered the two Asian men and had assumed they were involved with the smuggling. Instead they worked for the Immigration and Naturalization Service.

"Just before Christmas, I was approached by some of my contacts—here and in China—about being part of their smuggling operation. They had a system all worked out and wanted to include me. They thought I could manage to get them some sort of cover through my importing business. I went to the INS, who asked me to follow through. Or pretend to, at any rate."

Colette tightened her fingers around his. "You took a very big risk," she said in a tearful voice.

He grimaced. "I knew people were being exploited. I didn't feel I had much choice. However, I couldn't tell anyone—like you. For everyone's protection, this had to be completely covert."

"How did you finally get out? Did you escape?"

"I couldn't—they watched me day and night. I was in some kind of makeshift prison for two weeks. What a hellhole! I could even hear my guards arguing about the best way to kill me."

Colette was horrified at the thought. He would never have been seen or heard of again; she would never have known what had happened to him.

"I think the reason they didn't murder me right away," he went on, "is that I'm a fairly well-known businessman, and there might be repercussions if I simply disappeared. Still... I knew I probably wouldn't see you again. I expected to die, and just when I'd given up all hope, I was rescued by a coalition of American military and Chinese police."

Colette gave him a puzzled glance. She'd combed the newspapers for any information to do with China and hadn't seen a single mention of the undercover operation. "There was nothing about it in the papers."

"There won't be. The government wants to keep it quiet."

"For obvious reasons," she murmured.

Christian nodded.

"What about the anonymous letter I wrote?"

"I will say that letter stirred up a bit of interest," Christian said with a grin. "If anything, though, it worked to my advantage. It deflected any suspicion the smugglers might have had—at least the ones in North America." He gave her a solemn look, all traces of his smile gone. "I hated deceiving you, Colette, but I didn't have a choice."

She'd hated deceiving him just as much; like Christian, she didn't feel there was any option. She'd had to keep the baby a secret from him.

They moved into the living room; when he chose the sofa, clearly expecting her to sit there, too, she sat in a spindly antique chair across from him.

"Is anything wrong?" he asked.

When she shook her head, he frowned. "Then why are you over there and not next to me?"

"Because I have something important to tell you and I'm not sure how you're going to react."

"Okay," he said after a brief hesitation, "maybe you'd better tell me now."

She braced herself, struggling to come up with the

right words. In the end she just told the truth, without explanation or embellishment. "I'm pregnant."

The color drained from his face. The longest minute of her life passed before he responded. "Is the baby Steve's?"

She shook her head again, then looked up and held his gaze. "The baby's yours."

If she thought he was pale before, it didn't compare to the shock that showed on his face now. "I...asked," he reminded her. "After that night, I came to you and asked if you were pregnant, remember?"

"I know. I lied. I'd found what I felt sure was damning evidence against you. I was afraid I couldn't trust you. All I could think of was to get away."

He leaned forward and ran his fingers through his hair. "That explains so much." Still holding her gaze, he said, "I love you, Colette. I want our baby. I understand why you kept this from me, but please say you believe me now."

"I do."

"How can I prove to you that I'll be a good husband and father? Just tell me and I'll do it."

An involuntary smile came then, because she'd never dared hope Christian would want their baby, let alone her. Only in the last month had she begun to feel there might be a chance for them.

"What you found on my computer was only part of the reason you resigned, wasn't it?"

Not trusting herself to speak, she nodded.

"The baby played a role in that decision, too."

Again she nodded.

"Then you sold your house and moved because you didn't want me to find you?"

"Yes, but you did track me down," she pointed out, "and for someone with your resources, that couldn't have been too difficult." She shrugged. "I wanted a fresh start, a new life for me and the baby."

"The baby—that's why you came to see me the night before I left for China?"

"That, and because I'd fallen in love with you." Colette smiled. "It's why your aunt was trying to be a matchmaker. But by then, I'd decided I had to tell you."

"Aunt Elizabeth knows?"

"Three people know—my friend Alix, your aunt Elizabeth and now you. I admitted it to your great-aunt the first time we met." She'd never intended to, but such were Elizabeth's powers of persuasion… "All these months I'd kept this secret to myself. Not even my parents know. Then I met your aunt…and she figured it out."

"Good old Aunt Betty." It was Christian who smiled this time. "No wonder she demanded I marry you." He straightened with a startled expression. "I'd want to marry you, with or without the baby. A child—our child—is a bonus I never anticipated." He looked at her carefully. "You're six months along?"

"Five and a half. My due date's September twenty-first."

"I thought…you know, that you might've put on a few pounds, but I never guessed *this*. I…"

She sat beside him and reached for his hand, which she placed on her stomach. Their child responded as if on cue. The look of astonishment on Christian's face made her giggle. And then he smiled with such unreserved love and pride and joy, it brought tears to her eyes.

Holding her in his arms, he kissed her again and again, pausing only long enough to beg her to marry him.

"Yes," she told him, kissing him back.

"Soon?" he asked.

"Soon," she promised.

Thirty-Eight

Lydia Goetz

I'd hoped that after Brad and I confronted my sister, there'd be a marked change in Margaret's attitude toward Danny Chesterfield. My niece had made such a poignant plea to her mother that I couldn't see Margaret ignoring Julia's feelings.

Julia had impressed me with her insight, and what she'd said revealed wisdom far beyond her years. Julia knew she couldn't heal until her mother let go of her hatred; she couldn't move forward in her own life until Margaret did the same.

Unfortunately, I hadn't seen the change I'd hoped for in Margaret. This didn't completely surprise me, since my sister is rarely effusive. I hardly ever know what she's thinking, unless it's negative. Then there's never any doubt. The first day I opened for business was a good example of that. Margaret marched in and told me A Good Yarn was doomed to failure. After that cheery announcement, she promptly left.

I'll never forget her dire prediction (which of course didn't come to pass). I also recall, just as vividly, the day I realized how much my sister loves me. A few months after I opened the yarn store, I had a cancer scare. *Scare* is a mild word to describe what I felt. *Panic* is more like it.

I was in the hospital. Margaret, who hates hospitals, came to see me and dragged Brad in with her. In my hopelessness and despair, I'd broken up with Brad, but she simply would not believe I didn't want to see him again. So she'd taken matters into her own hands. That was a love so clearly spelled out I couldn't disregard it.

If I were to look for a turning point in our relationship, I'd have to say that was it. She wept with me when I learned I was cancer-free. In some ways, I think she was more relieved than I was. You see, I'd already made my decision. If the cancer had returned for the third time, I was going to refuse treatment.

It all seems rather melodramatic now. Thankfully, the decision was taken away from me and the truth of it is that I don't really *know* if I would've followed through. To refuse treatment meant almost certain death. No matter what I said, a part of me, even during the worst of the chemo, wanted to live. And now there's no doubt at all about the decision I'd make if cancer ambushes me again.

It was Tuesday, and I'd arrived at the shop early to pay bills and take care of some paperwork.

A lot had been happening recently. First, there was Alix and Jordan's wedding. Alix had looked lovely, so happy. But shortly before the ceremony, Pastor Turner, Jordan's father, announced that his mother had died that morning. He'd told us she had her family there, gathered around her, and how she was ready for death. His prayer was moving and what might have been a tragedy became a celebration as Alix and Jordan exchanged their vows and honored a woman they both loved.

Colette had mysteriously gone missing after the wedding, although I saw on the news that Christian Dempsey was back, and I suspected they were together. I caught a glimpse of her during the impromptu press conference at the airport on Monday. She was standing to the side and her eyes never left his face. I had to wonder if there was another wedding in the making.

Mom was nicely settled in at the memory care facility and had made yet another major adjustment. Every day I marveled at the transformation in her since she'd started getting the kind of individual care she needed. In barely two weeks, she'd improved noticeably, joining in the center's activities and having meals with the other residents.

The door opened at ten and Margaret walked into the store. She slapped the morning paper on the corner of my desk, where I'd been sitting with my cup of tea and a stack of bills.

"Did you read this?" she demanded.

"Ah…" I'd glanced at the headlines but little else. "I scanned the front page. Why?"

"Look in Section B." Margaret handed it to me. Arms crossed, she stepped back and waited.

It was all the routine local stuff—break-ins, accidents, police activities. Not wanting to admit I couldn't find what she wanted me to read, I shrugged.

Margaret rolled her eyes, then pointed to a small article at the bottom of the page.

Two lines into the piece, I read the name Danny Chesterfield.

"He was caught," I said.

"So it seems." There was no disguising the glee in Margaret's voice. "He pulled another carjacking, only this time there was a patrol car driving past. Danny Boy pushed the driver out of the way and took off. The cops chased him."

"He decided to make a run for it?" I asked.

"And put several innocent bystanders at risk," Margaret said. "Fortunately, no one, including the driver, was injured."

"But he didn't get away, did he?"

"No," Margaret replied, hardly able to contain her delight, "and the one involved in an accident was none other than Mr. Chesterfield himself."

My attention returned to the article. Apparently Chesterfield swerved in order to avoid a head-on collision with a second police car, lost control of the vehicle and flipped over at least twice.

"He won't be released for lack of evidence *this* time," Margaret said. "There's no need to get someone to give him an alibi, either."

I nodded and continued reading. "It also says he's in the hospital."

"Good. I hope he's in a lot of pain."

"Margaret!"

"Do you want me to lie?"

"No, but a little compassion wouldn't hurt."

"Compassion?" Margaret repeated. "I have as much compassion for him as he did for my daughter."

I refolded the newspaper and gave it back to my sister. I'd really hoped Margaret had listened to Julia, but evidently not.

"Don't look at me like that," she muttered.

"Like what?"

"Like I'm a big disappointment to you."

"Oh, Margaret," I said, growing tired of the discussion. "You aren't a disappointment. I don't have any love for Danny Chesterfield either, you know. He hurt Julia and his actions have affected our entire family. Even Mom's sensed that something's wrong."

"The article said he's in serious but stable condition."

I'd read that, too. "He'll live," I muttered.

"Better yet, he's going to jail."

I had to agree; learning Danny Chesterfield would soon be incarcerated didn't bother me any.

"You know what Julia said when I told her?" Margaret asked. She didn't wait for a response. "Julia said revenge wasn't for us to exact. Danny Chesterfield will pay for his crimes. In our justice system or a higher one…"

Once again, I felt there was much my sister could learn from her daughter.

The subject of Danny Chesterfield wasn't brought up even once as we charged through our day. Margaret turned over the Closed sign to read Open, flipped on all the lights and stopped to pet Whiskers, who'd taken his spot in the display window.

No sooner had she unfastened the lock than our first customer arrived. I hadn't finished with my paperwork, so Margaret waited on her.

Even at the best of times Margaret isn't a chatty person, but as the day wore on I noticed that she seemed quieter than usual. I knew our brief conversation that morning weighed on her mind. Frankly, it did on mine, too.

John F. Kennedy is reported to have said that we can forgive our enemies but we shouldn't forget their names. I wasn't forgetting Danny Chesterfield anytime soon, but to the best of my ability I'd forgiven him. I don't mean to sound like some spiritual giant who could magnanimously offer this man my pardon. For one thing, I had far less to forgive than my sister. Julia was my niece, not my daughter. This man had put Margaret and Matt through hell when he hurt Julia.

Toward the end of the afternoon, Margaret approached me. I'd returned to my office to complete some orders. "Can you come with me after work?" she asked.

I assumed she wanted the two of us to visit Mom. "Of course."

Margaret nodded and offered me a smile that wasn't quite a smile. "Thank you."

I almost asked, "For what?" Margaret was thanking me? *That* was a rare occurrence.

"You *were* talking about going to visit Mom, weren't you?" I pressed, suddenly unsure.

Margaret shook her head. "No, actually I was thinking of going to the hospital."

Sometimes I can be a little slow, but for the life of me I couldn't recall who we knew in the hospital. My confusion must have shown on my face because Margaret walked over to my desk, picked up the folded newspaper and waved it in front of me.

"You want to visit *Danny Chesterfield?*" I asked, so astonished I could barely get the words out.

"You aren't going to change your mind, are you?"

My immediate reaction was to do exactly that. I had absolutely no desire to see Danny Chesterfield. He probably had no desire to see Margaret and me, either.

"What possible good will that do?" I asked.

"Are you coming or not?" she demanded. "A simple yes or no will do."

"Ah…"

"Fine, suit yourself," she snapped, walking quickly as if she couldn't get away from me fast enough.

I took a couple of minutes to consider before I followed her. "I'll go," I said in as neutral a voice as I could manage.

"Don't do me any favors."

"I'm not," I told her, although this definitely felt like one.

While Margaret was busy helping a customer, I called Brad on his cell phone and told him I'd be home a bit later than usual and why.

"You're doing *what?*" he said when I'd explained Margaret's request. "Do you really think this is a wise idea?"

"Which? Margaret visiting Danny Chesterfield or me going with her?"

"Both!"

"I don't know," I answered honestly.

For a moment I thought Brad was going to try to dissuade me, but he didn't. I was grateful for that because I wasn't sure what I would've done if he'd asked me not to go.

After Margaret and I closed up shop for the day, we

decided to leave my vehicle in the parking area. Margaret could drive, since it seemed pointless to take two cars, especially during rush-hour traffic.

The first place we went was the information desk at Harborview, the hospital where, according to the paper, Chesterfield had been taken. The clerk there checked her computer. "Daniel Chesterfield was brought in two days ago by an emergency medical vehicle and released to local authorities this morning."

Margaret nodded.

I didn't have a clue what that could mean. "In other words, he's in jail now?" Apparently his injuries weren't significant enough to keep him hospitalized.

"He's in the King County Medical Facility at the jail," the woman said.

"Oh…"

"Thank you," Margaret said, and together we hurried out of the hospital.

"Well, that's that," I said, glad of the reprieve. I didn't understand why Margaret wanted to visit this criminal in the first place.

"We're going to the King County Jail," Margaret announced when we got back in the car.

I'd hoped she'd drop this and should have known better. "They won't let us see him," I said. "Why are we doing this, anyway?"

My sister ignored me. She was on a mission, which did not include informing me of her reasons. And little things like steel bars and gun-toting guards weren't about to slow her down.

Finding a parking spot and getting into the facility wasn't a task for the weak-willed. I was astonished by all the regulations we had to observe just to talk to an official.

When we finally met with a corrections officer, Margaret got straight to the point. "Can I see Daniel Chesterfield?" she asked.

He looked at her as if she'd requested an audience with the Pope. "No." He didn't elaborate. "It's way past visiting hours," he said with more than a hint of sarcasm. "In case you ladies didn't realize it, this is a correctional facility. Otherwise known as a *jail*. Mr. Chesterfield has been indicted on a class one felony charge."

"I'm glad to hear it." Margaret didn't spare any pity for Danny Chesterfield. "Could you give him something for me, then?"

"Lady, listen, I'm sure you mean well but—"

"As a matter of fact, I *don't* mean him well. I couldn't be happier that he's behind bars. I also know I can't allow my feelings toward this man to eat away at me any longer." She pulled a package from her large purse and literally shoved it at the corrections officer.

"What's this?" he asked suspiciously.

"It's a prayer shawl," Margaret explained. "I knit it myself. Give it to him and tell him…tell him," Margaret said in a choked voice, "tell Mr. Chesterfield I'm trying very hard to forgive him for what he did to my daughter. I'm praying for him and I'm praying for me because it isn't easy, you know?"

So that was it. This was why Margaret had wanted to see Danny Chesterfield. To give him the prayer shawl. I blinked back tears, moved by how far my sister had come. Difficult as it was for her, she'd taken Julia's words to heart.

I put my arm around her.

The correction officer's attitude changed instantly. "You don't know, do you?"

Margaret wiped her eyes as if it were a crime to reveal emotion. She shook her head mutely.

"Danny Chesterfield was in a car accident," he told us.

"That was reported in the paper," I answered for Margaret.

"What wasn't reported is that he's paralyzed from the waist down."

Margaret froze and stared up at the officer.

"He suffered a spinal cord injury. He'll be in a wheelchair for the rest of his life."

We left King County Jail soon afterward. Margaret seemed deep in thought as we walked to the parking lot and her car.

"I wouldn't have wished that on him," she said quietly.

"Of course you wouldn't," I told her.

Until recently I would not have believed that. Now I did.

Thirty-Nine

Alix Townsend Turner

Grandma Turner's funeral was truly a beautiful event, Alix thought. She hadn't known what to expect. Like so much else in life, she'd never experienced a real funeral. Even when her only brother died of an overdose, there'd been no one but her to mourn his passing. No one to pay for his burial, either, so it had fallen to the government. Her brother had been cremated and his ashes placed in a common grave without a marker. All Alix ever knew was the name of the cemetery where Tom's ashes were kept.

Alix had assumed that at Sarah Turner's funeral there'd be lots of sadness and tears. While that was true, and almost everyone wept, the mood was joyful, more like a celebration of a life well-lived, a woman well-loved.

Long before she died, Grandma Turner had made all her own burial arrangements, so the decisions hadn't been left to her children. She'd given specific instructions on which songs to sing and what Scripture verses to read. The only thing she hadn't indicated was which clothes she wanted to be buried in and that was decided by her two daughters-in-law.

Alix and Jordan had arrived back from Canada in time for the viewing, the night before the services. This was an unfamiliar ritual for Alix. In her heart she knew Jordan's grandmother had been ready to die, ready for her heavenly reward. What she hadn't expected was the rush of emotion as she approached the casket, hand in hand with her husband. Large floral arrangements surrounded it and when Alix looked down on this woman she'd come to love, she'd had to blink back sudden tears. Jordan's family had chosen to bury their mother in a lovely blue dress. They'd tucked Alix's prayer shawl around her shoulders.

Alix was moved by that.

Susan Turner came to stand next to her.

"Thank you," Alix whispered, barely able to speak.

Jordan's mother knew immediately why Alix was thanking her. "Sarah loved that shawl," her mother-in-law said in a low voice, "but more importantly, she loved you. Just as I do."

At the gathering in the fellowship hall after the funeral, Alix took care of the serving and cleaning up, thus allowing family members to visit with their guests.

Susan found her in the church kitchen, washing dishes. "Thank you for all your help, Alix," she said.

Alix finished rinsing the last of the dishes and released the drain at the bottom of the sink. "I was happy to do what I could."

Susan sighed, leaning against the counter. "Mom always knew."

Alix turned and cast a quizzical glance at her mother-in-law as she dried her hands. "Knew what?"

"Mom knew you'd be good for Jordan. I was the one with doubts, the one who questioned…. Well, you know that, but Alix, I was wrong."

"Susan, please, it's okay." She wished Jordan's mother would forget all that. Alix had.

"I know you've forgiven me, which also amazes me about you." Susan seemed in awe of her, and that only embarrassed Alix further.

"Listen," she said, "I'm no saint."

"Yes, but…"

"What you need to remember," Alix told her, "is that I realized if I was going to have a successful marriage, you and I had to come to a meeting of the minds. I didn't want to put my husband in the middle and demand that he choose sides. Besides, I don't have a mother of my own." Alix hesitated. "Well, I do have a biological mother—I'm sure you remember her—but she's no one I'd ever want as a role model."

Susan nodded, then looked away. "The family would like to thank you."

"For washing the dishes? No, really—"

"Not for that," Susan said, interrupting her, "but for the way you handled everything the day of the wedding. You were the only one who thought of calling the sheriff's office, for instance."

Alix shrugged off the praise. "When you've dealt with the police as much as I have, it's second nature to expect them in every situation."

Susan laughed, and then Jordan came into the kitchen. "People are starting to leave, Mom."

"Oh, thanks," she said, hugged Alix and left.

Jordan was grinning from ear to ear.

"What's so funny?" Alix wanted to know.

Jordan slid his arms around her waist. "You're pretty incredible, Alix Turner." He grinned again. "Pretty *and* incredible."

"Yeah, right."

"You think I'm joking?"

She had to admit she enjoyed listening to him sing her praises, deserved or not.

"I don't know what you did to win over my mother, Alix, but she's had a complete turnaround." Jordan arched his brows. "Are you going to tell me how you did it?"

Wrapping her arms around him, Alix smiled. "It was easy. All I had to do was love her son."

Jordan kissed her then, and it wasn't the short, affectionate kisses they so often shared in public or when family members were nearby. Her husband kissed her the way he had on their wedding day, the kiss of a man utterly captivated by the woman he'd married.

Alix leaned her head against Jordan's shoulder and looked out the kitchen door at the family gathered to honor the life of Sarah Turner. Many of them were people she barely knew, people she'd met once or twice before. Some of their names escaped her at the moment, and yet they were her family now. Not Jordan's brother or his cousins and uncles and aunts. *Their* cousins, uncles and aunts.

For the first time in her adult life, Alix belonged.

Forty

Colette Blake

Elizabeth Sasser invited Colette and Christian to dinner five days after his return from China. Since then, she and Christian had spent practically every minute together. He'd accompanied Colette to her ultrasound appointment and then to her doctor's, where he listened to his child's heartbeat. Already he was enthralled with the idea of becoming a father.

Colette was no longer working. Susannah had been sympathetic—and very excited for her. Chrissie, who was out of school now, would be filling in. Colette had offered to work out her two-week notice, but Susannah had said it wasn't necessary.

Elizabeth had invited Christian's father, Elliott, for dinner that same evening.

On Friday night, Elliott had arrived before Christian and Colette. The minute they pulled up outside the house, he stepped onto the porch to welcome them.

He smiled approvingly when Christian slipped

his arm around Colette's waist and guided her up the walkway.

"You're looking considerably healthier," Elliott commented. "And happier."

"I am," Christian assured his father.

"Are they here?" Elizabeth asked, poking her head out the front door. She smiled when she saw them on the porch, then frowned at Christian and shook her head. "You're late."

"Aunt Elizabeth, I am not late."

"Dinner's on the table," she said as though to prove him wrong.

The dining room had been set with a lace tablecloth, plus the china and silverware from the display cabinet. Doris had already carried in the serving dishes. In the center of the table was a sirloin roast, new red potatoes and fresh asparagus. The rolls appeared to be homemade.

"This looks delicious," Colette said as Christian drew out a chair for her.

He sat next to Colette and clasped her hand. It felt good to be linked to him, good and right.

After the blessing was given by Elliott, the serving dishes were passed around.

Elizabeth helped herself to a generous portion of roast beef, then set the plate down and glared at Christian. "Well? Are you going to keep me in suspense all night?" she demanded.

"Suspense about what?" Christian asked innocently. Beneath the table and out of view, he squeezed Colette's hand.

"Are you going to marry the girl or not?"

Elliott seemed equally interested in his response.

"We're talking about it." Christian glanced at Colette. "In other words, we're still negotiating."

"Negotiating," his aunt repeated scornfully. "Marriage is a commitment, not a contract to be *negotiated*."

"What's important, son," Elliott began, sounding far calmer than his aunt, "is that you two love each other. And just seeing you together, I can tell that you do."

"Of course he loves her," Elizabeth said irritably. "And she loves him."

"Then they'll reach the decision to marry in their own good time," Elliott assured the older woman.

Elizabeth picked up her fork. "Unfortunately, time is of the essence," she muttered and dug into her beef.

"Now, Elizabeth, be patient," Elliott cautioned. "You're going to be around for a lot of years yet."

Christian's great-aunt looked somewhat condescendingly at Elliott Dempsey. "My age has nothing to do with this."

"Dad," Christian said. "Aunt Betty—"

"Don't call me that!"

"Yes, dear," he said, struggling to hide a smile. He turned to his father. "I do have some news for you."

Elliott smiled expectantly.

"You're going to become a grandfather in three months."

Christian's father leaped to his feet, rushing over to congratulate them. But Elizabeth was not appeased. "If you don't marry this woman and give that baby your name, I swear to you right now, I'm cutting you out of my will."

"Aunt Elizabeth," Christian said, grinning. "That baby's a little girl and her name is Elizabeth Catherine Dempsey."

"I...I—" Elizabeth sputtered.

"We're naming her after you," Colette said, "and Christian's mother."

"You're getting married? For the love of heaven, *please* tell me you're getting married," Elizabeth cried. "The sooner the better."

Christian winked at Colette, but then his expression sobered. "Actually, no."

"No?" Elizabeth bellowed loudly enough to bring Doris running in from the kitchen.

"Is everything all right?" the housekeeper asked anxiously.

Stricken, Elizabeth nodded. "Everything's delicious, Doris, thank you. You can bring out dessert in a few minutes."

"What's for dessert?" Christian asked.

"Christian, don't be cruel," Colette said and held up her left hand, revealing the gold band on her ring finger. "Christian and I were married Thursday afternoon by my friend's husband."

"I certainly hope he's a minister," Elizabeth said under her breath.

"He is," Colette told her. "We got the license first thing Monday morning and Jordan Turner married us as soon as the waiting period was over."

"Thank God!"

"Then we phoned my parents and told them our news."

"*All* of it?" Elizabeth asked.

"All of it," Colette said. "They're pleased for us, more than a little surprised about the baby, but delighted." She paused. "Telling Derek's parents was more difficult, but they wished us well."

"A girl named after me," Elizabeth repeated slowly, proudly. "It's about time you did something right," she said, reaching for her fork again. "Even if you *didn't* invite me to the wedding."

Elliott raised his wineglass to congratulate them. "Under the circumstances, Aunt Elizabeth, I think we can forgive the oversight."

Colette turned to smile at her husband, the man she loved, the man whose child she carried. They'd decided to call her Beth, and when she brought her daughter home from the hospital, Colette would wrap her in the prayer shawl she'd knit with Lydia and her other friends.

Forty-One

"Granny was knitting a lovely lacy sweater. She had a piece of paper with tick marks and numbers on it. 'Where is your pattern?' I asked. She replied, 'A pattern? God gave you a brain, didn't he?' Granny was a thinking knitter. I wanted to be just like her."

—René Wells, Granny and Me Designs

Lydia Goetz

I was pleased that Julia and Hailey were with Mom when I visited. She chatted on endlessly about her childhood, and the girls listened attentively. It was a relief to see my mother in such high spirits. She was showing signs of improvement, I thought.

After about thirty minutes, the girls left and it was just Mom and me.

"You're looking so happy," Mom said as I brushed her hair, getting her ready for an early dinner. The prayer shawl I'd knit was tucked around her shoulders.

She wore it almost constantly these days and I found that gratifying. Of all the things I'd knit Mom through the years, this was the one I felt most strongly about because so many of those stitches held my hopes and prayers for her.

"Lydia?" she asked as I stroked the brush down the length of her hair.

"Yes, Mom?"

"Who were those nice young girls?"

I smiled, but it was a smile of sadness and resignation. "Those are Margaret's daughters, Julia and Hailey."

My mother sighed. "Oh, of course. What's the matter with me that I can't remember my own granddaughters?"

"Mom, don't worry. Julia and Hailey know who you are and that's what's important." The diagnosis was official now. Mom had Alzheimer's. As the disease progressed, I knew there'd come a time when Mom no longer recognized me. I'd deal with it; I would have no choice. I'd remember her as the young wife in photographs from the '60s and '70s, as the mother who'd walked me to school and sewed my Halloween costumes, as the grief-stricken widow and the old woman she was now. And all the moments in between. My mother.

"Is Margaret coming?" Mom asked in a tentative voice.

"Soon." My sister would come by sometime on Monday. We alternated visits, which helped. I was grateful for Margaret and the way taking care of Mom had strengthened the bond we shared as sisters.

"She's going to be a star," Mom told me.

I knew my mother was thinking about Margaret's

high-school days and her athletic success. I was the brains of the family, supposedly. I did take pride in the fact that I'd graduated with my high-school class despite missing almost my entire junior year while battling cancer.

After I finished brushing Mom's hair, it was time for dinner. Each of the residents was brought down to the dining room by a staff member. I waited until Mom was gone, then locked her room and left.

Brad, Cody and Chase were waiting for me at Green Lake. The three-mile walk around the lake was a favorite exercise of mine. Brad and Cody loved it, too, and Chase was quivering with excitement as he and Cody set off on their run.

"How's your mom doing?" Brad asked.

I thought about the question she'd asked me—who Julia and Hailey were—and shrugged. "She's in good spirits."

"I'm glad."

Brad knew I'd agonized over the decision to move Mom yet again, and so soon after her last move. Until Margaret told me, I hadn't been aware how long she'd been suffering from memory loss. But Dad had known and he'd been covering for her and I'd never suspected.

Brad and I started down the path, hands linked. He talked about one thing and another, and I responded at the appropriate times, but my mind was in a dozen different places.

I was thinking about Carol and her baby.

Colette, too.

It'd been a shock when she told me she was pregnant. And married! Needless to say, she'd moved out of the apartment and in with Christian. Which meant

I'd be looking for a new tenant soon, and that was fine. Susannah was going to miss her, but it seemed Chrissie enjoyed working in the flower shop, and she'd be there all summer.

Mostly I've been thinking about Brad and me adopting. Perhaps a baby would be unrealistic for us, but there are older children in need of a home, in need of love. That thought had come to me during a conversation with Alix. The state had declared her parents unfit and she'd been eligible for adoption. Only she was too old, she'd said, for anyone to want her. An older child—this was a possibility Brad and I needed to explore.

"You're very quiet," my husband said.

"I've been thinking…about a lot of things."

"Tell me one," he said.

I sorted through the most pressing of the thoughts dancing in my head. "I'm afraid my mother won't live much longer," I said and felt an immediate sense of pain. It was the first time I'd admitted this to Brad and the knowledge that I'd soon be without my mother left me feeling bereft and alone.

"That frightens you, doesn't it?"

"It does, more than I realized it would," I told him, but found myself unable to describe my feelings beyond this awareness of impending loss. Life without Mom—I could hardly imagine it. She was no longer the person she'd been, and yet she would always be my mom.

"Then treasure the time you still have with her," Brad suggested gently.

I nodded.

"Margaret phoned," he told me. "She wanted me to pass along the news."

"What news?"

"Danny Chesterfield's been sentenced."

Margaret had followed the case closely; according to her, Danny had reached a plea agreement with the prosecuting attorney's office. He would be serving a ten-year prison term. To my way of thinking, he was already serving his sentence, and it had nothing to do with his time behind bars.

"Mom, Dad!" Cody shouted frantically as Chase ran toward us, dragging his leash. "Catch him for me."

Brad reached out and grabbed the dog's leash. Laughing, Cody caught up with us and hugged his father. "Thanks, Dad," he said, breathless with exhilaration and joy.

Joy.

I felt it, too, in every cancer-free cell of my body. I was at peace with my life and with the future, whatever it held.

* * * * *